FUGITIVE LOVE

"You could have been killed," Genevieve said. "All it would have taken was for someone to recognize you and you would have been dragged into jail and hanged by nightfall."

Haydon regarded her with steady calm. She sensed his powerful attraction to her, felt it as keenly as if his hands were upon her and his mouth was over hers. She drew the blanket around her tighter, only to feel his heat and scent engulf her senses further. Her voice was barely a whisper. "Why?"

She studied him, waiting. Haydon felt as if she were trying to look inside him and understand who he really was. She had a right to know. She had risked herself and her beloved family to keep him safe. There was only one reason why he'd acted as he did, but he scarcely dared admit it to himself. And yet in that moment he could suddenly no longer contain it.

"I did it for you, Genevieve."

Her eyes widened. A terrible, desperate longing surged through her, the need to be held by him, to be kissed and stroked and covered by the glorious power and heat of him. With a little sob she ran to him, wrapped her arms around his neck, and crushed her lips to his as she drew him closer to her heart.

Also by Karyn Monk

The PRISONER

KARYN MONK

Bantam Books

New York Toronto London Sydney Auckland

THE PRISONER

A Bantam Book / June 2001

ISBN 0-553-57762-X

Published simultaneously in the United States and Canada

For
GENEVIEVE
with all my love

The

PRISONER

Chapter One

HE CRACKED OPEN A WEARY EYE, HIS VISION blurred by pain and fever.

"Evenin', yer lordship." A heavy set of iron manacles dangled ominously from the warder's grimy fist. "How are we keepin' tonight?"

Haydon regarded him warily and said nothing.

The warder laughed, exposing a jagged array of rotting teeth. "Quiet this evenin', are we?" With his muddy boot he nudged the dish of congealed porridge abandoned at the foot of Haydon's wooden bed. "What's this? Supper not to yer likin', milord?"

"The lad can have it." Haydon nodded at the scrawny figure opposite him hunched upon the frigid floor. "I'm not hungry."

The rawboned youth did not bother to look up, but remained huddled in a ball, his thin arms locked around his knees in a vain attempt to find some warmth.

"What say ye, Jack?" asked the warder, shifting his attention. "Are ye wantin' his lordship's supper to fill yer belly?"

The boy looked up, his gray eyes hard and glinting

with naked hostility. A thin white scar marred the otherwise smooth skin of his left cheek. "No."

The warder laughed. The rations provided in the prison were as foul as they were mean, and he knew the lad had to be hungry. "Hard little bugger, ain't ye? Don't need a thing from anyone—except for what ye steal, of course. Thievin' runs in yer blood just like whorin' ran in yer ma's, don't it, lad?"

The boy's lean body tensed. Haydon watched as his skinny arms tightened farther around his knees, fighting to keep his anger under control.

"That's the trouble with ye whores' bastards," continued the warder. "Ye're born with bad blood and ye die with bad blood, and in between ye do nothin' but stink and make life a misery for the rest of us. Well, today," he drawled, jangling his manacles ominously in front of the lad's face, "I'm goin' to see if I can't beat some of that bad blood out of ye."

A hint of fear seeped into Jack's cold gaze.

Haydon clenched his jaw as he slowly eased himself onto one elbow, fighting a wave of pain and dizziness. The beating he had received some two weeks earlier had broken several ribs, and fever had sapped him of much of his strength. Even so, concern for the lad made him force himself to a sitting position. "What are you talking about?" he demanded.

"Been sentenced to thirty-six stripes o' the lash, our young Jack has." The warder took perverse pleasure in the alarm that drained the blood from the youth's filthy face. "Did ye think I'd forgotten about that, lad?" He laughed, then spat on the floor. "The sheriff takes a dim view of scum like you stealin' valuables from honest folk. Thinks a little beating and a few years spent at a reformatory school in Glasgow might cure ye of yer evil ways. But we know different, don't we, Jack?" He sank his beefy hand into the boy's hair and hauled him roughly to his feet. "We know a filthy little shit like yerself can only end up dead, either killed by yer own kind, or hanged as a murderer, like his lordship over there." He shoved Jack hard against the wall. "Now, I suspect that bein' strapped to the whippin' table with yer wrists manacled and yer bare arse bleedin' beneath the lash of my whip ain't goin' to cure ye of yer wicked ways. All the same, I want ye to know," he finished, laughing, "that I am goin' to bloody enjoy it."

Rage, hard and hot, suddenly flooded the lad. With a quickness and strength that Haydon found surprising in a half-starved youth, Jack plowed his bony fist deep into the warder's flaccid gut. Sour air blew from the jailer's rotting mouth, part groan and part curse. Before he could recover, Jack had drawn his fist back and rammed it into his tormentor's jaw. The warder's head snapped back, cracking his decrepit teeth together with a sickening crunch.

"*I'll kill ye!*" the warder raged. He dropped his manacles and swung a heavy fist at the boy. Jack ducked just in time, deftly avoiding the blow. "Come here, ye rotten little prick!"

He swung a clumsy fist again, and Jack spun neatly beyond it, betraying an uncommon ability to evade assault. His fury augmented with frustration, the warder charged at the boy like an angry bull, ramming into him with all the power of his substantial girth. Jack went flying into the wall, his thin body and head crashing against the frigid stone surface. Pain glazed his eyes and he stood helplessly a moment, fighting to regain his strength and focus.

"I'll teach ye to dare raise a fist to yer betters!" roared the warder, pinning the boy against the wall as he prepared to smash the lad's face with his fist.

Powerful hands suddenly clamped upon the warder's shoulders with brutal force. In one swift motion, the warder was ripped from Jack and sent hurtling across the cell. He crashed into Haydon's wooden bed, shattering the structure beneath his considerable weight. With a groan, he extricated himself from the debris, then stared at Haydon with equal measures of surprise and fury.

"Touch the lad again," Haydon intoned softly, "and I'll kill you."

He forced his labored breath to come in shallow pants, trying to manage the pain tearing through his side. It was an effort just to stand, but Haydon could not let the warder see that or he would be finished. And so he stood tall and locked his legs beneath him, hoping to God that the dizziness swirling through his brain would cease before he was forced to succumb to it.

The warder hesitated. Haydon was a man of impressive stature, and a convicted murderer besides. Clearly his jailer was trying to assess his odds of besting him before he made his next move.

A drop of fevered sweat trickled down Haydon's cheek.

The warder's mouth split into an ugly smile. "Not feelin' well, are ye, milord?" Sneering, he rose to his feet.

"I'm feeling well enough to bash your skull in," Haydon assured him.

"Are ye now?" His opponent looked doubtful. "Somehow, I don't believe ye."

With that he grabbed a heavy wooden plank from the broken bed and smashed it with all his might against Haydon's injured side.

It was a blow that would have been debilitating for any man, but with his broken ribs and nauseating fever, it was unbearable. Haydon sank to his knees, fighting the agonizing pain racing through the muscle and bone of his fractured rib cage. Before he could shield himself from the next blow, the warder struck again. The heavy bat cracked against his spine, knocking him to the floor. Overcome, Haydon was unable to protect himself as the warder began to kick him savagely about the ribs and back with his heavy, mud-crusted boots.

"Stop it!" screamed Jack, springing onto the warder's back and pummeling him with his fists. "You'll kill him!"

The warder abandoned his attack on Haydon as he tried to knock Jack off his shoulders. He rammed backwards into the wall, effectively disengaging Jack's hold. "And I'm goin' to kill ye as well, ye stinkin' little son of a bitch!" He jerked the boy to his feet, locked his hands around his throat and began to strangle him.

"*Take your hands off him,*" commanded an outraged woman's voice. "*Now!*"

Startled, the warder released his grip on Jack.

"Good God, Sims," gasped the prison governor. "What the devil is going on here?"

With excruciating effort, Haydon turned his head. Governor Thomson was a short, round apple of a man, with a badly receding hairline. He compensated for the lack of hair on his head by proudly promoting the wiry gray bush that sprouted from his chin, which he kept neatly trimmed in the precise shape of a gardening spade. He was dressed from head to toe in his customary black, which Haydon supposed was appropriate attire for a man who spent his days within the forbidding walls of a prison. In a way, he mused, Governor Thomson was just as condemned by his profession as those whose pathetic lives he imprisoned.

"These two prisoners were tryin' to kill me!" yelped the warder.

"Governor Thomson, is it your policy to permit the use of brutal force on mere children?"

The woman standing beside the governor was an apparition in gray, her face sheltered by her bonnet, her slender body lost somewhere within the folds of the dark cloak that enveloped her. And yet there was a self-assurance to her that was unmistakable, a dignified confidence and barely contained fury that filled the frigid little cell with righteous energy.

"Of course not, Miss MacPhail," Governor Thomson assured her, his head shaking nervously from side to side to underscore the point. "All our prisoners are treated with fairness and dignity—unless, of course," he amended, glancing down at Haydon, "they pose a threat to others. In a situation like that, I'm sure you understand, Mr. Sims here is obliged to restrain them."

"They were tryin' to kill me!" the warder squawked, trying his best to look as if he had barely evaded death. "Attacked me like a pair of wild animals, they did—I'll be lucky if I haven't broken anything." He rubbed his elbow, evidently in the hope of eliciting some sympathy.

"And why do you suppose they did such a thing?" demanded the woman icily.

The warder shrugged. "I was just takin' the lad for his whippin', when he suddenly went mad and—"

"You were going to whip this boy?"

Haydon couldn't decide which was greater, her horror or her fury.

"The sheriff has sentenced him to be lashed," explained Governor Thomson, as if that somehow absolved him and the warder of any responsibility in the matter. "Thirty-six stripes, in addition to forty days imprisonment here. Then he is to spend a further two years in a reformatory school."

"For what crime?"

"The lad's a thief," Governor Thomson reported.

"Is he, now?" The woman's tone was blatantly caustic.

She turned and approached Haydon, releasing the ties of her bonnet as she did so. The dark headpiece slipped down her back, revealing a woman of far greater youth and beauty than he had initially suspected. Her face was pale against a mass of honey-colored hair tinged with red, which was carelessly escaping the pins she had used to try to contain it. Her eyes were large and dark against her milky skin, her features small and elegantly carved. Her beauty was as luminous as it was out of place in the foul darkness of the cell, as if a glorious flower had suddenly bloomed between one of the cracks in the filthy floor. Untroubled by the prospect of dirtying her clothes, she knelt beside Haydon, her brows drawn together with concern as she studied his pain-etched face.

"Are you badly injured, sir?"

Haydon regarded her in silent fascination. She was not so young after all, for the fine web of lines around her eyes and across her forehead were testament to a life lived at least twenty-five years, perhaps more. She had known trouble in those years, the faint shadows beneath her eyes and the furrows between her brows made that clear enough, but he sensed there had been much laughter as well. In that moment he longed for nothing more than to see her smile, to watch the warm light of amusement drift across her lovely face, and see the sweet lines around her eyes crinkle with pleasure.

"No," he murmured thickly. For all he knew, inside he was bleeding to death. It scarcely mattered. Dying upon the floor with this magnificent creature looking down upon him with such tender concern was vastly preferable to being hanged the following day before a jeering mob. He stared at her intently, willing her to stay near, afraid that if he so much as blinked she would be gone and he would be left to finish whatever remained of his miserable life alone.

She laid her hand against the rough growth of beard on his cheek, then placed it lightly upon his fevered brow. Her touch was soft and cool and sure. Somehow, it filled him with a kind of fragile hope. It must be the fever, he realized with vague disappointment. There was no hope for him.

"This man is gravely ill," she announced, her eyes never leaving his. "He is almost afire with fever and he has been badly beaten. You must send for a doctor immediately."

The warder snorted with laughter.

Governor Thomson was only slightly more courteous, regarding her as if she were utterly innocent in matters that were best handled by men. "I am afraid, Miss MacPhail, that this man has been found guilty of murder and is sentenced to hang tomorrow. Since his crime is of the most serious nature and his punishment but hours away, I'm afraid I cannot justify troubling the prison surgeon to examine him—especially considering he will not live long enough to benefit from any treatment that might be prescribed."

Her body stiffened, although she was careful to keep her expression composed. Clearly the mention of murder and hanging had affected whatever her previous assessment of him had been. She withdrew her hand and Haydon felt lost, as if the gentle thread of compassion joining him to her had snapped.

"No," he protested, grasping her wrist and pulling her toward him again.

Alarm flared in her eyes, and he realized his mistake. He could well imagine how he appeared to her; a battered prisoner sprawled on the floor of a dank cell, filthy and unshaven and perhaps crazed by fever, trying to hold her against her will. He closed his eyes in despair, still clinging to her slender wrist, but his grasp was gentle now, and she could have broken free if she wished.

She remained where she was, the skin of her wrist clean and cool against his grimy fingers.

"I am no murderer," he murmured, unable to fathom why it should matter to him that she know this.

She hesitated a moment, studying him soberly. "I am sorry, sir," she finally said in a soft voice, "but that is now a matter between you and God." Gently she extricated herself from his hold. "Jack, would you kindly help me move this man to that bed?"

"I'll move him," growled the warder.

"Thank you, but I think it would be best if the boy and I did it," she returned firmly.

Jack obediently went to Haydon's side. Together he and the woman helped him to his feet and onto the remaining bed.

"If you will not call for the surgeon, perhaps you will permit me to send my maid to tend to this man this evening," she said, adjusting the coarse folds of a foul-smelling blanket over Haydon. "I see no reason why he should not be permitted some measure of comfort on his final evening."

Governor Thomson stroked his thick gray beard uncertainly. "It really isn't necessary—"

"It would scarcely reflect well upon you or your prison were he not fit to stand during his execution tomorrow," Miss MacPhail pointed out. "It might give cause for some to question the treatment he received while he was entrusted to your care." She cast an accusing look at the warder.

"On the other hand, I see no harm to your maid paying him a visit," Governor Thomson relented.

"Very good." Satisfied that she had done all that was within her power to help Haydon, she turned her attention to Jack.

"Permit me to introduce myself, Jack. My name is Genevieve MacPhail, and I would like to speak with you—"

"I never stole nothin'," he spat vehemently.

"I don't care whether you did or not."

Surprise flickered in his gaze, but he was quick to shroud it with sullen indifference. "Then what do you want?"

"I live in a house in Inveraray with some other children who, like yourself, have been through some rather difficult times—"

"I'm not a child," he interrupted rudely.

"Forgive me. Of course you aren't. You must be what—fifteen?"

He straightened his posture, pleased that she had overestimated his age. "About that."

She nodded as if greatly impressed by this. "Well, I was wondering, Jack, if instead of staying here in prison and then proceeding to a reformatory school, you would be willing to come and live with me for the duration of your sentence."

Jack's eyes narrowed. "You mean like a servant?" His tone was openly scornful.

"No," she replied, untroubled by his hostile attitude. "But you would have chores to do, the same as everyone there does."

He regarded her skeptically. "What kind of chores?"

"You would be expected to help with cooking and cleaning and washing, and all the other things that are necessary to run a busy household. And you would be required to spend part of each day learning to read and write and cipher numbers. You don't know how to read, do you?"

"I get by," he assured her tersely.

"I don't doubt that. But my hope would be, Jack, that after you finished staying with me, you would be able to get by far better than you have been."

He was silent a moment, considering. "Could I come and go as I pleased?"

"Unfortunately, no. Should you decide to come with me, you would then become my responsibility. That means that I would have to know where you were at all times. I'm afraid I would have to insist that you agree to that," she added, as a scowl twisted his sharply chiseled features. "And your days would be structured, so you would not be permitted to simply wander off and do as you wished. I can assure you, however, that you would find your situation far more tolerable than what awaits you at reformatory school. You would be well fed and cared for. The others who have come to live with me actually find it quite pleasant."

"Fine."

His answer was just a touch too quick, thought Haydon, to be genuine. It was clear to him that the boy had decided that going with this Miss Genevieve MacPhail was infinitely preferable to getting thrashed by the warder and spending any more time in jail. Once he had relieved her of a warm set of clothes and a decent meal, he would steal whatever he could and be gone, by tomorrow at the very latest. Haydon wished he had time to speak to the boy alone, to make him understand the incredible opportunity he was being offered.

"Can you get him out as well?" Jack inclined his head toward Haydon.

Haydon looked at the lad in surprise.

"I—I'm afraid not," Genevieve stammered, startled by the question.

Her dark eyes were veiled with what appeared to be regret. Haydon thought that rather amazing, given all that she knew of him was that he had been convicted of murder. It was scarcely the kind of credentials that roused the more tender sensibilities of a gently bred woman like Miss MacPhail.

"Excellent," said Governor Thomson, pleased that

the two had come to an agreement. "Let us retire to my office and work out the necessary details of this arrangement, shall we?" He scratched his beard in anticipation.

So that was it, Haydon realized. This Miss MacPhail was securing Jack's release in exchange for payment of some kind to the prison governor. She wore no jewelry, and a closer inspection revealed that her cloak was void of ornamentation and the fabric was cheap and somewhat worn. Whatever she was paying for the dubious privilege of taking on the responsibility of a half-starved, lying, thieving urchin, it was clear she could ill-afford it. The certainty that Jack was planning to take advantage of her well-meaning intentions and then abandon her made him feel sad for both of them.

Governor Thomson was already on his way out the door, evidently anxious to have the transaction completed.

But the lovely Miss MacPhail hesitated.

"I will send my maid to attend to you as quickly as possible," she promised Haydon. "Is there anything special you would like?"

"Do not take your eyes off the lad until you are certain he will stay with you—otherwise he will be gone by morning."

Her dark eyes widened. Obviously she had expected him to ask for something simple and self-indulgent, like whiskey, or perhaps that a particular dish be prepared for him.

"There is one more thing."

She waited expectantly.

"I would like you to believe that I am innocent."

The warder snorted with amusement. "All ye murderers want the world to think ye're sweet an' pure as bairns—especially before ye're due to have yer neck snapped."

"Why does it matter to you what I believe?" she asked, ignoring the warder's jeer.

Haydon regarded her intently. "It just does."

She was silent a moment, contemplating his request. "I'm afraid I do not know the facts of your case, sir, and therefore can pass no judgment." Her voice was soft and laced with remorse, as if she would have far preferred to tell him that she believed him.

He nodded, suddenly feeling immeasurably weary. "Of course." He closed his eyes.

"Come, then, Miss MacPhail," said Governor Thomson, who was waiting impatiently for her at the cell door. "Let us have this matter of the lad settled."

"I will have my maid prepare something special for you," Genevieve promised Haydon, perhaps hoping that he would be somewhat consoled by this.

"I'm not hungry."

"Then she will do whatever she can to see to your comfort," she persisted.

"Fine. Thank you."

He sensed rather than saw her hesitate, as if there was something more she wished to say to him.

And then she left the cell, leaving him to face his final hours alone in the frigid darkness.

THE CONTRACT IS THE SAME AS THOSE TO WHICH YOU have previously agreed, except, of course, I have included the particulars of the lad's sentence," said Governor Thomson, laying a sheet of paper on the desk before her. "I'm certain you will find it is all in order." It was clear he was most anxious to have the document signed and receive his payment.

"I'm sure it is," Genevieve replied. "But it would set a poor example if I were to sign it without reading it first. One must always read a document thoroughly

before putting one's signature on it," she instructed Jack.
With that she began to carefully read the contract.

"Well, now, lad, this is a fortuitous day for you, is it
not?" asked Governor Thomson, lamely attempting to
fill the awkward silence.

Jack said nothing.

Genevieve glanced up at the boy. He was staring intently at the passage beyond the doorway of the governor's office, apparently transfixed by Warder Sims, who
was busy piling scummy porridge bowls onto a heavy
wooden tray. Perhaps, Genevieve reflected, the boy was
considering how close he had come to being beaten to
death by the horrid man.

"Jack, you must respond when someone asks you a
question," she instructed gently.

Jack blinked and looked at her in confusion. "What?"

"In polite conversation we don't say 'what,' we say
'pardon me,'" Genevieve corrected, deciding this was as
good a time as any to begin work on the boy's manners.

He regarded her as if she were crazy. "What are you
talkin' about?"

"Governor Thomson was speaking to you," she
explained, deciding to put the issue of "what" versus
"pardon me" aside for the moment.

"What did he say?" he asked, not bothering to look
at the governor.

Later she would explain that it was rude to speak of
someone who was present as if he weren't there. "He
asked you if you felt lucky to be leaving this place with
me," she said, realizing he would likely not understand
the word "fortuitous."

Jack shrugged. "Anythin's better than this pisshole."

Governor Thomson's gray brows shot up and his
face reddened with indignation. "Why, you ungrateful
little—"

"You're quite right, Jack," interjected Genevieve,

untroubled by either the lad's surly indifference or his colorful choice of words. If anything, she admired him for his honesty. "Anything is indeed better than here." She smiled at him, then proceeded to study the contract.

Looking bored, Jack slumped in his chair and began to bang the heels of his filthy, worn shoes against the elegantly carved legs.

"Here now, stop that, you'll scratch the wood!" protested Governor Thomson.

Jack shrugged. "It's just a chair."

"It may be just a chair to you, you filthy ruffian, but it is solid mahogany and cost more than you shall ever earn honestly in your entire life!" the governor snapped.

Oozing defiance, Jack kicked the chair again.

"Why don't you wait in the hall, Jack," suggested Genevieve, trying to avoid an altercation between the two. "The governor and I will have completed our business shortly."

Needing no further encouragement, Jack stomped out the door and began to pace restlessly up and down the corridor.

"You'll have your hands full with that one, mark my words," huffed Governor Thomson. "I wager he'll be back to his lawless, pilfering ways and in here again before the month is through. My recommendation, Miss MacPhail, is that you take a firm position with him—with a regular beating, just to keep him obliging."

"I am not in the habit of beating my children, Governor Thomson," Genevieve informed him coolly.

"The Lord tells us children must be beaten," Governor Thomson argued. " 'He who spares the rod hates his son, but he who loves him is diligent to discipline him.' Let the lad know in no uncertain terms that you own him now. If he gives you one whit of trouble, send him right back to me."

"What did he steal?"

"Pardon?"

"You mentioned in your letter to me that the lad had been found guilty of the crime of stealing. What did he steal?"

Governor Thomson pulled a pair of spectacles from his jacket and placed them on his nose before opening a file upon his desk. "He broke into a home and stole one pair of shoes, one blanket, one round of cheese, and a bottle of whiskey," he reported gravely. "He was later found asleep under the blanket in a neighbor's coach house. The whiskey and cheese were all but gone, the stolen shoes were on his feet, and the lad was thoroughly drunk." He regarded her seriously over the rims of his spectacles. "I'm afraid there was never any question of his culpability in the matter."

"And for the crime of being cold, hungry, and without decent shoes, he was to be imprisoned, lashed, and sent to reformatory school." Genevieve's tone was flagrantly bitter.

"We live in a lawful society, Miss MacPhail. Where would we be if everyone who was cold and hungry decided they could just walk into someone else's home or shop and help themselves to whatever they wanted?"

"No child should ever be that desperate," she argued. "We need laws to protect our children from starving, so that they don't have to resort to stealing food and clothing to survive."

"He did not starve while he was here, nor would he have starved at the reformatory school," Governor Thomson pointed out. "Regardless of whether you had decided to take him or not, his arrest was the best thing that could have happened to him. It usually is for strays like him. He claims his parents are dead and that he has no home or kin who might take him in. At least in a reformatory school he would have a roof over his head, a blanket to cover him at night, and three meals a day."

"Boys cannot live on thin gruel and water, and stealing some cheese and a pair of shoes scarcely merits being lashed and locked in a freezing cell with a murderer," retorted Genevieve. "As for our precious reformatory schools," she continued mockingly, "they are little more than a place where children are abused and forced to slave under intolerable conditions. If, somehow, they find the will and strength necessary to survive, they are then tossed onto the street with no appreciable skills or money, and callously told to get on with their lives. Which, of course, leads them straight back to thieving and prostitution."

"Regrettably, we who work within the system can only do so much, Miss MacPhail," Governor Thomson responded. "By bringing the lad to your attention, I hope I may have played some small part in the possibility of his salvation. The other children I have directed to your custody are doing reasonably well, are they not?"

"They are doing extremely well," Genevieve assured him. "Far better than they would have otherwise."

"And I don't doubt that you shall do your utmost to try to help Jack overcome his baser instincts and eventually, perhaps, lead a life that is both honest and productive. Let us hope so, at any rate, for his sake." He closed his file. "One more altercation with the law, and I'm afraid there will be nothing further that either of us can do except let him suffer the full burden of his sentence." He rose from his desk and regarded her expectantly, indicating that their business was all but finished.

Satisfied that all the details of their arrangement were in order, Genevieve signed the document, then retrieved the money she carried in the inner pocket of her cloak and handed it to Governor Thomson.

"Thank you, Miss MacPhail," he said, smiling as he quickly counted it. "I do hope this arrangement shall work out satisfactorily for you."

"I have no doubt that it shall." Genevieve rose and moved toward the door, ready to tell Jack that they were leaving.

And froze.

Having completed his task of collecting the dirty crockery from each of the cells, the abundant Warder Sims was now struggling to hoist his heavy tray onto his shoulder. His back was turned to Jack, leaving him blissfully unaware of the fact that the boy had sidled up to him and was stealthily slipping the ring of keys off the warder's belt.

"Here now, what the devil do ye think ye're doing?" the warder growled suddenly, spinning about.

"Nothin'," said Jack, casually stepping away from him.

"Open yer jacket and let me see what ye've got there," Warder Sims commanded, "before I rip it off yer skinny hide myself."

Panic gripped Genevieve. If Jack was found stealing before he had even left the prison, Governor Thomson would have no choice but to forfeit their arrangement. Jack would be lashed and thrown back in his cell to half-starve before suffering years of abuse in a reformatory school.

"Mr. Sims, watch out!" she screamed suddenly, her cry almost ear-splitting as it reverberated against the cold stone walls. *"There is an enormous rat by your foot!"*

Pure horror blanched the warder's face. "Where?!" he shouted, hopping awkwardly from one foot to the other, as he valiantly tried to balance his tray. "Where?!"

"Right *there!*" she shrieked, pointing at his ankles.

The next thing Genevieve knew, he was flying

through the air, yelping in fear, before crashing amidst a
mess of gluey bowls and lumpy porridge.

"Get him off me!" he screeched, scrambling to rise.
He raced toward her with outstretched arms, as if he expected her to save him. His foot got caught in a wayward
bowl which skidded on some porridge, sending him
barreling into Governor Thomson's office, where, fortunately, the governor's precious mahogany chair helped to
break his fall.

The chair itself did not fare so well.

"For God's sake, Sims, what the devil is the matter
with you?" thundered Governor Thomson furiously.
"Just look at what you've done to my chair!"

"Is it gone?" whimpered the warder, staring
frantically behind himself. "Is it?"

"I'm not sure," said Genevieve, searching the shadows of the hallway for Jack, who had disappeared.

"I don't see any rat," the boy reported calmly as he
emerged from the darkness around the corner. "It must
be gone."

He strolled past Genevieve into Governor Thomson's
office. "Too bad about your chair," he remarked, his voice
edged with sarcasm. He bent over to pick up the mangled
piece of furniture. "Maybe it can be fixed."

When the chair was precariously righted upon its
three remaining legs, Mr. Sims's prison keys were lying
innocently upon the floor, looking as if they had simply
fallen off when he crashed into it.

"My chair!" lamented Governor Thomson, turning
over the broken mahogany leg. "It's ruined!"

"I'm sorry, sir," apologized Warder Sims, looking
forlorn. "It's just that—I hate rats."

"If there is nothing further, then Jack and I must be
going," interjected Genevieve, anxious to have the boy
out of there before he tried to steal something else.

"Yes, fine," said Governor Thomson, looking as if he was torn between weeping over his chair and cracking Warder Sims over the head with its shattered leg. "As for you, young man," he said, regarding Jack sternly, "see that you abandon your lawless ways and do everything Miss MacPhail tells you. One misstep and you will be back in this jail and on your way to reformatory school, do you hear?" He shook the fractured chair leg at him.

"I'm sure Jack understands his situation," Genevieve swiftly replied, afraid to let the boy speak lest he offend Governor Thomson yet again. "Good evening, Governor Thomson. Warder Sims," she added crisply, nodding at the dejected jailer, who still had gray globs of porridge stuck to his uniform.

She put her hand firmly upon Jack's shoulder and steered him toward the door, trying not to think about what the boy had wanted with the warder's keys.

THE PRISON WAS CLOAKED IN A COLD, DANK BLACK, and quiet except for the dispiriting sounds of human misery. Long bursts of horrible, phlegmy coughing were intermingled with painful groans, and a soft, pitiful weeping filtered through the air from a desolate woman in one of the cells on the second floor. They were the feeble sounds of hopelessness, the death knell of shattered people who had been cast aside and all but forgotten.

Except by the ignoble Warder Sims, who made it a point never to forget any of his prisoners.

In his rather limited view, whatever circumstances had caused these men, women, and children to end up in his prison were entirely of their own making. And now that these castoffs of society had been relegated to his tender care, he was determined that they be made to pay for their crimes each and every minute. Further, they had to understand that he, and not the fatuous Governor Thomson, was the man in whose hands their miserable lives now rested. Only then could there be order in his prison. If he were to be utterly honest, which he rarely was, he would have also had to admit that he actually relished the act of goading and tormenting his charges.

It was one of the few perquisites of being a prison warder.

This need to affirm his status as the ruler of his domain was what drew him back to Haydon's cell soon after Governor Thomson had retired to his apartment for the evening, still mourning the destruction of his beloved chair. There was unfinished business between this prisoner and himself, and Warder Sims did not intend to let the matter rest—not when his lordship was scheduled to be hanged the following day. That murdering scum had dared to lay his hands upon him. Although Sims had managed to do him some damage, before that filthy strip of a lad had jumped upon his back, the matter was far from finished. It hadn't helped his mood any to have been attacked by an enormous rat and sent skating into the governor's bloody chair on a bowl of greasy porridge. The indignity of that moment, along with the humiliation of having to endure the governor's ire as he cleaned up the mess, had only whetted his desire to further pummel this murderer.

Especially since Sims knew his lordship was in no condition to fight back.

He opened the narrow inspection slide in the door and peered in. The cell was dark, save for a filmy veil of moonlight trickling through the iron bars of the window. The remnants of the demolished bed lay scattered upon the floor at one end of the chamber. Anger surged through him as he thought of himself being thrown into it. His lordship would pay dearly for that. His muscles tense with anticipation, he shifted his gaze to the other side of the cell.

And found it impossibly empty.

"What the hell—"

He fumbled for his key ring, grabbing the door handle as he did so, and was bewildered when the heavy oak portal swung open without the benefit of a key. He snatched a burning lamp from the wall and stepped cautiously into the cell, studying the vacant shadows with determination. For several long moments he stood there, searching wildly, as if he thought he might still find his prisoner if he only looked hard enough, perhaps under the narrow wooden bed, or hiding behind the chamber pot.

Finally the lamp sputtered and went out, leaving him alone in the darkness of the cell, desperately trying to think of how he should tell Governor Thomson that their most illustrious and dangerous prisoner had escaped.

Chapter Two

HAYDON COULD NOT STAND MUCH LONGER.

It had taken every shred of his strength just to follow Miss MacPhail and the boy here. He had not initially intended to do so. But the moment Haydon stood outside the prison walls clutching his injured side and gasping for breath, he realized he had absolutely nowhere to go. He knew no one in Inveraray, he was without money, and he was wearing a filthy prison uniform. Moreover, between his illness and his injuries, he knew he could not travel very far.

The sight of the compassionate Miss MacPhail walking with young Jack some distance ahead of him had offered his only hope. He had no illusions that Miss MacPhail would be interested in helping him. Although she was apparently generous and tenderhearted, she believed him to be a murderer. Aside from fearing that he might harm her, there was also the very real threat of her being prosecuted for aiding a criminal, should Haydon be discovered in her care. The lad, however, was another matter. By boldly stealing the warder's keys and unlocking Haydon's cell door, Jack had demonstrated that he was at least somewhat concerned about Haydon's fate. Much as he loathed to ask it of the boy, at that moment he desperately needed assistance. If he could only hide in Miss MacPhail's shed or coach house for a few days, with a little food and water brought to him occasionally, he could regain his strength.

Then he'd get the hell out of Inveraray and try to clear his name.

The fact that there had been no carriage waiting for Miss MacPhail outside the prison, coupled with the relative simplicity of her attire, had suggested that her financial situation was modest. Haydon was therefore surprised to follow her to this fashionable street and watch her enter a large, elegant house of smooth gray stone with numerous windows and a handsomely carved front door. The house was not grand by Haydon's standards, but it bespoke gentility and affluence, as did the homes surrounding it. Jack had appeared utterly indifferent to his new residence, striding up the stairs and into the building without sparing it a second glance. It was clear to Haydon that the boy had no intention of staying there. Perhaps when they had a chance to talk he would be able to make the lad understand what a rare opportunity he was being given.

The draperies in the house had been drawn, leaving only a soft, buttery glow permeating the fabric. Nearly overcome with exhaustion, Haydon had forced himself to stand in the shadow of a neighboring house and wait. After an hour or more, the curtains in an upstairs window parted slightly, and a pale young face stared out at the street below. Haydon retreated farther into the darkness, watching. The face hesitated a moment, then disappeared behind the draperies once again.

Haydon could not be certain it had been Jack. He thought it had looked like him. Did the lad suspect that Haydon had followed him? It was possible. Jack had lived much of his life on the streets, and was undoubtedly more attuned to his surroundings than those who had enjoyed more sheltered existences. On the other hand, the lad might simply have been curious about his new environs, and was taking a moment to contemplate his situation before climbing into a clean, comfortable bed.

Haydon raised a hand to his brow, fighting the dizziness that threatened to overwhelm him.

One by one the lamps in the house were extinguished, until all the windows were sheets of black. Shivering with fever and weary beyond measure, Haydon slowly emerged from the shadows.

Finally, realizing he had no choice, he picked up a handful of stones and began to fling them at the boy's window.

THERE IS A MAN THROWING STONES AT OUR WINDOW!" shrieked ten-year-old Annabelle, her pale blonde hair flying out behind her as she raced into Genevieve's room and leaped excitedly upon her bed.

"He's been doing it for a few minutes," Grace added, clumsily banging into Genevieve's nighttable before joining Annabelle on the mattress. Grace was two years older than her stepsister, but contrary to her name, she lacked the charming mannerisms that came to Annabelle so effortlessly.

"What do you think he wants?" wondered Charlotte, limping in after them. A quiet, serious child of eleven, she had glossy auburn hair and large hazel eyes. Unfortunately, few people noticed anything about her beyond the fact that she walked with a limp.

"Maybe he is a secret admirer of Genevieve's, come to profess his undying love," rhapsodized Annabelle dreamily.

Grace frowned. "Why wouldn't he come and profess

his undying love during the day, when Genevieve is awake?"

"Because then we would all be awake to see him and he wouldn't be a secret admirer anymore," explained Annabelle.

"But we're all awake now," pointed out Charlotte.

In fact, Genevieve was only half-awake as she fumbled to light the oil lamp by her bed. Nevertheless, Charlotte's point seemed a valid one. "There is a man throwing stones?" she murmured groggily, staring at the three excited little faces in bemusement.

"And he's terribly handsome!" added Annabelle breathlessly, clasping her delicate hands to her breast. "He looks like a prince!"

"You don't know that," Grace retorted. "You barely saw him."

"I did so see him," Annabelle argued. "And there was moonlight shining down upon his handsome face, and he looked as if his heart was broken."

"He did look a little sad." Charlotte carefully arranged herself on the edge of Genevieve's bed and rubbed her stiff leg.

"He wasn't wearing a hat," reflected Grace, frowning. "Don't princes always wear hats?"

"Princes wear crowns," Annabelle corrected.

"I thought kings wore crowns," said Charlotte.

"Kings wear bigger crowns," Annabelle informed her with great authority. "That is why princes want to become kings—then they get to wear the biggest crown."

"Are you girls certain there is a man there?" Genevieve wanted nothing more than to return to sleep. Morning came relentlessly early in her busy little household, and she treasured every moment of respite she could get.

"Come and see for yourself!" squealed Annabelle, tugging on her arm.

"Quick, before he leaves and decides to throw himself in the river!" Clearly Grace sensed Genevieve needed some added incentive.

Reluctantly Genevieve dragged herself out of bed and followed the three girls as they raced into their room.

"Stand there so he can't see you," Charlotte instructed, indicating the corner by the window.

"Why shouldn't he see her?" wondered Annabelle. "Her hair is a bit untidy, but other than that she looks very nice—like a princess."

"We don't know who he is, Annabelle," Grace cautioned. "For all we know he could be a dangerous cutthroat."

Annabelle's blue eyes grew round. "Do you really think so?" She sounded perfectly exhilarated by this new possibility.

"I only meant that a strange man shouldn't see Genevieve in her nightgown," explained Charlotte impatiently. "It isn't fitting—is it, Genevieve?"

"No, it isn't," Genevieve agreed. "Now, would you all please lower your voices before you waken the entire house."

The three girls obediently fell silent. Genevieve slowly drew back part of the curtain, then peered cautiously through the exposed sliver of window.

"Gracious me!" she gasped, whipping the curtain closed.

"Did you see him?" asked Grace excitedly.

"Isn't he handsome?" Annabelle squealed.

"He didn't see your nightgown, did he?" fretted Charlotte.

Jamie bounded into the room, his red-blond hair tousled and his eyes surprisingly alert for an eight-year-old lad who was supposed to be asleep. "What's going on?"

"Is someone sick?" piped Simon, who was three years older but not much taller, scrambling in behind him.

Jack followed the two boys in, scowling. "How does anyone get any sleep around here?"

"Genevieve has a secret admirer waiting for her outside," reported Annabelle.

"We think he's a prince," Grace added.

"Or maybe a cutthroat," finished Charlotte.

Jamie and Simon needed no further enticement. Before Genevieve could stop them, they tore across the room and ripped back the curtain to catch a glimpse of the mysterious stranger on the street below.

"I see him!" squealed Jamie, ecstatic. "Look!"

The other children swarmed around the window, knocking and jostling one another as they each fought to secure a better view.

"Hello down there!" called Simon cheerfully. He pressed his freckled nose against the glass and waved, inspiring all the other children to do the same.

"Hello!"

"Hello!"

"Hello!"

Genevieve stared in horror at Jack, her mind reeling. It was suddenly appallingly clear what the lad had wanted with Warder Sims's keys. Jack sauntered over to the window and took a cursory glance at Haydon. Then he looked at her.

"I didn't think he would come here." He shrugged.

"You know him?" exclaimed Simon, studying Jack with awe.

"Is he a prince?" asked Annabelle excitedly.

Jack snorted. "Hardly. He's a—"

"He's leaving!" interrupted Grace, diverting everyone's attention back to Haydon.

"Oh my," murmured Charlotte in a soft, sympathetic voice, "he can hardly walk."

"What's wrong with him?" wondered Jamie, concerned.

"He was badly beaten by the prison warder for tryin' to help me." Jack stared at Genevieve, his expression challenging.

"We have to stop him!" said Simon. "Come on!"

"Wait!" cried Genevieve as the children stampeded for the door.

Reluctantly, they stopped and regarded her with impatience.

"I'm not sure this is a good idea," she ventured, trying to grasp a moment to think.

"We are going to help him, aren't we?" asked Charlotte.

"Of course we are," Jamie assured her. "Genevieve always helps people."

"And if he helped Jack, then we should help him," reasoned Grace.

"We must stop him now," declared Annabelle, wringing her hands dramatically, "before he disappears forever!"

Genevieve looked helplessly at Jack.

He regarded her with cold contempt, as if her hesitation was no more than what he expected of her.

And then he turned and marched toward the stairs.

The children needed no further encouragement. They raced after him, flying down the staircase with their pale cotton nightgowns billowing around them like wings.

"Stay back!" barked Oliver, bursting suddenly from the kitchen wielding an ax in his wizened, trembling arms. "There's an unsavory rascal out there and I'm going to chop him into wee bits and have Eunice grind him into haggis!"

"Now, Ollie, ye should know better than to be scarin' the bairns with such talk," chided Doreen, the plentiful lines of her plain, thin face crinkled with disapproval. "However am I to get them to eat their food when ye're constantly fillin' their wee heads with such blather?"

"I'm of no mind to make haggis out of some poor, half-starved wretch," added Eunice, squeezing her bounteous form into the crowded hallway. "He's bound to be all string and gristle."

"Oh, Oliver, you mustn't kill him," pleaded Charlotte earnestly. "He's hurt!"

"And he's Jack's friend," Grace added.

"We're going to invite him in," explained Annabelle.

"Then could we have some tea?" asked Simon hopefully. "I'm starving."

"At this hour?" Eunice regarded Genevieve with dismay. "But we're scarcely fit to receive company, Miss Genevieve—we're all in our nightclothes!"

"He won't mind," Charlotte assured her.

"He's from prison!" chirped Jamie, as if this were a marvelous endorsement.

Jack threw the front door open. The children surged forward, only to find Haydon's figure slowly retreating down the street.

"Hello there!" Simon shouted.

"Come back!" cried Charlotte.

"We won't let Oliver chop you up for haggis!" Annabelle promised.

Realizing that Haydon might not find that particularly reassuring, Jack sprinted into the frigid darkness in his bare feet, catching up to Haydon just before he disappeared around the corner.

"It's all right," Jack told him. "You can come in."

Haydon stared at him in confusion. His vision was blurred by fever, and every step required excruciating effort. Even so, he had no desire to endanger Miss MacPhail and the flock of white-gowned children who were calling to him from the doorstep. This was not what he had planned.

"No."

"You must," Jack insisted impatiently. "You're too weak to walk, and soon all of Inveraray will be lookin' for you."

"Didn't want her to know." Haydon's tongue felt thick and clumsy as he labored to form the words. "Didn't want her to be part of it."

"She doesn't mind," Jack lied. He wrapped a thin arm around Haydon, supporting him. "She wants you to come in."

Haydon looked over at Genevieve. She was clad only in a creamy nightrail, her tall, slender figure rising above the excited, waving children clustered around her. His vision was too clouded to make out her expression.

In that moment she was as close to an angel as anything he had ever hoped to see.

"Just for tonight," he mumbled. "No longer."

Leaning heavily against Jack, he began to stagger back toward the house. Jack helped him through the door and into the hallway, where Haydon stared vacantly at the fascinated audience surrounding him.

And then crashed in a heap upon the floor.

"What's happened to yer friend, laddie?" Oliver frowned at Haydon over the blade of his ax. "He dinna look so good."

"He was beaten while trying to help me," Jack explained. "And he's sick."

"Sick, ye say?" scoffed Doreen. "He looks nigh fit to be buried."

Jamie looked up at Genevieve, his eyes wide with concern. "Is he going to die?"

"Of course not," she replied, affecting far more assurance than she felt. Even if she managed to nurse him back to health, the man lying on the floor of her hall-way was a convicted murderer. If he was captured, as he most certainly would be, he would be hanged.

She pushed the thought from her mind. All that mattered in that moment was that he was badly injured and needed their help.

"Oliver, please help Jack take his friend up to my room and put him on the bed," she instructed briskly. "Eunice, kindly warm some of that broth you made earlier, and bring it up with a pot of strong tea. Doreen, please fetch a jug of hot water, a jug of cold water, some soap, and a pot of ointment. Simon and Jamie, bring some wood up to my room and add it to the fire. Annabelle, Grace, and Charlotte, see if you can find an old, clean sheet, and tear it into narrow strips for binding."

Everyone immediately rushed in all directions to do her bidding.

Genevieve inhaled a slow, steadying breath before hurrying up the stairs to her bedroom.

"We'd best get him out o' these clothes," remarked Oliver after he had eased Haydon onto the bed. "Were ye wantin' me to burn them?" He regarded Genevieve meaningfully.

She nodded. Oliver was well acquainted with the ill-fitting moleskin jacket, trousers, cotton shirt, and braces that comprised local prison uniforms. Clearly he didn't want anyone beyond their household to recognize it as such—not even if it was tossed in the garbage.

"Here, lad, help me to sit him up so we can get these things off," Oliver said to Jack.

Their patient was an unusually large man, and it took the three of them to lift and turn him as they peeled away the filthy layers of his prison uniform. Finally he was stripped to the waist.

"Dear Lord." Genevieve stared in horror at the ugly purple and black bruises streaking his muscular torso. "Did that awful warder do all this?"

Jack shook his head. "He was hurt when he came to the prison. Said somethin' about being attacked. That's why Sims hit him in the rib cage." His voice was filled with loathing as he finished, "He knew it would make it worse."

"They're a nasty lot, prison warders." Oliver's expression was grim. "I've known my share, and they're all the same. Here now, lass, ye'd best look away while Jack and I pull off his trousers."

"I'll see what's keeping Doreen," said Genevieve, suddenly embarrassed.

She returned a few minutes later carrying a pile of thin towels, to find her bedroom in complete turmoil.

"Ye canna stack logs on a fire like bricks," Oliver was saying to Simon and Jamie as he poked violently at the hearth, which was merrily spewing thick gray smoke into the room. "Ye've got to give 'em room to breathe, or else they'll make ye sorry for it."

"Girls, can ye not find elsewhere to do that?" clucked Eunice, nearly tripping over Annabelle, Grace, and Charlotte, who were seated upon an enormous sheet as if they were having a picnic.

"I think we have to get off it if we're going to tear it up," reflected Charlotte.

"Nonsense," Grace said, struggling to start a rip in one corner. "It will be much better if we all sit on it to keep it steady."

"Look at me—I'm an Arabian princess!" Annabelle stood and draped a length of the threadbare sheet in front of her face. "Where, oh where is my handsome desert sheik?"

" 'Tis a shame we can't just toss him in a bath,"

remarked Doreen, staring at Haydon with her work-reddened hands fisted on her hips. " 'Tis the best way to get a man really clean."

"Or to drown him," quipped Oliver. He gave the fire one final thrust, then handed the poker to Simon, who immediately began to flail it around as if it were a sword. "Especially in his condition."

"I'll help to wash him," offered Jamie, pulling a sopping wet cloth out of the wash bowl and letting it drip water all over the bed. "I know how."

"That won't be necessary." Genevieve set down the towels and scooped up the dripping cloth from Jamie. "Oliver, Doreen, and I will take care of Jack's friend. The rest of you may go to bed."

Simon stopped his swordplay to regard her with a crestfallen look. "But we want to help."

"We won't make any noise," Grace assured her.

"And we won't get in your way," added Charlotte.

"Please," chimed Annabelle from behind her make-shift veil.

Genevieve sighed. "I appreciate your desire to help. But there are too many people in this room, and the best way you could help is by going to bed and getting a good night's sleep. There will be lots of other things for you to do tomorrow."

"Like what?" asked Jamie eagerly.

"I'll tell you tomorrow. Eunice, please take the children back to their rooms and make sure they are nicely tucked in."

"Come on, then, duckies." Eunice opened her slack, plump arms and gathered the children together like a flock of little birds. "If ye move smartly, ye each may have a special sweetie at yer plate in the morning."

Excited by that wonderful possibility, the children instantly abandoned their pursuits and raced from the room.

"Jack, you may also go to bed," Genevieve said, dipping her cloth in warm water. "We can manage."

"Are you going to report him to the police?" His voice was low and hard.

Doreen's aged eyes rounded in shock as she studied the man sprawled on the bed. "Sweet Saints," she gasped. "He's the one I went to see, isn't he? The murderer who escaped from the jail this evening?"

Genevieve wrung out her cloth and calmly began to wash Haydon's face. "If not for him, Jack would have been brutally beaten today," she stated quietly. "Isn't that right, Jack?"

"He had no reason to help me." His voice was low and fierce, as if he thought she might debate the matter. "But he did. Sick and hurt as he was, he pulled that bastard warder off me. Told him he would kill him if he touched me again. And then he got pounded for it."

Genevieve eased her cloth down the chiseled contour of Haydon's cheek. His face had the black growth of a week or more, and there were dark circles bruising the skin beneath his eyes. Even so, he was an uncommonly handsome man. A man convicted of murder, she reminded herself uneasily.

Who would rise to the defense of a helpless boy, when he himself could barely stand.

"Do ye ken who he is, laddie?" asked Oliver, his white brows knit with concern. "Or who he murdered?"

Jack shook his head. "I only shared a cell with him for a few days. He never talked much. But he's from money, judgin' by his speech. The warder used to call him 'his lordship.' "

"That doesn't mean anything," Doreen scoffed, grabbing a cloth so she could help Genevieve wash Haydon. "Warders are always makin' sport of their prisoners. It's part of how they have their fun."

Jack regarded her curiously. "How do you know that?"

"Because I've been in prison," she replied matter-of-factly.

"We all have, lad," added Oliver, sensing the boy's surprise. "Except for Miss Genevieve, of course." He chuckled.

"But Miss Genevieve knows the black ways of prison, make no mistake." Doreen cast Genevieve an adoring smile, then resumed her earnest scrubbing of Haydon's hand.

"The authorities are searching for him now," Genevieve mused, skimming her cloth with gentle care across the hot, bruised flesh of Haydon's chest. "And as Jack and I were the last ones to see him in his cell, they will undoubtedly want to question us when they fail to find him tonight."

"I won't talk to them," Jack spat fiercely.

"I'm afraid you will have to, Jack. We both will." She hesitated, studying Haydon's face.

I am no murderer, he had told her, his gaze boring into her with painful intensity. And in that moment, as he held her within his desperate grip, she had almost believed him. She knew nothing of the facts of the case—knew nothing about him whatsoever. Except that in his last hours upon this earth, he had been more concerned about the fate of a sullen, thieving boy than himself.

And when that lad was about to be savagely beaten he had intervened, and offered himself instead.

"What we tell the authorities, however," she finished in a soft, determined voice, "is another matter entirely."

.   .   .

Haydon FELT AS IF HE WERE ON FIRE.

He flung himself from side to side, desperately trying to douse the flames, or perhaps just find a shred of
cool air to ease the terrible burning. And yet he was
shivering, his teeth clattering together like loose peb-
bles, his jaw clenching so hard he thought the bones
would snap. There was pain, too, lashing against him each
time he shifted, a deep, racking torment that surged
through every inch of his body. He could neither move
nor lie still, for both were excruciating, and the frustration of it made him feel as if he were going mad. He
tried to cry out, a hoarse, desperate plea, wanting it to
end, even if that meant death. Surely even the cruelest
God could not expect him to endure such agony.

And then it occurred to him that perhaps he was
dead, and this was the abominable hell to which he had
been sentenced.

His cry died in his throat.

"Hush," soothed a voice, soft and achingly feminine. "It's all right, now."

A cold, wet cloth slid gently over his face, dousing
the flames in its path. It lifted away from his skin for a
moment and then returned, slipping across his searing
flesh, cooling the terrible, melting heat. The liquid chill
dribbled in silvery rivulets down the sides of his face,
into his hair, through his papery lips, into the dry parch-
ment of his mouth. A splashing of water in a basin and
the cloth was back, making slow, sure movements across
the battlefield of his broken body, swirling and caressing, like gentle waves lapping over him. Slowly, the fire
blazing through him began to wane. Finally he sank
deep into the softness upon which he lay, his breath
shallow but steady, his chills all but vanquished.

Perhaps he was not dead after all.

He dozed a while, vaguely aware of the sweet graze of the cool cloth across his burning skin. Along his chest and down his stomach it moved, then gingerly up the sides of his waist and ribs. Its touch was sure yet strangely tender, as if it sensed the injuries hidden beneath, and knew just how much pressure he could withstand. Again and again it traversed him, lulling him with its rhythmic caress, making him feel cool and clean and cherished, although he could not imagine who might think him worthy of such regard. A whisper of music filled the air, fragile and hushed, as if it was not meant for him to hear. He forced himself to lie utterly still, tried to even quiet the weak sigh of his breath so he could hear the lovely singing drifting like a feather on the air around him. It filled him with pleasure, wrapping around him in an ethereal embrace; tender, absolute, forgiving.

His sleep deepened.

Time seeped by. When he awoke it was by slow degrees, a languid peeling away of the hazy layers of confusion and weariness. Fresh, cool air filled his nostrils, tinged with the smoky, sweet scent of firewood burning. The mattress beneath him was soft, the sheets covering him, clean. The faint ticking of a clock lulled him, its quiet, perpetual song tapping lightly at his senses, speaking of reason, order, and logic. He sighed, taking immense comfort in the distilled quiet around him. He could not remember where he was or how he had come to be here, but one thing was utterly clear.

He was no longer rotting in a foul cell with death looming over him.

With enormous effort, he opened his eyes.

Dark shadows veiled the room, indicating it was still night. A low fire cast ripples of apricot light into the darkness, spilling across the carpeted floor, flickering over the rumpled plaid blanket covering his bed. He followed the shifting ribbons to the chair beside him, where they danced up a white nightgown, then dappled the creamy pale skin of the soundly sleeping Miss MacPhail.

She had curled herself into the padded constraints of the chair as best she could, tucking her legs up beneath herself and leaning over so she could use her slender arm as a pillow. Her coral and gold hair spilled lavishly over the snowy linen of her nightgown, setting it afire with strands of silken color. Her sleeves were rolled up to her elbows and her gown was copiously water-stained and wrinkled. It was she who had tended him through the night, Haydon realized, glancing at the porcelain water basin and abandoned cloths resting on the table beside her. The lines of her brow were deeply etched, and wine-colored shadows stained the delicate skin below the fringe of her lashes. Exhaustion had dragged her into a heavy sleep, too absolute to permit her to be roused by the cool breeze gusting through the window, or the discomfort of her position, or the fact that her patient had awakened. He studied her with reverent fascination, watching the slow rise and fall of her sweetly rounded breasts, the slight shifting of her slender body, the nearly imperceptible deepening of the lines between her brows as she buried her cheek deeper into her arm.

He could not remember a woman ever staying by his side to watch over him so.

He was unaccustomed to being helpless—especially before a female he scarcely knew. And it seemed he truly was helpless. The savage beating he had received at the hands of his assailants some two weeks earlier, followed by the illness that had gripped him in prison, and then that final beating from dear Warder Sims only hours ago had combined to reduce him to a weak and shivering invalid. He had no idea how he had made it from the prison to this home. All he could remember was Jack leading him, and the sight of the lovely Miss MacPhail standing amidst a cluster of angels who were waving and calling to him.

Perhaps sensing that she was being watched, she stirred, her eyes fluttering open. She studied him a moment, her enormous brown eyes void of either suspicion or fear, as if she was merely trying to recall how a battered, half-naked man had come to be lying in her bed.

And then she bolted upright and scrambled to find something with which to cover herself.

Clearly, she had remembered.

"Good evening," rasped Haydon, his throat painfully dry.

Genevieve grabbed the woolen shawl that had fallen onto the floor and hastily wrapped it over her shoulders and across her chest. How long had he been staring at her like that? she wondered nervously. And what was she thinking, falling asleep beside a strange, naked man, with her hair down and her feet bare, when she was supposed to be watching over him? She reached for the jug on the bedside table and poured him a glass of water, using the simple task to compose herself.

"Here," she said, modestly clamping her shawl closed with one hand as she held the glass to his lips. "Try to take a small sip."

The water trickled into his mouth and throat. Haydon took a swallow, then another and another, until finally the glass was drained. He was a man who had indulged heavily in the finest of wines and spirits, yet he could not remember ever finding a drink so enormously satisfying.

"Thank you."

Genevieve placed the glass on the table and self-consciously adjusted her shawl. "How are you feeling?"

"Better."

She glanced at the tray Eunice had brought up so many hours earlier. "Would you care to try some broth? It's cold now, but I could run downstairs and heat it—"

"Not hungry."

She nodded and fell silent, uncertain what to do or say next.

All night long she had tended to him, despite Oliver's and Doreen's adamant protests that they had done as much for him as anyone could possibly do. The matter of whether he succumbed to his injuries and his fever or not, they assured her, was now in God's hands. But it had been years since Genevieve had yielded matters that she believed to be at least somewhat within her grasp, solely to God. Regardless of who this man was or what he had done, she could not simply retire and leave him to suffer through the night alone.

And so she had stayed with him.

She had spent long hours swabbing his bruised, burning body with soothing cool cloths, alternately covering him with more blankets and peeling them away, pressing the softness of her palms against his searing forehead and roughly bearded jaw as she tried to ascertain whether she was winning her desperate battle against his fever. She knew every chiseled contour of his chest and shoulders and belly, the hard heat of his skin where it stretched tightly across his pectorals, the dark swirls of hair that formed a mysterious line beneath his navel before disappearing under the thin linen of the sheets. She knew he shifted and tried to curl onto his side when a chill began to grip him, and flailed his arms and legs wide when he was suffering unbearable heat. She knew just how much water she could drizzle from the edge of a cloth between his lips without making him gag or have the water leak down the sides of his face, and how much pressure she could render in her touch to soothe him instead of causing him pain. She was familiar with every bruise and scrape and welt upon him, and was reasonably sure of which ribs were broken and which were sore but solid. This intimate knowledge had made her strangely at ease in his presence as he slept, as if she had known him for years and had no reason to feel either threatened or self-conscious.

Now that he was awake, however, she didn't feel at ease in the least.

"Did you . . . help him?"

She regarded him blankly.

"The boy," Haydon explained, laboring to form the words. "Did you help him . . . free me?"

Her initial inclination was to assure him that she most certainly had not. But that wasn't quite true, she realized. She had watched Jack clandestinely lift the keys from the warder's belt. Instead of stopping him, she had created an enormous fuss to distract the jailer from noticing. In the ensuing melee, she had not set out to find Jack promptly and bring him back to Governor Thomson's office as she should have. Instead, she had waited nervously for him to finish whatever his business was and reappear.

Had she not at least suspected his intent—especially after Jack's insistence that she take this condemned man with her in addition to him?

"I am not in the habit of breaking convicted criminals out of prison." She was unsure if she was trying to convince herself or him.

"You took Jack out."

"By completely legal means, with Governor Thomson's knowledge and consent," she retorted. "Furthermore, Jack is only a boy, and should never have been sent to prison in the first place."

"Nor should I." It was an enormous effort just to talk. He wearily closed his eyes.

His brow was furrowed and his jaw clenched, indicating he was experiencing pain. Genevieve wet a cloth and pressed it lightly against his forehead, trying to ease his discomfort. A stifled groan escaped his lips. She removed the cloth, dipped it in cool water once more, and began to skim it over his face.

What kind of a man would rise to the defense of a young thief, when he himself was so racked with fever and pain he could barely stand? she wondered. Jack had told her that this man had been gravely ill and injured even before he rose from his bed, tore the prison warder off Jack and threw him across the cell. Surely he must have known that in his condition he could not possibly win a battle against Warder Sims. And he had not even befriended the lad. According to Jack, they had scarcely exchanged a half-dozen words with each other in the entire time they had shared a cell.

For a convicted murderer, he was capable of remarkable compassion and nobility.

His head dropped to one side and his breathing grew deep, indicating that he had fallen asleep. Genevieve leaned over him and gently lay her hand against his brow. He was still overly hot, but not with the same burning intensity he had suffered an hour earlier. Still, experience in dealing with the children's fevers had taught her that the body's temperature could drop and then suddenly flare again with alarming speed. She would have to monitor him carefully to try to make sure that didn't happen. She adjusted the blankets over him, then picked up the tray Eunice had prepared, intending to return it to the kitchen and bring up some fresh water.

"Stay."

His voice was rough, making it sound more a command than a plea. But his blue eyes were clouded with fever and desperation, and she knew that he was not trying to intimidate her.

"I shall only be gone a few moments," she assured him.

He shook his head. "They will come for me soon and I will be hanged. Until then, stay. Please."

"They will come and I will send them away," Genevieve returned emphatically. "They need not know you are here."

His eyes widened slightly in surprise. And then they closed, as if he no longer had the strength to keep them open.

Genevieve hesitated.

And then she set the tray down and returned to her chair, preparing to stay by his side for the rest of the night.

Chapter Three

CEASE YER POUNDIN'!" SHOUTED OLIVER IRRITA-
bly. "I canna move faster than this!"

That was, in fact, a matter of debate. Whoever was
rapping heavily upon the front door appeared to take
him at his word, however, and the insistent knocking
stopped.

"Have ye nae learned the virtue of patience?"
Oliver grumbled, grasping the latch with his gnarled
hands. "Did yer ma nae teach ye 'tis no proper to be
breakin' down an old man's door?" He swung the door
open, finishing crossly, "Have ye no more manners than
a stinkin', hairy—oh, beggin' yer pardon, Governor
Thomson."

"Kindly inform Miss MacPhail that Police Constable
Drummond and I must speak with her at once on a most
urgent matter," said Governor Thomson impatiently.

Oliver leaned against the door and idly scratched his
white head. "What's amiss, then? Did someone finally
take a torch to that nasty pile o' rubble ye call a jail?"

Indignation nearly turned the roots of Governor
Thomson's wiry beard pink. "I'll have you know I run
a respectable prison, which meets with all the current

recommendations of the Inspector of Prisons for Scotland. Second, what I choose to discuss with Miss Mac-Phail is none of your concern. And third, if you had learned anything whatsoever about being a butler since you left my prison, you would open this door this minute and escort the constable and myself into the drawing room to await Miss MacPhail's company."

Oliver snapped his brows together in a snowy scowl. "Is that so? Well, I'd wager yer precious inspector would make a far different list of recommendations if he'd been made to actually stay in that stinkin' cesspool a week or so. Second, I'm nae in the habit of lettin' anyone enter this house without havin' them state their business first. And third, as Miss MacPhail is my mistress, I'll be lettin' her decide whether ye'll be sittin' in her house or standin' out here biding yer time on the doorstep." He slammed the door in their startled faces.

"Let them stew over that for a moment." He chuckled. "Are ye ready, then, lassie?"

"Almost," said Genevieve, lifting her skirts as she hurried down the staircase. She had been tending to her patient, who was still sleeping, and had needed a moment to straighten her appearance before facing the authorities. "You may show them into the drawing room, Oliver." She rushed into the room and seated herself.

Oliver waited another moment, just to further annoy Governor Thomson before finally opening the door. "Miss MacPhail will see ye both in the drawing room." He raised an arthritic arm and gestured grandly at the modestly appointed room.

Regarding him with irritation, Governor Thomson removed his coat and hat and held them out for Oliver to take.

" 'Tis kind o' ye to offer, but I canna say I'm particularly fond of black," Oliver told him. "Makes ye

look like a corpse, Guv'ner, if ye dinna mind my sayin'
so. Besides, ye'll only be wantin' them again when ye're
leaving."

Governor Thomson huffed with exasperation and
marched into the drawing room, carrying his rejected
attire. Constable Drummond removed his own hat and
followed behind him, his thin mouth pressed into a line
of disgust, as if Oliver's rudeness was no more than
what he expected.

"Good morning, Governor Thomson," said Genevieve pleasantly. "Constable Drummond. Please, sit down.
May I offer you some refreshment?"

"That won't be necessary," Constable Drummond
replied before Governor Thomson could accept.

"Forgive us for disturbing you this morning, Miss
MacPhail," Governor Thomson apologized, plopping
his corpulent backside into a chair, "but I'm afraid
something terrible has happened. Lord Redmond has
escaped."

Genevieve regarded him blankly. "Who?"

"The murderer who shared a cell with the boy you
took home with you last night, Miss MacPhail," Constable Drummond explained. "He was Lord Haydon
Kent, Marquess of Redmond. I believe you exchanged
some words with him before leaving the prison."

Constable Drummond was a tall, dour man of some
forty years, with unfashionably long hair that dripped in
a scraggly fringe below his collar. More hair oozed in
two dark stripes along the sides of his face, which only
served to accentuate the thinness of his somber features.
Genevieve had first met him when she had gone to rescue Charlotte a year earlier from prison, and she had
taken an immediate dislike to him. It was he who had
arrested the poor child, who was all of ten at the time,
for the criminal offense of stealing a turnip and two

apples from a garden. It was Constable Drummond's impenetrable conviction that those individuals who did not uphold the law deserved to be dealt the harshest of consequences, be they adult or child, and he had not been supportive of Genevieve taking Charlotte into her tender custody.

"Of course. I was not aware of his name." Somehow Genevieve managed to keep her expression neutral. *The warder used to call him "his lordship."* Jack had said. Her own father had been a viscount, and her former betrothed was an earl, so she was not easily impressed with aristocratic titles and the preposterous implication of social, moral, and intellectual superiority that accompanied them.

Nevertheless, it was somehow disconcerting to think that the naked man whose battered, aching body she had swabbed throughout the night was a marquess.

"My maid told me when she returned from the prison last night that the prisoner from Jack's cell was missing." She drew her brow together in feigned worry. "I had hoped you would have found him by now."

"Rest assured, he can't have gone far," said Governor Thomson, shifting uncomfortably in his seat. His waistcoat was straining tautly against its buttons, which looked as if they might suddenly fly off at any moment. "Not in his condition."

He appeared to be trying to convince himself as much as her. Clearly it did not reflect well upon his abilities to have a dangerous murderer escape from his prison the very night before the man was to be executed. It occurred to Genevieve that the governor might well be in danger of losing his position for such a grave blunder. The possibility was troubling. Whatever his faults, she had carefully cultivated a valuable partnership with him over the years. With Governor Thomson running the prison, she was always informed when there was a child sentenced to languish behind its foul walls. She could not be certain a new governor would be nearly so accommodating—or so open to bribery.

"I will find him." Constable Drummond spoke with a harsh resolve that Genevieve found unsettling. "Have no fear of that. I expect he will be locked up again before nightfall, and hanged first thing tomorrow."

She managed what she hoped was a sufficiently bright smile. "How very reassuring. Just hearing you say that makes me feel much better. As I'm certain you can appreciate, a woman with young children becomes most anxious when she hears that a dangerous killer is lurking on the streets. Until you have succeeded in your capture of him, I shall be sure to keep careful watch over all of my family. Thank you both for taking the time to come here to warn me. It was most kind of you." She rose, as if presuming their discussion was finished.

"Actually, that isn't the sole purpose for our visit." Governor Thomson shifted awkwardly once again. Genevieve thought he looked like a giant egg wobbling back and forth. "We wanted to speak to the lad."

She arched her brows in confusion. "You mean Jack? Why?"

"It is possible your new—" Constable Drummond's mouth tightened as he searched for a palatable noun "—*charge* can provide us with some clue as to where Lord Redmond may have gone." The word "charge" was laden with scorn.

"What makes you think he has any knowledge of such a thing?"

Constable Drummond leaned back and steepled his long fingers together, studying her. Genevieve regarded him with brittle calm.

"They must have talked about something, Miss MacPhail." His manner was infuriatingly condescending, as if he were trying to explain the obvious to a dullard. "Lord Redmond is not from Inveraray, and was arrested for his brutal crime shortly after he arrived here. This leaves us with limited clues as to where he might be hiding. Given his severely weakened condition at the time of his escape, we do not believe he can have traveled very far. We know he did not return to the inn where he was staying prior to his arrest, or to the tavern at which he became intoxicated on the night of the murder. We need to find out from the lad if Lord Redmond made any mention of his acquaintances in Inveraray, or discussed some place where he might go were he to escape."

"I have known Jack only a short while, but I can tell you he is not a boy who engages much in conversation." Her tone was light as she finished obligingly, "However, if you believe he may be of some assistance, of course you must speak with him. Oliver, would you be kind enough to fetch Jack and ask him to join us?"

Oliver poked his scraggly white head around the door to the drawing room. "Aye."

He disappeared and returned a moment later, with Jack reluctantly following.

The lad who entered the room bore scant resemblance to the filthy urchin who had left the prison the previous night. His skin had been scrubbed clean with fragrant soap and a brush, and his greasy tangle of brown hair had been washed, trimmed, and neatly combed. He was dressed in a tailored jacket, white shirt and dark pair of trousers, and on his feet were a pair of worn but well-polished shoes. His jacket hung a little too loose on his thin frame, and his shorter hair was springing into curls that had completely resisted Doreen's efforts to make them lie flat. At first glance he looked like a perfect, albeit somewhat uncomfortable, young gentleman.

Only the raw animosity burning in his gray eyes and the scar across his left cheek suggested otherwise.

"Jack, you remember Governor Thomson," said Genevieve.

Jack glared at the governor.

"And this is Police Constable Drummond," she continued, ignoring the hostility emanating from the boy. She would educate him on his manners later. At the moment, she was more concerned that he not lose his temper or say anything that might give their visitors reason to be suspicious.

"Actually, Jack and I are well acquainted." Constable Drummond regarded the boy with obvious contempt. "Aren't we, Jack?"

Jack gave the constable a single curt nod.

"These gentlemen would like to ask you a few questions about Lord Redmond," Genevieve continued. "He's the man with whom you shared your cell at the prison," she explained, realizing that Jack would be unfamiliar with his title. "As Doreen mentioned on returning from the prison last night, he has escaped."

Jack said nothing.

"Tell us, lad, did Lord Redmond ever mention anything to you about his plans for escape?" asked Governor Thomson hopefully.

"No."

Constable Drummond regarded him with barely contained derision. It was his unflinching conviction that Jack was a liar and a thief, and therefore could not be trusted. "Ever talk about having acquaintances in Inveraray?"

"No."

"Did he ever mention any place in Inveraray at all—a tavern he was familiar with, or an inn where he might have taken a meal?" Governor Thomson prompted.

"No."

Constable Drummond tapped his fingertips thought-fully on the arm of his chair. "Did he talk at all about his family or friends?"

Jack shook his head.

"Well, then, just what did you talk about?" asked Governor Thomson, perplexed.

He shrugged.

"You must have talked about something." Constable Drummond's voice was vaguely menacing. "All those hours you spent together."

Jack flashed him a look of undiluted loathing. "He was sick most of the time, and just lay on his bed. And I wasn't there to make friends with a bloody murderer," he finished bitterly.

There was a moment of uneasy silence.

"Yes, well, fine then," said Governor Thomson, somewhat chagrined at having the fact that he had placed a mere boy in the same cell with a deadly killer pointed out. "I guess that's that, then." He regarded Constable Drummond hopefully. "Is it?"

"That's all for the lad—for now." Constable Drum-mond met Jack's glare with cool disdain, neither con-vinced nor impressed by his protest of ignorance. "I should like to ask Miss MacPhail a few questions, how-ever."

"Thank you, Jack." Genevieve gave the boy an en-couraging smile. "You may go."

He hesitated, as if he wanted to stay and hear what she was going to say. It was obvious he was not con-vinced that he could trust her. Genevieve suspected there had been far too many betrayals in his life for him to believe that she would keep her word and protect the man lying helpless in her room.

"Come on, then, laddie." Oliver placed his hand upon the boy's bony shoulder. "Let's see if we canna convince Eunice to give us a chunk of that shortbread she just took from the oven."

Jack shot Genevieve a final hard look before permitting himself to be led from the room.

Constable Drummond's thin mouth curled in disgust. "He's a liar and a thief, and he always will be—no matter how hard you try to clean him up. You would be best to return him to the prison, Miss MacPhail, and let the iron fist of the law deal with him."

"Jack has been under my roof for only a few hours, and already he is being questioned by the police, even though he hasn't done anything," Genevieve replied evenly. "One could hardly expect him not to be angry and defensive."

"Even so, I'd wager the lad knows more than he's letting on." Governor Thomson stroked his gray beard, trying to appear astute. "You must watch him at all times, and let us know if anything seems amiss. Anything at all."

"I can assure you, I have every intent of keeping a very careful watch over Jack. And I have no intention of returning him to the prison system, or letting him come to any further harm. What will you do now about finding Lord Redmond?" she asked, changing the subject.

"At this moment we have men visiting every tavern, inn, store or other place of business in Inveraray, asking if anyone has seen him," replied Constable Drummond. "We're searching the coach houses and sheds of each home in the surrounding area, and are questioning people to see if they have noticed anything strange—particularly if any food or clothing has gone missing. We are also keeping careful watch over the coaches leaving Inveraray, in particular those that are traveling to Edinburgh and Glasgow. Dangerous criminals often flee to the cities to find work and disappear amidst the thousands of people there. Of course, we are sending word to the authorities in Inverness to arrest him immediately should he turn up there. The marquess has an estate just north of there."

"Nasty piece of business, the murder he committed," commented Governor Thomson. Finally surrendering to his girth, he released one of the straining buttons of his waistcoat. "Truly horrid."

Constable Drummond regarded Genevieve intently. "As brutal a slaying as I've ever seen in over twenty years."

She didn't want to hear this. She was certain of it. After all, she couldn't believe that the man lying so helplessly upstairs in her bed could be capable of such a thing.

Even so, she could not help but ask, "What happened?"

"Bashed some poor fellow's head in with a rock." Governor Thomson shook his head in disbelief. "But that was a mercy, because Lord Redmond had already beaten him half to death."

Bile began to seep up the back of Genevieve's throat. Was it possible that the man she had permitted into her home and was trying to protect was actually a vicious murderer? *I would like you to believe that I am innocent.* She wanted to believe him. But a man was dead, and a jury had decided that he was responsible.

"Who did he kill?"

"The authorities were unable to identify him." Constable Drummond's dark eyes seemed to be boring into her as he finished, "His face was all but gone."

Hands filled her mind. Large, powerful, elegantly formed. With long fingers that she could imagine stroking the keys of a piano, or perhaps caressing the softness of an adoring woman's cheek. She had carefully bathed and dried those hands, had washed them clean of all trace of the prison's filth, and placed them gently upon the cool linen that covered him. At the time she had thought of them as the caring hands that had come to Jack's rescue.

Were they also the savage hands that had beaten a man to death?

"Did anyone see him do this?" Her mouth was suddenly dry, making it difficult to force the words out.

"There were no witnesses to the actual murder," Constable Drummond allowed. "But several people saw Lord Redmond running from the docks where the body was found. It was amply clear from his bloodied hands and clothes that he had been involved in a brutal assault. They served as witnesses at his trial."

She pretended to be distracted by an imaginary speck of lint upon her gown, trying to appear no more than mildly curious. "And what was Lord Redmond's explanation?"

"Just exactly what you would expect him to say. That he had been set upon by several men, and had, unfortunately, killed one of them. He claimed to have no knowledge of who they were or what their motive might have been for attempting to kill him, other than simple robbery. The jury did not accept his explanation."

She looked up. "Why not?"

"There was no one who could substantiate his claim that he was attacked by four men instead of just one. If there were four assailants, how could he possibly have emerged the victor? Nothing was taken from him during the course of this alleged robbery. And if he was rightfully defending himself, then why didn't he contact the authorities afterward, as any innocent person would do, instead of running away? Finally, he was unable to secure anyone to come and testify on behalf of his good character."

"Surely he had some family to speak for him—or perhaps a close friend?"

"No one, except for his lawyer, who traveled from Inverness for the trial. For their part, the prosecution was able to secure statements from numerous acquaintances establishing that Lord Redmond is well known to have a dangerously volatile temper that is frequently roused by his inordinate fondness for drink. There were witnesses who testified that he had been drinking heavily in a tavern on the evening of the murder, and had nearly engaged in a fight with the owner before he was thrown out."

"A shame," said Governor Thomson, who had rolled back in his chair and laced his pudgy fingers over the bloat of his belly. "To be blessed with a title and fortune, and have so little self-control." He sounded as if he thought that he should have been so blessed instead.

"Indeed." A sickening coil of fear was unfurling in Genevieve's stomach. If the man lying in her chamber upstairs was as dangerous as these men suggested, then she must tell them immediately, so they could arrest him at once and take him back to the prison. But if she confessed to helping him, they would have no choice but to arrest her too. What would become of the children? she wondered desperately. Oliver, Eunice, and Doreen would gladly stay to look after them, but her arrangement with Governor Thomson did not permit for anyone other than herself to have custody. He certainly would fail to convince the court that their wardship should now be transferred to three elderly criminals.

"Since the boy is of no help to us and Miss MacPhail has not noticed anything amiss, we should be moving along," suggested Governor Thomson, bobbing forward in his chair. He regarded Constable Drummond uncertainly. "Shouldn't we?"

"Not just yet." Constable Drummond's gaze was riveted on Genevieve. "With your permission, Miss MacPhail, I would like to conduct a search of these premises."

Terror streaked up Genevieve's spine.

"More specifically, I wish to inspect your coach house," he clarified, oblivious to her sudden alarm. "Although it is unlikely we shall find our prisoner there, as I mentioned we are searching all such outer buildings, in the hopes of finding some indication as to where Lord Redmond may have spent the night."

Genevieve exhaled the shallow breath trapped in her chest. "Of course. Oliver can escort you to it."

"That won't be necessary," said Constable Drummond, rising. "I'm sure we can find it."

"All the same, I'll be showin' ye round the back." Oliver appeared suddenly in the doorway. "I'll nae have ye trampin' through my garden while ye wander about—the plants may be in their winter sleep, but they dinna like it. I'll just go fetch my coat." He disappeared.

"There's another one you will never change," commented Constable Drummond, stroking his forefinger along the dark strip of hair on his cheek. "I do hope, Miss MacPhail, that you are prudent and take appropriate care of your valuables with all these criminals living under your roof. It would be a pity to see you robbed after you had extended such generosity to them—however misguided it may be."

"The only true valuables I have, Constable Drummond, are my children," Genevieve replied evenly. "Everything else is entirely replaceable. And no one in this household, including Oliver, would ever dream of taking anything from this house—or from any other house, for that matter."

"Let us hope so." He put on his hat. "For their sakes as well as yours. Good day to you." He nodded curtly to Genevieve before striding from the room.

An icy wind surged into the vestibule as he opened the front door.

"Good day, Miss MacPhail," added Governor Thomson, wrestling with his coat and hat as he hurried out behind him.

"Here now, ye're not goin' out there without me!" Oliver crammed a battered felt hat on his head and shuffled out as fast as his ancient legs would carry him.

Genevieve closed the front door and leaned heavily against it, trying to calm the anxious pounding of her heart.

And then she lifted her skirts and began to slowly make her way up the stairs.

Lemony ribbons of sunlight poured over him, drenching him with soothing heat. It permeated the clean blankets covering him, seeping through his skin and into his heavily bruised muscles and bones. Gentle as a caress, the soft warmth seemed to liquefy the stiffness of body, penetrating every fiber and joint and rib, easing the terrible throbbing that had tormented him all night. A veil of exhaustion cloaked his mind, making his wakefulness come in lethargic stages. The clock was still tapping away at time in neat, precise intervals. Somewhere in the distance people were talking, but their voices were too muffled for him to hear what they were saying. It didn't seem to matter. The sweet fragrance of baking bread drifted lazily around him, tangling with the spicy aroma of simmering meat and vegetables. He was reluctant to open his eyes, for fear that with one reckless lifting of his lids he would find himself back in the fetid squalor of his cell, with nothing to look forward to except his execution.

The door opened and he heard the silky whisper of skirts crossing the room. A citrus scent wafted upon the air, a tantalizing mixture of orange and soap and some wonderfully exotic blossoms he couldn't begin to name. He lay perfectly still, even though his mind had snapped to near crystalline clarity with the entrance of the lovely Miss MacPhail. Despite his weakness and injuries, his body began to stir. He longed to feel the softness of her cool palm pressing against his skin, the aching awareness of her lush breasts as she leaned over him to adjust his blankets, or perhaps even the agonizing swirl of her wet cloth as she drew slow circles across his hungry, burning flesh.

She did not touch him. Instead she remained at a distance, silent and still. Sensing that something was amiss, he opened his eyes.

And saw that everything between them had changed.

"Good morning, Lord Redmond."

Her voice was cool. It was her expression, however, that disturbed him most. Gone was the sweet distress that had filled her eyes the first time he had gazed into them as he lay upon the prison floor. He could not accurately remember how she had looked upon him last night, but he felt reasonably certain it had not been with this tense animosity. How could she have tended to him with such quiet devotion all those long hours, and now be looking upon him with such inimical contempt and wariness?

"What has happened?" he demanded hoarsely.

"I am going to ask you a question, Lord Redmond," she began, ignoring his query. "And I will have your word that you will answer me honestly, regardless of what the consequences may be. That is, I feel, the very least you can do for me, given the extreme risks I have taken to help you. Do I have your word?"

Cold despair leaked over him. For a moment, somewhere within the hazy, treacherous veil of slumber, he had been lulled into thinking that he was almost safe. But he wasn't. He was too weak to move, and if this lovely, agitated woman chose, he could be handed over to the authorities and executed before sundown. He was not a man accustomed to weakness or vulnerability, and the fact that his life now hung so precariously before him filled him with helpless rage.

"You have my word." There was no point in lying to her, Haydon decided. It was clear that she already knew about his crime anyway.

She hesitated. She seemed to be struggling with her question, as if she was afraid to ask it.

"Did you kill that man?" she blurted out suddenly.

"Yes."

To her credit, she did not run screaming from the room, but remained rooted where she was. Even so, he could see by the wavering of her stance that he had affected her deeply, and he was profoundly sorry for that.

"Why?" Her voice betrayed her distress.

"Because he was trying to bury a knife in my chest and I didn't much care for the idea."

She regarded him with skepticism. "Why did he want to kill you?"

"If I knew that, or who he and his three friends were, I might have had a more agreeable verdict at my trial. Unfortunately, the men who attacked me did not bother with the niceties of a formal introduction." He winced as he shifted his position, trying to sit up.

She made no move to help him. "Constable Drummond said there was no evidence that there were any other assailants."

"Constable Drummond is a malicious, loathsome, frustrated man whose personal lack of pleasure and comfort in his life causes him to heap undue infamy upon nearly every individual who crosses his path," Haydon retaliated darkly. "It is immensely fortunate that he is not a judge, or the entire town of Inveraray would be locked up."

Genevieve regarded him in surprise. It was not often that she heard someone beyond the members of her own household articulate similar thoughts on the constable. The fact that Constable Drummond was a malevolent brute did not make the man lying before her innocent. It did, however, remind her that she had not yet heard Lord Redmond's side of this sordid tale.

"Perhaps you could tell me exactly what happened that night, Lord Redmond," she suggested, clasping her hands expectantly before her.

Haydon sighed. He had been through this countless times, and without exception, no one had believed him—not even the expensive lawyer he had sent for all the bloody way from Inverness. Even he was starting to question what exactly had transpired that hellish night.

Miss MacPhail was watching him from across the room, her back rigid, her expression guarded. It was obvious she didn't trust him enough to get too close. After caring for him all through the night, after bathing and caressing nearly every inch of him with her gloriously soothing strokes, after filling his senses with singing and soft words and the tangy scent of soap and blossoms, it was somehow unbearable that now she was afraid to even be near him. He scarcely knew her, Haydon reminded himself impatiently.

Even so, the loss of her gentle trust cut him deeply.

He closed his eyes, fighting the terrible pounding invading his skull. Was this how his miserable life was to end? he wondered bleakly. As an infamous convicted murderer whose very presence struck fear into the hearts of women and children? Just when he had thought he couldn't possibly be any more loathsome, he had gone and sunk a knife into someone, adding murder to his litany of sins.

At that moment he was nearly glad that Emmaline was dead. He did not think his beautiful, troubled daughter would have been able to bear this additional anguish in her already wretched life.

"Lord Redmond?"

There was no way out of it, he realized wearily. He would have to tell Miss MacPhail his rendition of the events that had landed him in prison awaiting his execution.

And she would either believe him, or have him hauled out of here and sent back to prison.

"I had only just arrived in Inveraray that afternoon," he began in a flat, resigned voice. "I had come to investigate the possibility of investing in a new whiskey distillery to be built just north of here. Being somewhat tired after my long journey, I decided to take refreshment at one of your local taverns. After I left, I suddenly found myself attacked by four men who knew me by name, although I did not recognize any of them. They seemed to have no interest in robbing me, but merely wanted to cut my heart out. In the course of defending myself, one of them was killed and the others ran off. I was subsequently arrested, charged with murder and convicted, despite the fact that there was no apparent motive for me to walk out and kill a perfect stranger."

"Were you drunk?" Her mouth was taut with disapproval.

He found her smug self-righteousness extremely irritating. What right had she to judge him? The prim-faced, gray-gowned spinster before him had no doubt led a placid, sheltered life of chaste, dull comfort. What could she possibly know of the challenges and agonies of life, of the cruelties that could gnaw away at a man's soul until he felt he couldn't bear to face another moment without the fortification of drink?

"Very," he snapped. "But I have been drunk numerous times before, Miss MacPhail, and to my knowledge I have still refrained from murdering anyone."

"Constable Drummond said you got into an altercation with the owner of the tavern and had to be thrown out."

"That is true."

"He also said that—" She stopped suddenly, uncertain whether it was wise to continue.

Haydon raised an inquiring brow. "Yes?"

"He said that the man you killed was beaten beyond recognition." Genevieve's stomach twisted as she finished in a halting voice, "They said that you smashed his skull in."

Pure, cold rage hardened his features, making him look truly fearsome. In that moment Genevieve could absolutely believe that he was capable of murder.

"That," he managed with barely leashed fury, "is a filthy lie."

She stared at him, clasping her hands together so tightly they began to ache. She desperately wanted to believe him. After all, he had saved Jack from a horrible lashing, only to be beaten himself. And her new ward, who regarded everyone with suspicion and contempt, apparently liked and trusted this man—to the point that he was even willing to risk his own chance at freedom in order to help Lord Redmond secure his. But at that moment, Lord Redmond's fury was surging through the room in a terrible dark wave, and she could not help but be frightened. Her instincts warned her that if he was provoked, this man could be extremely dangerous—regardless of his illness and injuries.

"I stabbed the man, Miss MacPhail," Haydon said brusquely. "With his own blade. The blade he was trying to sink into me. And in the course of our struggle, I managed to land a blow or two to his face. I also did some damage to the other three. And after I killed their friend, I withdrew the knife and charged at them. They ran off, but I suspect it was more because they heard voices approaching and did not wish to be caught, rather than out of any fear of me. When I looked down and realized that my assailant was dead, I dropped the knife and got the hell out of there as fast as I could."

"If you were merely defending yourself, then why did you run away? Why didn't you alert the police?"

"Because in my experience, Miss MacPhail, the authorities always look for the easiest answers," he replied tersely. "I was a stranger to Inveraray. I was drunk. I had just killed a man. My attackers were nowhere to be found, and between the darkness and my guttered state, I would not have been able to provide any useful description of them. And there were no witnesses. I'm sure you will agree it was not the most auspicious position to be in. At that moment I wanted nothing more than to find a room, fall into bed, and sleep off my stupor. I suppose in my inebriated condition I imagined that there would be time enough to go to the authorities in the morning, at which point I could explain the situation with some modicum of sober credibility. Given the way things have turned out for me, you can hardly argue that my concerns were not well-founded." His tone was cynical.

Silence stretched between them for a long, frozen moment.

"You have no reason to believe me," he finally acknowledged.

"I don't know you—"

"It wouldn't matter if you did," he interrupted harshly. "You would no doubt only think worse of me."

She turned her gaze toward the window, unable to bear the wounded fury burning in his gaze.

Haydon closed his eyes, wishing to hell that everything was different.

"I'm sorry," he murmured. "I never intended for you to put yourself at risk. I thought I would spend a night or two in your coach house and then be gone. You were never to know I had even been there."

"Then Constable Drummond would have found you and arrested you early this morning," Genevieve told him. "The police are presently performing a search of all the coach houses and sheds in Inveraray, looking for you."

"Jesus Christ." He gripped his throbbing ribs with one hand and awkwardly threw off his blankets with the other. "If they decide to start searching the houses and find me here, you will be charged. I suspect you will have a hard time explaining how I came to be lying naked in your bed if it was supposedly your intent to deliver me to the police." Clenching his jaw against his nausea and pain, he stood, stark naked.

Genevieve's eyes widened.

She had considered herself to be reasonably well acquainted with the male anatomy, having nurtured a love of painting and sculpture from the time she was a little girl. But other than the frozen subjects of painting and sculpture, her experience with the male body was strictly limited to the cherublike appearance of little boys. Although there had been ample opportunity to study every marble-hard plane and chiseled curve of Lord Redmond's physique last night, she had quite properly refrained from glimpsing at him *there*.

Now that she was suddenly presented with this

startling exhibition of his masculinity, there seemed to
be no other place she could look.

Haydon was too absorbed with the extraordinary
effort it was taking him to stand to notice her sudden
fascination with him. "Do you know where my clothes
are?"

Propriety returned to her in an icy rush. She gasped
and whirled around, vainly trying to obliterate the
memory of what she had just seen.

Haydon stared at her in confusion, wondering what
the hell was the matter with her.

And then it suddenly penetrated his fever-soaked
brain that he was standing stark naked in front of a
virgin.

"Forgive me." He jerked a plaid blanket off the bed
and clumsily wrapped it around his waist. "I did not
mean to frighten you."

His voice was gruff, but his remorse seemed genuine. It struck Genevieve as paradoxical that he was more
concerned about his nudity frightening her than the
fact that he had stabbed a man to death. There was an
earnestness to his apology that touched her, somehow.
It was clear that Lord Redmond was a man of at least
some sensitivity.

"I'm decent now. You may turn around if you
wish."

In truth, she would have liked another moment to
compose herself, for she was certain that her cheeks
were blazing with embarrassment. But she could scarcely
stand there staring at the wall after he had invited her to
turn, or else she would seem like a ridiculous prig,
which she most certainly was not. Fixing her face with
what she hoped was an expression of relative serenity,
she slowly turned.

He was leaning heavily against the bedpost, using it
for support as he clutched a rumpled swath of plaid

around his waist. Sunlight blazed upon his magnificent body, highlighting every niche and curve of his powerfully carved chest and thickly muscled arms and legs. There was a raw, savage beauty to him as he stood before her, all sinewy ripples and hard planes, his body battered and bruised, but still exuding strength and determination. In that moment he reminded her of a medieval warrior—fierce, uncultivated, dangerous. She felt the urge to reach up and place her hands upon the powerful breadth of his shoulders, to splay her fingers wide over the solid flat of his belly, to feel his warrior blood pulsing hot beneath her palms as she pressed herself against him.

Appalled by the direction of her thoughts, she looked away.

"My clothes," repeated Haydon, who was sapping every ounce of his strength just to remain upright, and had no inclination of the effect he was having upon her. "I need them."

"Oliver burned them," she managed in a small voice. "We could not risk having someone find a prison uniform."

"Then I will need something else to wear."

She turned. His forehead was pressed into the bedpost as he struggled to stay on his feet, and his face was drawn with pain. Concern tore through her, instantly dousing both her ardor and her fear. All through the night she had tended this man, constantly worrying that he might suddenly succumb to his injuries. He was still extremely ill and weak. There might well have been blood leaking into the inner depths of his body as he stood there.

How could she even consider making him leave in such a state—especially when he seemed to be doing so out of concern for her?

"Please get back into bed, Lord Redmond."

Haydon regarded her warily. "So you can call Constable Drummond back and have him drag me out of here?"

"Because you look as though you are about to faint and I don't think I can lift you by myself."

"I cannot stay here."

"You're right, you cannot. But neither can you leave here in your current state. At this point you can barely stand, so I hardly think you're well enough to manage on your own. Which leaves us with the only logical choice, getting you back into bed."

He shook his head. "If the police come here—"

"There is no reason to think that the police will return," Genevieve pointed out. "Constable Drummond wanted to speak with Jack, and he learned nothing from that conversation except that Jack despises everyone and has no desire to help the authorities. Since there was nothing to be found in the coach house, and there are many other places that need to be searched, I suspect the police will be too busy to come back here."

Haydon leaned heavily against the bedpost, forcing his breath to come in small, measured gulps. His skull felt as if it were about to split open with pain, nausea was churning his stomach into a vortex, and every breath put almost excruciating pressure on his bruised and broken ribs. If he somehow managed to hobble out the door of this house, he had no idea how he would even make it down the street, much less where he would go with the entire town now looking for him.

The idea of simply sinking into a soft mattress and closing his eyes was extremely appealing.

"Please, Lord Redmond." Genevieve stepped forward, peeled back the rumpled blankets of the bed, then smoothed down the sheets with quick, expert strokes. When the linens were arranged to her satisfaction, she regarded him solemnly. "You will be safe here. I promise."

"How do I know you're not just going to bring Constable Drummond back here to arrest me as I sleep?"

"I give you my word that I will not."

He made no move to lie down. "Why should you want to help me?"

She could not blame him for not trusting her. None of her children had trusted her when they first came into her care, except for Jamie, of course, who had been a mere infant. Trust, Genevieve had learned, was a delicate, elusive thing that could neither be summoned nor given simply because someone demanded it.

"You helped Jack, and Jack is now a part of my family," she explained. "Consider it a debt of gratitude."

He shook his head, unconvinced. "Anyone would have done what I did."

"You're wrong." Her voice was taut. "To most people around here, Jack is nothing more than a common thief and a bastard, who deserves every agonizing stroke of his thirty-six lashes, and all the hunger and misery he can endure in prison. Many even wish that he would just disappear altogether. There isn't another man in all of Inveraray who would dream of fighting on his behalf—especially a titled gentleman like yourself." She stared at him a long moment, studying the rugged beauty of his battered body, and the lines of exhaustion etched into his face. "But you chose to risk yourself to help him," she continued quietly. "And because of that, Lord Redmond, I am choosing to help you."

"You are placing yourself in danger by doing so," he reminded her.

"I know."

Her eyes were wide and velvety, and her pale cheeks

were charmingly flushed. The mouth that a few moments earlier had been set in a flat, disapproving line
was now imploringly curved. Her loveliness reached out
to him like a gentle caress, drawing him nearer to her.

"I will only stay long enough to regain my strength,"
he finally relented.

"Of course."

He moved slowly toward her, awkwardly holding
the swath of plaid around his hips. Genevieve reached
out and placed her hand upon his arm, thinking only to
steady him as he lowered himself onto the bed. The
heat of his flesh seeped into her palm, making her feel
flushed once more. The moment he was lying down she
relinquished her hold.

"You must rest a while," she instructed, careful not
to so much as graze his skin as she briskly arranged the
blankets over him. "I will have Eunice prepare a tray for
you."

"I am not hungry."

"Even so, you must eat."

Haydon closed his eyes. "Perhaps later."

His brow was lined with weariness and pain and his
jaw was clenched. Genevieve turned away and drew the
curtains. It would be easier for him to rest if the room
was darkened. After she left him she would go downstairs and have Eunice prepare some broth and toasted
bread for him, she decided. He might not want to eat,
but the lack of nourishment would only make him
weaker than—

"I would never hurt you."

She turned and stared at him in surprise.

"Not you, nor any of your children," he continued,
regarding her seriously. "I give you my word, Miss
MacPhail." Without waiting for her response, he closed
his eyes once more.

Genevieve remained where she was, watching as he drifted into a deep, uneasy sleep.

And then she hurried from the room, knowing well that despite Lord Redmond's feverish assurances, his very presence had already placed her and the children in grave danger.

Chapter Four

BY THE TOES OF SAINT ANDREW, THERE'S NAE worse task in the world than gutting a stinkin' slippery fish," complained Oliver, wrinkling his nose with distaste.

"If ye'd gripe less and gut more, the job would be nigh done by now," chided Eunice. She scooped a slippery pile of glassy-eyed fish heads into a bucket of cold water, then plunged her arms in up to her elbows and briskly began to rinse the bobbing faces clean.

"Ye can scarce expect a man to nae complain when he's been forced into doin' a woman's work," Oliver retorted, sawing fiercely at a hapless haddock's head. "I'm sure ye'd have somethin' to say if I told ye to go out back and chop a pile of wood, or lay the fires, or clean the silver."

"Ye've not chopped a piece of wood in three days—not since ye discovered 'twas the only chore Jack would do without twisting his face into a black knot," Doreen pointed out, as she vigorously scraped the skin off a carrot. "Ye've got Jamie and Simon fightin' over which of them can have the fun of layin' the fire next, and just yesterday ye convinced the lassies that if they set to work polishin' the few silver pieces Miss Genevieve has left, they would no doubt conjure up one of them magic genies Annabelle was reading about in one of her fairy tales. I've never seen the silver gleam so bright." She gave him a look of mock disapproval.

"I was just tryin' to let the wee ones have a little fun," Oliver protested innocently.

"Ye were tryin' to get them to do your work," Eunice countered. "Now, I've nae objection to ye teaching the children to do chores, but seeing as there's little for ye to do today and I'm up to my ears in fish heads and sheep's pluck, I see no reason why ye canna help Doreen and me put three meals on the table and take some food up to his lordship besides. Sweet Saint Columba, I've never known a man to eat as much as he does," she marveled, tossing the shimmering fish heads into an enormous pot on the stove. "Been here just three days and already he's finished off two pots of broth, four loaves of bread, a dozen bannocks, three pans of tatties with onions, and an entire boiled haggis." She doused the heads with a jug of fresh water.

"'Tis a good sign that he's hungry," Doreen remarked, attacking another carrot. "It means that he's farin' better."

"If he eats like this when he's feelin' poorly, I scarce want to think about what he'll eat when he's well." Eunice dropped a few sprigs of parsley into the soup pot and covered it, then checked the pot in which a sheep's lungs, heart, liver, and windpipe were simmering. Satisfied that everything was faring well, she went to the table and continued rolling out the oatcakes she planned to cook on the flat, cast-iron griddle heating over the fire. "Between his lordship and Jack, there will be nothing left in the larder by week's end."

"Now, Eunice, ye know 'tis just because they're newly released from prison," said Oliver. "We've all felt what it is to have hunger gnawing at our bellies in that foul place. I can still remember when Miss Genevieve first brought me here." His mouth curved in an affectionate smile. "She sat me down at this very table and served me a dish of your fine rabbit stew with dumplings. Upon my soul, I thought I had died and entered the gates of heaven." He scooped the purple-and-gray guts out of another fish.

"And so ye had," said Eunice, banging her rolling pin against a mound of dough. "There's few who could ever resist one of my stews. Lord Dunbar always used to say 'twas my cooking that made the dinner parties he and his wife were so fond of giving among the most sought after invitation in all of Inveraray."

"Aye, I'm sure it was." Doreen's voice was edged with anger. "A pity he couldn't see his way to payin' ye a decent wage for all yer years of hard work."

"Well, he's the one sufferin' for it now," remarked Eunice, pummeling her dough into a thin sheet. "Miss Genevieve told me she'd heard that Lord Dunbar had dismissed yet another cook, apparently for serving a tainted chicken that made every one of his fancy guests violently ill. Poor Lady Barclay didn't even make it out the door before spewin' up the rotten meal all over Lord Dunbar's shiny new shoes."

The three burst into laughter.

"Forgive me for interrupting."

Startled, they looked up to see Haydon standing in the doorway, naked except for the plaid from his bed.

It was a combination of restlessness and boredom that had finally roused him. His fever gone and his body healing, he had started to find the confines of Genevieve's pleasant, tidily arranged chamber almost as stifling as his prison cell. It was with some effort that he managed to hoist himself off the soft mattress and onto his aching legs, but once his initial dizziness had waned, he found that he did not feel so weak after all.

Encouraged, he went to the wardrobe in search of his clothes. Upon discovering nothing beyond a few modest gowns and some carefully folded mounds of feminine undergarments, he decided that the plaid from the bed would have to suffice. He draped it clumsily around his waist and then, not quite knowing what to do with the extra fabric, tossed it carelessly over his shoulder, thinking it would serve until something better could be found.

"Your pardon, ladies," he said, seeing by their wide-eyed stare that he had shocked them with his state of undress. "I'm afraid I was unable to find my clothes."

"That's because we burned them, laddie," Oliver informed him cheerfully. "Miss Genevieve didna want to risk having anyone find a prison uniform lyin' about."

Haydon vaguely remembered Genevieve making some mention of this. His senses were suddenly overwhelmed by the spicy sweet fragrances wafting through the kitchen air. He looked longingly at the pots simmering on the stove. It had been over two hours since he finished the bread and broth Genevieve had brought up to him, and he was extremely hungry. "Is that meat cooking?"

"It's sheep's pluck," Eunice replied, "but it's not cooked yet. I'll be mincing it fine and making haggis from it once it's boiled and cooled. It'll be ready by dinnertime."

"What about the other pot?" Haggis was fine and well, but Haydon was looking for something a little more substantial.

"Steer far from that one, laddie," warned Oliver, chuckling, "unless ye can stomach the sight of a lot o' beady little eyes starin' up at ye."

Haydon's stomach lurched. Just what the hell had been in all the soup he had consumed since coming here? "You're cooking eyes?"

"It's fish heads," Eunice said, casting Oliver a disgruntled look. "I'm making ye a lovely fish soup. I thought 'twould make a nice change."

"That's very thoughtful of you." Haydon was almost certain that if he faced one more bowl of broth he would retch. "Do you happen to have some roasted beef, or perhaps some glazed chicken?" His mouth began to water in anticipation.

"I'm afraid not," Eunice said, shaking her head. "It's Thursday."

Haydon was perplexed. "Thursday?"

"No meat left on Thursday," explained Doreen. "Except, of course, the pluck."

"I see," said Haydon, although in fact he did not.

"Tonight we'll be havin' fried haddock and haggis with tatties and peas," Eunice elaborated, sensing his confusion. "Then tomorrow night it'll be my fish soup. On Saturday I'll be seein' if I can't find a nice piece of cheap beef to cook in the pot with parsnips, cabbage, and potatoes. Sunday I'll have made stew and dumplings with whatever is left, and on Monday I'll have turned that stew into a rich soup. By Tuesday I'll be shopping for a piece of meat again, and maybe I'll find some neck cutlets of lamb or perhaps an oxtail that the butcher is willing to part with for a fair price. Whatever it is, it'll have to be made to feed ten people—eleven, includin' yourself—over three days. And that's why there's no meat left on Thursday night—we always finish whatever I started cooking on Tuesday by today's luncheon."

Haydon was utterly unfamiliar with the workings of his own staff and kitchen, and quite accustomed to being served a selection of freshly prepared fish and meat dishes three times a day. The idea of having to buy cheap cuts of meat and then stretch one meal into another was completely foreign to him.

Eunice took pity as she saw disappointment clouding his handsome face. "But that doesn't mean ye'll be going hungry, milord—there'll be fresh oatcakes in just a few minutes, and I've some sweet butter and sharp cheese to go with it. That should tide ye over nicely 'til dinnertime."

"Why don't ye sit down on that chair while ye're waitin', lad," suggested Oliver, who had just finished decapitating his last victim. "Ye look like ye're nigh ready to fall down anyway."

Haydon adjusted his plaid as he seated himself. Cheese and oatcakes would have to do, he supposed, until the haggis and haddock were ready. "Where is Miss MacPhail?"

"Taken the children to see the paintings," said Doreen. "She likes to take them to an art gallery once a week."

"The lass thinks it's good for them to see art." Oliver furrowed his white brows in bafflement as he rinsed his fish corpses in a tub. "Says it helps them to see the world around them, or some such blather."

"I don't know why they need to look at paintings for that," said Eunice, greasing the surface of the griddle with a piece of suet wrapped in muslin. She slapped her oatcakes onto the griddle's glossy surface. "All they need do is open their eyes. They'd be better off here, learnin' how to make a decent clootie dumpling, or helping me to wash the linens."

"Ye say that because ye once lived in a fine house that was full of paintings, Eunice," Doreen countered. "But until Miss Genevieve took me to that gallery, I scarcely knew such pretty things existed. Miss Genevieve wants the children to see that there's more to the world than what they'll find here—like great ships and angels and battles and such."

"Angels indeed," huffed Eunice, watching as her oatcakes began to brown and crisp. "Flyin' about half-naked with their bare bosoms out for all the world to see—it's plain disgraceful, to my way of thinking, and certainly not a fitting sight for children."

"How many children does Miss MacPhail have?" asked Haydon curiously.

"There's six of them now, including Jack," replied Doreen. "Three boys and three girls."

"Are any of them actually hers?" Although Genevieve was unmarried and exuded an aura of sexual innocence, it occurred to Haydon that she could still be the mother of at least one of her brood.

Oliver's eyes crinkled with amusement. "Well, lad, if ye'd ask her that question she'd tell ye flat that they are all hers, and make no mistake about it. But if ye're askin' how many of them has she actually borne, the answer is none of them."

"She might as well have borne Jamie," observed Eunice, banging a plate with three golden oatcakes and a wedge of cheese before Haydon. "She's cared for him since he was but hours old."

"Aye, and a fine job she's done of it too," declared Doreen loyally. "If not for her, the poor lad would be dead—and no one would have cared a whit."

Haydon cut himself a chunk of cheese and balanced it on a warm oatcake. "Why is that?"

"Jamie is the bastard of Miss Genevieve's dead father, Viscount Brynley, and one of his maids," explained Oliver. "No one here cares about a maid's bastard."

"Surely Genevieve's father cared," Haydon protested.

"He was dead long before the bairn arrived,"

replied Eunice. "I suppose had he lived, he might have made provisions for poor Cora and wee James."

"Or he might have just turned her out with a few quid and told her it wasn't his problem," Doreen countered angrily. "Men can be all pretty words and kisses when they're tryin' to find their way under a lass's skirts, but they start singin' a different tune quick enough the minute they discover they've left somethin' growin' in there."

"A pretty thing, Cora was," reflected Eunice, "with hair like fire and laughing eyes. I was working for Lord Dunbar then, and I used to see her sometimes down at the market. 'Tis no surprise the viscount took her to his bed."

"I expect 'twas a bit of a surprise for Miss Genevieve's stepmother to discover that her maid was carryin' her husband's bairn after he died," mused Doreen. "Tossed Cora out on her ear, she did, with nothing but a swollen belly and the clothes on her back."

" 'Twas quite a scandal at the time," said Eunice, laying more cakes on the griddle. "Everyone in Inveraray could talk of nothing else. Of course, no respectable household would take the poor lass in. And so she left. Most folk thought she had family that she could go to, but if she did, they dinna let her stay, for a few weeks later she was back again, round as a melon with no work and no money. And then she stole some apples and a bun, and she was sentenced to two months in jail."

Haydon paused in his eating, appalled. "They put a pregnant girl in jail for stealing some apples?"

"Makes ye wonder about what they call justice, don't it, laddie?" Oliver shook his head in disgust.

"What happened then?"

"Well, Cora knew Miss Genevieve had a soft heart,

and so she sent word to her," continued Eunice. "And when Miss Genevieve went, Cora begged her forgiveness, and asked her if she could see it in her heart to take the bairn when it was born."

"How could Genevieve take the child if she was dependent upon her stepmother's charity?" wondered Haydon.

"She couldn't. And that's what she told poor Cora. Miss Genevieve was scarcely eighteen years old at the time, and was betrothed to the Earl of Linton. Her father had arranged the match afore he died, and because he believed her future was secure, he hadn't taken the precaution of leavin' her any money. He did give her this house an' a few paintings and such—perhaps in the hope that they might be passed down to his future grandchildren. Miss Genevieve's stepmother got all the money."

"Miss Genevieve told Cora that the minute she got out of jail she would help her to find a position," said Oliver, who was now hacking Doreen's carrots into uneven chunks. "And then Cora would be able to work and look after the bairn herself."

"Don't forget, at that time, Miss Genevieve was young and had scarce notion of what life was like for those not of her station," explained Doreen, anxious to defend her mistress for her ignorance. "Nor had she any ken of how much work a bairn could be. She probably thought it would just sleep all day while Cora did a few easy chores."

"But when Miss Genevieve went next to visit her, she discovered that poor Cora had died in her cell while birthin' the bairn." Oliver paused in his chopping. "The warder told her the bastard was a sickly runt that would not last through the night, which would save them the trouble of sendin' it to the orphanage, where it would just die anyway. Miss Genevieve demanded to see the bairn. When they brought him out, she took wee Jamie in her arms and said, 'This is my brother and I'm takin' him home,' just like that." Oliver's wrinkled face beamed with pleasure, as if he could just imagine Genevieve doing such a thing.

"What did her betrothed think of that?" wondered Haydon.

"At first he thought she must be suffering from some sort of woman's ailment that had made her touched in the head," scoffed Doreen. "Thought she was just grievin' over her father's death. Brought in a doctor all the way from Edinburgh to examine her and make her right again. After a week the doctor presented his lordship with a huge bill, and told him there was nothin' wrong with his betrothed except, like most new mothers, she was very tired."

Eunice chuckled. "He even insisted the earl consider hiring someone straightaway to help her with the bairn, since she seemed to know nothing whatsoever about caring for bairns, other than what he had shown her."

Haydon found himself smiling. From the moment she had appeared in his cell like an outraged angel, he had known Genevieve was a woman of unusual strength and conviction. Even so, for a gently bred, inexperienced girl with no apparent income to take in a bastard baby in the face of both her stepmother's and her betrothed's opposition demonstrated remarkable compassion and courage. "And did the earl hire someone?"

"No." Oliver's expression grew dark. "The miserable swine broke their engagement and walked away. Told everyone that she had gone off her head and he wasn't to blame for whatever might become of her."

"Then the viscountess packed up and left as well," added Doreen. "Which was the best thing, except that she took all of Miss Genevieve's father's money with her and dismissed the remaining servants, leavin' Miss Genevieve with nothing but this old house and a pile of debt."

" 'Twas hard on her, that first year," said Eunice, placing a fresh batch of oatcakes before Haydon. "Living all alone in this house, with no one to help her or show her how to care for a bairn. The folk who used to pretend they were her friends stopped callin' upon her or inviting her to their parties and such, because they didn't want to be tainted with the scandal. Until I finally came to live here, the poor lass was just barely managing, all by herself."

"How did you come to be employed here?" asked Haydon.

"Well now, I'm afraid that was another bit of a scandal." Eunice's plump cheeks, already pink from the warmth of the fire, reddened with embarrassment. "Miss Genevieve had heard that I was about to be released from the prison, ye see, after servin' time for stealing a brooch from my former employer, Lord Dunbar."

"Because they wouldna pay her a decent wage so she could put some quid aside for when she was too old to work," interjected Doreen, wanting to make it clear that Eunice had had a very good reason to steal. "Instead they expected to her slave for them from morning 'til night, and then when they'd no more use for her they would toss her onto the street like an old rag without so much as a thank e."

"Miss Genevieve bundled up Jamie and went down to the prison and asked if she could speak to me," continued Eunice, smiling affectionately at Doreen. "Very sweet and polite she was, not at all like all the other rich folk I had known. And after we had talked a while, she asked me if I had any plans for when I got out of prison. I told her I hadn't, but 'twas certain no one would hire me, as I was guilty of stealin' from my former employer and therefore would forever be considered a dangerous criminal and untrustworthy. And she asked if I might consider coming to live with her and Jamie, and said she hoped I would, because they really needed my help to get along. Made it sound as if I would be granting her a wonderful boon. Said she couldn't pay me much, but that I would have a warm roof over my head and good food to eat, and if I ever needed more of anything I only had to ask her and she would see if she could provide it. And here I am, thankin' the good Lord each and every day that he sent Miss Genevieve to me, because if he hadn't, I dinna know what would have become of me." She fished an enormous handkerchief out of her apron pocket and dabbed at her eyes, then trumpeted her nose noisily into it.

"Then came the rest of us," said Doreen, taking up where Eunice had left off. "Miss Genevieve took a special concern for any child that had nowhere to go after spending time in the prison. First came Grace, then Annabelle, then Simon and Charlotte. She asked me to come here after I was jailed for liftin' a wee bit of brass from the customers at the tavern where I used to work for slave's wages." She snorted with contempt, as if it was beyond comprehension how she could have been imprisoned over such a trifling matter. "Said she could really use my help, since I knew about servin' and cleaning up after crowds of people and such."

Haydon looked at Oliver. "What about you?"

"Well, lad, I'm proud to say I'm the only true professional amongst the lot of us, descended from a long and distinguished line," Oliver declared loftily.

"Your father was a butler?" said Haydon, somewhat astonished.

"A thief," Oliver corrected him, amused. "And one

of the best in the county of Argyll, I might add. Began teachin' me the family business when I was but a wee lad of seven. I could ask a gentleman, 'What time is it, sir?' an' lift his watch and billfold before he'd finished giving me the answer," he boasted, chuckling. "Because I had an uncommon talent for it, my da had me breakin' into houses and robbing coaches at an early age. There isn't a lock in all of Inveraray I can't get past. 'Course there's no honor to it anymore," he finished, scratching his white head wistfully. "Thieves today just bob a pistol or a blade about and terrify people into givin' everything over. I ask ye, where's the bloody sport in that?"

"And Miss MacPhail took you from the prison as well?"

Oliver's expression softened. "Like a bonny angel she was," he said. "Cold had seeped into my bones in that miserable place, and I was plagued with a nasty cough that made me sure I was about to take my dying breath. And she marched into my cell and asked but one thing: Did I like children?"

Haydon absorbed this in silence. How had one small slip of a girl found the strength and the resources to salvage the shattered lives of all these people? he wondered. And how did she manage to support all of them? Clearly money was tight, as was evident by Eunice's thrifty approach to meal preparation. These three were obviously not paid much, but even so, to maintain a home and feed, clothe, and otherwise provide for ten people would be very costly. And that cost was only exacerbated by his presence, he suddenly realized. A stab of guilt penetrated his reflections. It was Genevieve's uncommon concern for others that had enabled him to lie shivering upon her bed for the past three days, just one step ahead of the law.

He needed to get out of here soon, before his presence placed her and her family in any further danger.

"Well, laddie, if ye've eaten enough to tide ye over 'til dinner, ye'd best be thinkin' about getting yerself back in bed," Oliver suggested. "If Miss Genevieve were to come home and find ye wandering around naked but for a plaid about yer waist, I'm sure she'd have somethin' to say about it."

"What time will she and the children return?"

"She usually takes them to a tearoom after their gallery visit, where they have to mind their manners and sit still and learn how to behave in public," said Doreen, banging her pot of mutilated carrots on the stove. "They'll likely be gone another two hours or more."

Haydon rubbed the dark growth of beard on his chin. "It appears I am in need of a shave and some clothing." He raised an inquiring brow to Oliver. "Do you think you might have something that would fit me?"

"Only if ye dinna mind havin' yer shirts stop at yer elbows and yer trousers end at yer shins," he joked, amused by the idea. "I'm thinkin' we'll have to do a sight better than that if we don't want to have ye arrested for indecency."

"What about the viscount's clothes?" suggested Doreen. "There's two whole trunks of them up in the attic. Very fine things, too, I might add—Miss Genevieve has been keeping them so that the boys might wear them one day, providin' the fashions haven't changed overmuch."

"Well, now, that just might do," said Oliver, critically studying Haydon. "From what I understand, the viscount was nae as tall as you and he carried a fair bit of pudding on him, but with a nip here and a tuck there, we might be able to make ye look tolerable. Both Eunice and Doreen know a thing or two about needle and thread, and I can shine up a pair of boots until they look like glass."

"I'm thinkin' a lovely bath might do you a world of good as well," said Eunice. "Why don't you take him upstairs and fix him one, Ollie, while Doreen and I see what we can find amongst the viscount's clothes? If we all work together, we'll have his lordship cleaned up and looking presentable before Miss Genevieve comes home with the children."

"All right, then, laddie," said Oliver, delighted to have a task that released him from his duties in the kitchen. "Let's see if we canna get ye lookin' more like the gentleman ye were before this whole sorry murder business began."

THE FRONT DOOR CRASHED OPEN AS A GIGGLING, yelping crush of children surged inside.

"I win! I made it in first!" declared Jamie, triumphant.

"Only because you pushed me out of your way," Simon complained, shoving at him hard. "You cheated."

Grace sniffed the air. "I smell ginger biscuits."

"That's not ginger, it's allspice," said Annabelle, wrinkling her nose in distaste. "Eunice is making haggis again."

"Maybe she made biscuits and haggis." Charlotte's expression was hopeful as she limped through the door.

"If she did, she won't let you have a biscuit now," Jamie told her with certainty. "She'll tell you it's too close to dinnertime."

"Tell her you saw some naked ladies in the paintings today," suggested Annabelle. "Then she'll give you a biscuit to make you forget about it."

"If you want to discuss the paintings you saw today with Eunice that's fine," said Genevieve, walking through the door. "But you just had tea and scones, and that should suffice until dinnertime."

"I only had one cup of tea, and Simon had two," complained Grace. "That wasn't fair."

"Fine, next time we go you shall have two cups," Genevieve assured her, trying to restore the balance of justice. "Then you'll be even."

"Can I sit beside Jack next time?" asked Jamie, smiling at Jack as he sauntered in.

"I believe you shall have to ask Jack that."

Jamie gazed at the older boy with worshipful eyes. "Can I, Jack?"

Jack shrugged and looked away.

Genevieve studied him, taking in his careless stance and averted gaze. Throughout the afternoon, he had remained cool and removed from the children, always standing just beyond the cluster she had instructed them to maintain, barely answering them when they asked him an excited question. It was as if he was uncomfortable with their obvious fascination with him, and was trying to maintain his distance. He was still planning to run away from her, she realized, troubled by the thought. Jack was older than the others had been when they came into her care, and therefore had a greater sense of his own maturity and independence.

She could only hope that he would realize the benefits of staying with her far outweighed the freedom and autonomy for which he apparently yearned.

"All right, everyone, let's put our coats and hats in the cupboard and then we shall go into the drawing room and continue our reading of *Gulliver's Travels*," she said, releasing the ties of her bonnet and cloak. "Simon, would you please hang this up for me?"

The elfin lad sprang forward to retrieve her heavy

cloak, which practically buried him within its voluminous folds. His thin little arms could carry no more, so
she popped her bonnet on his head, much to all the
children's delight.

"Look at me—I'm Genevieve!" he squealed, spinning around so they all could see.

"Mind that you don't crush the fabric," Genevieve
warned with mock severity. "All right, now, everybody
ready? Let's go inside." She pushed open the doors leading to the drawing room.

And gasped as a tall, elegantly attired man rose to
greet her from the chair in which he had been comfortably ensconced.

"Good evening, Miss MacPhail," Haydon said, tilting forward in a mannerly bow. "I trust you and the
children have had a pleasant day?"

Gone was the savagely handsome warrior with the
dark, tousled hair and the roughly bearded cheeks who
had found it an effort just to remain upright. Haydon's
jaw had been scraped clean, revealing a strong, chiseled
line that might have been rendered by a Renaissance
artist, and his thick, coal-black hair had been washed
and trimmed, causing it to curl at the edge of his collar.
His muscled body had been fitted into a charcoal frock
coat, dove-gray waistcoat, white shirt and loosely cut
trousers, with an expertly tied cravat arranged around
his neck. They were her father's clothes, Genevieve
realized as she studied them, but somehow they had
been adjusted so that they clung to her patient's immense frame in long, fluid lines. His carriage was tall
and sure, and his movements were no longer burdened
by pain. Indeed, he looked every inch the fashionably
refined gentleman, ready to host a dinner party for
thirty, or perhaps simply depart for his favorite club.

Or for his home near Inverness.

A bewildering sense of loss swept through her, as if

something she was beginning to treasure had suddenly been wrenched away.

"Genevieve took us to see some paintings of naked people," reported Jamie, bounding past Genevieve and flopping into a chair beside the fireplace, where a cheerful fire was burning. Like all the children, Jamie had been in and out of Haydon's bedroom countless times while he convalesced over the last few days, and was not affected in the least by his transformation.

"Really?" Haydon raised an amused eyebrow at Genevieve. "And did you enjoy it?"

Jamie shrugged. "The pictures of the ships were better."

"The best part was when we went for tea," Simon decided. "I had two cups with milk and honey, and finished one of Charlotte's currant scones when she said she wasn't going to eat it."

Charlotte cast Haydon a shy smile. "One is enough for me."

"And I'm going to have two cups next time," added Grace, "just so it's fair."

"And I'm going to sit with Jack next time," said Jamie, clearly excited by the prospect. "Isn't that right, Jack?"

Jack was slouched by the doorway, poised for escape the moment Genevieve would permit it. "I suppose."

"The nudes were very beautiful," Annabelle declared, affecting a worldly air as she carefully arranged the folds of her skirts upon the sofa.

"I don't know how those women lie about with no clothes on," remarked Simon, frowning. "Don't they get cold?"

"They only pose like that in the summer," Grace explained with great authority. "The hot air keeps them warm."

"It's their love for the artist that keeps them warm,"

rhapsodized Annabelle, clasping her hands to her heart. "That, and the knowledge that together they are making great art."

Haydon felt a smile tugging at the corners of his mouth. "A fascinating point of view. What do you think on the matter, Miss MacPhail?"

Genevieve blinked, trying without success to tear her gaze away from the impossibly attractive form of Lord Redmond. "What?"

"In polite conversation we don't say 'what,' we say 'pardon,'" chirped Jamie.

The children giggled.

"Yes, of course, I meant pardon," Genevieve said, feeling flustered. What on earth was the matter with her? She raised her hand to smooth down a stray hair, and felt that her cheeks had become flushed. "What was it you were saying, Lord Redmond?"

"Miss Annabelle suggests that a woman can be warmed by the euphoria of love," Haydon elaborated, amused by the fact that Genevieve seemed to be so disconcerted by the change in his appearance. "Do you agree?" His gaze was dark and faintly teasing.

"I really don't know," she managed with what she hoped was a modicum of levity. "I suppose so."

"Have you ever been in love, Genevieve?" asked Charlotte.

Genevieve regarded her helplessly, wholly unprepared for such a question.

"Of course she has," Haydon replied, coming to her rescue. "After all, she loves all of you."

"I don't think it's the same." Jamie's little brow furrowed in thought. "I mean, it's not the kind of love that makes you lie about naked in front of a man, like those ladies in the paintings."

"I really think we've discussed the naked ladies

enough for one day," said Genevieve, desperate to change the conversation.

"If ye hadn't shown them all that indecency, they wouldn't be blatherin' on about it at all," admonished Eunice, waddling into the drawing room with a plate of shortbread. "Here, duckies, have a wee sweetie and try to forget about it."

The children happily swarmed around her, their eager little arms outstretched as they grasped at the biscuits.

"Mind ye don't knock poor Eunice over," Doreen chided, entering the room with Oliver.

"Sweet saints, ye act as if ye were starving," said Oliver. "Did Miss Genevieve not take ye for tea?"

"That was hours ago," countered Jamie.

"I only had one cup," Grace explained.

"I let Simon have my second scone," added Charlotte.

"The scones were very small," Simon pointed out.

"And had hardly any currants in them at all," finished Annabelle.

"Well, duckies, tonight we're havin' fried haddock and lovely haggis with tatties and peas, so that should fill yer wee bellies nicely," said Eunice, keeping the plate low so the children could help themselves to another biscuit. "That is, of course, unless his lordship eats it all afore Doreen can get it to the table—his appetite is so big, I'm thinking we'll soon need to hide the furniture!"

"Actually, I was thinking that Simon's chair might be rather tasty," Haydon reflected, looking longingly at it, "especially if it had a little of Eunice's fine gravy drizzled over it."

The children burst into giggles.

"Your pardon, Miss MacPhail. We did not mean to interrupt."

The merriment permeating the room instantly disintegrated. All eyes fell in horror upon the sight of Constable Drummond, Governor Thomson, and the Earl of Linton, Genevieve's former betrothed, who were standing at the drawing room entrance.

"The door was ajar and no one heard us knocking," explained Governor Thomson, looking somewhat embarrassed by the liberty they had taken.

"And I assured the governor and the constable that you wouldn't mind if we let ourselves in," Charles added smoothly.

The handsome, fair-haired earl regarded Genevieve with a superior, faintly pained look, as if he found the sight of her laughing with her servants and children objectionable. He was dressed in the very height of fashion, with an exquisitely tailored black coat over tightly fitted checked trousers and immaculately polished chestnut boots. Over this ensemble he sported a heavy charcoal overcoat of the finest Scottish lamb's wool, the lapels of which were trimmed in ebony velvet. At thirty-eight he was beginning to show the evidence of his affluent lifestyle, for his waist and thighs were sagging from a constant diet of overly rich food and minimal physical exertion, and his golden hair was sadly thinning across the top of his forehead. After critically studying Genevieve, he swept a cursory look over the children and elders.

Then his gaze joined that of Constable Drummond, who was staring at Haydon with predaceous fascination.

It was over, Haydon realized, his chest constricting. He could not run. Even if there had been some available path to the door, he would never risk anything that might endanger either Genevieve or the children. And so he simply stood there, despair crashing over him in a great, dark wave. Why had God granted him this short reprieve? he wondered bitterly. Why had He prolonged his torment by granting him this fleeting taste of freedom, only to rip it so cruelly from him?

Because his sins were great, he reminded himself with grim harshness. He might have killed his attacker in self-defense, but he had a long list of other transgressions that stained his soul and shattered any hope for forgiveness. The worst, of course, was his abandonment of his daughter, Emmaline. He had no right to the slightest shred of mercy after what he had done to her.

It was best to leave here quietly, without creating a scene.

He glanced at Genevieve, who stood frozen, her luminous brown eyes large and filled with anxiety. Suddenly there was much he wanted to say to her, and now he never would. He wanted to thank her, not just for her tender care and shelter, but for something far more. For showing him that there were people in the world who were genuinely good. That had been an extraordinary revelation for him, and he was glad that he had learned it before his impending death. He also wanted to thank her for rescuing Jack from that cesspool of a prison and offering him a chance to make a new life. And for believing, however briefly, that there actually might have been something worth redeeming within Haydon's own battered soul.

He stared at her, shrouding his emotions with cold indifference, not wanting the others to have any inkling of his feelings toward her. He would not implicate Miss MacPhail in this matter any more than was absolutely necessary. He would tell Constable Drummond that he had forced his way into this home. He would say that he had threatened to kill all of them in the most hideous manner if they didn't do his bidding. He regarded her intently as he swiftly formulated this plan, his expression hard, hoping that she would somehow sense what he could neither show nor speak.

Then he pulled his gaze away and calmly regarded his captors, his relaxed stance betraying no hint of the agonizing regret coursing through his veins.

"I beg your pardon, sir," said Charles with forced civility as he stared up at Haydon, "have we been introduced?"

"No," interjected Genevieve firmly before Haydon could respond. "You have not."

Her heart pounded wildly against the wall of her chest, making it difficult to breathe. Until that moment she had been too overwhelmed with shock and fear to have any clear thought on how to handle the situation. But the fact that Charles honestly did not know who Haydon was shook her from her numbness. Charles had never met Lord Redmond, she realized. A quick look at both Governor Thomson and Constable Drummond revealed that they, too, were not entirely sure that the elegantly attired man standing with such assured composure before them was the dangerous murderer they sought. It was this slight uncertainty, this faint possibility that there was a sufficient difference in Haydon's appearance and manner and dress, that spurred her to action. When she had first seen Lord Redmond rising from the chair in her drawing room, she had found the changes in his manner and appearance dramatic, and she had had the opportunity to study him at length as he lay upstairs in her relatively well-lit chamber. She could only hope that for Governor Thomson and Constable Drummond, who had viewed the man before them only as a filthy, feverish drunk with scraggly hair and many days' growth of rough beard lying in a ragged uniform inside a miserably lit cell, the difference was even more compelling.

Everyone was staring at her expectantly, including Haydon, who could not imagine what tale she was about to weave. Her mind swiftly considered and rejected a list of possibilities of who Haydon might be. Cousin. Uncle. Friend. Acquaintance.

Ultimately there was only one role that she believed would offer him the requisite protection he so desperately needed.

"Gentlemen, I should like to introduce you to Mr. Maxwell Blake—my husband."

She did not know who within the crowded drawing room looked more shocked—her children, her uninvited guests or Eunice, Doreen and Oliver, who were blinking in astonishment.

"Married?" sputtered Charles, his watery, gray eyes nearly popping from his head. "You got married?"

"Yes." She moved to Haydon's side and looked up at him, smiling brightly, surreptitiously pleading with him to play along with her ruse. Haydon stared back at her, careful to keep his expression composed as he considered this inconceivable turn of events.

And then, realizing he had no choice, he placed his hand at her back in a gesture that clearly intimated the proprietary rights of a husband. She trembled beneath his touch, and it pained him deeply to think of how great her fear was at that moment.

"Yes," he said, firmly drawing her against the solid wall of his body. "I'm afraid we did."

His powerful arm wrapped about her like a heavy shield, and the heat of his flesh penetrated the thin fabric of her dress, helping to ease her shivering. Genevieve knew she had set them upon a treacherous path, but at that moment she could think of no other way to save him. Drawing strength from the hardness of him pressing against her, she inhaled a steadying breath and forged ahead.

"Maxwell," she continued pleasantly, "this is Lord Linton, an old friend who I'm certain will want you to call him Charles, and Governor Thomson, the esteemed governor of our jail, who in the past has been so supportive of my efforts to help the children. And this is Police Constable Drummond, who works hard to keep the streets of Inveraray safe for all of us."

"It is a pleasure to finally meet you, gentlemen." Haydon extended his hand to each of them. "Especially you, Charlie." Haydon enjoyed the flash of irritation that tightened Charles's mouth. "My wife has spoken to me about each of you at length."

"But—how?" demanded Charles, whose face had reddened to an extraordinary shade of scarlet. "When?"

"Actually, we were married a few months ago," Genevieve supplied, her mind whirling as she struggled to fabricate a credible sequence of events. "You may remember, Charles, that I had to travel to Glasgow to oversee some business matters regarding my father's estate. Maxwell and I met at an art gallery there."

"My wife and I share a similar passion for art." Haydon smiled fondly at her.

"I'm afraid our courtship was rather brief," Genevieve added, frantically trying to work out the details in her mind.

"I asked for her hand the very day that we met," continued Haydon smoothly. "As I'm sure you gentlemen can appreciate, I was utterly overwhelmed by her beauty, and was absolutely determined that she not escape my grasp." He cast a thoroughly self-satisfied look at Charles, indicating that he was well aware of his wife's prior relationship to him.

"She wouldn't have me at first," he confessed, chuckling. "Fortunately, I am not a man who backs down easily from a challenge—especially when the rewards promise to be so great." He caressed her cheek lightly with the back of his fingers, then smiled with husbandly amusement at the rosy blush that flooded her skin.

"Well, I believe congratulations are in order," managed Governor Thomson, who still looked utterly astounded.

"Thank you, governor," said Haydon. "Your good wishes are most welcome."

"I'm confused as to why you failed to mention your recent marriage when we called upon you a few days ago." Constable Drummond's gaze bore into Genevieve, trying to delve beneath the surface of her breathless performance.

"I'm afraid I am responsible for that," Haydon asserted, unfazed. "Business matters in London have kept me from joining my new family until now, and my wife and I had decided that we would not tell anyone of our marriage until I had actually settled in a bit here in Inveraray. We were particularly concerned that the children might grow inordinately anxious about my impending arrival if they knew about it too far in advance. As I have only been here a few days, and we have been keeping mostly to ourselves, my wife has been reticent to announce our union. On the morning you unexpectedly called," he continued, making only a slight emphasis on the fact that they had not been invited over, "I had not yet finished dressing and was therefore unable to come down and be properly introduced. Finally, I don't believe my wife has grown quite accustomed to her new status as a married woman—have you, Mrs. Blake?" He flashed her a devastatingly charming smile, which had the immediate effect of flooding Genevieve's cheeks with color once again. "I'm sure you gentlemen can understand our desire for privacy after such a lengthy separation," he finished, grinning broadly.

"Ah yes, of course," said Governor Thomson, looking thoroughly uncomfortable with such a delicate subject. He cleared his throat. "Absolutely."

Charles glared at Haydon with barely concealed acrimony. "Of course," he bit out stiffly.

His loathing was palpable to Haydon. It was clear to him that the earl was painfully unresolved about his decision to break his betrothal to Genevieve. Perhaps he had long soothed his ire by convincing himself that no one else would ever want her. The thought infuriated Haydon. He found himself wondering what vacuous, servile chit poor Charles had found to marry in her stead.

The sound of a stomach growling filled the uncomfortable silence.

"Are we going to have supper soon?" Simon wondered, rubbing his belly. "I'm starving."

"Sweet saints, I've forgotten my haggis!" burst out Eunice. "Here it is, nearly supper time and I've nae mashed my tatties. Do excuse me, Miss Genevieve— and of course you, too, Mr. Blake . . . sir." She bobbed a quick, clumsy curtsy at the two of them, then bustled out of the room.

"Oh my, I didn't realize 'twas so late," Doreen added, glancing at the clock on the fireplace mantel. "Come, my chicks, ye can help me lay the table for supper." She headed toward the door, then stopped suddenly. "Providin', of course, that's all right with ye, Mr. and Mrs. Blake." Her knees cracked like dry kindling as she also dipped awkwardly before her supposed employers.

"That is fine, Doreen." Genevieve was thankful to Eunice and Doreen for making it clear to their unwanted guests that it was late and their visit should come to an end. "Mr. Blake and I will be in the dining room shortly."

"Off we go, then, children," said Oliver. "Let's see if we can get some of the grime off yer hands afore ye start touchin' all those plates and forks."

The children hesitated.

"Come and see how well I can fold the napkins, Mr. Blake," Jamie pleaded, taking Haydon's hand. "I've been practicing."

"And I want to show you how well I polished the teapot." Charlotte limped over to Haydon and tentatively laid her fingers upon his sleeve.

She was shivering, Haydon realized. Something told him that her fear was not solely for his fate, but also for her own. A quick perusal of their guests revealed that Constable Drummond was staring at her with particular contempt. An unfamiliar feeling of protectiveness seeped through Haydon. He released his hold on Genevieve to pull Charlotte between them, then laid his hand with gentle reassurance on the fragile child's thin shoulder.

"I would very much like to see that, Charlotte," he murmured, his voice low and sure.

"Oliver said a genie would come out if we polished the silver long enough, but nothing happened," complained Annabelle, winding an arm around Genevieve's waist. "Do you believe in genies, Mr. Blake?"

"Everyone knows there's no such thing," Simon scoffed. He took his place beside Jamie, thereby completing the shielding ring of children around Genevieve and Haydon. "There's no scientific evidence to prove it."

Although each of the children had befriended him by wandering into his room over the past few days to see how he was faring, Haydon knew this demonstration of protection was for Genevieve, whom they all adored. Genevieve was trying desperately to safeguard him, and the children were doing their utmost to help her. Despite the fact that they were not acting out of any affection for him, Haydon found himself profoundly moved by their actions. Even Jack, who had slunk into a corner when the unexpected visitors arrived, was now leaning against the wall with his fists clenched, as if he intended to attack Constable Drummond should he suddenly decide to arrest Haydon.

"Do forgive us, gentlemen, but I'm afraid dinnertime around here is very much a family endeavor," Haydon said apologetically. "Was there something you needed from my wife and myself?" His question made it clear that as Genevieve's husband, he would be privy to any discussions they might wish to conduct.

"We wanted to ask the boy a few more questions." Constable Drummond fixed his formidable gaze upon Jack.

Jack stiffened.

"About what?" asked Genevieve with forced calm.

"About the prisoner who escaped from jail," Governor Thomson explained.

"Ah, yes, my wife mentioned that to me." Haydon lifted a bemused brow to Constable Drummond, as if he felt such a simple matter must surely have been resolved. "Have you not found the man yet?"

"Unfortunately, no."

"That is unfortunate." Genevieve's voice was tense as she continued, "And by your presence here it seems you have some compelling reason to think that Jack might be able to shed some light on the man's current whereabouts?"

"Of course we will try to assist you with your investigation in any way that we can," Haydon interjected, giving Genevieve a reassuring squeeze. "Won't we, Jack?"

Jack shrugged. "I already told them, I don't know nothin'."

Haydon frowned. "Are you absolutely sure?"

Jack nodded.

Turning to Constable Drummond, Haydon queried,

"Do you have any specific questions you want to ask him—other than, of course, the ones you have already posed in your previous meeting?"

Constable Drummond hesitated, evidently confused by the restriction Haydon had put upon him. "Well, no, not exactly—"

"Forgive me if I'm being overly protective of my new family, constable," Haydon interrupted, "for I can assure you, we want to assist you with your investigation in any way that we can. As I'm sure you realize, however, my wife and I are firm believers in the merits of trust. It is only by trusting our children that we can, in turn, teach them the lesson of treating that trust with care. If you intend to ask Jack questions to which he has already provided you with answers, then that means you have come into my home to suggest that a member of my family has lied to you. Is that your intent?"

Constable Drummond's expression tightened. "No."

"We merely wanted to know if any of you have noticed anything unusual over the last few days." Governor Thomson sensed that they were on the cusp of offending Haydon, and that he was not a man who would take such an offense lightly. "Anything at all."

Haydon regarded the circle of children around him. "Have you, children?"

They innocently shook their heads.

"Then I regret that we cannot be of any assistance to you today, gentlemen," Haydon said, making it clear that his guests' visit was at an end. "We shall be sure to keep you informed should any of us notice anything that we think might be pertinent to your investigation."

"Our apologies for disturbing you, Miss MacPhail— I mean, Mrs. Blake," Governor Thomson hastily corrected himself.

"Not at all, Governor Thomson." Genevieve looked at Charles in feigned confusion. Each time she rescued a child from the prison, Charles made a point of calling upon her to tell her what a hideous mistake she was making, and what a ridiculous mess she had made of her once promising life. Obviously Charles had heard about Jack joining her household, and had come over to share his objection with her. "Was there a purpose to your visit, Charles?"

The earl hesitated. "I wanted to know if you would paint a new portrait of my daughter," he improvised suddenly. "The one you painted three years ago no longer depicts her accurately. That is, of course, if your new husband will permit you to continue painting portraits." He gave Haydon a challenging look.

Charles was trying to determine her new husband's ability to support her, Genevieve realized. Over the years she had struggled constantly with her limited financial resources. By painting portraits of the children of those wealthy aristocrats who had once welcomed her into their homes as a guest, she had managed to help pay for some of her household expenses, thereby slowing the sale of her family's most prized possessions. Although she enjoyed painting immensely, she had been forced to swallow a lifetime of pride the day she had walked into Charles's magnificently appointed home, not as his betrothed or even an honored guest, but as a lowly employee.

She suspected that Charles had only offered her the commission because he derived perverse and bitter delight in seeing her reduced to that position.

She was reluctant to turn down the possibility of earning some money, but she also did not want to make it appear that her new husband was unable to support her and the children. To do so would only invite unpleasant speculation about him. "Maxwell and I have not yet discussed it—"

"You must do whatever pleases you, my dear,"

interrupted Haydon, immediately sensing Genevieve's dilemma. "If you would find it amusing to paint Charlie's daughter, then by all means, you should go and enjoy yourself."

The redness on Charles's face effused up to the sparse roots of his pale hair. "My name is Charles," he managed tautly.

Genevieve hesitated a moment, as if she were trying to decide. "Very well, Charles," she finally relented. "I do enjoy painting portraits, and your daughter is a lovely subject. I would be happy to do this for you." She smiled, pleased that it had sounded as if she were granting him a favor.

"And now, gentlemen, if you will excuse us, I'm afraid we have kept our children from their dinner long enough," said Haydon. "Oliver, would you kindly show our guests to the door?"

"Aye, Mr. Blake, sir," drawled Oliver, who had been itching to perform that very task from the moment they had arrived.

"A pleasure to meet all of you," Haydon said, as Oliver ushered their guests through the corridor. "I hope to see you again soon."

"Just don't make it too soon," muttered Oliver, banging the door shut behind them, "ye miserable bunch of bloody, boot-licking—"

"Did you see that?" Jamie demanded excitedly. "They really believe you're married to us!"

"I'm proud to say I had a hand in that," said Eunice, beaming merrily as she returned from the kitchen. "Did ye like the way I curtsied ever so nice for ye?"

"Aye, and me too," Doreen added, following behind her. "And dinna think 'twas easy on these poor old knees!"

"I'd wager they heard them crack all the way up in Oban," said Oliver, chuckling. "I thought it was the floorboards breakin' beneath Governor Thomson's bulk!"

"That Constable Drummond is the nastiest-looking man I have ever seen," remarked Annabelle. "He looks as if he just bit into a lemon."

"At first, I thought he had come for me," Charlotte confessed. "He was so mad when Genevieve took me out of the prison last year."

The knowledge that Charlotte had been afraid caused Genevieve to momentarily dismiss her own fear. She knelt down so she could look Charlotte straight in the eye. "No one is ever going to take you away from me, Charlotte," she told her adamantly. "You must believe me when I tell you that. I will never let anything happen to you—do you understand?"

Charlotte nodded.

"Good." She wrapped her arms around the girl and held her close. "Now go with your brothers and sisters and get ready for dinner. I'll be along in a few minutes."

Haydon waited for the last child to depart before he closed the drawing room doors. He pressed his forehead against them and inhaled deeply, fighting for calm. Finally he turned to face Genevieve.

"Why in the name of God did you tell them I was your husband?"

"Because I didn't want them to drag you away in front of my children and hang you. And I believed it was the only choice that would adequately explain how you came to be sleeping under my roof."

"You could have said I was your uncle—or even a distant cousin, for God's sake!"

His anger took her by surprise. "That would have invited too many questions," Genevieve argued. "If you were any other relation to me they would have immediately asked you about where you were staying, when did you arrive, and what was your business while you were here. Any claim of your being an uncle or a cousin could easily be proven false. I am an outcast here, Lord Redmond, and my penchant for doing the unthinkable is well known. Believe me, the people of Inveraray will have little trouble believing that I married a man I had known for only a few days. I have created an entire family out of thieves and urchins I had known for scarcely more than a few minutes. To marry a stranger on a whim is entirely in keeping with the impossibly irrational woman I have become to them."

She was right, Haydon realized, drawing no pleasure from the conclusion. The woman before him had severed her ties with respectability and acceptance the moment she chose to single-handedly raise a thief's bastard over a life of tedious comfort with that primping, fatuous peacock, Charles.

A stab of irritation pricked his already dark mood. Just who the hell did that idiot think he was, barreling in here and acting as if he had some exclusive right to her? The idea that Genevieve had actually been betrothed to that sniveling, spineless fool filled him with fury. Whatever her father's attributes may have been, it was clear he had not been a discerning judge of character. It had taken nearly every ounce of Haydon's self-control to refrain from booting the pompous imbecile out the door on his expensively wrapped backside.

"I would have thought you might be a little more grateful for the risks I have taken on your behalf," Genevieve continued, incensed that he dared to criticize her. "Did you think that after tending you night after night and making sure you didn't bleed to death or die from fever I would merely stand back and watch as they led you away? If so, then you do not know the first thing about me, Lord Redmond."

Anger had stiffened her stance and heated her cheeks. She looked as if she wanted to strike him. The fact that she faced him so readily, unwilling to back down, touched a deep chord of admiration within him. The irrepressible Miss MacPhail was a woman of astonishing strength and conviction, who would not retreat when she believed she was right. And more, despite the terrible crimes of which he had been accused and convicted, she was quite clearly not afraid of him in the least.

He felt an urge to touch her in that moment, to pull her into his arms and press his mouth to hers, to feel her soft, slender form against him, his hands roaming the firm swells of her breasts as she opened her mouth and invited his tongue inside. His body stirred and hardened, filling him with a desire that had long lain dormant, flooding his senses with restless, impossible need.

Appalled, he turned away abruptly. Here he was, in a crowded household filled with children, a hairsbreadth away from being hauled off and executed for murder, and all he wanted to do was bury himself in the woman who was responsible for saving his life.

Clearly, he was losing his mind.

"I did not mean to offend you, Genevieve," he said, raking his hand through his hair. "It's just that I wonder if you have considered the ramifications of the picture you have painted here. You have told the authorities that you and I are married. If I leave now, everyone in Inveraray will know that you have lied. Do you understand what that will mean for you? The relentless Constable Drummond will be breaking down your door, demanding your arrest for hiding an escaped prisoner. Given that justice here finds it appropriate to jail an expectant mother for stealing an apple, I can well imagine what punishment they will decide to inflict upon you. In addition to sending you to prison, they will deem you to be an unfit parent and take your children away."

Genevieve paled, her anger suddenly chilled by this very real possibility. What had she been thinking? she wondered. That Haydon would simply stay with her forever, and no one would ever learn of their lie?

She sank into a chair, trying to stifle her panic.

Haydon braced one hand against the mantel and stared grimly into the flames of the fire.

He wanted to leave this place and try to clear his name by solving the mystery of who those men were who had attacked him the night this whole ugly mess began. That would mean having his barrister hire someone to investigate the matter for him, and remaining in hiding far from Scotland until the puzzle was solved. He was certain the authorities had frozen his bank accounts, but between his lawyers and his accountants, he was sure they could find some way to access some funds for him under the guise of legal fees. Once his attackers were brought to light and the charges against him were dropped, he could return to his prior life as Lord Redmond.

It could take years, he realized bitterly, assuming the investigation was successful at all. And in the meantime, the beautiful, intelligent, selfless woman before him would be arrested and imprisoned for her role in helping him to escape.

It was unthinkable.

"It seems I am trapped here."

Genevieve looked at him in surprise. "Do you mean you're going to stay?"

"For the time being, yes. I will stay and play the role of your husband. But I will only do it long enough to firmly establish our relationship to the people of Inveraray. Then, perhaps in a month or two, once the search for me has tired somewhat and everyone has come to believe that we are the blissfully happy couple we shall portray ourselves to be, I will be called away to

England on business. And there, after a separation of a few weeks, I will unfortunately meet my demise in an accident. You will have a suitable period of mourning, and then you will pick up and go on, now with the added respectability of being a tragic young widow."

Genevieve considered his plan a moment. "And what will happen to you?"

It did not surprise him that she remained worried for his welfare. Concern for others was woven deep into the fabric of her very being. It was part of what made her so desirable to him, as firelight played upon her pale cheek and sweetly furrowed brow.

"I will either eventually succeed in proving my innocence and reclaiming my life, or spend the rest of my days trying to keep one step ahead of the law. Either way, I am determined that neither you nor the children should suffer for trying to help me. And therefore you must promise me something, Genevieve." His expression was deadly serious. "I would have your word that if I am discovered while I am staying with you, you will say whatever you must to establish your own innocence in the matter. You will tell them I forced you to take me in. You will say that I threatened you cruelly and relentlessly, that I even beat you, and that your fear for your own life and the lives of the children was so great that you felt your only option was to succumb to my demands and say I was your husband."

Genevieve adamantly shook her head. "If I do that, no one will believe in your innocence."

"If I am discovered here, my innocence won't matter," Haydon told her flatly. "I cannot risk investigating the matter myself while I am supposed to be the newly wedded Maxwell Blake. And if Constable Drummond and Governor Thomson realize that your adoring husband is actually their escaped prisoner, their fury at being duped will overshadow any willingness to reconsider my innocence. All they will be interested in is my immediate execution, so that the embarrassment of my escape and my subsequent masquerade can be buried with me."

"I won't pretend that you are some sort of monster when you're not," Genevieve argued. "If you're caught, then I will go to the courthouse and explain to them what happened. I will ask the judge to reexamine your case and—"

"Listen to me, Genevieve," he said, kneeling before her. "I know you are a fighter, and that is why you are unwilling to accept injustice. But I could not bear the thought that you and the children were made to suffer because of me. Do you understand? My death does not concern me nearly so much as the idea that I will have destroyed your life as well."

His expression was harsh as he spoke to her, almost as if he was trying to intimidate her into agreement. But it was his eyes that captured Genevieve's attention. There was anger there, laced with the frustration of a powerful man who was not accustomed to having to demand something more than once. But there was a terrible pain there as well, an overwhelming sadness that swirled through the icy blue depths, suggesting a wound that was still raw deep within him. It was this that she focused on, for it seemed so haunting and familiar, almost as if she were looking into a reflection of herself.

"Very well," she said quietly, knowing full well that she would never honor his request. "I will do as you wish."

Haydon eyed her speculatively. She returned his gaze steadily.

"Good." He rose to his feet and crossed the room, suddenly anxious to have some distance from her. He felt as if he had inadvertently revealed some part of himself to her. It was not his habit to disclose anything about himself to anyone.

"Shall we go into the dining room and join the children for dinner?" Genevieve asked.

"If you'll forgive me, I think I will retire upstairs and lie down for a while. I find myself somewhat tired." Instead of moving toward the door, he gripped the mantel and stared at the fire.

"Would you like me to bring you something?"

"No." Realizing his tone was gruff, he added, "Thank you."

"Perhaps later, then."

"Perhaps."

He had drifted away from her, she realized, surprised by how much she felt the loss. For one brief moment she had looked into his soul, had almost felt as if she could reach out and touch him and know that he would not mind, that he might have even welcomed the feel of her slender arms about his enormous shoulders, offering him comfort and refuge. Her experience with men was limited to her utterly proper courtship with Charles, which had included a few disappointingly passionless kisses, and one rather fumbling grope of her breasts. Although her blond betrothed had seemed handsome enough to her when she was an inexperienced girl of eighteen, neither his perpetually disapproving face nor his increasingly pulpy physique could begin to compare with the darkly chiseled lines of Lord Redmond's visage, or the powerfully cut ripples and planes of his warrior physique. She had seen him standing before her with nothing but a blaze of sunlight warming his skin, had swabbed almost every inch of his beautiful body with her gentle touch, and she knew that Lord Redmond was strong and hard and sleek, like a wild panther. She found herself wondering what it would be like to have his arms wrapped tightly around her, to feel herself pressed against his chest as he lowered his head and pressed his mouth to hers.

Heat flooded through her.

She rose and hurried toward the door, bewildered by the strange sensations coursing through her veins. Her relationship with Lord Redmond was one of unfortunate but necessary circumstance, and nothing more, she reminded herself.

Even so, the urge to stay with him was strong as she stole a final glance at him standing by the hearth, his powerful form silhouetted against the dying shadows of the fire.

Chapter Five

O VER THE NEXT FEW DAYS, HAYDON AND JACK were introduced to the duties expected of them as members of their new household. Haydon gained an appreciation for the seemingly endless tasks that had previously been the exclusive domain of his servants.

Jack plotted ways to escape his chores.

When Genevieve had been forced to fend for herself and a newborn infant at the tender age of eighteen, she had been handicapped by her lack of knowledge about even the most basic of household tasks. There had always been a cook, a housemaid, a butler, a valet, and a gardener to tend to every detail of running her father's home, enabling Genevieve to pursue her studies and her interest in painting. But after her father's death and Charles's subsequent rejection of her, she had been left entirely without an income, which meant that she could no longer afford the luxury of employing servants.

It was then that she realized how very limited her education had been.

She could well remember those exhausting early days as she struggled to look after little Jamie by herself.

The kitchen was shrouded in a perpetual smoky haze, a combination of her inability to make a decent fire and the charred remains of all the food that she had put on the stove or griddle and subsequently abandoned as she ran to soothe Jamie's cries. Laundry sat in great heaps around the house in various stages of soaking, washing, drying and folding; silky gray layers of dust accumulated on the carpets, furniture and artwork; and lamps were burned until their chimneys were black and the oil had run dry. Precious food was improperly preserved and had to be thrown out, and the meals that she did manage to prepare for herself were either boiled to a pulp or burned beyond edibility. There never seemed to be enough hours in the day to tend to Jamie and see to the hundreds of other tasks that needed to be done, and even if there had been more time, Genevieve was simply too weary to get to them. She would fall into bed each night on the verge of tears, not knowing where she was going to find the strength to get up and face another morning.

Then she would turn toward Jamie's cradle and study his beautiful little face as he slept, his tiny, perfect hand fisted beside the chubby softness of his cheek. In those moments nothing seemed to matter except the steady, shallow whisper of his breath and the certainty that despite the dust and disorder around her, Jamie was clean and happy and completely loved. She would trace her fingers down the petal velvet of his skin, resolving to be stronger and more capable the next day.

On the morning Eunice first arrived from the jail, the elderly woman had clucked her tongue sympathetically as her gaze swept over the disarray. She immediately donned an apron and set to work organizing the kitchen, baking bread and fixing a simple but nourishing stew. At first she had tried to banish Genevieve to the drawing room, saying she needed only to look after "the wee lamb," as Eunice called Jamie, assuring her new mistress that she would take care of everything else herself. While it was extremely tempting to be coddled and waited upon once more, Genevieve had refused. Self-sufficiency, she believed, was going to be key to her survival if she was going to make a happy life for herself and Jamie. And so she had created a little play area for her brother a safe distance from the hearth and the stove, and set about learning from dear old Eunice all she could about cooking, cleaning and otherwise managing a household.

This belief in the absolute necessity of self-sufficiency now extended to her wards, all of whom had come to her with scant knowledge of what it was to live in a household where one was clean and properly nourished. In addition to their lessons in history, reading, writing, science, and arithmetic, her brood was required to spend part of each day performing household chores. Although Oliver, Doreen, and Eunice would have much preferred to have the children out of the way so they could see to the tasks themselves, Genevieve was insistent that the youngsters be their apprentices. It was her firm conviction that children should learn to appreciate the hard work and knowledge that was required for maintaining a pleasant, orderly household. Beyond that, she knew they would need these skills when they eventually left her home. With neither the benefit of a prestigious pedigree nor abundant funds, each child was going to have to rely upon his or her own resources to make their place in the world, and to keep their own homes clean and well-maintained. Even if they were one day fortunate enough to employ servants, Genevieve believed they should still have a thorough understanding of and regard for the multitude of vital tasks that servants performed.

"There now," said Oliver, watching as Grace and

Annabelle fished acrid lengths of wick out of a bowl of strong vinegar. "Now ye leave them to dry well, and ye'll find the lamps will scarcely smoke at all the next time we burn them. In the meantime, let's see ye take those funnels and fill the founts with oil, and mind ye dinna spill any."

"This smells *horrid*," complained Annabelle, laying a vinegar-drenched wick down upon a sheet of yellowed newspaper.

"It can't be as bad as this awful stuff." Simon wrinkled his nose as he poked at a creamy paste in a pot over the stove.

"What is it?" asked Grace.

" 'Tis a mixture for removing scorches from linen," Doreen said, pouring a half pint of vinegar into the pot. "And if ye'd been mindin' yer business instead of blatherin' on to Charlotte while ye was ironing that tablecloth, we'd be havin' no need of it."

Simon sneezed as the acidic fumes tickled his nose. "I think this smell is dissolving my brain."

Jamie looked up from rubbing a blackened flatiron with a gritty polish of bees wax, salt, and powdered bath brick. His face, hands, shirt, and hair were completely covered with greasy soot, making him look like a chimney sweep. "What's in it?"

"The juice of two onions, a half ounce of white soap, two ounces of fuller's earth, and a half pint of vinegar," replied Doreen. "We'll boil it well, then let it cool before we spread it over the scorch mark on the cloth, and it should take it out nicely."

"Either that or it will burn a hole right through the cloth," Haydon predicted dryly. "All right, Charlotte, you hold the teapot steady while I fix this handle on it."

Charlotte obligingly pinned the heavy china piece firmly against the table. "Like this?"

"Perfect." His brow creased with concentration,

Haydon carefully placed the final fragment of the broken pot into position. "There now, I think that's done it," he said, feeling enormously satisfied with himself. "You may go back to using this handsome teapot, Eunice, confident in the knowledge that it has been expertly repaired by both Charlotte and myself." He lifted it up to show her.

The handle slipped off and the delicate pot smashed to pieces on the floor, leaving Haydon staring in bewilderment at the scattered remnants of his work.

The children burst into laughter.

"Oh my," said Charlotte, trying to contain her smile in light of Haydon's evident disappointment. "I'm so sorry, Lord Redmond. I don't think it was quite ready to be lifted."

"Well, lad, 'twas a fine job ye did, make no mistake," Oliver assured him, shaking his head with amusement. "Next time, ye might consider lettin' the paste cure a wee bit afore ye start waving things about."

Haydon frowned. "It had to cure?" He gave Eunice a sheepish look. "I'm sorry, Eunice."

"Now, don't be fretting over it," soothed Eunice. "Bad mistakes provide a man wi' quick experience," she declared philosophically, handing him a broom and a dustpan. "If we cried over every wee thing that got broken in this house, we'd be sailin' a ship up the stairs! Since ye're finished with that now, Charlotte, would ye mind creamin' that butter over there?" She pointed a floury finger at a bowl.

"Not at all." Charlotte gave Haydon a gentle smile of encouragement before limping to the other side of the table and seating herself in front of the bowl.

Jack emerged from the cellar bearing a pitcher of milk and a bowl of eggs. He set them on the table, then surreptitiously tried to slink out of the crowded kitchen.

"Ye can take them over to Charlotte, Jack," directed

Eunice, not bothering to glance at him as she mixed some marmalade and lemon juice together. "Crack two eggs into the bowl, then after Charlotte has beaten them in, ye can add the flour and some milk—not too much, mind, just enough to make the pudding nice and soft."

Jack scowled. Earlier that morning Oliver had set him to work chopping wood, which was the one task he had performed so far that he actually enjoyed. He liked the solid weight of the ax in his hands, the hard flex of his muscles as he swung it in a silvery arc over his head, and the satisfying crack a log made as it split open, filling the air with the loamy fragrance of woods and earth. The day before he had even helped Oliver clean and grease the carriage, and that had been a decent enough job, except for the fact that Genevieve had sent him to scrub his hands three times afterward before she deemed his fingernails acceptable. But preparing food was woman's work, to his way of thinking, and he certainly was not about to stand around and crack goddamn eggs into any bloody bowl. His body rigid with defiance and his hands clenched into fists, he opened his mouth to set Eunice straight on that.

"Please, Jack," pleaded Charlotte softly. "If you wouldn't mind, could you help me to cream this butter? I fear it's far too hard for me to have much effect on it, and I know with your strong arms you can do it easily."

He looked at her in surprise.

Of all the children in the household, Charlotte was the only one who rarely spoke to him. Jack intuitively understood that this was not meant as any slight to him, but rather was because Charlotte was the shyest and the least self-assured. He did not know the nature of the injury that had caused her to limp, but suspected that she had suffered abuse at the hands of some brute—possibly even her own father.

If he had been there when it happened, he would have killed the pissing bastard.

The sight of her perched awkwardly upon a chair, her injured leg stretched out before her as she tried with limited success to beat the block of butter Eunice had given her, chipped at the shell of his resistance. Several strands of her thick auburn hair had strayed from the faded green ribbon tying it back, and her milky skin was flushed with effort, as if she found even the simple task of creaming some butter tiring. But it was her eyes that captivated him most. He had never noticed how unusually large and pretty they were, a clear swirl of brown flecked with green, rimmed with a feathery sweep of charcoal lashes. She continued to study him, her gaze slightly wary, as if she was worried that his response might be to snarl at her, or perhaps to simply glare at her with contempt and say nothing. Certainly he had treated everyone else in the household to just such a response at one point or another.

Shame chiseled away another little piece of his armor.

Without a word, he went over to Charlotte, took the bowl and spoon from her hands, and began to pummel the resistant butter.

"Thank you." Charlotte's voice was barely audible above the sound of the spoon thrashing mercilessly against the bowl.

He gave her a brisk nod. When the butter was finally beaten into submission, he went to retrieve the eggs and milk.

"Here," he said, handing her an egg. "You crack them into the bowl, and I'll beat them in for you." He regarded her intently, wanting to make it clear that he was doing it for her, and not because Eunice had told him to.

A hesitant smile crept across her face. She did not

wait for him to acknowledge it, but bowed her head and gently tapped the delicate white shell against the rim of the bowl. "I do believe it's going to be a splendid sponge pudding," she predicted softly.

"Good afternoon, everyone." Genevieve smiled at her busy little brood as she entered the kitchen. With so many faces and activities to look at, it was not difficult for her to keep her gaze averted from Haydon.

Although it had been impossible to avoid Lord Redmond completely over the last few days, after that night in which she had experienced such intense and bewildering feelings toward him, Genevieve had made absolutely certain that they were never alone. Haydon had recovered sufficiently to no longer require either her bedchamber or her constant attendance at his bedside. Doreen had generously offered to move onto a cot in Eunice's room, and Haydon had been given Doreen's room. At first Genevieve had worried that being relegated to the relatively cramped third floor servants' quarters would not please Lord Redmond, who was obviously accustomed to opulent and spacious surroundings. On the contrary, the arrangements seemed to suit him well, and he assured Doreen that he was most grateful and hoped he wouldn't be putting her out for too long. Genevieve supposed that after spending several weeks in a dank, frigid cell, Doreen's bright, tidy little room was almost luxurious.

"My goodness, Jamie, you look like you fell into the coal bin!" Genevieve looked at her brother's blackened face and hands in amusement.

"I'm cleaning the black off the iron," Jamie reported proudly.

"So I see. The question is, who is going to clean the black off of you?"

Jamie looked down at his impossibly filthy shirt, arms, and hands. "It's not that bad," he assured her brightly. "I think it will come off with a bit of Eunice's soap."

"More like we'll be needin' a whole kettle of soap," Doreen predicted. "Dinna fret, Miss Genevieve, I'll be tossin' him in the bath the moment he's finished, and won't let him touch a thing on the way upstairs."

"That's fine, Doreen." Genevieve gently ruffled her hand through the one patch of Jamie's berry-tinged hair that looked relatively clean. If there was one thing she had learned in eight years of raising children, it was that if there was a mess to be either made or found, her boys were sure to get into it. "After you have all finished your chores, I thought it might be nice for us to bundle up in our coats and hats and take a walk. It has started to snow and—"

A loud rap upon the door interrupted her.

"Oliver, would you kindly see who that is?" She struggled to control the shrill thread that snaked through her voice every time someone had come to their door since Haydon's arrival a week earlier. Even the regular delivery of their milk and butter filled her with panic that somehow Lord Redmond had been found out and they were all going to be dragged away to prison.

"Right, ye lassies wipe down the lamps well with these rags, then screw the tops on and place the chimneys back," instructed Oliver, demonstrating his typical lack of urgency about going to the door. "Once they've had a chance to dry we'll put the wicks in, an' I promise ye'll be amazed—"

"The door, Oliver?" Genevieve persisted. The knocking was growing louder.

"I'm gettin' to it, lass," Oliver assured her. He cast a speculative eye at Haydon. "Were ye wantin' to slip out the back, lad—just in case?"

Haydon shook his head. If the authorities had somehow deduced that Maxwell Blake was in fact their missing prisoner, he would not abandon Genevieve and her family to try to explain why they had protected him. He would stay with her and make sure the police understood that he had forced her to help him.

"Very well. I'll make a lot of noise if I'm thinkin' 'tis someone ye might not be so keen to meet." Oliver stood and carefully straightened his frayed jacket before heading out of the kitchen to the front door.

"All right, then, duckies, let's keep working," said Eunice, trying to alleviate the pall of anxiety that had settled over the kitchen. "Being busy improves yer mind and cheers yer heart."

Everyone in the kitchen continued with their chores in uneasy silence.

"It's that old codger Humphries from the bank," Oliver reported, shuffling in a moment later. "Says he needs to speak with ye urgently, lass—an' yer husband, Mr. Blake, as well. It seems news of yer marriage has traveled through Inveraray. No doubt he's come to offer his congratulations." His tone was scornful.

"Thank you, Oliver." Genevieve regarded Haydon uncertainly. "I imagine Mr. Humphries would think it strange if I were to meet with him now without my husband—but of course if you'd rather not, I understand."

"I would be delighted to meet my wife's bank manager." He regarded her steadily as he offered her his arm.

Genevieve tentatively laid her hand upon his sleeve. She could feel the heat and strength of him shifting beneath her palm, like the muscles of a panther poised to strike. She found herself wanting to grip him tighter, to feel the marble hardness of him flexing against her grasp. She resisted the impulse and lightened her hold on him, until her trembling fingers barely grazed the finely woven fabric of his dark coat.

"Mr. Humphries, how pleasant to see you," she said as they entered the drawing room. "I should like to introduce my husband, Mr. Maxwell Blake. Maxwell, this is Mr. Gerald Humphries, manager of the Royal Bank of Scotland branch here in Inveraray."

Haydon blinked at the bank manager in astonishment.

Mr. Humphries was a shriveled little raisin of a man, with twiglike arms and legs that looked wholly insubstantial for supporting the fragile frame over which his loose-fitting coat and trousers were arranged. His thinning white hair was carefully parted just above his left ear, then painstakingly scraped up and over his shiny pink pate and liberally pomaded into place. Unfortunately, some of the slicked-down strands had separated, making it look as though his bald head were bursting through a fibrous white helmet. He required the assistance of a polished black cane to rise from the chair in which he had been seated, and upon rising to his feet he began to quiver so alarmingly Haydon was worried that he was going to topple right over.

"A pleasure to meet you, Mr. Humphries," said Haydon, striding forward with his hand outstretched so that he could catch the ancient little gnome if he fell.

Mr. Humphries grabbed Haydon's hand in his clawlike fingers and held on, steadying himself. "And you, sir," he said cheerfully. "A great pleasure indeed." He gazed at Haydon with eyes like blackberries, aged but alert. "When I first heard that you had married dear Miss MacPhail here, I said to myself, that's a fine man who would take on an impossibly heavy burden like that. A man of principle. A man of generosity. And, I daresay, a man of considerable means." He gave him a sly wink. "Of course, Miss MacPhail is exceptionally lovely," he hastened to add, smiling fondly at Genevieve, "but it takes a remarkable man to see the beauty not just in her, but in all those children as well. Six, now, isn't it, counting that new lad? And you're so young." He looked faintly envious as he eyed Haydon up and down. "Lots of years ahead of you. Marriage, children, money." He shook his head, nearly overcome with the pleasure of it all. "You're a lucky lass, Mrs. Blake, to have found this handsome knight, here. I wish you and Mr. Blake here years of happiness."

"Thank you, Mr. Humphries." Genevieve tried to remain patient as her bank manager espoused the joys of marriage. For Mr. Humphries to make a personal call upon her could only mean there was a problem with her account. She seated herself upon the sofa, feeling a knot of tension stiffen her back. "Can we offer you some refreshment?"

He waved a gnarled hand in the air. "Thank you, no. I don't wish to intrude upon you young newlyweds. I only wanted to offer my congratulations, and to inform you and your new husband of a small development regarding your account with the bank." He permitted Haydon to ease him back into his chair.

"Which is?"

"Your account is, regrettably, empty."

Genevieve regarded him in shock. "But—it can't be . . . I deposited a substantial sum of money into it just two weeks ago. There were sufficient funds there to last at least four months."

"And so there were," Mr. Humphries agreed. "I registered the funds myself." He smiled at Haydon, exposing a row of brittle yellow teeth. "I may have attained the position of bank manager, but I do try to offer my personal service with certain special clients, like your charming wife here. Why, I've known her from the time she was in nappies. Used to handle all of her father's accounts, God rest his soul. A most charming and cultivated man, Viscount Brynley was, and so proud of his bonny wee lass—"

"Forgive me for interrupting, Mr. Humphries," said Genevieve, who was anxiously clutching the armrest of the sofa, "but what has happened to my money?"

Mr. Humphries pulled his white brows together in puzzlement. "Money? Oh, yes, indeed. Those funds had to be taken and applied to the past-due payments on your mortgage, my dear. Only made a small dent in them, to be sure, but every little bit counts." He turned to Haydon, chuckling. "I'm sure you're aware, Mr. Blake, if you take a wee penny here and a wee penny there—"

"But why?" Panic was rising fast within her. "You knew that money was set aside to cover our living expenses over the next few months—as the money in that account always is. Why would you use it to make a payment to the mortgage?"

Mr. Humphries sighed. "Well, my dear, unfortunately the decision was not mine. I received written instructions from our Glasgow offices directing me to address the issue of your arrears immediately. Most emphatic they were on that point. It seems we have gone on a bit too long in ignoring your mortgage payments, which, as you know, have increased considerably over the years as you have required further loans. I had tried to explain to them that you are just getting settled and that the payments will be forthcoming in the future, but they were having none of it. Said that the terms I had extended you were contrary to the Royal Bank of Scotland's policy." He scowled with indignation. "Imagine—I've been with the bank over fifty years, and some milk-fed pup is trying to tell me about bank policy. Insulting, I call it," he railed, thumping his cane on the floor. "Had I the time to make the trip, I'd go there myself and take this lad to task. I'd tell him that I've been managing the bank's affairs in Inveraray since he was puking in a cradle, and I don't need some stripling to tell me how to do business."

Genevieve's mind was reeling. "We were depending on that money to get us through the next few months. What am I going to do?"

Mr. Humphries blinked. "Do? Why, just have your husband cover the balance," he answered happily, pleased to have the solution. "I can open an account for you today, Mr. Blake, and you can arrange to transfer the funds to discharge both the mortgage and the arrears, and the whole matter shall be resolved. We'll close your account, my dear," he added, looking fondly at Genevieve, "and you need never worry your bonny head about these dreary financial matters again. Won't that be a relief?"

Of course, thought Haydon, watching in grim silence as the last tint of color drained from Genevieve's face. Mr. Humphries had heard that his client was married. And if the town gossips had been doing their job, he had likely been informed that she had married an older man of nearly forty, who was well dressed and cultivated—apparently a man of some means. As a husband was responsible for his wife's debts, Mr. Humphries had come to the utterly reasonable conclusion that Mr. Maxwell Blake would simply pay off Genevieve's debts and that would be that. And therefore he had emptied Genevieve's account, as directed, which was the bank's right to do if she had defaulted on her mortgage payments.

"What is the figure for the amount owing?" Haydon asked calmly. Whatever happened, they must give no indication that they were unable to honor their debts.

"You'll forgive me if I am unable to provide you with the exact figure here," apologized Mr. Humphries. "If you would make an appointment to come and see me at the bank, I shall be able to calculate it more accurately."

"Approximately."

Mr. Humphries frowned, as if he thought it unseemly of Haydon to pursue such a delicate matter beyond the hallowed sanctum of a bank. "The monthly mortgage has not been paid for nearly two years—but I applied the funds in Mrs. Blake's account to that, which covered nearly two months. Therefore there is some twenty-two months still owing—plus interest, of course."

"How much?" persisted Haydon.

Mr. Humphries scratched his pointed chin, thinking. "Let's see, this house was already mortgaged for some five hundred pounds at the time of the viscount's death. Your wife has taken out numerous additional loans against the remaining equity over the years, which have been paid only infrequently until the year before last. That was when Mrs. Blake came to me and asked if she could avoid making payments at all for a few months. I was, of course, most anxious to be of assistance, and told her not to concern herself with the loans until she was able. I do try to be accommodating to my clients," he assured Haydon.

Haydon had to fight to keep from raising his voice. "How much?"

"I believe the mortgages now total some two thousand seven hundred pounds. The arrears are in the vicinity of approximately four hundred and forty pounds, including principal and interest."

Genevieve felt as if a clamp had tightened around her chest. How would she ever come up with such an enormous sum?

"And what terms is the bank offering?" asked Haydon, his expression utterly composed.

"I'm afraid the arrears must be paid at once,"

replied Mr. Humphries. "And henceforth—and I do apologize for the stringency that the bank feels it must invoke here—henceforth the monthly principal and interest against the mortgage is to be paid without fail on the first of every month." His blue-veined lips flattened into a thin line, as if his next words tasted unpleasant. "I hope you will forgive me for bearing this most disagreeable message to you, but the bank has said that if you do not honor the arrears in full within the next thirty days, it shall be forced to bring proceedings against you to sell the house and secure all the moneys owed on it. But that, of course, won't be necessary, now that you have Mr. Blake here to take care of things for you." He beamed happily at both of them.

"No," Genevieve murmured, feeling sick. "That won't be necessary."

"Excellent." Leaning heavily upon his cane, he managed to extricate his spindly frame from his chair. "Well, then, Mr. Blake, shall we meet at my office tomorrow at, say, eleven o'clock, and get this matter settled?"

"That would be fine." Haydon smiled, giving no indication that he was concerned in the least about the state of his wife's finances. "Thank you so much for coming here today in person to bring this matter to our attention. Permit me to see you to the door."

"As always, it is a pleasure to see you, my dear," said Mr. Humphries, giving Genevieve a creaking bow. "Marriage clearly agrees with you—you look positively radiant."

Genevieve managed a wan smile.

Haydon escorted his guest to the door, then returned to the drawing room and closed the doors.

Genevieve stared vacantly at the hem of her skirt against the threadbare carpet. Her gown was a brown,

ugly fabric that she had never liked, and the hem was
badly worn. She had already turned it up once to pro-
long her use of it. There was not enough length remaining to enable her to turn it up again.

"I had no choice."

Haydon said nothing.

"For a while I was able to manage if I was very
careful," she continued, somehow feeling the need to
explain. "I had no income, and my father had neglected
to leave me any money to manage the house or pay the
mortgage. I suppose he thought that perhaps I would
rent it out or simply sell it after I was married to Charles.
I'm certain he thought of it merely as an investment,
nothing more. He never dreamed that Charles would
break our betrothal."

You are lucky he broke it, Haydon found himself
thinking. *He would have tried to destroy you, and you were
too fine to be sentenced to a life lived beneath the heel of that
peacock's polished boot.* "And so you kept increasing the
debt against the house to survive," he surmised soberly.

She nodded. "At first I thought I might sell it and
move to a place that was cheaper. Mortgaging the house
further seemed like I was just taking an advance on
money that I would have when I sold it, and the debt
would be paid."

It was a reasonable enough plan, Haydon realized.
Anyone in the same position might have done the same.
"Why didn't you sell it?"

She traced her finger along the armrest, feeling
where the threads were about to split apart and expose
the stuffing inside. She could remember curling upon
that very sofa as a small child, tucked safely beneath her
mother's slender arm as they studied books together.
Then the sofa had been new and expensive, and she'd
had to be careful to not let her pretty embroidered shoes
touch the fabric, or let anything spill upon it.

"I was all alone—except for Jamie, of course. My father had just been killed in a riding accident. My mother had died after a lengthy illness when I was twelve, and my father made the mistake of marrying my stepmother barely six months afterward, before he had a chance to delve beneath the congenial facade she so artfully presented. My stepmother was outraged that I had dared to take my father's bastard son in as my own, so she left, taking what little remained of my father's money with her. She had gone through quite a lot of it during their marriage. Charles had broken our engagement and proceeded to tell everyone in Inveraray that I had gone soft in the head. And people began to turn away from me." She paused for a moment, watching her finger draw swirls upon the shabby, faded fabric. If she closed her eyes, she could almost smell the fragrance of her mother, a light, fresh scent of citrus and roses. "This house was the only home I had ever known. I didn't want to leave it."

Of course you didn't, Haydon thought, infuriated by the impossible situation she had been put in. *You were like an abandoned child, and you wanted at least the comfort and familiarity of your own home.*

"Later, of course, I started bringing home other children from the jail, and I needed the space the house provided. Mr. Humphries was kind enough to grant me agreeable terms, and to not mind if I paid late or even missed a payment or two entirely. Every few months I would sell some artwork or a piece of silver or some other thing that we didn't really need, and that would keep us for a while. And of course I painted portraits of other people's children. That didn't pay much, but it helped."

"But it was never enough," surmised Haydon.

She shook her head. "The children always needed new shoes, boots, gowns, coats, books, paper. We have always tried to make do with what we have and pass things down from one child to another, but some things just have to be purchased. Then there's all the food we eat, and a hundred other little things, like candles, lamp oil, firewood, and blankets—"

"I'm sure you did what you felt was necessary, Genevieve," interrupted Haydon. He did not mean to be abrupt, but they had a serious problem and he was impatient to devise a plan for dealing with it. "No one can fault you for the care you have provided for the children, or for how well you have managed on very little. But it was reckless and unprofessional of Mr. Humphries to extend you the terms he did, knowing that you could not possibly make regular payments, or ever get caught up."

"He was just being nice to me." Genevieve was taken aback by his brusqueness. "If not for Mr. Humphries, I might have been put on the street."

"And by being so nice, he has now put you in an extremely precarious position. The bank wants its money, and it is determined to get it by whatever means necessary. For the moment, Mr. Humphries believes he can get it from me, and I don't intend to enlighten him on that point. In my life as Lord Redmond, I am a man of some means, although through an abundant measure of my own stupidity, I have managed to throw much of it away." He raked his hand through his hair in frustration. "I have enough funds to take care of your debts, Genevieve. Unfortunately, given my current situation, it is impossible for me to access them."

Genevieve looked at him in amazement. Did he honestly believe she would accept money from him? "I don't expect you or anyone else to pay my debts," she told him flatly.

"Had I the money available, I would not give you any choice in the matter," Haydon retaliated. "But since

I cannot provide the funds, we must think of someone who can. Have you any other relatives who might be willing to come to your aid?"

"No."

Haydon frowned. "No one at all? Perhaps an uncle or a cousin—a relative of your father's?"

She shook her head. "My father's family was small— he had just one brother, who died a few years before he did. My mother had no brothers or sisters, and none of my grandparents are living."

"What about your stepmother?"

"I would never ask her for anything, and she would never agree to help me." Her voice was steeped in bitterness. "She was a selfish, evil woman who despised me from the day my father married her. After they were wed, she withdrew the affection she had lavished upon him during their courtship, leading him to seek companionship elsewhere. She told me I should have left Jamie in the prison to die the night I brought him home. I have no doubt that she would take great pleasure in the knowledge that I am in this position, and have no interest whatsoever in trying to help me out of it."

Haydon considered this in silence. The only other choice was obvious, but somehow he could not bring himself to make the suggestion.

You're being a fool, he told himself angrily. *He has lots of money and it's clear he still has feelings for her.* Swallowing his distaste for the only remaining option, he forced himself to say, "Then you must ask Charles for a loan."

She stiffened. "Absolutely not. Charles has gone to great pains to constantly inform me that I can't possibly manage to care for these children on my own. When I took Jamie in, he was horrible. He told me he wasn't about to raise some whore's bastard, regardless of who his father was. Then he forbade me from keeping him.

Forbade me." Her hands gripped the armrest. "I told Charles I had no intention of giving up my brother. He became enraged, and told me to choose between him and the baby I was holding in my arms. And I did."

Haydon said nothing. It was easy to despise Charles for being selfish, stupid, and cowardly. Easy to condemn him for his overbearing, narrow-minded stance, and to think that he did not deserve a beautiful, rare, and determined woman like Genevieve.

What was difficult was admitting what he himself would have done eight years earlier, had he been presented with the same situation.

Self-loathing filled him. In many ways, he realized miserably, he and Charles were not so different.

"If you went to Charles and asked him, do you think he would lend you the money?" Haydon persisted.

"No. He'd only take enormous satisfaction in the idea that he had been right."

"Charles wouldn't want to see you and the children put on the street," he argued. "If you asked him for help, I believe he would give it to you."

"You don't know him as I do," Genevieve replied. "Charles would derive great satisfaction from seeing me lose my home and forced to give up my children to orphanages or workhouses. Such a devastating outcome would soothe his pride over my public rejection of him, and reinforce the presumption amongst everyone in Inveraray that I have been a complete fool."

"You don't know that—"

"Your concern is appreciated, Lord Redmond," Genevieve interrupted. "But this is my problem and I shall deal with it as I think best."

"And what do you propose to do?"

"I shall find something to sell."

Haydon swept his gaze over the heavily worn furniture and the two inconsequential paintings that decorated the otherwise naked walls. "It doesn't appear that you have much left of any value."

"I still have a few things," Genevieve assured him defensively.

"Enough to come up with four hundred and forty pounds by eleven o'clock tomorrow morning?"

"No. But Mr. Humphries said I had thirty days, and I'm certain the bank will give me more time."

"Mr. Humphries expects me to pay the total of your arrears tomorrow. Moreover, more time for what?" he demanded. "More time to miss yet another mortgage payment and have your debts pile even higher?"

"More time to consider my situation and find a way to address it," Genevieve retorted. "I will sell some things. That will appease the bank somewhat while I find a way to repay the outstanding debt."

Haydon shook his head. "The Royal Bank of Scotland isn't run by your adoring little friend, Mr. Humphries. All they care about is getting their money. If they say they will take proceedings against you to sell the house in thirty days, then that is what they will do. Your home will be swiftly sold for a fraction of its value, the money collected will go to pay off your debts, and you and your children will be on the street. In the meantime, the bank has emptied your account, which means at this very moment you don't have the means to buy so much as a pint of milk or an egg."

"Thank you for clarifying my situation for me, Lord Redmond," said Genevieve tautly, rising to her feet. "I believe you have enough concerns of your own at present, without having to trouble yourself over my situation as well. Tomorrow I shall meet with Mr. Humphries at eleven o'clock, and explain to him that I need more time. I shall say that my husband's funds are currently tied up in investments, and cannot be accessed for a week or two. That should give me enough time to sell a few things and accumulate enough money to keep the bank at bay for a while."

Haydon was unconvinced. Even if Genevieve came up with the money to satisfy the immediate outstanding debt, there was still the matter of the monthly payments which she was clearly unable to honor, and beyond that, the money needed for daily household expenses. Although he could understand her desire to help all the lost waifs and stray elders she had taken in, at some point she should have realized she lacked the means to support so many people. But then, her generous spirit was at the heart of her. If not for her singular determination to help others, he would not be standing here arguing before her in her drawing room, almost healed and, for the moment, safe.

"I will go with you," he told her.

"That isn't necessary."

"Yes, it is." He found her stubbornness profoundly irritating. "People believe you are a married woman, Genevieve, and as such, whether you like it or not, your debts are now my responsibility as far as the rest of the world is concerned. We will meet with Mr. Humphries together, and convince him that we have the funds, but they are not immediately available. Let us hope that we are able to obtain an extension of a week or more. And then," he finished, glancing in frustration at the nearly bare walls, "we had best hope that you find diamonds hidden in the frames of these paintings."

. . . AND THEN LORD REDMOND SAID THE BANK WAS going to keep all the money from selling the house, and we would all be on the street."

Jamie, Annabelle, Grace, and Charlotte stared at Simon in horror, their faces like a row of little pale moons against the darkness of the boys' bedroom.

"Genevieve won't let that happen," said Jamie, trying to feign greater assurance than he actually felt. "She'll find a way to pay the bank its money."

"She can't, because the bank stole all her money," Simon countered. "Lord Redmond said we don't even have enough to buy an egg."

"Oh my." Grace's eyes grew wide with anxiety. "What are we going to do?"

"We are going to starve to death," Annabelle declared matter-of-factly. "We shall grow weak and tired and gradually waste away, and when we finally die we shall be so small, they will place all of us in one simple, pine coffin, and then they shall lay us to rest forever in an unmarked grave, because Genevieve will not be able to afford a proper gravestone. Instead she will plant a scarlet rosebush on it, and she will come every day and water it with her tears, and every year there will be six lovely roses blooming for her, one for each of us." She hugged her knees to her chest and sighed rapturously.

"Don't count me in that coffin." Jack was stretched out upon his bed with his hands laced behind his head. "I'm not stayin' around here to starve."

Jamie looked at him in surprise. "You're not?"

"I'm leavin' tomorrow. Never planned to stay this long anyway."

"But where will you go?"

He shrugged his shoulders. "Glasgow, maybe. There's plenty of quid to be made there."

"You mean in a factory?" Simon was intrigued. He liked the idea of all that complicated machinery pressing and squeezing and hammering away at a myriad of tasks before spitting out a button or a kettle at the end.

Jack snorted with contempt. "I'd never work in one of those places. You might as well be in prison—or dead."

"Then how will you make money?" wondered Jamie.

"Same way I always have. Glasgow's full of fancy folk just waitin' to have something lifted off them. Most of them are so rich, they don't even notice if a wallet or watch goes missing, an' if they do notice, they don't care."

Annabelle's pink bow of a mouth tightened with disapproval. "You mustn't go back to stealing, Jack. You might get caught and end up back in prison."

"How would Genevieve ever find you all the way in Glasgow?" added Grace. "The prisons there must be very big."

"I don't need Genevieve to find me," Jack retorted. "And I won't end up back in prison. I've been stealin' my whole life and never got caught—except," he grudgingly allowed, "for this one time. I know how to snatch something and slip into the shadows. Most times folk don't even know they've been robbed. You can make a bloody good living at it, if you're clever and quick."

Simon regarded him curiously. "Does that mean you weren't clever and quick when you got caught?"

"I made a mistake," Jack grumbled. "I won't make it again."

"If you run away, you will get Genevieve into a lot of trouble."

Charlotte's quiet, earnest statement had the effect of instantly silencing the room. None of the children wanted anything bad to happen to Genevieve.

Jack shifted uneasily on his bed. He did not relish the thought of adding to Genevieve's troubles, but he did not feel that was reason enough for him to stay. After all, he had to look out for himself first. It had been that way from the moment he was born, and it wasn't about to change just because Genevieve had been kind enough to take him out of prison and save him from being lashed by that bastard of a warder. Even if she had subsequently risked herself to help Haydon as well, and stayed by his side while he burned with fever, and then lied and told everyone he was her husband when it seemed for certain he was going to be arrested. She had taken risks for both of them, sure, but that didn't mean Jack was obliged to stay there.

Guilt gnawed at his conscience.

"If Genevieve gets into trouble because of you, Jack, they might take us all away from her," added Grace soberly.

"They can't." Jamie looked stunned by the possibility. "Can they?"

"I don't think they would be able to take you away, Jamie," Simon said, wanting to reassure him. "You've never been in jail."

"I was born in jail." His little voice trembled with pride, the result of many long talks with Genevieve in which she had instilled an unyielding sense of dignity in the lad regarding his heritage and the unfortunate circumstances of his birth.

"That doesn't count," Annabelle told him. "You didn't steal or break any laws like the rest of us. The court can't take you away just because of where you were born."

"If they take our house away and we've no food to eat, they're going to put all of us in a reformatory school or workhouse," concluded Grace. "Genevieve won't be able to stop them."

"I can't." Charlotte swallowed thickly, trying hard to be strong and not to cry in front of the others. "I can't possibly go to live in a place like that. I know they'll be cruel to me because of my leg, and they'll make me do things I can't do, and when I fall behind they'll beat me and tell me I'm lazy and stupid. . . ." Tears began to drip down her cheeks in two anguished streams. "And I won't have any of you with me to help keep me strong—"

"Hush, now," soothed Grace, wrapping her arms around Charlotte and pulling her against her slender form.

At twelve, Grace was barely one year older than Charlotte, but the life she had endured thus far had given her a tenderness and maturity that was years beyond her youth. She had run away from an uncle who tried to molest her at the age of eight, and then spent a year working with a small ring of pickpockets before she was finally caught and rescued from the jail by Genevieve. "Whatever happens, I won't let them separate us, Charlotte—do you hear?"

"Nor will I," added Annabelle fiercely, laying her head affectionately upon Charlotte's trembling shoulder.

Like Grace, Annabelle also knew what it was to be utterly desperate and alone. Her mother had died long before she could remember, and her father had been a drunk who seemed to despise her very presence. He beat her often, once throwing her across the room into a table and knocking her unconscious. She still bore a scar on her temple from that vicious attack, and was most careful to arrange her blonde hair so that it was hidden from view.

"Me neither," said Simon.

"I'm going to go with you too." Jamie's expression brightened suddenly. "Do you think they might let Genevieve come with us as well?"

Charlotte inhaled a ragged breath, as another tear spilled down her face.

"None of you is goin' anywhere," growled Jack suddenly.

The little group looked at him in confusion.

It was Charlotte's tears that had decided the matter for him. They shimmered upon her cheek in a liquid trail of pain and fear that cut straight into his heart. He could not remember anything affecting him so much before. He had vowed not to care about any of these children when he first arrived. At the time, it had been an easy enough oath to make. He had thought he could leave this house the moment it suited him and not look back. But the thought of Charlotte—or any of the children, for that matter—being beaten and abused in some filthy, evil reformatory school was impossible to contemplate. He had only the flimsiest knowledge of their circumstances before they came to live there, but he was well aware that each of them had suffered the pain of rejection, fear, and hopelessness in their brief lives. Then Genevieve had rescued them. She had pulled them from the wintry ashes of their existence and brought them into her home, where she had cleaned them and fed them and held them in her arms, making them feel wanted and safe.

Jack was not about to stand by and watch them be torn from the only person who had truly loved them, only to be tossed onto the refuse heap of life once more.

"All we need to do is get the money to pay off the soddin' bank," Jack said succinctly, "and you can all stay together in this house."

"But where will we find the money?" asked Jamie.

"Genevieve believes she might have something to sell, but Lord Redmond said whatever she has won't fetch enough," reported Simon. "He said she had better find some diamonds."

"I don't think Genevieve has any diamonds," Annabelle reflected. "I've never seen her wear any jewelry of any kind."

"She once had a ring and a necklace that belonged to my grandmother," said Jamie, "but she sold them down at Mr. Ingram's antique shop just after Simon came. You remember that, don't you, Simon?"

Simon nodded. "She was trying to pretend to be very happy about it afterward, but I could see that she was really sad. She took us out for tea and let us order lemon tarts instead of scones, saying that it was a special occasion and we had to celebrate."

"I'm not going to find any money here," Jack said impatiently. "I'm going to have to find it there." He tilted his head meaningfully toward the window.

"In the curtains?" asked Jamie, confused.

Jack rolled his eyes. They were practically babies, he reminded himself. "In the streets."

"Do you mean you're going to steal it?" Grace bit her lip, uncertain of the idea.

He nodded.

"We can help you," offered Simon, excited by the possibility. "We've all got experience at picking pockets— except for Jamie, of course—but I suppose he can learn."

"Picking pockets won't be enough," Jack informed him. "I need to steal something really valuable. Like a piece of jewelry with lots of fancy stones in it, or maybe a statue or a painting."

"I think it would be hard to steal a painting," reflected Grace with her customary pragmatism. "They're much too big to hide beneath your coat."

"We would have to break into a house to find those things," added Annabelle. "But how would we get in?"

"I know how to blow up a lock," volunteered Simon. "I did it once to get into a house."

Jack raised a brow, suitably impressed. "What did you steal?"

"I ate an enormous ginger cake, half a date pudding with sticky sauce, four crumpets with marmalade, a plate of cold lamb and peas, a bag of raisins, a bowl of butter, a chunk of sugar, a pint of double cream, and a jug of ale."

"Weren't you sick?" asked Jack, amazed.

"All over the prison warder's trousers," Simon reported. "He was most anxious for Genevieve to take me away."

"Genevieve will be sorely mad if she finds out you were blowing up things again, Simon," said Annabelle. "The last time you tried to blow the lid off of Eunice's roasting pan, you set fire to the good carpet in the dining room. Genevieve said it was lucky you didn't burn the entire house down."

"That was an accident," replied Simon dismissively. "I know how to do it better now."

"Oliver says we shouldn't need to resort to things like exploding locks," said Charlotte. "He always says there isn't a lock in Inveraray that can't be picked, as long as you've the patience and the charm to coax it."

"He taught us to open both the front and back doors of this house without a key," Jamie told Jack proudly. "But we're not to ever do it in front of Genevieve, because Oliver says she might not think that's a fitting skill for us to have."

"The trouble with breakin' into a home is, I can't be certain there's going to be somethin' there that's really valuable," reflected Jack. "I need to go somewhere where I know there's somethin' worth taking."

"Why don't you steal something from Mr. Ingram's store?" suggested Annabelle. "He has a suit of armor that a brave knight used to wear. Genevieve says it may have even belonged to Sir Lancelot. He was one of the knights at a round table."

"I don't think I can steal a suit of armor without anyone noticing," observed Jack dryly. "Besides, who'd want it?"

"Mr. Ingram has other things as well," Grace assured him. "That's where Genevieve sometimes takes things from our home to sell."

"She showed us a case filled with broken pots from ancient Egypt," said Simon. "The paint was badly chipped and the pots couldn't be used, but Genevieve made us study them anyway. She said they were worth a fortune."

Jack was unconvinced. "If someone wants a pot, why not just buy one that isn't all dirty and chipped?"

"They're worth more because they're old," Annabelle informed him with great authority. "People like the fact that other people have used them."

"I know someone who will give me money for what I steal, but he won't want a lot of broken rubbish from Egypt," said Jack. "He prefers things that look expensive."

"Mr. Ingram has jewelry too," Charlotte reflected.

Jack raised a querying brow. "Made of diamonds and rubies?"

"He keeps it in a special case at the back of the store made all of glass, and he gets sorely mad if you press your nose against it and make a mark."

"Genevieve sometimes looks at that case while she's waiting for Mr. Ingram to pay her," supplied Jamie. "She says most of the jewelry came from families who used to live in castles in France and had to run away so they wouldn't have their heads chopped off."

This was definitely starting to sound like a possibility, Jack decided. "Is the case locked?"

"I don't think so," said Grace. "But you have to go around to the other side of the counter to open it."

"There's a lot of pretty things in that case," added Annabelle. "I'm sure Mr. Ingram wouldn't notice if you took something."

"I would need to take a few things," Jack decided,

"just to be sure I could get enough money to pay the bank."

"If it isn't enough, we could always just go back and steal something else," Simon suggested.

"No, *we* couldn't." Did they actually think he would take them with him? "I'm doing this alone."

The children regarded him in dismay.

"But we want to help," protested Jamie.

"We'll be able to help you," Grace insisted.

"And we won't get in your way," Simon vowed fervently.

"I can't risk any of you gettin' caught." Jack's voice was flat. "It's better that you just let me take care of it."

"But what if you get caught?" asked Annabelle.

"I won't."

"But what if you do?"

He shrugged. "I'm older than all of you. If I'm caught, I can take care of myself. I'm not used to any of this." He gestured to the comfortably furnished room around him, with its dark-green curtains blocking the chill from the windows and the richly patterned carpet that felt like brushed silk against his bare feet. "Wherever they put me, I'll be able to get on."

Grace firmly shook her head. "You may be older, but you haven't been here as long as I have. You must at least let me go with you. I will watch out for you, and let you know when Mr. Ingram is about to look."

"Well, I've been here three years, and that's only one year less than you, Grace," said Annabelle, her chin set with determination. "Since I'm an actress, I will go and create a distraction for Mr. Ingram, which will make stealing the jewelry easy."

"I can make a better distraction than you," scoffed Simon. "I'll blow something up."

"We want to steal from Mr. Ingram's shop, not burn it down," pointed out Annabelle.

"I won't burn it down," Simon retorted, insulted.

"I would also like to go." Charlotte regarded Jack earnestly. "People always stare at me when I walk by, so that might help to take their eyes off of you."

"I don't want people starin' at you," growled Jack, infuriated by the idea.

"It won't bother me, Jack," she assured him in a small, soft voice, "if I know it's going to help Genevieve."

"I don't want to be left out," lamented Jamie. "Couldn't I help too, Jack?"

Jack stared at the imploring crescent of faces before him.

His first impulse was to tell them that they were too young to accompany him. But he had survived on his own since he was nine, which was but a year older than Jamie was. That was when he had finally realized that his mother was never going to keep her promise to rescue him from the hellish existence he was enduring with the vile husband and wife she had placed him with shortly after he was born. Over time her brief visits had grown less frequent, but when she appeared she was like a warm wash of sunlight in his otherwise cold and miserable life. Heavily powdered and rouged, her amply fleshed body squeezed into overly tight corsets and faded gowns that revealed a generous knoll of snowy bosom, she was always unbearably soft and lovely and exotic to Jack. She would ruffle her fingers through his hair and draw him close, holding him tight as he inhaled the mysteriously sweet scent of her, a fragrance that reminded him of flowers and honey, but which he later came to recognize as cheap whiskey. *It won't be much longer, my sweet lad,* she would promise him. *Only a wee bit more to save and then we'll buy a fine cottage and live in it together, as cozy as two mice in a teacup.* After she was gone the old man would drink and beat Jack until he could barely stand, saying his mother was nothing but a drunken whore and he couldn't afford to give her little bastard his charity any longer. Finally her visits stopped and the savagery of Jack's beatings grew, until one day something within him snapped and he decided to fight back, with a shovel.

That was the day he ran away, uncertain whether he had become a murderer or not.

Jack was accustomed to surviving on his own and stealing by himself, without the comfort or complication of knowing that there was someone else working with him. But his customary solitude had worked against him recently, resulting in his arrest and imprisonment in the Inveraray jail. There might be merit to having accomplices on this particular job, he decided. After all, every pair of eyes could keep a sharp watch and warn him of any trouble brewing. And if something did go wrong, it could prove helpful to have others there to create a distraction, as Annabelle had suggested.

"Fine," he relented finally. "You can all help. But you must do exactly as I tell you—is that clear?"

The little band of aspiring thieves solemnly nodded.

Chapter Six

SNOW FELL IN RAGGED WISPS OVER THE BLACK rooftops and cobblestone streets, dressing the town of Inveraray in a foamy white cape. It fluttered over the gray, choppy waters of Loch Fyne, dancing upon the chilly air before it kissed the frigid water and disintegrated, and piled in frothy layers upon the elaborate hats of the ladies and gentlemen walking through the frosty streets, making them look as if they were balancing enormous cakes upon their heads.

Jack stamped his feet, vainly trying to restore some heat to them. The boots Genevieve had given him were far too big and the snow had seeped through the worn leather, soaking his stockings. He wished he had thought to stuff some newspaper in them. He could not remember ever having a pair of shoes or boots that fit him well. Over the years he had utilized a variety of techniques for either filling up the excess, covering cracks or relieving blistering pressure. A cushion of newspaper would have made his boots more comfortable and had the added benefit of increasing their insulation. Their previous owner had obviously not spent much time standing about in the freezing wet snow, he reflected irritably.

He would have preferred not to do the robbery on such a miserable day.

Fresh snow had the distinct disadvantage of leaving a trail of footprints, particularly if one tried to escape down a previously untrod lane. It also reduced the number of people milling about and shopping, which would make it difficult for him to lose himself in the crowd once the jewels were safely in his pocket. Unfortunately, a delay in their plans was impossible. According to Simon, the bank had insisted upon payment immediately. Genevieve and Haydon had arranged to meet with the bank manager that very morning; therefore, the children had been excused from their regular studies. Jack had quickly offered to take them out for a walk in the falling snow, a suggestion that Oliver, Doreen, and Eunice agreed to happily, thinking it would enable them to get their own work done without having all the children getting in their way. Jack did not mention that they would be going to Inveraray's main street. If anyone questioned their presence while they were there, he could easily explain that they were merely enjoying the Christmas decorations adorning the shop windows.

"There's an old man and his wife in the shop now, looking at a pair of silver candelabra on a table," reported Grace, returning from her stroll past Mr. Ingram's window. "Mr. Ingram is helping them."

"Are they anywhere near the jewelry case?" asked Jack.

Grace shook her head. "The table is at the front of the store."

"Can we go inside now?" Jamie had been amusing himself by forming little mountains of snow with his boots and then pretending to be a giant and crushing them flat. "I'm cold."

"Jack said we had to wait until the store was crowded with people," Annabelle reminded him.

"But we've been here forever, and there are never more than one or two people in the shop," Jamie complained. "Mr. Ingram should try selling something better than all that old stuff—like cups of hot tea and chocolate."

"Why don't we go to the tearoom and have something to eat?" suggested Simon. "I'm hungry."

"You're always hungry," teased Charlotte.

"We can't go to the tearoom—we haven't any money," Annabelle pointed out.

"We could go back home and ask Oliver to give us some," said Simon.

"Oliver's not about to give us money for tea when we're already at home," argued Jamie, scraping together another mountain with his feet. "He'll just make us sit in the kitchen and eat something that Eunice has made."

Simon's mouth began to water. "Maybe she's made some treacle scones."

"We're not goin' home," Jack said firmly, "until we've done what we came to do. Now pipe down and pay attention."

The children obediently quieted.

"Mr. Ingram is havin' a bit of a slow day, so we're going to have to go ahead with our plan with just that old couple in the store. Does everybody know what they have to do?"

They nodded.

"Good. Make lots of noise as you go in—we don't want Mr. Ingram to think you're tryin' to sneak about. I'll come in by myself a moment later. Grace will keep watch for me while I get into the case. The rest of you do whatever you have to do to keep Mr. Ingram's attention

away from me. The most important thing to remember
is, if anything goes wrong and I'm caught, all of you get
out of there as fast as you can. Don't try to help me—
understand? Just keep movin' and go home."

Charlotte's eyes widened. "But Jack—"

"If you won't swear to me that you'll do this, we'll
bloody well go home right now," Jack snapped.

Charlotte dropped her gaze to her wet boots.

Jack instantly regretted his tone. He had to learn to
be more gentle with Charlotte, he realized in frustration. She didn't have the same confidence and resilience
that the others enjoyed. It was clear to him that she had
been deeply affected by the life she had led before
Genevieve took her in. He had no desire to further
erode her already fragile countenance.

"I'll be fine, Charlotte," he assured her, his voice
low and edged with apology. He reached over and
tipped her chin up, making her look at him. "Trust me."

Charlotte stared at him, her gaze glistening with
emotion.

He held her chin a moment, staring deep into the
swirl of her brown-and-green eyes. There was fear
there, fear and regret and something else that he could
not quite understand. He frowned and studied her
longer, holding the delicate round of her jaw in his fingers. Snow was drifting like goose down around her,
forming a lacy pattern on her hat and coat and in the
auburn silk of her hair. A flake settled upon her cheek,
an exquisite work of the finest frozen lace. She seemed
more perfect to him in that moment than any of the
ladies in the paintings Genevieve had taken such pains
to show to him; more beautiful than anything he had
ever seen. Her skin was cool and pale, but there was sufficient heat to melt the intricate snowflake, turning it
into a single, silver tear. And suddenly he understood
what he was seeing in Charlotte's enormous eyes.

Charlotte *cared* about him.

A slender ray of warmth shot through him.

"Everything is going to be fine, Charlotte," he said gruffly. He released his hold on her chin to gently brush the silvery tear from her cheek with the back of his fingers. Then he cleared his throat. "I promise."

"I'm getting cold," complained Jamie, rubbing his stiff little hands together.

"We're going now," Jack decided. "Keep your hats low and your scarves up around your face, so no one gets a clear view of any of you. The snow is comin' down hard, so people won't think it strange that you're bundled up. When you see me movin' away from the jewelry case, that's your signal to leave. Don't race out in a pack—go to the door nice and slow, as if you've finished whatever you were lookin' at and are now moving on to another shop. We'll meet by the church at the end of the street and go back home together. Does everybody understand?"

They nodded.

"Good." He swept a critical gaze over them, trying to be certain that there was nothing about any of their appearances that would give anyone pause. They were all reasonably well dressed, with freshly scrubbed faces and cheeks chilled pink from the cold. None of them looked like a ragged, starving urchin who might be about to filch something.

"Let's go, then."

A little brass bell tinkled cheerfully as the door opened, heralding their arrival. The six children poured into the shop, giggling and chattering as they made a great show of stamping the snow from their boots and brushing it from their shoulders. Once they had given Mr. Ingram time to appraise them and realize they were relatively well dressed and were not trying to escape his notice, they each wandered into different areas of the

store, so that the shopkeeper would have to keep shifting his gaze to keep track of what each of them was
doing.

Jamie went to stare in awe at the gleaming suit of
armor that stood guard in one corner of the store, while
Annabelle adopted a tragic expression as she studied a
painting of a heartbroken young woman cradling her
murdered lover in her lap. Charlotte limped over to a
bookcase and became engrossed in several leather-
bound volumes that had their titles stamped in gold on
the spines, and Simon frowned at a statue of two naked
men battling each other. Why the artist had chosen to
have them fight without any clothes on was absolutely
beyond his comprehension—he thought they looked
ridiculous. Grace went to the back of the store and
made a show of examining a pretty set of blue-and-
white plates that had been carefully arranged upon an
elaborately carved sideboard, not too far from where the
jewelry cabinet stood.

". . . and you're absolutely sure, Mr. Ingram, that
these candelabra are from the palace of Versailles?" in-
quired the bloated gentleman in the black felt hat and
enormous overcoat.

His flaccid-faced wife apparently suffered from an
equal fondness for rich foods, and had barely been able
to squeeze her colossal, crinolined backside into the al-
lotted space beside the polished mahogany table upon
which the enormous pair of candelabra were displayed.

"Belonged to King Louis the Fourteenth himself,"
Mr. Ingram assured his prospective buyer. He was a
compact little man of slightly less than average height,
with a neatly combed mat of carefully arranged graying
hair upon his head, and a slightly strained expression
upon his face. Clearly he did not enjoy having the au-
thenticity of his wares questioned. "Truly a magnificent
pair, and extremely rare. Stolen by a French duke who

was an adviser to Louis the Sixteenth at the time of the Revolution. Poor chap barely made it out of France with his head on his shoulders. One can only imagine the remarkable events in history to which these hand-some pieces were witness," he continued, embellishing his sale with a whiff of intrigue. "The workmanship is so superb, I almost hate to part with them," he added wistfully.

Jack sauntered nonchalantly toward the back of the shop. An ancient, battered sword caught his eye, and he paused for a moment to study it. He didn't think an old, rusted weapon like that could be worth very much, but he decided that if he ever had a home of his own, that was the kind of thing he might like to hang on the wall. All the other ornate furnishings around him made him feel uncomfortable, as if the furnishings themselves thought they were better than him.

"Pssst!" Grace tipped her head slightly in the direc-tion of the jewelry cabinet.

Jack nodded once. He glanced back to make certain that Mr. Ingram was still engrossed in making his sale.

"Think of the dinners they have overheard—the drama, the mystery, the romance that has unfolded be-fore their elegant presence," Mr. Ingram continued, making it sound as if the candelabra had eyes and ears. "What an impressive addition to your home these pieces will make—you shall be the envy of all those who see them. . . ."

Feigning interest in several objects that lay between himself and the jewelry cabinet, Jack surreptitiously continued his trek to the back. One more quick glance to make sure that Mr. Ingram was still engrossed in making his sale.

Then he slipped behind the cabinet and ducked down, unobserved.

Grace had been wrong, he realized, cursing silently. A small padlock clamped the door to the case closed. Jack had not yet mastered the skill of opening a lock without the benefit of a key. He thought he could probably break it off easily, but that would make too much noise.

Better to unscrew the pins holding the hinges in place.

He raked his gaze over the table behind him, where a number of objects were waiting to be cleaned and tagged before being put on display. A small, gleaming dirk lay in a nest of packing straw. Checking once more to make certain Mr. Ingram remained occupied, Jack snatched the dirk and bent down to set to work.

The point of the blade fit almost perfectly into the head of the screws. Working quickly, Jack twisted the blade round and round, releasing the small screws and setting them silently on the floor. Finally the hinge to which the lock was linked was freed. Jack pulled it off and eased open the door to the cabinet.

A dazzling array of jewels sparkled before him. Glittering rubies, sapphires, diamonds and emeralds of every size and color were artfully arranged in glorious necklaces, brooches, rings, and earrings. Within that single case there was sufficient wealth to keep him comfortable for his entire lifetime—or possibly two. One quick sweep of his hand across the blue velvet-lined case and he could be on his way to a new life—one that was free of perpetually searching for food and wearing blistering boots and sleeping on the streets. He wondered what the penalty for such a tremendous theft would be. Would they hang him if he was caught, or worse, put him in jail for the rest of his life?

". . . I don't know," the boiled dumpling of a wife was saying, shaking her head until her powdery jowls trembled. "I had been hoping to find something bigger, perhaps with a bird or two worked into the pattern—or maybe even some fruit. . . ."

Jack hesitated, torn between stealing a few pieces or just taking the whole bloody lot. He had never been presented with such a fabulous amount of wealth, and the allure of it was overwhelming to the point of making him feel sick. He might never know what it was to be starving and desperate again, he realized numbly. He could buy a home, fill it with food, and keep the lamps and fireplaces burning day and night if it pleased him. He could buy clothes as fine as or better than the ones that fat old codger at the front of the store had stuffed himself into, and never have to worry about where he was going to sleep that night, or finding food in the morning. He could be truly free, in the way that he believed only great wealth could make a man. He fantasized about this for a long, heady moment, tempted to the point of dizziness by the possibility of the life that lay shimmering before him.

And then he remembered that if he took everything, Mr. Ingram would certainly notice, and be bellowing for the police within a matter of minutes. Jack would be caught, and Jamie, Simon, Annabelle, Grace, and Charlotte would be implicated by their presence in the store at the time of the robbery. Genevieve would lose everything, including the children she so obviously loved. After all of her unexpected kindness to him, Jack could not risk hurting her so terribly.

There would be other jewelry cases, he assured himself philosophically.

Exhaling the breath he had been holding, he quickly selected two rings with enormous diamonds at their centers, a stunning sapphire-and-diamond necklace and a brilliant diamond brooch. He crammed them in his coat pocket, then quickly rearranged a few of the remaining pieces so there was no discernible gap in the cabinet. He closed the narrow door, repositioned the lock, and began to swiftly twist the screws back into the wood with the tip of the dirk.

". . . if it's fruit you're looking for, madam, then I believe I have the very thing," Mr. Ingram continued, temporarily abandoning his battle to convince his customers of the merits of the candelabra. "There is a magnificent silver serving tray at the back of the shop that dates from the sixteen hundreds, which once belonged to King Charles the First himself. If you'll just permit me—"

"*Jack!*" whispered Grace frantically as Mr. Ingram turned toward the back of the store. "*Jack!*"

There was no time to replace the last screw, Jack realized in frustration.

"You there!" barked Mr. Ingram suddenly. "What the devil do you think you're doing?"

Had he been given an opportunity to reply, Jack might have been able to fabricate an almost credible answer.

Unfortunately, Jamie decided to help him by sending the heavy suit of armor crashing noisily to the ground.

"*Run!*" Jamie screamed, darting down an aisle, toward the door.

"Stop him!" roared Mr. Ingram, momentarily forgetting about Jack.

The corpulent couple at the front did their best to oblige. The portly man stuck out his walking stick as Jamie raced by, neatly tripping him. Unfortunately, this sent the lad plowing straight into the voluminous hooped skirts of his abundantly sized wife. The impact caused her to fall flat on her backside between the table and the wall, effectively trapping her amidst the endless layers of her petticoats and the expensively wrought metal cage supporting them.

"Help!" she shrieked, her arms and legs flailing as she bobbed about like a great, overturned turtle.

"Got you, young ruffian!" huffed the man, snatching up Jamie by his shoulders.

Simon launched himself at Jamie's captor, wrenched his walking stick away from him and began to whack him soundly in the shins. "Take your hands off him!"

"Help—murder!" cried the man, releasing Jamie in favor of trying to defend himself. "He's trying to kill me!"

Mr. Ingram abandoned Jack so he could offer assistance to his poor customers. As he rushed past Annabelle, who was looking magnificently serene in the midst of all the chaos, she leaped lightly onto a chair, pulled the painting she had previously been admiring from the wall, and smashed it upon Mr. Ingram's utterly startled head.

"Why, you little—"

He did not finish whatever he might have thought to call her, but began to chase her along the narrow aisle instead. Unfortunately, with the frame wrapped about his neck and shoulders like a cumbersome gilded collar, he sent a trail of elegant teacups, delicately cut crystal wineglasses, and several heavy decanters that had been painstakingly arranged on a magnificent sideboard smashing to the floor in his wake.

"Look over here!" called Charlotte, as Mr. Ingram was but an inch away from grabbing a fistful of Annabelle's silky blonde hair.

Momentarily distracted, Mr. Ingram looked.

A fine Venetian tablecloth sailed toward him and landed squarely upon his head before draping over the picture frame, giving him the appearance of a small, high table with a round ball sitting on it.

"*I'll kill all of you, you vile wretches!*" he roared, turning about and clawing furiously at the delicate fabric as he struggled to free himself. Chairs and small tables fell every which way as he churned himself in a mad circle.

"Everybody get the bloody hell out!" shouted Jack, causing the little bell above the door to jangle merrily as he tore it open. "*Now!*"

The children scrambled to navigate their way through the litter of broken china, fallen armor, and overturned furniture. They tore through the store in a desperate streak, too frightened to even glance behind to see if Mr. Ingram had managed to free himself and follow them.

"Run!" commanded Jack as they spilled onto the street.

The children needed no further encouragement. Each dashed off in a different direction, easily darting around carriages and shoppers as they made their escape. Jack raced across the road, then turned to take a final look to see if any of the children were being followed.

And felt his heart slam to a stop as he watched Charlotte trip just as she reached the shop's threshold, only to be wrenched to her feet by the enraged and triumphant Mr. Ingram.

Chapter Seven

"WHERE'S GENEVIEVE?" DEMANDED JACK, HIS LUNGS heaving for air as he burst through the door.

"Sweet Saint Columba, just look at the snow ye're troddin' all over my clean floor!" scolded Doreen, who was on her knees scouring the floorboards at the end of the hall. "Do ye not know to take off yer boots when ye come inside?"

"Genevieve!" shouted Jack, ignoring Doreen as he threw open the doors to the drawing room. He spun around in frustration on finding it empty and ran to the stairs. *"Genevieve!"*

"What's all this commotion?" demanded Oliver, appearing from the door to the kitchen with a boot in one hand and a greasy brown rag in the other. His gaze fell upon Jack's panicked face. "What's happened, lad?"

"Here now, all of ye, stop and take yer boots off!" commanded Doreen, tossing her brush in her bucket in frustration as Annabelle, Simon, Grace, and Jamie stampeded into the house, depositing muddy snow everywhere. "Have ye all taken leave of yer senses?"

"Oliver, where is Genevieve?" Jack's pale face was glistening with sweat and his eyes were wild and frantic.

"Why, she's in the cellar, lad," said Oliver, realizing that something was terribly wrong. He glanced at the children to be sure no one was hurt, then frowned. "Where's Charlotte?"

Jack tore through the kitchen and sprinted down the cellar stairs. There he found Genevieve sitting on a crate, wearily rifling through the contents of a trunk that lay open before her. She appeared to have been analyzing the contents of the cellar for a considerable length of time, and was surrounded by a veritable mountain of musty-smelling boxes, paintings, chests, and discarded furniture.

"You've got to get her back." Jack's voice was curt and desperate. "She didn't do anythin'—she just went along because she wanted to help. I was the one who stole the jewels." He wrenched the stolen jewelry from his pockets and shoved it carelessly into Genevieve's hands. "That's all of it—I swear I didn't take anything else. Just take that to Mr. Ingram and make him let her go."

Genevieve looked in horror at the beautiful pieces glittering in her hands. "My God, Jack," she whispered, suddenly feeling as if she couldn't breathe, "what have you done?"

He blinked hard, fighting the tears threatening to spill from his eyes. "I stole this jewelry from Mr. Ingram's shop," he confessed miserably. "I was goin' to sell it and give you the money, so you could pay the bloody bank and keep your house and no one would be put on the street. But Mr. Ingram spotted me before I had left the shop and everyone started to run and then Charlotte tripped and fell and he wouldn't let her go."

The other children came racing down the cellar steps, followed by Oliver, Doreen, Eunice, and Haydon.

"I don't understand." Genevieve fought to remain

calm as she tried to make sense of what Jack was telling her. "Why would Mr. Ingram detain Charlotte?"

"Because she was the only one of us that he could catch." Grace's face was drawn and pale against the dim light. "I know I should have made her go before me because of her leg, but I was closer to the door and I thought she was following right behind—and she was— but then she tripped and—I'm sorry, Genevieve." She brushed angrily at the tears pouring down her cheeks.

Suddenly all the children began to speak at once, the voices shrill with fear and agitation.

"We thought we would go in and out without any trouble—"

"But when Mr. Ingram saw Jack by the jewelry case, I knocked the knight's armor over—"

"—And then that fat old man tripped Jamie with his walking stick and his wife went down like a top—"

"—And I told him to let Jamie go, but he wouldn't, so I hit him in the legs with his stick—"

"—And I broke a painting over Mr. Ingram's head and he started to chase me—"

"—So we threw a tablecloth over him, which made him sorely mad—"

"—And then we all ran out—"

"—Except for Charlotte."

Genevieve stared at her brood in shock. "You attacked Mr. Ingram?"

"It was *my* idea," said Jack adamantly. He wanted to spare the children from Genevieve's anger and disappointment. "I made them come with me."

"That's not true!" protested Grace.

"We all wanted to go," Simon assured Genevieve.

"And we had to make Jack see that it would be better if he didn't do it alone," Annabelle elaborated.

"They were going to leave me behind, but I wouldn't let them," finished Jamie.

"I see." Genevieve knew she should be angry with them, but there was no time for that now. Later, when Charlotte was safely back home, she would find the strength to be utterly furious with all of them. All that mattered in that moment was that she return the stolen jewelry and bring Charlotte home.

"Come, Genevieve." Haydon's voice was reassuringly calm and steady. "We shall return the jewels to Mr. Ingram, apologize profusely for the trouble the children have caused him, agree to pay for anything that was damaged, and bring Charlotte home."

Genevieve shook her head. "She won't be at Mr. Ingram's anymore," she said with dull certainty. "The police will have come and taken her away. She is at the prison."

"Then we shall go and retrieve her from there. Come." He extended his hand to her.

"You cannot accompany me." She slowly rose to her feet, unable to accept his help because her hands were still clutching the stolen jewels.

"Of course I can," Haydon argued flatly. "As your husband I'm sure they will expect me to be at your side."

She shook her head, overwhelmed by her fear for Charlotte. "We have already courted disaster by letting you be seen by Governor Thomson and Police Constable Drummond. We deceived them once, but that doesn't mean they will be misled a second time. There is also the risk of having that awful warder recognize you—or an officer of the court, or even another prisoner in the jail. We cannot take that chance."

"I'm afraid the lass is right, lad," said Oliver soberly. " 'Tis a strange fact that those of us who have spent time in prison have a far keener sense of things than bumbling lackwits like Governor Thomson, or even that suet-headed Constable Drummond."

" 'Tis a skill that comes from sitting all day and night in a dirty, cramped cell with naught but yerself for company," explained Doreen. "It makes ye more aware of yer surroundings, and of people as well."

"I hardly think one of the other prisoners is going to recognize me," objected Haydon. "I look entirely different than I did when I was there."

"They won't have to look at you," Eunice assured him. "They'll be able to tell who ye are just by listenin' to your voice, or the sound of yer steps as ye walk down the hallway. That's something even I learned to do during my time there. Ye start to pay attention to all the little things, like who scrapes the edge of their heels as they pass, or how heavy a person's step is, or what a voice sounds like as it bounces off the cold stone walls. It helps to pass the time."

"Then I shall disguise my voice and alter my stride," said Haydon stubbornly.

"No." Genevieve's tone was resolute. In truth, she would have taken comfort in Haydon's strong presence at the jail, but the possibility that he might be discovered as Lord Redmond and hauled back into his cell was too great. "I already have one member of my family in jail, Haydon—I won't risk having you arrested as well."

"Then I'll go with you," said Jack. "I'll tell them Charlotte had nothing to do with the robbery. They can arrest me instead. Old Thomson is just dyin' to have me lashed and sent away, and so is that bastard Constable Drummond. Whatever they do to me, I can take care of myself far better than Charlotte can."

Genevieve looked at Jack in surprise. His gray eyes were glittering with determination and his hands were clenched at his sides. She had always known he was capable of empathy for others. The fact that he had risked his own freedom to help Haydon escape had been ample testament to that. Even so, his willingness to sacrifice himself for Charlotte moved her deeply.

"I'm afraid I can't let you do that, Jack. I know you want to help Charlotte, but I don't believe the Governor will let you trade yourself for one of his prisoners. If anything, you'll be arrested along with Charlotte, and then there will be two of you to worry about. I will go on my own, I will return these jewels and I will make Governor Thomson and Constable Drummond see that they have no reason to detain Charlotte further. And after Charlotte is safely at home once again," she finished, raking her gaze over her dejected-looking children, "we shall further discuss the matter of your trying to rob Mr. Ingram."

CONSTABLE DRUMMOND REGARDED GENEVIEVE WITH spurious sympathy over the skeletal steeple of his fingers. His hands were unusually large with a taut sheet of pale skin stretched over them, and his fingernails were long and not quite clean. Given his hands and the greasy length of his hair, it was clear he was a man who did not concern himself overmuch with his personal ablutions. Of course, there was the black swath of hair that he curried and combed alongside each cheek, but even that was in need of a good trimming. Genevieve had long assumed that he had neither wife nor mistress, but until she sat across from him in Governor Thomson's office, uncomfortably aware of his musky, unwashed odor, she had not realized that he had no interest in attracting a member of the opposite sex into the narrow, cheerless parameters of his life.

"I'm sure you must realize, Mrs. Blake, that the accused's involvement in the brutal attack on Mr. Ingram and Lord and Lady Struthers completely nullifies any arrangement you may have with Governor Thomson regarding her custody." Constable Drummond didn't quite smile, but Genevieve knew he derived intense satisfaction from making the statement.

"It is my understanding that Charlotte neither stole anything nor actually attacked anyone," Genevieve argued. "Since I have returned all the missing items and intend to fully compensate Mr. Ingram for any damages he may have suffered, I believe the matter is largely resolved. I therefore see no reason why Charlotte needs to be detained further. If you will just take me to her, I will escort her home and deal with the matter privately."

"Unfortunately, Mrs. Blake, the situation is not quite that simple," said Governor Thomson, who was nervously scratching his beard.

It did not reflect well upon the governor to have one of the children he had released but a year earlier into Genevieve's care commit a serious crime against three of Inveraray's most influential and upstanding citizens. When this incident was combined with the recent escape of Lord Redmond from his prison, it seemed clear to Governor Thomson that he would imminently be called before the prison board to explain his extravagant failures. It was absolutely critical, he realized soberly, that he demonstrate to all that he realized the gravity of these recent mishaps, and that he take steps to ensure that they never happen again.

"The gang of thieves who attacked Mr. Ingram's shop stole jewelry that was extremely rare and of great value. In the process of doing so, they attacked Lord and Lady Struthers, two of our most distinguished citizens in Inverary. Lord Struthers has sent word that his wife is severely traumatized by the incident. She has been examined by Dr. Hayes, who has prescribed that she be confined to absolute quiet and bed rest for at least a month, to help her overcome her hysteria and any other injury to her person."

Genevieve bit down hard on her lip, fighting to refrain from making any comment. Jamie had told her how he had accidentally barreled into Lady Struthers after Lord Struthers tripped him with his walking stick. In her opinion, any woman who could afford the luxury of taking to her bed for a month after being knocked on her backside by an eight-year-old boy did not have enough responsibilities to keep her out of it.

"There is also the matter of the accused's unwillingness to assist me with my investigation, which clearly demonstrates the weakness of her moral fiber," added Constable Drummond. "She refuses to give me the names of her accomplices, despite the fact that I have indicated that the judge might view her case more leniently should she do so. Of course, we have deduced from Mr. Ingram's descriptions that the other children involved in this attack were your wards, but it would be helpful if the girl would confirm that."

Genevieve regarded him in disbelief. "Are you saying that you expect Charlotte to accuse her brothers and sisters?"

His jaw tightened with contempt, as if he found Genevieve's description of the other children as siblings both distasteful and ridiculous. "I am saying that should this girl demonstrate even a modicum of remorse by assisting me with my case, I would be more inclined to believe that there was some hope of your rehabilitating her. As it is, however, I can only conclude that a substantial length of time spent in prison and then reformatory school will be the best course of action for all concerned. Although I have decided not to pursue the matter with the other thieves, this girl must be made an example. Society cannot afford to let dangerous criminals inspire fear and unrest without due punishment."

"We are talking about an eleven-year-old child." Genevieve's outrage was tempered with her rapidly swelling fear. "She is scarcely a dangerous criminal."

"On the contrary, we are talking about a young woman with a criminal past who, despite all that you have misguidedly offered her by way of a home and a fine moral example, cannot seem to overcome her own corrupt instincts," Constable Drummond retaliated. "As I have told you before, Mrs. Blake, these things are in the blood, passed down from one generation to the next. No amount of coddling or comfort will cleanse the impure souls of the children in your household. It is best to treat them with a hard hand. Your unwillingness to do so has resulted in the unfortunate incident that has occurred today, in which several innocent citizens have suffered."

"I don't deny that the children were wrong in what they did today, Constable Drummond," Genevieve allowed, trying to mollify his unsparing attitude by agreeing with him. "But they were not doing it out of greed or any inherent need to steal. They were doing it solely because they wanted to help me—"

"Whatever the accused's reasons were can be presented at the time of her trial," Constable Drummond interrupted.

"Her name is *Charlotte*," said Genevieve, fighting to maintain a civil demeanor. She disliked the way Constable Drummond kept referring to Charlotte as if she were bereft of an individual identity, like a dog or a pig. "And you cannot possibly believe that anything good will come from imprisoning an eleven-year-old child in this foul place and forcing her to stand trial—"

"Unfortunately, Mrs. Blake, there is nothing more that we can do." Governor Thomson's voice was shadowed with regret. "If it were the lass's first offense, perhaps we could afford to be somewhat lenient. Unfortunately, the girl has a well-documented history of stealing—that is what led her to be incarcerated in my prison in the first place."

"It was her father who was stealing," Genevieve corrected, feeling the taut threads of her composure begin to snap. "He was forcing Charlotte to show her crippled leg as a way of distracting a crowd while he picked their pockets—a leg that is malformed because he beat her so severely in one of his drunken outbursts that he broke it."

"There is no question that the lass has had a difficult time of it," Governor Thomson acknowledged. "But as you are aware, one of the conditions of your arrangement with the prison is that once the children are released to your custody, they must not break the law again, or else you will lose custody and the child must suffer the full punishment of our justice system. It is only by enforcing this provision that I am able to provide some assurance to both the court and to the citizens of Inveraray that the children will pose no further threat to our society. Charlotte has broken the law, and I am therefore bound by our agreement to relieve you of custody and pursue the matter through the court. I'm afraid there is nothing else to be done." He looked as if he wished it were otherwise. "If we were to overlook this matter, the citizens could dispute my arrangement with you and insist that all the children currently serving the remainder of their sentences under your roof be returned to the prison system immediately. I'm sure Lord and Lady Struthers would be among the first to instigate such a petition."

He was right, Genevieve realized. Sick despair tightened around her chest.

"The Sheriff Court will sit again in three days,"

continued Governor Thomson. "At that time you will be able to plead your case on the lass's behalf. Perhaps you can appeal to the sheriff for lenience."

Three days. An eternity for a child to spend trapped in a prison. But it was time enough for Genevieve to try to get Mr. Ingram and Lord and Lady Struthers to view Charlotte sympathetically, and to provide testimony on her behalf. If the victims were willing to be compassionate, she did not see how the sheriff could not be.

She swallowed her fear and slowly rose from her chair. "I would like to see her now," she said, forcing herself to appear calm. She must give Charlotte the impression that everything was going to work out just fine.

"Of course." Governor Thomson rolled out of his chair and jerked the creased fabric of his black waistcoat over the swell of his belly. "I shall escort you to her myself."

LEADEN STRIPS OF LIGHT WERE FALLING THROUGH the narrow bars of the tiny window, casting the frigid cell in a somber caul.

Charlotte sat upon her wooden bed with her back against the wall and her crippled leg stretched out stiffly before her, the foot resting upon an overturned chamber pot. She was wearing her hat and coat, and had taken the two thin blankets that the governor's wife had provided her with and wrapped them tightly around herself in a desperate effort to stay warm. She knew she should try to walk around a bit to restore some heat to her flesh, but her leg was aching, so she did not think she could manage it just yet. Her injured limb was always worse when it was cold, or damp, or when she first awoke in the morning and it had grown rigid from repose. It also pained her badly at night after she had forced it to drag after her all day.

She could not remember a time when it had not hurt, although she knew that she must have once enjoyed the luxury of being whole and free of pain, for she had not been born this way. The memory of her actual injury had waned, however, and she was infinitely glad of that. That was the advantage of being young, she supposed, although there were times when she felt far older and wearier than her mere eleven years could account for. When one was a child, a year or two seemed nearly a lifetime away. While that made the wait for the privileges of being, say, thirteen, almost unendurable, it did have the benefit of blunting at least some of the sharp torments and cruelties of the past. The memory of her father's brutality seemed less immediate to her now, and although the dreams still haunted her, she no longer wakened to find her heart racing and her sheets soaked with a mortifying combination of urine and sweat.

"Stop yer starin', ye wicked whore of Satan, or I'll cut yer heart out and crush it in my hand!"

Charlotte glanced uneasily at the woman with whom she shared her cell.

Margaret MacDuffie was a short, sturdy woman of some forty years, with a plain, masculine face that scowled from beneath a filthy brown scarf which she wore tightly wrapped around her head. Her nose was large and misshapen; it started out between her eyes well enough, but then it rose in a stiff knob before flattening into a listless pulp just above her upper lip. In one of her slightly more lucid moments Margaret had told Charlotte that her husband used to beat her regularly, and that he had broken her nose more times than she could remember. This had aroused a great deal of sympathy on Charlotte's part, for she knew what it was to be at the mercy of a man who drank, and spoke with his fists.

She had tried to imagine how Margaret might have been before her husband began to brutalize her. Surely she could not always have been the raving madwoman she was today, or else he would never have married her. It was possible that Margaret had once even been somewhat attractive, although that required a rather substantial leap of the imagination. Charlotte was wise enough to know that most marriages were not based upon the romantic love that Annabelle described when she rhapsodized about her actress mother and the Scottish noble she claimed was her father. Even so, it seemed to Charlotte that when two people married, even if they did not love each other, they had to like each other, at least a little. In the case of Margaret and her husband, it seemed clear that they had not liked each other quite enough. Duncan MacDuffie drank and pummeled his wife nearly every day of their marriage, until one morning Margaret refused to tolerate his poor treatment of her any longer. On that particular day she rose before her husband awakened, washed her face and hands, then laid a fire in the stove and put a kettle on to boil. Then she went back into their bedroom, sliced open his throat with his own razor, dragged him into the barn and left him for the pigs to feed on. After she had washed away the blood, she sat at her kitchen table and enjoyed a strong cup of tea, a boiled egg, and two thick slices of oat bread spread with strawberry preserves. It was nae but a fitting end, she had told Charlotte, for a man who had been nothing but a swine his entire life, and certainly not worth missing breakfast over.

Unfortunately, Margaret was unable to bring the

judge and jury presiding over her trial round to her way
of thinking. In its wisdom, however, the jury did sense
that there was something about Margaret that was not
entirely sound—perhaps because of the way she wept so
pitifully when she described how one of the poor pigs
choked to death on a rather tough piece of her husband. Her ability to feel empathy for that animal, but
see nothing wrong whatsoever with what she had done
to her spouse, persuaded the jury to find her insane.
Thus her life was spared, but she was sentenced to be
confined as a prisoner for all the remaining days of her
life. She had spent nearly two years in the Inveraray jail,
and if her healthy appetite and robust constitution were
any indication, it seemed she would spend many more
there, although she was slated to eventually be transferred to a prison in Perth with a separate criminal lu-
natics section.

"I know what yer thinkin'," Margaret hissed, eyeing
Charlotte suspiciously. "Yer thinkin' to have my share
when the warder comes. Well, I won't allow it, do ye
hear? I've a farm to run when I leave this place, and I
need to keep myself well and fed. The pigs are waitin'
on me," she concluded, nodding happily.

Charlotte drew her blankets tighter and dug her
chin into her chest, ignoring her. It was better to ignore
Margaret when she ranted or talked nonsense. Charlotte
had learned that answering her just seemed to make her
further agitated.

There were footsteps coming down the hall, and a
jangling of heavy keys. A pale waver of candlelight
seeped into the dark cell as the door creaked open.

"Genevieve!" cried Charlotte, nearly tripping over
the chamber pot in her haste to rise.

Genevieve swiftly crossed the cell and wrapped her
arms tightly around the trembling child.

"Charlotte, my love," she breathed, kissing the top of her head before pressing her cheek against Charlotte's soft hair. "Are you all right?"

"Yes." She buried her face into the reassuring warmth of Genevieve's cloak, which smelled like soap and cinnamon. "Can we go home now?"

Genevieve swallowed thickly. She wanted to say, "Of course we can," and turn around and lead Charlotte out of the dark, cold little chamber, and away from the strange woman crouched in the corner who was staring at her with such unnerving fascination. She wanted to march past that vile Warder Sims, who was watching her embrace her daughter with such obvious derision, and by Governor Thomson, with whom she was unaccountably angry, even though she understood that he had been put in an impossible situation. She wanted to take Charlotte home, see that she had a soothing warm bath to wash away her fear and the foulness of this place, and then send her to bed with a tray laden with all of Eunice's specialties. And tomorrow morning Charlotte would be allowed to rest as long as she wished, and then she would join the rest of the family by a fire in the drawing room, and she would tell them about her terrible ordeal, and they would all hug her and tell her how good and strong and brave she had been to have endured such an awful thing.

Instead she held her child fast, stroking her hair as she desperately tried to think of what she was going to tell her.

"I'll leave you to visit, then," said Governor Thomson, placing the candle on a small wooden bench. He stroked his wiry beard a moment before adding, "You may stay as long as you like, Mrs. Blake,." It seemed he was at least trying to be accommodating. "Just call for Sims when you are ready to leave."

The door slammed shut.

"Where's my supper?" screeched Margaret, lunging at the door like a wild animal and banging on it with her fists. "I want my porridge! Ye'll nae steal it from me, ye greedy whoreson. I'll have it if I have to kill ye first—do ye hear? The pigs are waitin' on me, Sims, and they're waitin' on you, as well, unless ye bring me my pissin' supper!"

Charlotte burrowed her face even deeper into Genevieve's cloak, trying to lose herself in its warm shelter.

"Let's sit down over here," said Genevieve, steering Charlotte toward her wooden bed. "There, now," she said, drawing her into the cradle of her arm and kissing the child's forehead. "That's better."

"That's better, that's better," cackled Margaret, scurrying back to her corner.

"I'm not going home, am I?" Charlotte's face was pale as she looked up at her.

Genevieve's heart clenched. "Not just yet," she replied softly. "I'm afraid you're going to have to stay here for a few days—but I shall come to visit as often as I can, and we'll find some way to make them go fast. We have to wait for the next session of the Sheriff Court. Then we shall be able to talk to the sheriff and make him see what a dreadful misunderstanding this whole thing is. Once he realizes how terribly sorry you are for what happened in Mr. Ingram's shop, I shall able to take you home and everything will be all right."

"I'm going home too," Margaret said, tying and untying the oily scarf around her head. "My pigs are waiting for me."

Charlotte trembled. "I stood before Sheriff Trotter once before, and he sentenced me to prison and reformatory school."

"That was because he believed you had nowhere else to go." Genevieve's voice was soothing. "After I have explained to him that you now live with me and that except for this unfortunate incident your behavior has been absolutely faultless, I am certain he will see that the best thing for everyone is for you to come home."

"Come home, come home, come home," chanted Margaret before bursting into giggles.

Genevieve tightened her grip on Charlotte. "I am also going to speak to Mr. Ingram, and see if I can get him to speak kindly on your behalf."

"I don't think he'll be willing to say anything good about me," reflected Charlotte soberly. "He was sorely mad after Annabelle broke a painting over his head. Grace and I had to throw a tablecloth over him to stop him from grabbing her, and that just made him even angrier."

"After he has had a little time to calm down and consider the situation, he may see things differently," said Genevieve, although she feared the possibility was remote. "At any rate, I don't want you to worry. I just want you to try to eat and stay warm and think about how all this will be over in a few days. When I come tomorrow I shall bring you some books and some food, and we shall have a nice long visit."

Alarm flared in Charlotte's eyes. "You're not leaving now, are you?"

"No," Genevieve said, giving her a reassuring squeeze. "I shall stay for as long as you like."

Charlotte relaxed a little and settled herself against Genevieve once more. "Is everyone else at home all right?"

"Everyone is fine. Of course, they were horribly concerned when they realized what had happened to you. Your brothers and sisters came crashing through the door like a herd of mad elephants, flinging mud and snow all over Doreen's freshly washed floor."

Charlotte managed a wan smile. "That must have made Doreen upset."

"I do believe she was far more distressed by the fact that you had been arrested than a bit of wet mud on her floor. Poor Jack was particularly shaken by it all. He wanted to come down here and offer himself to Governor Thomson in exchange for your release. Oliver had to practically chain him to the stove to stop him from doing so."

"Oh, you mustn't let him do that, Genevieve." Charlotte regarded her imploringly. "I know he thinks he could stand prison better than I, but Jack is far more likely to make the warder or the governor angry, and then they might lash him. At least they won't lash me, because I'm a girl."

Genevieve regarded Charlotte in surprise. When had this special, selfless bond developed between Charlotte and Jack, she wondered, and why had she not been able to see it? Charlotte was an extremely gentle, reticent child who was typically wary of new people. And Jack was a detached, suspicious, angry young lad who seemed determined not to have feelings for anyone, lest it interfere with his jealously guarded independence. Yet here the two of them were, each apparently determined to sacrifice themself for the sake of the other.

"I'm not going to let him do it," Genevieve assured her, feeling a sense of wonder that these two abused children could be so protective of each other. "I made him realize that he would be very lucky not to have Constable Drummond arrest him as well, and then I would have the both of you to worry about in here."

Regret shadowed Charlotte's gaze. "I'm sorry for what I did, Genevieve. It's just that Simon overheard you saying that the bank was going to take our house from us, and then we would all be sent away. None of us wanted that to happen. We thought that if we could just find enough money to pay the bank, then you wouldn't have to worry anymore."

"I don't want you to concern yourself about that, Charlotte. I will find a way to pay the bank, and no one will take you or any of your brothers and sisters away from me. Do you understand?"

Charlotte nodded.

"Good. Now I want you to lie down and try to sleep."

She helped Charlotte to pull her legs up onto the hard slats of the bed, then arranged the thin blankets over her. Seating herself once more, she placed Charlotte's head on her lap and began to sing in a soft, lulling voice as she gently caressed the child's cheek.

"Sing to me," pleaded Margaret, who was watching her from her corner. "Sing, sing, sing."

"If you want me to sing to you, then you must lie quietly upon your bed and promise not to yell out or frighten Charlotte," Genevieve said. "Can you do that?"

Margaret obediently crawled onto her bed and closed her eyes.

"Sing, sing, sing," she pleaded softly.

Genevieve resumed caressing Charlotte's cheek and began to sing once more, and did not stop until the candle had burned down low and both prisoners in the barren little cell had drifted into the fleeting sanctuary of slumber.

HAYDON PROWLED THE CONFINES OF THE DRAWING room like a caged beast.

He never should have permitted Genevieve to go to the prison without him, he realized furiously. It would have been dangerous, but the threat of being discovered and thrown back into a cell would have been far better than this goddamn interminable waiting. She had been gone for hours now, the streets were pitch-black and it was taking every shred of his self-restraint to keep himself from going out to find her. The fact that she had not returned immediately with Charlotte could only mean that bastard Drummond or whoever the hell had been responsible for her arrest had refused to release the terrified girl. Haydon could only imagine Genevieve's horror when she realized that one of her children was going to be detained in the foulness of that jail. She had probably decided to stay with Charlotte, to try to calm the poor child's fears. Perhaps she even intended to remain with her through the night—or until Governor Thomson had her bodily dragged out of Charlotte's cell. It would be just like her to do something like that. Genevieve MacPhail was not a woman who would easily leave the side of a child whom she knew to be in jeopardy. Her determination to help others was a trait he had respected and admired in her from the first moment he saw her standing in his cell.

He wished he had possessed the same indomitable resolve with Emmaline.

He cursed and downed the last of his whiskey. Thank God Oliver kept a bottle in his room, "for medicinal purposes." After watching Haydon restlessly pace the drawing room for nearly an hour, the old man had suggested that perhaps Haydon needed a wee drop to help calm himself. Haydon had drunk well over half the bottle and still didn't feel the least bit calm. If anything, the need to take action was like a fire in his gut. If Genevieve was spending the night in the jail, then she should have sent word to him so that he wouldn't worry, he decided furiously. How was he supposed to be calm with Charlotte in prison and Genevieve wandering the streets of Inveraray alone in the dark? The streets were crawling with all kinds of vicious scum at this hour, a fact to which he could well attest. For all he knew, she had set out to come home hours ago, and on her way home had been attacked or abducted.

He banged his glass down upon a table and strode toward the front door, determined to find her.

Before he had reached it, a key twisted the lock and the door slowly swung open. Relief flooded through him as he saw Genevieve standing before him, her face shadowed by the brim of her bonnet and the dim light spilling from the single lamp burning in the hallway. Paradoxically, the realization that she was safe and whole only fueled the wrath now blazing within him.

"Where in the name of God have you been?"

His voice lashed at her like a whip. She did not flinch, but tilted her head up, until the small, pale oval of her face was exposed to the dusky light.

"They refuse to release her," she murmured, her voice a wisp of sound against the stillness of the night. "They have locked her up in a cell with a murdering madwoman who screams and babbles constantly. They intend to keep her there three days, at which time she will be made to stand trial. I went to plead with Mr. Ingram to speak on her behalf, and he refused. He said Charlotte must serve as an example to all the other undesirables in our society. Then I swallowed my pride and went to Charles, to beg him to hire a good lawyer for us. And he said it was up to my new husband to pay for my brats, and that I had made my choice the day I chose to keep a whore's bastard over wedding him. He said he has always known that my life would end in disaster. He knows about the bank, you see, knows that I am in grave danger of not only losing my home, but my children as well. And he doesn't care. He thinks that this is what I deserve."

Pain was etched with haunting beauty upon her delicate features. Rage churned through Haydon at Charles's cruelty, but in that moment it was Genevieve's suffering that mattered most. Ashamed for speaking to her so brusquely, unmanned by his own inability to be at her side to help her endure all that she had been through that night, he stood there, paralyzed.

And then, not knowing what else to do, he held out his arms to her.

For a long moment neither of them moved. The air between them hung frozen, suspended by fear and grief and need. *I can bear this alone,* thought Genevieve, desperately grasping at the last vestiges of her composure. *I have endured worse.* But she could not remember ever feeling so lost, so heavily burdened by the responsibility of saving Charlotte from the fate that was swiftly unraveling before her and all the rest of her children. She was losing control, she could feel it, and she knew that if she did so, all would be destroyed. And so she stood utterly still, feeling as if she were about to shatter, terrified that if she shifted or spoke or did anything at all, the carefully constructed facade of her brave independence would begin to crumble.

Haydon watched her as she struggled with her emotions. It had not been his intent to add to her burden, and the thought that he had apparently done so wounded him more than her obvious rejection of him. He lowered his arms.

And then Genevieve cried out and flew to him, burying her forehead against his chest as she broke into agonized sobs.

He clamped his arms tightly around her, encircling her with his strength.

"It's all right, Genevieve," he said, his voice low and sure as he held her fast. "Everything is going to be all right."

He had no grounds to make such assurances, yet he continued to murmur it over and over, soothing her the way he might a small child. He guided her into the

drawing room and closed the doors so that no one else
in the household would hear her weeping, knowing her
distress would only increase if the other children were
witness to it. He gently removed her hat and cloak,
which were cold and soggy with snow, then seated her
on the sofa before the fire. Her flesh was chilled, as if
fear and weariness and all the hours spent at the prison
and arguing with Ingram and Charles had sapped her
blood of heat. He went to the hearth and threw two
logs on the fire, then blew upon the coals, quickly coaxing fresh flames to life. Returning to her side, he pulled
her into his arms once more, vainly wishing he could
somehow wash away all the terrible things she had been
through.

"We will hire a lawyer without Charles's assistance,"
he began firmly, stroking the soft silk of her pale hair as
he spoke.

"We cannot afford to hire a lawyer," sobbed
Genevieve, "and the ones that the court provides for
those who are unable to pay fully expect the children
they are defending to go to jail. They imprison eight-
year-olds for taking an unripe apple to fill their bellies,
or a pair of old stockings to warm their raw, blistered
feet. And then they send them to reformatory school,
where they are forced to work and are starved and
beaten and only learn more about violence and stealing.
But no one cares about their fate, as long as they are
not sullying the streets and threatening the precious
welfare of fine, upstanding citizens like Lord and Lady
Struthers." Her tone was bitterly scornful.

"It is not the same with Charlotte," Haydon argued. "She has a fine home and a mother who loves and
cares for her—and there is also the matter of her injured
leg. Surely the judge will demonstrate compassion, and
realize that it is far better for Charlotte to return here
than to go to jail."

"Sheriff Trotter is due to preside over the court that day, and he has sentenced Charlotte once before," Genevieve informed him. "She was only ten, and had been arrested with her father for stealing. The drunken brute used to force her to hobble about and lift her skirts to show her crippled leg and beg people for money. And while they shook their heads in false sympathy and crowded round with cruel fascination, her father would slither in and out amongst them, picking their pockets."

"Where is her father now?"

"He was sentenced to four years in prison, which he is serving in Perth. And for the crime of being a victim of his greed and violence, Charlotte was sentenced to forty days in prison, to be followed by three years in a reformatory school." Her voice was ragged as she finished, "How can we expect compassion from a sheriff who could be so cruel?"

Haydon said nothing. He was appalled that any judge could impose such a harsh sentence on a girl who was so obviously at the mercy of an abusive father. On the other hand, perhaps Sheriff Trotter had genuinely believed that he was doing the best thing for the girl. At least in prison and reformatory school she would have a roof over her head and three meals a day, however meager and unpalatable they might be.

"But you took Charlotte before she was sent away," he surmised.

She nodded. "Over the years I have worked out an arrangement with Governor Thomson, and the court has always agreed to it. He lets me know when there is a child in his prison who has no parents or family willing to intervene on their behalf. Providing the child is not guilty of a violent crime, he has permitted me to assume custody."

Haydon thought of how anxious Governor Thomson

had been for Genevieve to take Jack out of prison. "And what benefit does Governor Thomson extract from this arrangement?"

"I pay him a fee for his trouble."

"You mean a bribe."

She sighed. "I suppose you could call it that. I sign an agreement assuming full responsibility for the child for the remainder of his or her sentence. The document stipulates that if the child breaks the law or runs away while under my care, our arrangement is void and the child must be returned to the jail to serve the full extent of their original sentence. Governor Thomson said that was why he and Constable Drummond couldn't release Charlotte. He fears there will be a public outcry, because everyone knows Charlotte has violated the terms of our agreement."

"More likely he fears that there would be an investigation and someone might find out that he has been, in effect, selling these children to you," reflected Haydon.

"Either way, Charlotte is shivering upon a hard wooden bed tonight, and there is nothing I can do to save her." Fresh tears welled in her eyes. "I have failed her," she whispered, her voice breaking.

"No, Genevieve, you have not." He laid his hands upon her slender shoulders, forcing her to look at him. "From the moment you retrieved her from the prison you have provided with a warm home and decent food and a loving family. You may not realize it, but by doing so, you have armed Charlotte with something she did not have before, and that is hope. You have also shown by your own example that women can be strong, courageous, and persevering, which will help her to endure the next few days."

"But what about the next few years? Charlotte cannot endure the hardships and cruelties she will be made to suffer in reformatory school—"

"Tonight you were unsuccessful in your pleas to have her released, but the matter is far from finished," Haydon vowed. "If we cannot afford a decent lawyer, then we can at least assist the one the court gives us in the preparation of Charlotte's defense. We will show the court that until this incident, Charlotte has been the very model of gentleness and lawful behavior. While we have to be careful not to implicate our other children, I will argue that Charlotte's role in this incident was in actuality very small, and that this is a matter best resolved by her parents. I will also argue that society will not be served by sending her to prison, which will cost public money and compromise any hope for her future, and therefore the wisest judgment would be for her to be returned to her home, where she will be shown the error of her ways and disciplined accordingly."

Genevieve regarded him through a veil of tears. "You cannot accompany me to the court, Haydon— someone might recognize you there."

"I will take that chance," Haydon told her flatly. "As your new husband and Charlotte's stepfather, the court may be willing to listen to me—out of perverse curiosity to hear what I have to say, if nothing else. Because I was charged with murder, I was tried before the larger Circuit Court, which I understand meets here but twice a year. While some members of the local Sheriff Court may have attended those proceedings, I can assure you that between my beatings, my illness, my prison uniform, and my unkempt state, I looked very different from the man who now appears before you. Also, I did not speak in my defense, at the suggestion of my lawyer, who felt that I was more likely to antagonize the jury than elicit any sympathy from them. Therefore, there is little danger that anyone present will have heard me speak."

"But—"

"The matter is settled, Genevieve." Haydon was adamant. "I have no intention of permitting anyone to jail Charlotte, and no intention of letting you go down to that courthouse alone. We will deal with this matter together, and we will see that Charlotte is brought home safely. Is that understood?"

His face was harshly cut in the flickering firelight, a rough sculpting of shadows and light. The lines between his dark brows were deep, as were those creasing his forehead and webbing the skin beneath his eyes. There was pain there, and a rawness of emotion that surprised her, for although she had sensed that Haydon had grown fond of Charlotte, she would not have expected him to be so agonized over a child he had only known for over a week.

As she stared at him, she suddenly sensed that he was reacting to something that had happened long before he had ever come to Inveraray. Something that had wounded him deeply. There was so much about him Genevieve didn't know, yet in that hushed, firelit moment she felt she knew him better than he perhaps even understood himself. It made her want to lay her hand against his cheek and feel the heat of him beneath her palm, to trail her fingers along the dark bristle shadowing his jaw, to lean close and feel his warm breath upon her skin, just as she had during those long nights when he had solely belonged to her.

Unable to restrain herself, she leaned into him and pressed her mouth to his.

Desire shot through Haydon. It was just an uncertain little kiss, he understood that, an inexperienced pressure of one mouth to another, but he could not remember ever having been so aroused by one simple touch. Of course he had been impossibly stirred by Genevieve during all the long hours she had tended him and bathed him, soothing every inch of his aching body with her skillful caresses and unbearably soft hands. His body was aching now, but it was with the rigid need to be touched again, to be stroked and kneaded and clutched, not gently, but with desperate, gasping hunger. He fought to control himself, struggled to endure the sweet graze of her mouth and the clean scent of her hair and the feathery brush of her fingers against his clenched jaw. If she would but pull away he might be all right, might be able to maintain the tightly shackled control he had been exerting over himself every time he saw her, or thought of her, or inhaled the lingering summery fragrance of her after she had left a room. But she did not pull away. Instead she increased the pressure of her lips, as if she was trying to elicit a response from him and was not quite sure how to go about it.

With the fragile uncertainty of a woman who had never been properly kissed, she parted her lips ever so slightly, inviting him to taste her.

Haydon groaned and crushed his mouth to hers, wrapping her in his powerful arms as he dragged her against him.

He plunged his hands in the strawberry-gold of her hair, plucking away the pins until the heavy mass poured like liquid silk into his rough palms. His tongue swept along the coral of her lips and then slipped inside, tasting her deeply as his hands roamed the elegant curve of her jaw, the fine silk of her cheek, the slender column of her throat. Much to his pleasure, she did not fight him, but instead moaned and grasped the back of his neck, pulling him even closer as her own desire flamed.

Her gown was a primly buttoned affair of slate-gray, unadorned and inexpensive and well-worn, yet as Haydon cupped the soft swell of her breast, he thought it the most mysterious and erotic fashion he had ever seen. One by one the tiny black buttons at the front were freed, until finally the creamy expanse of her breasts was exposed, barely veiled by the transparent fabric of her chemise. His tongue twined with hers as his hand wandered over the lush mounds, aroused by the flimsy barrier of linen separating his rough skin from hers. He rained a hungry path of kisses along the pulse of her throat, over the delicate structure of her collarbone and down into the valley below. Her chemise was loose and dipped in a low crescent over her, enabling him to slide it across her skin with little more than a sigh, releasing the beauty of her breasts to the shifting coppery light of the fire.

Genevieve felt as if she were melting, as if her skin and flesh and bone had been transformed to molten honey. She wanted to taste Haydon's mouth again, to swirl her tongue around the whiskey-sweet wetness and heat, and feel the low rumble of him moaning against her as his hands laid claim to her body. She tried to pull him up to her once more, but he was consumed with circling his tongue across her tingling skin, setting it afire with slick little caresses. And suddenly he closed his mouth over the peak of her breast and began to suckle, sending a deep shiver of pleasure surging through her. She gasped and threaded her hands into his hair, tilting her head back as she held him at her breast and shamelessly offered herself to him. She felt her nipple tighten into a taut bud of pure sensation, and just as she thought she could bear no more he broke away and flicked his tongue over the other peak, licking and suckling until both breasts were full and aching.

He eased her back against the cushions of the sofa and continued to worship her, trailing up and down from her breasts to her mouth, while his hands roamed across the ample layers of padded crinolines and skirts that cocooned her belly and hips and thighs. Suddenly his fingers were circling her ankle, and then they were trailing up, along the thin wool of her stocking, barely grazing her calf as they found the edge of her drawers. Up and up they moved with swift certainty, and then they stole through the opening of her undergarment and began to caress the downy soft mound between her thighs.

Genevieve gasped, but Haydon only kissed her more deeply as he stroked the intimate triangle, awakening it to a myriad of glorious sensations. Hot, dark pleasure bloomed inside her, and when he lightly traced his finger along the cleft of her womanhood, he found her slick and anxious to be touched. He eased his finger inside, fondling the slippery folds of her with slow, patient strokes, teasing her and rousing her as he devoured her mouth. His own hardness was pressing against her, and she tentatively laid her hand against it. He groaned and drove his finger deeper, shocking her, exciting her, filling the terrible void that had begun to throb from the very core of her body. In and out he moved as he suckled from breast to breast. His fingers circled the honeyed petals of her in swift swirls before slipping ever deeper inside again. He altered his rhythm and his touch, teasing her, coaxing her, distilling her awareness until it was nothing but a ripple of ever-increasing pleasure, tightening and intensifying until she couldn't move, couldn't think, could only take the smallest sips of air.

Her modesty forgotten, she gripped his hardness through the wool of his trousers and restlessly shifted her hand up and down, wanting to torture him as he was torturing her. But it was impossible to concentrate on what she was doing, because the sensations swelling within her were growing hotter and deeper and tighter, until she was certain she could bear no more. And then she was shattering into a thousand sparkling pieces and she cried out, a cry of ecstasy and wonder, and Haydon crushed his mouth to hers and held her tight.

It took every fragment of his self-control to keep

himself from taking her right there on the sofa, with her breasts spilling wantonly from her spinsterish gown and her ruffled skirts tangled in frothy disarray about her thighs and hips. Genevieve had ignited a desire within him that had long lain dormant, and he wanted to slake it, here, now, quickly, before the flames of her passion cooled.

He had no right to her, he reminded himself.

She was innocent and pure, a woman who had devoted her life to saving lost children from a bleak and unforgiving world. What could she possibly want with a selfish bastard like him, who had wasted most of his life in a drunken orgy of pleasure, gambling and drinking and rutting? He had carelessly permitted his family's fortune to dwindle until it was less than half of what he had originally inherited from his staid, thoroughly responsible brother. He had recklessly copulated with a married woman and created an unwanted child who was doomed to a life of loneliness and misery, until she finally decided she could bear the cruelties of this world no more. Now he was running from the law, accused of murdering a man he did in fact kill, albeit in self-defense, afraid to be known by his own name, without so much as a penny for food or shelter. In the midst of this appalling situation, he was selfishly ravishing the woman who had risked everything in her world to try to help him.

Hating himself, he rolled off of her. He stood and began to straighten his clothing, staring morosely into the fire.

Genevieve's senses began to return. Her heated flesh was suddenly cold and shockingly bare now that the comfort of Haydon's powerful body stretched over her was gone. Mortified, she rose from the sofa, pulling down her skirts before she clumsily began the task of buttoning up the gaping bodice of her gown.

"Forgive me," said Haydon tautly. "I should never have touched you."

What could she possibly say to that? she wondered miserably. Obviously he was trying to spare her feelings, for surely he could not have forgotten that it was she who had kissed him. But she had never imagined that a simple, tender kiss could burst into such a frenzy of heat and lust, of wanting to touch and taste and grope and feel, deep within, the sensations that had flooded her body with such glorious abandon. No kiss that she had shared with Charles had ever exploded into such a breathless, spinning vortex of erotic desire. And even though her skin was now chilled by Haydon's abandonment of her and her own shame, the area between her legs was still mysteriously wet and aching for more.

"I must go," she managed in a tiny voice, wishing the floor would open up and swallow her whole. And then, because her breeding and her irrevocably instilled civility would not permit her to do otherwise, she added awkwardly, "Good night, Lord Redmond."

Haydon closed his eyes as he listened to the door close behind her, excruciatingly aware of her summery citrus fragrance upon the air, his clothes, his skin.

He would never touch her again, he vowed fiercely. He had already destroyed one innocent life by following the torch of his lust, and he'd gladly burn in hell before ever doing so again.

Chapter Eight

THE INVERARAY COURTHOUSE WAS AN ELEGANTLY spare building of precisely cut blocks of biscuit-colored stone. Completed in 1820, it had been designed by the architect James Gillespie Graham, who had been sensitive enough to realize that men who were cooped up in a chamber with the onerous burden of dispensing justice all day long might appreciate a little light and air. Therefore, several large, paned windows filled the relatively spacious courtroom with either inspiring cheer or oppressive gloom, depending on the weather.

On the cold December day of Charlotte's trial, a thick gray mantle of cloud effectively blocked any hope of sunlight. This left the courtroom both freezing and dark, forcing the sheriff, lawyers, and clerks to bundle themselves in extra layers beneath their black robes. With their yellowing sausage-roll wigs perched precariously upon their heads and their wrinkled robes ballooning out around them, they looked like a flock of bored, fattened ducks ready to be plucked and roasted upon a spit, Genevieve thought.

". . . and since that terrible day I've not been able to

have an easy moment, either in my shop, or on the street, or even in my own bed at night," Mr. Ingram mewled pitifully. "Those young ruffians beat me so badly I suffer constant pain. The doctor has told me I will have to endure it for the rest of my life." He rubbed his gray head and winced, as if he were afflicted at that very moment, then gave the sheriff a mournful look.

"Thank you, Mr. Ingram," said Mr. Fenton. The prosecuting counsel was a pasty-faced man with a sharply pointed beak of a nose, beneath which he sported an enormous lobster-red mustache. "You may step down."

Mr. Ingram made a great show of hobbling as slowly and stiffly as possible to his seat on the hard wooden benches where the audience sat. Genevieve had an almost irrepressible urge to yell out "fire!" and then see how quickly Mr. Ingram was able to flee the confines of the building. When she had paid him a visit but three days earlier he had flapped his arms with athletic vigor as he scrambled about pointing to the damages his shop had incurred. His current physical impairment had mysteriously manifested itself since then.

She glanced at Charlotte, who sat with her back straight and her small hands tightly clenched upon her lap in the prisoner's box. Her long days in prison had leeched her of color, giving her skin an almost luminescent quality, as she silently listened to the witnesses bear testimony against her. Genevieve had brought her a gown of dark-green wool to wear, which did not fit particularly well, but was clean and appropriately modest. Eunice and Doreen had enhanced it with a snowy ruffle of lace at the cuffs, which had been stripped from one of Genevieve's old gowns, and helped to make Charlotte look less like the rough street urchin Mr. Ingram and Lord and Lady Struthers were claiming her

to be. Her auburn hair had been neatly brushed and
pulled away from her face with the assistance of a satin
strip of emerald ribbon, and Genevieve had taken care
to ensure that her face and hands were well scrubbed
with fragrant soap and then rubbed with Eunice's special olive-oil cold cream until they glowed with ladylike
softness. Appearances were important when one was
being judged, and Genevieve wanted Charlotte to look
every inch the gentle young lady who had no place in
either a prison or a reformatory school.

"If it please the court, Your Honor, the defense
would like to call Mrs. Maxwell Blake," said Mr.
Pollock, the defense counsel.

The sheriff wearily leaned over his bench, planted
his bulbous chin in his hand and nodded. While his ele-
vated position gave him an excellent view of everyone
within his courtroom, it had the distinct disadvantage of
putting him on perpetual exhibit, precluding the possibility of closing his eyes for a few moments. He had already presided over five cases that day, and there were
six more to follow after this one. It didn't help that he
had been suffering from a most uncomfortable digestive
upset since luncheon, which was making him feel de-
cidedly impatient with both the solicitors' and their
witnesses' theatrics. All he wanted at that particular moment was a nice, restorative cup of tea, and perhaps a
sweet bannock to help settle his stomach. There was this
case to finish and then one more concerning a drunken
brawl in a tavern, he decided stoically, before he could
order a recess and retire to his chamber for a brief
respite. He sighed and tapped his foot restlessly upon
the floor, determined to make sure that things started to
move along at a faster clip.

Haydon watched as Genevieve inhaled a steadying breath before rising to take her place on the witness stand. She had not permitted anyone but him to

accompany her to the courthouse, and even his presence had elicited considerable argument. Ever since their passionate interlude a few nights earlier, she had done everything she could to avoid him, much to the bemusement of the rest of the household. When she had occasionally found herself in the same room with him, she had quickly found some urgent reason to be elsewhere. While Haydon sympathized with her discomfiture and had no wish to further aggravate it, he had been utterly resolute that they attend Charlotte's trial together. Regardless of the complexity of their relationship when they were in private, to the rest of the world they were Mr. and Mrs. Maxwell Blake, blissfully happy newlyweds. He could well imagine how tongues would flap if they did not attend together something as momentous as their daughter's trial. The image of respectful domesticity they could present as a couple would only support their argument that Charlotte should be restored to them, he told Genevieve firmly, and ultimately she had accepted the wisdom of his argument.

Beyond what the rest of Inveraray thought, Haydon could not bear the thought of leaving poor little Charlotte to face her ordeal without him. He supposed on some level this was a manifestation of the guilt he carried around with him every day of his life. He had made a point of giving her encouraging smiles throughout the proceedings, and while she was clearly too distressed to smile back, he sensed that Charlotte was glad of his presence. When that listless fool of a judge finally deemed her not guilty, Haydon was going to scoop her up into his arms and take both her and Genevieve home, where they bloody well belonged.

"I swear by Almighty God and as I shall answer to God at the Great Day of Judgment that I shall tell the truth, the whole truth and nothing but the truth."

Genevieve's voice was tense but clear as she repeated the oath after the sheriff.

"Mrs. Blake, you are currently the guardian of the accused, are you not?" asked Mr. Fenton, the prosecutor.

"I am."

"Would you kindly explain to the court how you came to have responsibility for her?"

"Unnecessary," interjected the sheriff with an impatient wave of his hand. "I am aware of Mrs. Blake's arrangement with Governor Thomson and this court. I believe that arrangement clearly stipulates that should the children in her care break the law again, her custody is nullified and the children are returned to the charge of the court—is that not so?"

"It is, Your Honor." Mr. Fenton's mouth curved with satisfaction. "Therefore the prosecution moves that the accused be returned to the prison system immediately to serve the remainder of her sentence and any additional sentence Your Honor may elect to impose upon her at this time."

"No!" cried Genevieve.

"If it please Your Honor," interjected Mr. Pollock in a weary drone. The defense counsel was a sleepy-looking man whose aged eyelids had sagged to the point where his eyes were mere slits against the folds of flaccid skin, making it difficult for Genevieve to assess whether or not he was actually awake. "The defense respectfully suggests that the defendant has fared well in Mrs. Blake's home, this unfortunate incident notwithstanding. As the appropriated goods have been restored and Mrs. Blake has agreed to make full restitution to Mr. Ingram for any and all damages he may have suffered to his shop, I respectfully submit that there is no merit to sending the accused back to prison—not when she has a decent home to go to. Mrs. Blake has pledged that she will take pains to ensure that the accused understands the grave error of her ways, and that nothing such as this unfortunate incident will ever happen again."

"Mrs. Blake is in no position to make such a sweeping assurance," countered Mr. Fenton warningly. "At present she has six children to care for, all of whom have been implicated in this heinous assault, and have stood before this court previously for committing serious crimes—"

"That's not true," protested Genevieve. "My brother Jamie has never been charged with a crime."

"I beg your pardon, Your Honor," he apologized, his lobster-colored mustache twitching with irritation. "Apparently Mrs. Blake does have custody of one child who thus far does not have a criminal record. We are still investigating his role in this barbaric attack upon Mr. Ingram and Lord and Lady Struthers, however, along with the actions of Mrs. Blake's other wards." He glanced meaningfully at Genevieve.

Genevieve's heart sank. It was clear he was inferring that he would dearly like to see the rest of the children charged.

"At any rate," he continued in a briskly pleasant tone, "the fact that the defendant has returned to her unlawful ways makes it amply clear that the environment that Mrs. Blake has created in her home has not been advantageous for the accused, and therefore she should be returned to prison so that she may be appropriately punished—for her own sake, and for the sake of the society in which we all live."

"With all due respect, Your Honor, to return the defendant to prison would serve neither this child nor society at large," argued Mr. Pollock. "Her best hope of understanding her error and to subsequently be rehabilitated is to send her home to her mother and father, where she can be taught by the example of a loving and law-abiding family."

"The so-called law-abiding family is comprised entirely of thieves and urchins, Mr. and Mrs. Blake themselves notwithstanding," interjected Mr. Fenton scornfully. "The children are attended to by two women and a man who have all been imprisoned for stealing. It is scarcely a model of lawfulness and propriety, and clearly not a fitting environment for the accused, who has demonstrated her inability to control her innate criminal tendencies."

"She doesn't have innate criminal tendencies," objected Genevieve fiercely, trying to seize the opportunity to say something on Charlotte's behalf. "She's just a child who made a mistake—"

"Mrs. Blake, I fear I must remind you that you are only permitted to answer questions that are directly asked of you by either counsel or myself," interrupted the sheriff.

"Then someone should ask me something!" she flared hotly.

The sheriff blinked, clearly astonished by her belligerent tone. "Mr. Pollock, do you have any questions for your witness?"

The defense counsel consulted his notes for a moment. "Mrs. Blake, would you kindly tell the court why you believe that Charlotte should be returned to your custody?"

"When Charlotte came to live with me a year ago, she barely spoke to anyone," Genevieve began. "Her life with her father had been a misery. He was a drunken brute who beat her and forced her to assist him with his stealing, which was how she came to stand before the court in the first place—"

"And how did she change while living with you?" prodded Mr. Pollock, sensing that the sheriff's attention was growing severely strained. Tales of children being neglected and abused by their parents or guardians were commonplace, and scarcely grounds for leniency when it came to the law.

"She became a different girl," Genevieve replied. "Once she finally realized that no one in her new home was ever going to raise a hand to her, she slowly permitted herself to be the child she was. She began to talk a little, and then smile, and then she even started to laugh. Now she participates in her studies extremely well, and has learned how to read and write with amazing speed. She performs her household chores with cheer and grace, and she attends church with the entire family every Sunday. She is a serious, studious child who shows an enormous capacity for love and devotion. I know she has made a grave error in judgment, Your Honor," she said, looking at the sheriff, "but I implore you to demonstrate compassion and return her to me. I can promise you that nothing like this will ever happen again."

"Thank you, Mrs. Blake." Mr. Pollock nodded with satisfaction. "I have no further questions, Your Honor."

The sheriff stifled a yawn. "Does the prosecuting counsel have any questions for this witness?"

"Actually, yes." He sauntered over to Genevieve and scratched his scalp beneath the edge of his wig. "Mrs. Blake, I must confess that I am somewhat confused. If the home that you have provided for the accused is such a paradigm of virtue and stability, in which everything she could possibly need has been duly provided, why then was she caught in the act of stealing from Mr. Ingram's shop?"

Genevieve hesitated. She sensed she was being led into a trap, and she wanted to answer in a way that would not assist the prosecutor's case.

"Was there something she desperately needed that you refused to provide for her?" he prodded.

"No, of course not—"

"Then what caused her to behave in such a supposedly uncharacteristic manner?"

Haydon watched with concern as Genevieve struggled to formulate a response. If she confessed that she was in dire financial trouble and that her children had been trying to help, it would open the door for the court to examine her ability to maintain and support all of the children in her custody. But if she said she didn't know why Charlotte had participated in the raid upon Mr. Ingram, it would suggest that there was something inherently wicked about Charlotte, especially in light of the evidence that Charlotte had been well cared for and permitted to want for nothing.

"Charlotte believed she was helping me," Genevieve began hesitantly.

"By stealing?"

"She didn't actually steal anything—"

"Come now, Mrs. Blake, let us not dally with words. The accused was part of a gang of thieves who worked together to steal several precious pieces of jewelry from Mr. Ingram, and in the process did hundreds of pounds worth of damage to the contents of his shop. The fact that she did not actually have the stolen goods on her person at the time of her arrest is scarcely relevant. Are you saying she was trying to help you by stealing this jewelry?"

Genevieve paused. "I believe so," she finally allowed.

"I see. Forgive me, Mrs. Blake, if this question seems impertinent, but it seems to me the court must know if you are suffering some sort of financial crisis. Are you?"

"I have every ability to support my household, Mr. Fenton," she assured him evenly.

"Then you must agree that the accused had no compelling reason to rob Mr. Ingram's shop, and therefore must have been driven by her own immoral tendencies, which you, despite your very best efforts, have not been able to curtail," summarized the prosecutor.

"That's not true!"

"I have no further questions, Your Honor."

"But what he said was a lie——"

"Mrs. Blake, your testimony is finished," said the sheriff. "You may return to your seat."

Genevieve forced herself to regain control of her emotions. She did not want Charlotte to think that all was lost, and surely she would if she saw Genevieve ranting or weeping before the court. She gave Charlotte an encouraging smile before slowly making her way back to her place beside Haydon.

The sheriff studied the papers laid out before him for barely an instant before rendering his verdict. "As there seems to be no dispute regarding the accused's participation in the aforementioned robbery, I have no option other than to find her guilty of the charges against her. What remains to be decided is her sentence. It seems clear that despite Mrs. Blake's best efforts to keep her upon a path of good and lawful conduct, the accused has been unable to overcome her inherent tendencies toward thievery and her lack of respect for the law. Therefore, for her own betterment and to give her the opportunity to correct her apparent lack of moral fortitude, I hereby sentence Charlotte McCallum to sixty days imprisonment, to be followed by four years in a reformatory school in Glasgow."

"No!" cried Genevieve, stunned. "Please, you must listen to me——"

"The accused will step down so that we may begin the next case," said the sheriff, pushing the papers concerning the case aside. He was most anxious to get on with things so he could have his tea.

Charlotte stared at Genevieve, her enormous hazel eyes sparkling with fear. "Genevieve?"

"It's all right, Charlotte," Genevieve called, desperately trying to be reassuring in the midst of her own terror. "Everything is going to be fine."

Charlotte gave her a single, silent nod, filled with love and sorrow and a haunting courage.

And then she turned and permitted herself to be led away, leaving Genevieve clutching Haydon's arm for support as she stared in agony after her.

Chapter Nine

GOVERNOR THOMSON LOOKED UP FROM HIS PLATE of kippered herring in astonishment as Haydon marched into his dining room.

"Forgive me for interrupting your breakfast, madam," Haydon apologized, graciously bowing toward Governor Thomson's flaccid-faced wife, "but your husband and I have a serious matter to attend to that simply will not wait. I do hope you will accept my sincerest apologies for stealing him away from your lovely presence at such an unearthly hour."

Janet Thomson was a stout little melon-shaped woman whose face was screwed into a perpetual expression of pained disapproval. As prison matron, she continuously found ample reason to feel vastly superior to most of the world around her, and it was only by virtue of her deep religious convictions that she felt there was any hope for humanity at all. She was a pragmatic woman who had accepted at an early age the severe limitations of her lack of physical beauty, and saw her union with her husband and her life at the prison as little more than a trial by God, for which she expected to be duly rewarded by receiving a particularly exalted place in the hereafter.

Her moral resolve did not mean, however, that she was above being titillated by a morsel of feminine flattery, particularly when it was offered by such an uncommonly handsome man.

"Mr. Blake," she cooed, as Haydon pressed his lips to the solid bulk of her hand, "it is a pleasure to finally make your acquaintance."

"The pleasure is all mine, madam," Haydon assured her.

"I am so sorry to hear about your wife's ward," she continued, looking appropriately aggrieved. "I have spent some time talking to Charlotte since her return to our prison, and I have found her to be a generally sensible girl, despite the obvious low moral character of her father. After nearly a lifetime spent working with those who have fallen from the path of righteousness, I have learned that the wicked turbulence of the blood cannot be bridled by mere charity. *'The righteous shall be preserved forever, but the children of the wicked shall be cut off.'* Your wife is, of course, certainly to be commended for her efforts."

"Thank you." Haydon barely restrained the urge to tell her to keep her damn theories on wickedness to herself. "My wife and I are firm believers in the essential goodness of children, and so far, we have not been disappointed. It is to your husband's credit that he has shown both wisdom and compassion in the past by bringing these lost children to my wife's attention— especially when he seeks no reward other than the salvation of the child. It must be spiritually uplifting to share one's life and work with such a selfless and dedicated man." His voice was edged with contempt, which completely eluded Mrs. Thomson's notice.

"Oh, it is indeed," Mrs. Thomson agreed, thoroughly

pleased that a well-bred man of such obvious moral character was praising her husband. "My husband and I may be far from rich, Mr. Blake, but God has charged us with the difficult task of trying to help these poor sinners find the road to piety. *'Trust in the Lord and do good; so you will dwell in the land, and enjoy security. Take delight in the Lord, and he will give you the desires of your heart.'* Our wealth is in the work we do and the respect we have earned over so many years within our community."

"A most admirable philosophy," commended Haydon. "One can only hope that nothing ever happens to erode that community respect. It would be nothing short of tragic if you were to find a lifetime of work destroyed."

Mrs. Thomson permitted herself a confused half smile. "Whatever do you mean, sir?"

"I am certain Mr. Blake is merely making conjecture for the sake of discussion," interjected Governor Thomson hastily. "Aren't you, Mr. Blake?"

"I must say, you have some very handsome pieces in here, Governor Thomson," Haydon remarked, ignoring his question. He paused to examine a magnificent gold clock positioned on the mantel. "What a glorious antique—it's Swiss, isn't it? Looks to me like it's from the early eighteenth century. A truly exceptional work. Is it a family heirloom?"

"Oh gracious, no," answered Mrs. Thomson. "I'm proud to say that both my husband and I come from very modest beginnings, sir. That clock was purchased by my husband just last year, during a trip we made to Edinburgh."

Haydon arched his brow. "How very interesting."

Governor Thomson pushed his plate of cold kippers away. "Would you excuse us for a moment, my dear? It seems Mr. Blake and I have some business to discuss."

"I promise not to detain your husband overly long."

Haydon gallantly assisted Mrs. Thomson as she rose from her chair. "As a newly married man, I understand how time weighs heavily when one is separated from one's lovely wife."

Color flooded Mrs. Thomson's cheeks. "Of course, Mr. Blake," she said, her hand flitting at her throat as she regarded him with girlish infatuation. "I do hope we shall have the pleasure of a visit from you again. Good day to you, sir."

"Get your hat and coat," Haydon ordered curtly the instant she was gone. "You are coming with me to see Sheriff Trotter."

Governor Thomson scratched his gray beard in nervous confusion. "Why?"

"You are going to support the appeal that I am about to make to him to reverse his decision yesterday to send my eleven-year-old daughter to prison and reformatory school. You are going to tell him that in all your years of work as a prison governor, you have never known a more exemplary prisoner. You are going to tell him that you take particular interest in Charlotte's case because she is such a sweet and virtuous child, and that having known her personally from when she was first imprisoned over a year ago, you are astounded by the positive changes in her since she has been in my wife's tender care. You are going to tell him that Charlotte is the very model of morality and obedience, and that given these attributes, combined with the unfortunate state of her health, you cannot in good conscience condone her spending any more time in your prison. You will confess that your prison is torturously cold and damp and foul, and that Charlotte is at risk of falling victim to any one of a series of deadly conditions should she remain under its roof even one more night. You shall make it sound as if she could expire at any moment, Governor Thomson, and you will tell Sheriff

Trotter that if she dies, it is he and not yourself whom the public will hold accountable."

Governor Thomson stared at him with bulging eyes, completely flabbergasted. "I can't do that!" he sputtered.

"You can and you will," Haydon assured him in a tight, savage voice. "And if by the end of our discussion with the sheriff you have not managed to convince him to alter his sentence and return Charlotte to the custody of my wife and myself, I will go straight to the newspaper and alert them that there needs to be a thorough investigation of the prison at once. I will tell them of the abuses that go on in this place—from the beatings and torments doled out by Warder Sims to the foul water, insufficient food that a dog wouldn't eat, vermin-ridden uniforms and bedclothes, freezing dark cells with chamber pots overflowing with filth—"

"That isn't true!"

"Actually, I have a firsthand account. Jack spent time in your festering sewer just a couple of weeks ago, and he has enlightened my wife and myself on many of its less ingratiating points."

"My prison is a model of modernity," Governor Thomson retaliated defensively. "I'll have you know it is run in accordance with the recommendations of the Inspector of Prisons for Scotland!"

"Then you won't mind an inspection being conducted by the newspaper this very afternoon, including a thorough analysis of your financial register." Haydon picked up a handsomely wrought sterling silver carving knife and turned it over in his hands. "I suspect the people of Inveraray would be very interested to know just exactly how much you earn, Governor. It might give them cause to wonder how you are able to afford such lavish furnishings. I know my wife has some fascinating insight on that subject, which, if Charlotte is not safely restored to us by the end of the day, I shall feel obliged to share with Sheriff Trotter and the Prison Board."

Governor Thomson's face blanched. "If you will just permit me to fetch my coat, I shall be pleased to express my opinion to Sheriff Trotter on the matter of your daughter, Mr. Blake. The prison system can barely afford to support the inmates already within its confines, and is certainly not a fitting place for a gentle young lady of delicate health." He deposited his linen napkin beside his plate of cold kippers and stood.

Haydon nodded with satisfaction.

GENEVIEVE PUT DOWN HER PEN AND PRESSED THE heels of her hands hard against the hot, aching sockets of her eyes.

There was nothing to be gained by crying, she reminded herself fiercely, and everything to be lost if she allowed herself the luxury of wasting time by sitting around weeping. And so she dabbed her eyes for the hundredth time with her sodden handkerchief and dipped her quill in the inkwell, determined to finish this last letter to Queen Victoria, in which she pleaded, as both a woman and a mother, for clemency on behalf of Charlotte. She had already made an impassioned plea in letters to Sheriff Trotter and to Viscount Palmerston, the prime minister. She realized the chances were remote that Her Majesty might actually read her letter, but she intended to write her every day nonetheless. At some point one of her ministers or secretaries would be compelled to bring the matter to her attention. Surely any woman with children would be horrified to learn of the cruelty of sending a mere child to prison for the relatively paltry crime of theft? Or would the queen think that lower-class children who ran afoul of the law were the basis of all that was wrong with the world, and that they were best locked up in dark prisons and forgotten, so the rest of society could go on safely about its business?

The treacherous tears began to leak from her eyes, unstoppable as rain, until the desperately scrawled letter began to dissolve beneath wet blotches of salty ink.

Someone knocked upon her door.

"Please go away," Genevieve managed, fighting not to sound as if she were on the brink of hysteria. Her children depended on her to be strong and sure and in control of herself. She could not let anyone see her in her current condition.

"I need to speak with you, Genevieve." Haydon's voice was low and insistent. "It is a matter of great importance."

Genevieve swallowed and blotted at her eyes with her crumpled handkerchief. She did not want to see Haydon. She did not want to see anyone. Why couldn't they understand that? All day long Eunice, Doreen, and Oliver had been pounding relentlessly at her door, bringing her trays and begging her to go downstairs and eat something. She did not want to eat. How could she ingest even a sip of clean water knowing that Charlotte was sitting in a cell being offered putrid milk and sour porridge? And despite all their kind intentions, she did not want to talk to anyone. Her heart was shattered, and nothing anyone could say or do was going to ease the terrible pain ripping through her.

"Please go away," she repeated.

"I'm afraid I cannot do that, Genevieve. Open the door."

"I am not feeling well," she insisted. "Just leave me alone."

There was a moment of silence.

The door began to open.

Genevieve turned from her desk, poised to lash at him in anger and despair, to scream at him for being so callous and cruel when all she asked for was to be left to suffer her agony in solitude.

And then she saw Charlotte standing in the door-way, her precious face lit with a hesitant smile, as if she was not entirely sure that Genevieve would be happy to see her.

A cry pierced the air, the sound of utter joy mingled with pain. Genevieve tore across the room, grabbed Charlotte, and wrapped her arms around her before kiss-ing her cheeks, her forehead, her hair, touching her all over to make sure she was well and whole. Jamie, Anna-belle, Grace, and Simon giggled and yelled out as they burst from their hiding place in the hallway.

"Surprise, Genevieve!"

"Aren't you glad Haydon opened the door?"

"See, you told us Charlotte would be coming home again, and now she has!"

"Don't you want to let her take her hat and coat off?"

"Why are you still crying, Genevieve?"

Genevieve buried her face in Charlotte's hair and began to sob, the long, heaving sound of emotions that have suddenly burst free from their fetters and then can-not be restrained. The children watched her in strick-en silence, unable to comprehend her apparent misery when there was so much to celebrate. Only Charlotte seemed to understand, for she began to weep as well, and the sound of both of them crying vanquished the merriment that had filled the other children with such tittering anticipation as the entire household traipsed se-cretly up the stairs.

"Come, duckies," said Eunice, wiping her nose with the hem of her apron as she fought back her own tears. "Let's leave Miss Genevieve and Charlotte to have some time on their own."

Doreen sniffled loudly. "There's some nice warm bannocks in the kitchen."

"I'm thinkin' a wee walk might be just the thing," suggested Oliver, his voice choked.

"No." Genevieve shook her head as she held fast to Charlotte. "I want my children with me." She opened her arms, beckoning them to come and be enfolded in her protective embrace.

The children surged toward her in a crushing wave, engulfing both her and Charlotte in a ring of love. Genevieve hugged and kissed all of them, feeling desperately protective, promising herself that she would never let any of them so much as leave her sight ever again.

It was only as Oliver closed the door that she suddenly realized that Jack was not amongst them and that Haydon had silently slipped away, leaving her noisy, clamoring family strangely incomplete.

NIGHT HAD SPREAD ITS VELVET WINGS OVER THE house, leaving Genevieve to make her way up the narrow wooden stairs by the pale waver of her candle flame. The children were all sleeping safely in their beds, and judging by the steady rumble of phlegmy snoring that greeted her on the third floor, so were Oliver, Eunice, and Doreen. She stood outside the door of Haydon's room and listened, her flesh chilled by the cold night air. She did not hear anything. She did not know whether she was glad of that or not. If he had been snoring loudly, she would have swiftly descended the stairs and retreated to her room, telling herself that she would speak with him another time. But the silence

beyond his door was deafening. Somehow she knew
that he did not sleep, but was awake, listening to her
standing lost and alone in the corridor. She hesitated a
long moment. Finally, she poised her knuckles to tap
upon the wood.

Before her skin brushed against the panel, the door
opened and Haydon stood before her, naked except for
the plaid from his bed, which he had carelessly draped
around his waist. His muscular arms, chest, and torso
were sculpted in the wintry shadows of the night and
the flickering glow of her candle. He regarded her intently, his expression guarded but composed, as if he
had been expecting her.

Her courage began to fail as she stared at him. She
wanted to leave, she was certain of it. Instead she adjusted the soft woolen shawl she had wrapped around
herself and slipped past him into the room, filling the
inky space with a wash of golden light. She set the candle upon the small table that stood by the narrow, rumpled bed.

There was a plain wardrobe in one corner of the
room, with a door that wouldn't close properly. Doreen
had asked Oliver numerous times, if he could fix it and
while he always assured her that he could, he never
seemed to find the occasion to do so. Within the wardrobe hung several neatly arranged jackets, shirts, and
folded pairs of trousers. Obviously Eunice and Doreen
had been trying their best to outfit Haydon in the midst
of keeping up with all their other household responsibilities.

There was a low washstand in another corner,
which needed a fresh coat of paint. On it sat a chipped
jug and basin that was decorated in a clumsy pink rose
pattern. It had all seemed clean and cheerful enough
when the room was prepared for Doreen, but for a man
of Haydon's enormous physical stature and wealth, it

was hopelessly cramped and shabby and spartan. The Marquess of Redmond was undoubtedly accustomed to spacious, luxurious surroundings, and here he was sleeping in a servant's room without so much as the benefit of a chair. A shiver rippled through her and she realized the room was also gruelingly cold, as it lacked even a tiny hearth to generate some heat.

"Here," said Haydon, jerking the remaining plaid off the bed. "You're shaking."

She held her breath as his hands grazed her shoulders, steeling herself against the potent eroticism of his touch. The wool was suffused with the masculine scent and warmth of his body, and she realized he had been lying naked beneath it before she came. It seemed shockingly intimate to have his warmth wrapped all around her, but the sensation was so comforting she made no move to take it off. Instead she retreated to the far corner of the small room, no great distance in terms of space, but enough that she felt marginally safer.

From herself or Haydon, she wasn't certain.

Haydon could not imagine what had prompted Genevieve to seek him out in the middle of the night, dressed in nothing but a thin nightdress and shawl, but it was clear that something was troubling her. He realized that she had suffered horrendously over the last few days, and even though Charlotte had been safely restored to her that afternoon, her emotions were still ragged. For this reason he vowed he would keep his distance from her. Even as he made this oath, every fiber of his body was awakening to the memory of her lying lush and hot beneath him, writhing and pulsing against his touch. All he wanted to do was strip that flimsy nightrail off her and crush her to him, to lay her on the floor and bury himself inside her and lose himself to her silken heat and strength and staggering beauty. He was disgusted with himself for having such base desires, and yet he could not stop them, could not keep his body from growing hard and beginning to ache with need.

"No one has ever fought for me before," Genevieve murmured, her voice soft and yet raw, as if it pained her to speak.

Haydon said nothing.

She swallowed thickly, trying to find the words. "For over eight years, I have had to fight alone for my family. I have fought to feed them, clothe them, educate them, and give them a sense that they are loved and worthy." Her voice cracked slightly as she added, "And there have been some dreadful pitfalls along the way."

Haydon could well imagine that there had been. Aside from the constant threat of deadly childhood illnesses, there had been the unending battle to find funds to maintain the household, and the painful contempt and censure of the entire community around her.

"I think most of the people around here have always wanted to see me fail," she continued, her words tinged with bitterness. "Of course, they would never admit to having such uncharitable thoughts, but secretly, they believe my failure is inevitable. They delight in their conviction that my children are lowborn, and that their sinful natures cannot be overcome. And that is why everyone was so ready to send Charlotte back to prison. Everyone felt it was no more than what she deserved. Most of the citizens of Inveraray undoubtedly believed it would ultimately do her good, to lock her up with others who are just as irrevocably flawed and base as she is. But you didn't believe that."

She regarded him as if she were looking at him for the first time and didn't understand what she saw. "You could have been killed, Haydon. All it would have taken was for Governor Thomson, or Warder Sims, or some lowly clerk at the courthouse to recognize you, and you would have been dragged into jail and hanged by night-fall."

Her gaze bore into him, trying to delve beneath the layers to find out who he really was. Haydon regarded her with steady calm. She sensed his powerful attraction to her, felt it as keenly as if his hands were upon her and his mouth was raking hard over hers. She drew the blanket around her tighter, only to feel his heat and scent engulf her senses further. Her voice was barely a whisper as she finished, "Why?"

It seemed a simple enough question, and yet there was no easy answer. Haydon wasn't sure he understood his actions himself. All he knew was that he couldn't bear the thought of Charlotte being imprisoned so much as one more day. If the governor and the sheriff had not released her, then Haydon would have gone into the jail and stolen her out of there himself, and damn the bloody consequences. He felt a special affinity toward Charlotte and had wanted to protect her, but he knew that wasn't the sole reason why he had acted as he did. The memory of Emmaline, and how utterly he had failed his fragile daughter, had played a significant role. But he could never admit that to Genevieve. She seemed so pure and good and selfless to him, he could scarcely imagine the contempt she would have for him were she to learn of his selfish, cowardly history.

She stood there, studying him, waiting. He felt as if she were stripping away the layers of him, trying to pull him apart and look inside and understand who he really was. It was understandable that she would be curious, or might even feel that she had a right to know. After all, she had risked both herself and her beloved family to protect him and keep him safe. But he had no desire to have his deepest secrets and failures ferreted out and exposed to the light. She had found him lying in the filth on a prison floor, convicted of murder, and had been told nothing but ghastly stories about his brutality and lack of worth. He wanted her to think him nobler than that—not perfect or free of sin, but at least capable of acting out of a clean, unadorned desire to help others. Beyond that, there was only one reason to explain why he had acted as he did, and it seemed so incredibly simple yet complex that he scarcely dared admit it to himself. And yet in that shadowed, silent moment he could suddenly no longer contain it, could not bury it beneath the crushing depths of his past and his present and whatever little remained of his future.

"I did it for you, Genevieve."

Her eyes widened. And then she waited for him to qualify it, to say that he had done so because he felt a sense of debt toward her, that he owed her something for all the risks she had taken and the trouble she had gone to on his behalf, and now their account was settled and they could part on equal terms.

He said nothing.

It was this that cracked the wall of resistance she had so carefully constructed against him. A man like Charles would have blathered on incessantly about the whys and wherefores, and what all of this must now mean between them. He would have expected payment of some kind, although not with anything so crass and simple as money. No, Charles would have expected a debt of gratitude, in which he would forever own some part of her, and whatever she gave of herself would never be sufficient to render the debt paid. But Haydon merely stood there, strong yet strangely vulnerable. It was as if he had opened some long-hidden part of his soul to her, and was now waiting to see whether she would trample upon it or treat it with care.

A desperate longing surged through her, the need to be held by him, to be kissed and stroked and crushed by

the glorious power and heat of him. She was suddenly
aware of the thinness of her nightdress and the cool
air upon her bare legs, the worn, frigid floor beneath
her slippered feet, and the promise of warmth from
his flesh. She had lived for over eight years amidst a
constant blur of people who needed her, children and
adults who relied upon her to provide for them, to
show them how to be strong and fight back against a
world that seemed determined to reduce them to rubble. But until that moment, as she stood staring into
Haydon's heart, she had not understood how terribly
alone and afraid she had been. And suddenly she could
not bear it a moment longer.

With a little sob she ran to him, wrapped her arms
fiercely about his neck and crushed her lips to his, losing herself to his powerful longing as she drew him
closer to her heart.

Haydon moaned and hauled her slender body
against him. The plaid he had wrapped around his waist
slid down his legs and puddled upon the floor, leaving
him naked. He pressed himself against her, madden-
ingly aroused by the soft caress of the woolen blanket
that was slipping down Genevieve's body. Her thin
shawl followed, until finally she was garbed in nothing
but the transparent linen sheath of her nightgown,
which was worn and plain and thoroughly arousing. He
began to fumble with the closures at her neck, kissing
her deeply as he did so, but his ardor made his fingers
clumsy and the tiny buttons refused to yield. With a
growl of frustration he tore the fabric apart, exposing
her silky cool skin. The night rail trickled down her
body with a whisper, leaving both of them naked in the
flickering peach light.

"Genevieve," he murmured, his voice rough with
awe.

He lifted her up into his arms, enjoying the softness

of her cradled against his own muscled body, then kissed her ravenously as he laid her upon the narrow bed. Her hair spilled in glorious red-gold waves across the pillow, and her flesh was luminous against the sun-bleached sheets. He stretched out over her and covered her with himself, plunging his hands into her hair as he stroked and tasted the deepest recesses of her mouth. She was all softness and curves and coolness and heat, and he could not seem to get enough of her.

His hands roamed across her milky flesh, touching and swirling and caressing, learning every inch of her as his tongue swept along the ivory column of her throat, down the fine structure of her collarbone, over the lush hill of her breast. He drew a claret-colored peak into his mouth and suckled long and hard, causing her to moan with pleasure, then went to the other breast and suckled it as well, until both nipples had tightened into swollen buds.

From there he journeyed down, brushing his lips across the flat of her belly, caressing the velvet cream of her thighs, then pressing his face into the dark triangle between. Genevieve gasped and tried to push him away, but he gripped the slender bones of her wrists and held her firmly. Imprisoning her against the mattress, he dipped his head low and flicked his tongue deep inside her hot, slick opening. She gasped again, but this time it was with pure, undiluted pleasure.

He began to lap at her, tasting her with slow, languid strokes, swirling his tongue in and out, and over the sweet pink petals of her. He found the pearly nub in which her pleasure was centered and he sucked gently upon it, causing her to arch suddenly against him, raising herself up so that he might taste her better.

Genevieve jerked her wrists free of Haydon's grasp and threaded her fingers deep into the ebony mane of his hair, pulling him closer as she opened her legs and wantonly offered herself to him. She felt as if she were melting, and yet she had never felt so incredibly tense. She wanted him to touch her and kiss her and lick her everywhere, to devour her whole, until there was nothing left of her that did not belong to him. The pleasure roiling within her was unbearable, but it wasn't enough, for the more Haydon's tongue and lips swirled and stroked the intimate depths of her, the more she wanted him to taste her faster, harder, more deeply. A terrible ache was blooming far inside her, a tight hollowness that could not be filled by the magnificent caresses he was raining upon her hot, wet womanhood. And then he slowly pressed a finger deep inside her and began to move it in and out in leisurely, deliberate thrusts, dancing in rhythm with the agonizing caresses of his mouth. It was more than she could bear, she was certain of it, and yet it wasn't enough, and so she closed her thighs around the roughness of his jaw and held him fast, taking pleasure in the sandy feel of his cheeks against her silky skin, the scalding slickness of his mouth on her hot, coral cleft, the gloriously deep penetration of his finger as it slipped in and out, exploring and worshiping her until there was nothing but Haydon and the magnificent wet fire that was raging within her.

Suddenly she was gasping for air, tiny, desperate sips of breath that could not fill her bursting lungs, for everything was strained and tight and reaching for more, and Haydon's tongue licked in rapid little strokes at her liquefying flesh while his finger drove deep inside her. And then she was bursting into a shower of stars, which rippled over her in hard, breathless waves. She cried out, a desperate cry of joy and wonder, and as the ripples eased, she clawed at Haydon's shoulders, pulling him up until his powerful body was covering her with naked, hard heat.

Haydon fought for control as he felt his manhood

pressing against Genevieve's exquisite wetness. He wanted to plunge deep inside her and take her fast, to slake the unbearable lust that was surely going to kill him if he did not sate it immediately. She was a virgin, he reminded himself fiercely, and she required gentle care. And so he claimed her mouth with rough hunger, as his hands roamed the silky hills and valleys of her body, rousing her again until her nails were biting into his rigid shoulders and her legs had twined with his. Unable to bear the torment a moment longer, he entered her, just a little, feeling as if he had died as the scalding slickness of her closed over him.

Genevieve's eyes fluttered open and she regarded him with smoky desire. Then she wrapped her arms tightly around him and opened her legs wider, raising her hips, drawing him farther within. Despite his determination to go slowly, Haydon felt the last thread of his control snap. With a groan he drove himself deep inside, sheathing himself in her hot tightness.

Genevieve gasped.

"I'm sorry, Genevieve," Haydon managed, cursing himself. What the hell was the matter with him? he wondered furiously. He had no more control than a schoolboy. He held himself perfectly still, resolving not to move until she had grown accustomed to the feel of him within her. "I think, if we wait a bit, the pain will pass."

Genevieve blinked and nodded.

"I also think you should breathe," Haydon added after a moment.

Slowly, she exhaled the breath she had been holding. "Better?"

Actually, it was much better, Genevieve realized, especially when she allowed her body to relax. Longing to be back to where there were no words, she threaded her fingers into his hair and pulled him down so she could kiss him.

Haydon moaned as his tongue tangled with hers. He began to flex slowly within her, swearing to himself that he would be gentle, that he would give her time to be roused once more. But she seemed to be roused already, for she was kissing him deeply as her hands swept across the rigid curves of his shoulders and back and buttocks, pulling him into her as she thrust her body against his, opening herself to him and closing herself around him until there was nothing but wetness and heat and the silver sheen that was shimmering on their skin. Again and again he drove into her, overwhelmed by the silky river of her red-blonde hair, the summery hot scent of her skin mingling with the fragrance of her passion, the soft, lean beauty of her elegantly sculpted breasts and hips and legs.

She was everything he had ever wanted, he realized with piercing clarity. And the realization was agony, because he knew she was not his and never would be. He had killed a man and lost his identity, and he could not stay without endangering her and the children to whom she had devoted herself.

Yet if he ever succeeded in reclaiming his life as the Marquess of Redmond he was certain she would not want him, for that selfish, careless bastard was not worthy of a woman like her. The realization wounded and enraged him, for if he had but known that she existed he might have lived his life differently, might have refrained from drinking and gambling and heedlessly spreading his seed, creating children to whom he had no right and who he could not protect.

He wanted to join Genevieve to him, wanted to drive himself inside her and kiss her and hold her and cover her until neither knew where one ended and the

other began, wanted to meld their flesh and their breath
and their blood so that nothing could ever come between them. But there was just this moment that would
quickly be over, and the realization filled him with despair.

He tried to slow himself, tried to make this brief,
stolen interlude between them last longer, but she was
writhing and stretching beneath him, opening herself to
every aching thrust with hot little pants of breath and
her nails clawing desperately at his back, meeting his
penetrations with gasps of pleasure as she gripped him
in her tightness, until finally he couldn't bear it a moment longer. He shoved himself deep inside her, burying himself within the magnificently taut clench of her
beautiful body. And then he groaned and poured his
essence into her, feeling as if he were dying, and not
giving a damn, as long as he could stay joined to her,
with her heart pounding rapidly against his chest and
the whisper of her breath gusting soft and sweet against
his skin.

They lay joined together a long moment, each
afraid to move for fear of severing the fragile bonds between them. But as his flesh cooled, his reason returned.
What had he been thinking? Haydon wondered, his
mind suddenly reeling with self-loathing. It was not
enough that he had selfishly created one unwanted
child—because of his lack of control, he may well have
started another. He had not lived the life of a monk since
his torrid affair with Cassandra, but after Emmaline's
death he had vowed never to create a life so casually
again. Yet instead of withdrawing before his own climax,
as had been his rule these past two years, he had buried
himself within her.

How could he have been so careless?

He rolled off her and rose from the bed. He picked
up his fallen plaid and wrapped it around his waist, then

went to the window and stared grimly out at the infinite blackness of the night, cursing his own stupidity.

"Jesus, Genevieve," he said, his voice low and harsh, "I'm sorry."

Shame washed over her. Genevieve grasped the edge of the blanket and wrapped it around herself, shielding her body from Haydon's perusal as she gathered up her nightgown and shawl. She turned away and dressed beneath the tent of her blanket. Tonight she had shown herself for what she really was, she realized, trembling with humiliation—a wanton slut who would writhe on a bed beneath a man's touch. She had kissed Haydon and held him and opened herself to him, drawing him into her body with no thought to the consequences. He was not her husband, she reminded herself miserably, and he never would be. He was a fugitive from the law, a convicted murderer, and he could not stay there a moment longer than was necessary. Even if he did eventually reclaim his life as the Marquess of Redmond, he would never return to marry a woman like her. No man of decent station or normal sanity would marry an impoverished spinster with five young thieves and one maid's bastard for children.

She wanted to say something, but no words could articulate her emotions. He had apologized, but it seemed grossly hypocritical to accept that apology when it was she, in fact, who had sought him out, venturing to his room in the middle of the night in nothing but a nightrail and shawl. She had wanted to talk to him, to understand what had compelled him to take such enormous risks on Charlotte's behalf. She had also hoped to strip away some of the veils that shrouded the man whom the rest of the world believed to be her husband. But these were not the only reasons she had gone to his room, she realized, nearly sick with shame. The passion that had flared between them several nights earlier in the drawing room had awakened powerful feelings in her that she hadn't known she possessed. Despite her efforts to lock them into a dark corner of her mind, she had longed to experience those feelings again. On some level that was incomprehensible to her, she had wanted Haydon to touch her, had been desperate to know what it was to have him kiss and caress and worship her body, and to fill her to the core with his heat and strength and passion.

She flew across the room and jerked open the door, desperate to be away from him. The corridor was cold and black as she stepped into it, leaving all the heat and light that had flamed with such joyful brilliance but a moment earlier fading in the chamber behind her.

. . . A FTER THAT HE LEFT THE JAIL WITH THE GIRL AND returned to Mrs. Blake's house at approximately four o'clock."

Mr. Timmons scratched a rather alarming pimple on his nose as he closed his notebook, indicating his report was finished. "I remained on the street until eleven o'clock this evening—just before I came here. Mr. Blake did not leave, nor did any of the other inhabitants of the household."

Vincent Ramsay, the earl of Bothwell, drummed his manicured fingers thoughtfully upon the scratched surface of the small table in his room. Then he rose, withdrew an envelope from an inner pocket in his coat, and slid it across the table. "Thank you, Mr. Timmons. I shall be in touch if I find I have further need of your services."

Mr. Timmons's mouth gaped open as he glanced at the thick pad of notes bulging within the envelope. "Thank you, Mr. Wright, sir," he gushed, overwhelmed by the generosity of his mysterious employer. "I'm happy to be of service to you. If there is anything else I can do—perhaps I should watch Mr. Blake again to-morrow. . . ."

Vincent opened the door to his hotel room, anxious to have the wheedling little man gone from his sight. He despised men who made their living by prying into the lives of others, and disliked Mr. Timmons in particular because his very presence was an intrusion into Vincent's own life. He had paid him well to ensure his discretion, but the earl was not foolish enough to believe that his confidentiality was absolutely assured.

"That will be all for the moment." Best to let the little toad think there might be more work coming his way. That way he would be more inclined to keep his tongue still. "Good night." He shut the door abruptly, leaving Mr. Timmons standing in the hallway with the envelope clutched in his hand.

Vincent poured himself a glass of insipid sherry, took a sip and cringed. He was not accustomed to drinking such cheap vintages, but he had made every effort since his arrival in Inveraray to do nothing to draw undue attention to himself, and that included not indulging in his fondness for discriminating wine. Hence he had registered in this decrepit little hotel as Mr. Albert Wright, a businessman from Glasgow who was on his way north to investigate the production of charcoal in the hills north of Taynuilt. He dressed modestly and kept to himself, giving no one any reason to notice him except when they served him his stringy, grease-laden meals, either in his room or in the dreary restaurant below—with its copiously stained rug and hopelessly tarnished flatware—that he felt obliged to patronize on occasion. He presented himself as a quiet, polite, wholly uninteresting man, who he hoped was

forgotten the moment he was out of sight. He had no
wish to make an impression of any type on anyone during his stay here.

Except, of course, for the missing Marquess of
Redmond.

When he first received word that Haydon had actually managed to fend off the attackers he had hired to
kill him, Vincent had been infuriated. Ultimately he
consoled himself with the view that hanging was just as
fitting an end for the rutting bastard. The fact that
Haydon was paraded before a court like a common
criminal and found guilty of murder seemed ironically
appropriate. There had been the added pleasure of
imagining him languishing for weeks in a fetid, vermin-
infested cell, surrounded by the scum of humanity, undoubtedly beaten and abused, all the while desperately
protesting his innocence to no avail. Vincent had dallied
with the idea of traveling to Inveraray to attend the
hanging, but ultimately decided that the whole miserable business was best left to play out in his absence. He
had wanted Haydon dead, but he had not felt any compelling need to witness it himself. All he had desired was
some small measure of retribution for the unspeakable
humiliation and suffering the marquess had so casually
inflicted upon his own life. It had cost a substantial sum
and had taken some discreet arranging, but ultimately
Vincent had been certain that both the funds involved
and his time were well spent.

What he had not anticipated was that Haydon
would escape his death a second time.

The idea that his deceased wife's lover had managed
to elude the sharp talons of justice and was roaming
about, hunted but free, grated mercilessly upon him.
After waiting impatiently to see if he would be recap-
tured, Vincent ultimately realized he had no choice but
to take the matter into his own hands. He had traveled

to Inveraray and hired Mr. Timmons, an experienced investigator whose discretion, like almost everything else, could be reasonably assured for a price—at least for a time. Mr. Timmons was easily able to secure information on Haydon's trial and his sojourn in the jail. What struck Vincent as most interesting was the fact that a pretty, well-meaning spinster had been the last person to visit the marquess in his cell before he escaped. According to the warder, who had been eager to talk to Mr. Timmons when he realized the investigator was willing to buy him unlimited pints of ale, his lordship had looked little better than a filthy, broken beggar on the night of his escape. Vincent had suspected that may not have mattered to the eminently altruistic Miss MacPhail. The Marquess of Redmond had always had a talent for enchanting and seducing women, regardless of the circumstances. That was what had enabled him to crawl between the legs of his lovely Cassandra.

He took another bitter swallow of sherry.

The humiliation of his wife's affairs still had the power to enrage him. He reminded himself that she had been a selfish, spoiled bitch, and Vincent had been glad to be rid of her when she died some two years earlier, after some ignominious doctor had tried to scrape the progeny of her latest lover from her womb. The shambles of their marriage had ceased to matter after Emmaline was born eight years prior. With her wonderful, miraculous arrival, everything else in his life had suddenly diminished in importance.

When Vincent had learned that Cassandra was finally pregnant after more than six years of marriage, he had unashamedly hoped for a son. A son would inherit his title and his holdings and leave an important mark upon the world. When little Emmaline was handed to him in his study an hour after her birth, her face all pink and shriveled and squalling, he had known a moment of wretched disappointment. He tried to give her right back to the nurse, but the frazzled woman said she had to fetch something immediately for his wife and bolted from the room. And so he was forced to carry Emmaline up the long staircase himself to deliver her back to his wife's bedroom. Somewhere along the way Emmaline stopped crying and settled contentedly in his arms. She opened her blue eyes and regarded him with quiet satisfaction, as if to say that she had only been crying for him, and now that she had found him, all was well. It was in that moment that Vincent discovered what he had believed was the purest form of love.

The knowledge that he had been wrong burned a deep, agonizing hole through him.

He set down his glass and went to the window, pulling back the cold, musty drape so he could look out at the frozen street below. He did not know for certain that the man known as Maxwell Blake was, in fact, the Marquess of Redmond. Tomorrow he would keep vigil near the house, and every day after that, until he caught a glimpse of him and determined his identity.

If he did turn out to be the man who had destroyed his life, then Vincent would make very sure that this time he succeeded in killing him.

Chapter Ten

HERE'S A BONNY ONE OF SOME BOATS ON LOCH Fyne." Oliver placed the painting on the worn sofa in the drawing room so that Haydon could better appreciate it. "That would be good for someone who fancies the water—don't ye think?"

"Possibly," Haydon allowed, critically examining the work. The brush strokes Genevieve had used were quick and soft, giving the boats and the loch a fluid, almost dreamy feeling.

"I like this one better," declared Annabelle as she and Grace plopped a rendering of a vase of flowers onto a chair. The amethyst and pink blossoms were drooping slightly, and a single petal had fallen onto the linen of the table on which the vase stood, marring its otherwise pristine surface. "The flowers look so terribly sad—almost as if they were crying." She sighed with pleasure.

Haydon had to agree. Genevieve made no effort to execute a precisely realistic rendition of what she saw, but instead filtered her work through her own emotions and sensibilities. The result was stirring.

"Here's one that she painted of me and Simon last

summer," said Jamie, dragging his corner of the painting along the floor, while Simon supported the other.

"She said it was of two men getting ready to sail the world," explained Simon proudly.

In the painting the two boys were sailing their little wooden ships upon a stream. They were shown from behind, with their clothes rumpled and their hair ruffled by the same wind that was fluffing the sails of their small boats. The scene was sunny and had an almost tangible lethargy to it, as if the afternoon would never end. But a narrow strip of clouds painted in the distance was ominously leaden, suggesting that the boys' game, and perhaps by extension their childhood, would soon be brought to an end.

"I like this one." Jack deposited a portrait of Charlotte on the sofa beside the painting of the boats. "It really looks like you, Charlotte."

Charlotte regarded the painting with shy uncertainty, secretly pleased that Jack thought her as pretty as the girl on the canvas. "Do you think so?"

Genevieve had painted Charlotte seated in a chair, quietly reading a book. Her gown was drawn tight about her narrow waist before it fell in a generous puff to the floor, giving no hint of where her legs might be beneath it. But upon the floor by the hem of her skirts lay a single, creamy rose, with thorns protruding in sharp green spikes along its stem. If Charlotte bent to retrieve the rose, it seemed certain that she would prick herself upon its thorns. But if she left it where it lay, the rose would wither and die. It was a simple enough quandary to the casual observer, but Haydon found the image troubling, for he sensed that the rose was a metaphor for Charlotte's crippled leg.

It was clear that Genevieve could not help but infiltrate her work with her private perception of the world around her. It was this seductive, haunting quality that Haydon hoped would make an indelible impression on prospective buyers.

"That's the last of the wee ones," huffed Doreen, planting another painting beside the two that were already precariously balanced upon the mantel. "Jack and Ollie will have to bring up the rest."

Eunice planted her hands upon her plump hips as she inspected the makeshift exhibition. "There's no more room in here, so we'll have to start piling the rest of them around the dining room—"

"What in the world are you doing?" demanded an astonished voice.

Haydon's chest seemed to constrict when he saw Genevieve standing in the doorway.

The flame-gold hair that had poured like warm silk over his hands and across his pillow the night before was now tightly pinned into a proper arrangement, and the dark, chastely buttoned gown she had selected would have been appropriate for the most formidable of dowagers to wear to a funeral. Had he not experienced the passion that had blazed between them, he might have thought he was in the presence of a virgin nun. Genevieve's skin was pale and the dark circles that bruised the area beneath her eyes suggested that her night had been as sleepless as his. He knew it had taken courage for her to come down to the drawing room and face him, and he had no desire to make it any more difficult for her. All he sought now was to restore some security and comfort to her and her household.

Once he was certain she would not lose her home he would leave, so as not to put any of them at further risk.

"His lordship here thinks he can get someone to buy yer paintings," said Doreen excitedly.

Oliver scratched his white head, unconvinced. "I suppose they're a sight better than most o' the dribble and rot some folk hang on their walls."

"At least the people in them are decently dressed." Eunice surveyed the canvasses with approval. "Ye could hang them anywhere and nae be ashamed, or need to drape a cloth over them when there are ladies and wee ones present."

"If Haydon sells enough of them, then we'll have the money to pay the bank and we won't have to worry about being on the street," added Jamie happily. "Isn't that wonderful?"

Genevieve affected a frozen calm as she looked at Haydon. She had remained in her chamber for as long as she felt she could that morning, trying to summon the composure she needed in order to face him without betraying her shame over the intimacies they had shared the night before. Unfortunately, the sight of him coolly analyzing her precious paintings, which he had apparently ordered the rest of the household to dig through and line up around the house, shattered that composure.

"Why are you doing this?" Her voice was brittle.

"Because we need to find a way to meet your obligations to the bank," Haydon replied. "I have been through all the other items that are stored in your cellar, and unfortunately, there is really nothing there of any consequence. Your paintings, however, are extremely well done. I believe if we can get a gallery to show your work, you will be able to sell enough canvases to satisfy a significant portion of your debt."

"My work isn't good enough to sell," Genevieve informed him, feeling exposed and humiliated. Her work was very personal, and she had no illusions about its value. "It's only portraits of the children and simple little scenes of boats and flowers and landscapes. No one

would want to buy them. People prefer paintings that
are grand and heroic in their subject matter."

"Unless there are naked ladies in them," piped Jamie.
"People seem to like that."

"Here now, that's enough of that talk," scolded
Eunice.

"I believe you are wrong, Genevieve," Haydon
countered. "There is a growing movement away from
painting gods and heroes and violent episodes of history
and mythology. Your paintings reflect the scenes of your
life—modest, quiet, fleeting moments, to which many
people can easily relate. And more, they are suffused
with emotion. One cannot look at any of your paintings without being drawn into them and feeling something."

"He's right, lass," said Oliver. "I look at these boats
here and I'm thinkin', 'twould be nice to have fish for
dinner tonight."

"Ye know there's no fish to be had tonight," Eunice
scolded. "It's Sunday."

Genevieve stared warily at Haydon, wondering if
he was being sincere. Deep within, it pleased her to
think that he had looked at her paintings and thought
that they were more than just the pleasant work of a
woman who amused herself by dabbling with a paint-
brush. She had sketched and painted for as long as she
could remember, but after her father died and she had
taken Jamie in, her painting had changed dramatically.
Isolated and afraid, she had needed some way of expressing her joys and fears and frustrations, and painting
had become that venue. Every work within that drawing room held special significance to her that went far
beyond the depiction of its subject matter. It was as if
her happiness and her suffering were saturated into the
very paint, and each stroke bonded some small part of
her forever to the canvas.

Was it possible that Haydon was able to sense the passion with which she had created these canvases? And if he could, did that mean that perfect strangers would be able to recognize it as well, and be willing to pay for them?

No, she suddenly realized, angry with herself for being so foolish. "No one in Inveraray would ever host an exhibition showing the work of a woman," she told him flatly. "Nor would anyone here think that my work was of any value. People may be willing to pay me for painting their children's portraits, but that is far different from purchasing my other work solely based on its own merits."

"You're right," Haydon agreed. "But I do not intend to secure an exhibit for your work in Inveraray. There is not enough of a market here to command the prices I believe your paintings warrant. I am going to try to arrange for a showing in Glasgow."

It was clear to Genevieve that Haydon did not understand the intrinsic male exclusivity of the art world. "No art dealer in Glasgow will grant a woman artist an exhibition either."

"Which might be a problem, were I to reveal that this work is by a woman." Haydon stood in front of the portrait of Charlotte, considering. "I'm thinking a French name would work well. In my experience, Scottish art dealers have a great fondness for representing something that was created elsewhere. It instantly gives the work a certain credibility and mystique."

"That's true for them that buys the paintings as well," said Eunice. "Lord Dunbar's house was full of all kinds of pictures, and not one of them was by a good, honest Scotsman. They all came from Italy and France and England—as if those lads know more about slappin' paint on a piece of cloth than our own." She huffed with disapproval.

"Are you suggesting that we say that my paintings were created by a Frenchman?" Genevieve wasn't certain she cared for that idea.

"I realize it isn't the perfect solution," Haydon acknowledged. "But if we hope to secure a showing of your work and create some interest in it, I believe that is our best strategy."

"I think it's very romantic," Annabelle decided with approval. "French names sound so elegant."

"I think they sound silly," said Simon. "Like someone is trying to spit something up from the back of their throat."

"I won't do it, Genevieve, unless you are in agreement." Haydon regarded her intently. "But I believe this is your best chance of raising the money to pay off your debts."

Genevieve stared at her precious canvases haphazardly arranged around the drawing room. Each one represented some private facet of her life, and by extension, her children's lives. She didn't care for having her world put on display for others to gawk at and analyze and possibly ridicule. And she found the idea of having her work accredited to some fictional man, because the fact that it had been created by a woman undermined its merit in the eyes of others, was truly offensive.

Jamie, Annabelle, Grace, Charlotte, Simon, and Jack were watching her, waiting for her to make her decision. Their expressions were utterly trusting, as if they believed that should she refuse to sell her paintings, then she would just come up with some other way to pay her debts and keep their household going. Oliver, Eunice, and Doreen looked more concerned. They had a far better understanding of the precariousness of their situation.

Ultimately, she realized she had little choice.

"Very well, Lord Redmond," she said, lamely trying

to instill some fragment of formality back into their relationship. "Just tell me with what name you would like me to sign them."

ALFRED LYTTON TOOK OFF HIS SPECTACLES, POLished them vigorously with his crumpled handkerchief, and then wired them around his generously sized ears once more.

"Extraordinary," he murmured, bending to take a closer look at the painting. "Utterly extraordinary." He straightened suddenly and jerked his spectacles off again. "You say this Boulonnais is a friend of yours, Mr. Blake?"

"An old friend," Haydon assured him. "We met some ten years ago when I was traveling in the south of France. Of course, at that time his work was completely unknown. I had the privilege of visiting him at the crumbling old farmhouse he still uses for his home and studio. Even then, I had the sense that he was going to develop into a very fine artist. I had no idea at that time, however, just how great his talent would be."

"Indeed." Mr. Lytton raked his gaze over the five paintings that Haydon had brought to his gallery.

"Of course, when I wrote to him about the idea of exhibiting his work in Scotland, he was not immediately enthusiastic." Haydon wanted the art dealer to feel as if he were achieving a remarkable coup by arranging the exhibition. "I'm afraid it is well known that he is something of a recluse. Never married. Rarely ventures from his home. He deplores everyone and anything that might take him from his work, you see. Likes to paint at all hours of the day or night, without stopping to eat or sleep. I suppose one might say he is a bit of an eccentric, really."

"As so many artists are," Mr. Lytton remarked sagely. "It makes one wonder if madness is the price of genius." He studied the paintings further. "I have heard of Boulonnais," he murmured, lest Haydon think he was not up-to-date on the current talk of the art world, "but this is the first time I have had the pleasure of actually seeing his work. There is no question that it is most impressive. His sensibility toward his subject is quite unique."

Haydon smiled. He had anticipated that Mr. Lytton would feign familiarity with his phantom artist rather than admit ignorance. "As I'm sure you are aware, the name Georges Boulonnais is presently being heralded amongst the salons and art dealers of Paris. His works are sold the very day they go on exhibit, with many collectors begging for a chance to bid on whatever he might produce next. The esteemed art critic, Monsieur Lachapelle of *Le Parisien*, has predicted that Boulonnais will quickly become one of the most celebrated artists of this century."

"One would have to be blind not to see that," agreed Mr. Lytton. "I am most grateful to you, Mr. Blake, for bringing your association with this wonderful artist to my attention. I have no doubt that I will be able to sell all five of these paintings. The Duke of Argyll is perpetually looking for interesting work to add to his already impressive collection, and I shall be pleased to invite him for a private viewing as soon as possible. I'm sure we can arrange an exhibition of any other works Monsieur Boulonnais may choose to send to me."

"How refreshing to meet a man who is only interested in promoting art within his community, rather than realizing his maximum potential for profit. You are a credit to your profession," Haydon told him.

Mr. Lytton blinked, confused.

"I have no doubt you will get an acceptable response here and I respect you for wanting to keep the exhibition within Inveraray instead of arranging for a much larger showing at your affiliate gallery in Glasgow." Haydon rose as if their meeting was finished. "There is no question that once a burgeoning artist such as this is introduced to the art world in a major city, the spirituality of the art becomes lost amidst the frenzy of exposure and profit. One need only look at what happened at Monsieur Boulonnais's latest showing in Paris to understand."

Mr. Lytton's eyes widened. "What happened?"

"Why, every work was sold within hours, with people begging the dealer to accept bids of two and three times the listed price. Such spectacles may draw celebrity and financial gain to the gallery, but in my opinion they do little to preserve the sanctity of the work itself—as I'm sure you must agree."

"To a certain extent, yes." Mr. Lytton swiftly began to reassess his potential profit on the venture. "But I also believe that great art deserves to be shared with as large an audience as possible," he qualified carefully. "Moreover, such an enthusiastic response can only help to secure an artist's financial future, which in turn provides him with the time and the means to create more momentous works. I can assure you, Mr. Blake, that I am thinking only of Monsieur Boulonnais's welfare when I suggest that perhaps we are being hasty in limiting ourselves to an exhibit in Inveraray. I feel upon reflection that an exhibition in Glasgow is far more appropriate. If you are in agreement, I would be happy to arrange it."

Haydon looked doubtful. "Do you really believe that will be better?"

"Absolutely. An artist of the caliber of Monsieur Boulonnais should be introduced to the Scottish art world in a major city of industry and refinement. Glasgow is a far better choice for his inaugural exhibition. Shall we aim for a date in, say, eight months?"

Haydon thought about the bank's impending fore-
closure on Genevieve's house.

"Unfortunately, I'm afraid Monsieur Boulonnais is
quite temperamental, and such a delay would only give
him time to change his mind," he said, apologetic.

"But even my gallery is fully booked until summer of next year. I couldn't possibly arrange an exhibition of Boulonnais's work before then," protested Mr.
Lytton.

"Then I'm afraid I shall have to decline your offer
of an exhibition," said Haydon. "I have at this moment
over twenty paintings in my possession ready to be ex-
hibited. As there is no shortage of dealers in Paris anxious to take them, Boulonnais has instructed me that if
they cannot be shown immediately here, then I am to
return them to France. It is a pity we could not come to
some arrangement." He extended his hand.

"Twenty paintings, you say?" Mr. Lytton's myopic
eyes fairly danced as he considered his share of the prof-
its on such a sale. "In that case, Mr. Blake, let us see
how quickly we can have them crated and sent to
Glasgow. I do believe I can arrange with my associates
to find some space to hang them."

JACK SCOWLED AT THE WORDS ON THE PAGE BEFORE
him, looking as if he might tear the leaf out at any moment and shred it in frustration. Finally he slammed the
book closed and shoved it across the table.

"I'm finished." He folded his arms and regarded
Genevieve defiantly.

"Would you like me to review any of the words
with you?"

"I know them all," he assured her, his jaw set.

"But we always read until teatime," objected Simon,

peering up from his book. "The clock says we've another fifteen minutes yet."

"I don't give a damn what the bloody clock says,"
Jack snapped. "I'm finished."

"I don't want to read anymore either," said Jamie,
wanting to be supportive of Jack. "Can we do something else now, Genevieve?"

Genevieve hesitated. If she told the children they
had to continue reading it would now seem like a punishment, and she didn't want that. "You may put your
books away and spend the next few minutes drawing, if
you wish. Since you are finished for the day, Jack,
would you mind coming with me? I want to show you
something." She rose and went down the corridor to
her father's library, leaving him to follow.

"I have a book here that I think you might enjoy,"
she said, scanning the heavy leather-bound volumes
crowding the shelves. She pulled a large, worn edition
down from the top shelf and handed it to him.

Jack frowned at the mysterious gold letters forming
words on the cover, pretending to read them.

"It's called *Ships Through the Ages*." Genevieve took
the book and opened it, revealing a page in which a
magnificent Viking ship with a menacing serpent's head
at the prow sliced through the waters of an azure ocean.

"Bloody hell," swore Jack, impressed. "That looks
just like a dragon."

"That is a Viking ship from nearly a thousand years
ago. The Vikings were known as the Lords of the Sea, because of their remarkable ability to build light, streamlined
ships that could sail the most dangerous seas and strike terror into the hearts of those who saw them coming. They
were extraordinary explorers and brutal conquerors. At
one point, great parts of Scotland and Ireland fell beneath
their rule."

Jack studied the macabre ship in fascination.

"One of the most ingenious aspects of the Viking ship was the complete symmetry of the bow and stern," Genevieve continued, pointing them out on the engraving. "While this gave the craft a graceful look, it also played a role in its movement. The mast was placed precisely in the center of the ship, thereby enabling it to easily sail forward or backward, which was of great benefit during battle. The fact that the ships weren't heavy meant that if they were traveling on a river, and waterfalls or rapids blocked their passage, the Vikings would lower the mast, pull in the oars and rudder and roll the ship over land, using tree trunks beneath it."

Jack tried to imagine plucking a ship from the water and pushing it along land. "They must have been bloody strong."

"They were strong and determined," Genevieve agreed, electing not to suggest that he should try to curb his use of profanity.

She was well aware that Jack did not yet feel as if he belonged with her and her family, and she had no desire to further alienate him by constantly criticizing his language and manners. His attempt to help her by leading the other children on their failed robbery attempt, however misguided, had demonstrated to her that he did harbor at least some measure of concern toward her and the members of her household, whether he realized it or not. It was this that had kept him from running away—coupled with his ever-growing fondness for Charlotte.

Although Jack had remained steadfastly silent on the details of his past, Genevieve knew that it had been both hard and brutal. The thin white scar that snaked down his left cheek was evidence of a savage fight, and, on the night of his arrival, Oliver had seen the faded scars of a whip marking his thin back as he peeled away his filthy prison clothes. Genevieve suspected it was this

sickening familiarity with fear and violence that drew
Jack to Charlotte.

All of the children had suffered abuse at the hands
of adults before they came into Genevieve's care, but it
was Charlotte who had been damaged the most physi-
cally and emotionally, and who would never be able to
conceal her injury from the rest of the world. Her
frailty roused Jack's protective instincts in the same way
he had been motivated to help Haydon the night he escaped from the prison. This inherent empathy for others touched Genevieve deeply, and made her ever more
determined to keep the boy within the realm of her
protection until he was fully educated and equipped to
make a life of his own.

"The Vikings came to know a great deal about sailing and navigation," she continued. "They had to be
able to read the wind and the waves, and to use the position of the sun and the moon to help them understand
where they had come from and where they were going.
They thirsted for greater lands and riches, and in order
to find it, they had to constantly expand their knowledge. That determination enabled them to pack some
dried meat and fresh water into a ship and sail across the
ocean all the way to America—without even knowing
what they would find, or if they would in fact ever
come to land. On the way they battled terrible storms
and illness and heat and cold. And still they kept going,
when most men would have simply given up and gone
home."

Jack stared in silence at the image of the ship.

"The thing we often forget, Jack," Genevieve continued softly, "is that everyone comes into this world
with very little knowledge. No one is born knowing
how to read or write, or build a ship or sail the ocean.
These are all things we have to learn. Some people have
the advantage of starting earlier than others, and so it

may seem that they are smarter than us, but in fact they are not. They have just had more time to absorb the information."

He was quiet for a long moment. "They think I'm stupid," he finally growled in a low, angry voice.

"They don't think that at all," Genevieve countered. "Jamie and Simon are fascinated by everything you do and say, because to them, you seem so worldly and experienced. Annabelle and Grace are old enough to remember a time when they couldn't read either, so they understand. And Charlotte is so fiercely devoted to you, she thinks everything about you is absolutely perfect."

Jack said nothing.

"I realize it has been difficult for you to give up the independence you had when you were living on the streets," Genevieve acknowledged, refraining from pointing out that he would have had far less freedom at this moment were he incarcerated in a prison cell. "And I know you dislike having to study. You think you have managed well enough without knowing how to read or spell or add two numbers together on a piece of paper, and so you can't see why you should be bothered trying to learn these things now, when you are almost an adult."

"Lots of people can't read," he informed her with brusque authority. "And they manage. You find ways."

"I'm sure you do. But there is so much you will miss if you don't learn to read, Jack. Books can tell you how to build a ship and cross the ocean. They can show you the muscles and organs inside a man's body, or describe the greatest paintings in Italy, or tell you what life was like five hundred years ago. Books can open up worlds for you that you may have never imagined and may never see otherwise. Beyond that, knowing how to read and cipher will help you to make a success of yourself in this world."

"You don't understand." His brow twisted in frustration. "I'm older, so I should know more than them. And when they see me lookin' at some dumb word that looks so simple to them, and I don't know what it is, even though you've already told me five times, they can't help but think I'm stupid. Bloody hell, even I think I'm stupid."

"First of all, there is no doubt that you're exceptionally clever," countered Genevieve adamantly. "No one could have survived on the streets as long as you have and not be gifted with plenty of shrewdness and intelligence. Learning to read and write takes time, and that's all there is to it. If it bothers you to have your lessons with the other children, then you and I can study privately in here. That way you don't need to be concerned about what others are thinking. Would you prefer that?"

Jack looked at her in surprise. He had not thought that Genevieve would be interested in going to such lengths to help him. He had thought she would tell him to just do the best he could and not to mind the other children, and leave the matter at that. After all, why should she care whether or not he learned to read or write?

She was watching him expectantly, waiting for his answer. And suddenly it seemed very important to him that he not disappoint her.

"Yes," he said. "That would be better."

"Very well, then. You may keep that book, if you like. Although you may not be able to read it yet, there are lots of fine pictures of ships in it that you will enjoy. After we have our lesson, we'll take some time to look at them and I'll tell you more about the men who built them and all the wonderful places they visited. Perhaps one day you will travel to faraway countries on a ship. Maybe you will even go to America." She smiled.

"Then you will write to me and tell me about all the marvelous things you have seen."

Jack stared at the image of the Viking ship. It had never occurred to him that he would ever set foot on a ship. He had never even imagined that he might one day see the world beyond Scotland. But hearing Genevieve speak of it made him feel strangely excited, as if this was a dream that might well be within his reach. And why not? he wondered fiercely. Genevieve said he was smart, and he knew he was a hard worker when it suited him. Perhaps one day he would find work on a ship, and spend his days with nothing but the sky for a roof and the waves rocking beneath him. He studied the turquoise ocean in the engraving and wondered what it would be like to swim in warm water with the sun sparkling on the waves like fallen stars.

Genevieve resisted the impulse to reach out and brush a dark brown curl off Jack's temple. He seemed so young and vulnerable to her in that moment, the desire to wrap her arms around him and hold him was great. But he was not a little boy, she reminded herself, and he would surely resent her attempt to treat him as one. He was a fourteen-year-old youth who had lived a life of constant hunger, instability and need, who had managed to survive on the streets with nothing but his wits and pure determination. In some ways, Jack was far older and more worldly than she was. She only hoped he would ultimately decide to stay with her—at least until he didn't need her protection or her guidance any longer.

"Genevieve." Jamie was giggling as he called through the door. "We have something for you."

She smiled, wondering what game the children were playing. "I suppose we have locked ourselves up in here long enough, Jack, and the children are anxious for their tea."

Jack closed the precious book on ships. "That's all right." He was feeling strangely privileged at having been able to spend some time with Genevieve alone. "Can we look at this book again tomorrow?"

"I would like that very much."

"Genevieve, let us in!" pleaded a chorus of voices in the hall, as they banged upon the door.

"Come in," she said.

The door burst open and the children practically shoved Haydon inside.

"Tell her!" they shrieked, dancing around him. "Tell her right away!"

Haydon reached into his coat pocket and withdrew an envelope, which he placed in Genevieve's hand.

"What's this?" she asked, puzzled.

"Two tickets for the coach to Glasgow. We leave on Friday of next week."

Her brows drew together in bewilderment. "We're going to Glasgow?"

"We are indeed. The eminent artist Georges Boulonnais is about to have his inaugural Scottish exhibition next Saturday evening. We must select fifteen more of your best paintings and take them over to Mr. Alfred Lytton's gallery tomorrow. He is going to have them shipped to his affiliate gallery in Glasgow, and they will see to it that the works are suitably framed."

"But we can't afford to go to Glasgow," Genevieve protested. She was having trouble coming to grips with what Haydon was telling her, so her mind focused on the more mundane aspects of his pronouncement. "We don't have the money."

"Actually, we do. Mr. Lytton was astute enough to realize that it would be a major coup if the reclusive Monsieur Boulonnais were to make an appearance at this opening. While I could not guarantee such a thing, I did mention that my eccentric friend might be more

apt to attend were I there. Since I am newly married
and most reticent to travel without my charming wife,
Mr. Lytton was kind enough to offer to pay for all our
expenses."

Genevieve stared at him in disbelief. The idea of actually seeing her work for sale in an art gallery was simply inconceivable. "But I cannot leave the children—"

"Of course ye can, lass," interrupted Oliver. "I'll
take good care of them."

"Dinna let that thought frighten ye," said Eunice,
chortling. "Doreen and I will make sure the children
are warm and fed and in their beds by eight o'clock. Ye
just go to Glasgow and have a grand time. Dinna worry
about a thing."

"Just think," said Simon, grabbing her hand with
excitement, "your paintings are going to be on display
for the whole world to see!"

"Yet no one will know that you are the true artist,"
reflected Annabelle dreamily. "One day I shall write a
play about it and then perform in it, without ever revealing your true identity."

"And I'll make all the beautiful costumes for you,"
offered Grace, "and people will be so taken by my de-
signs that they will become all the rage in Paris soon
afterward, and I shall become rich and famous." She
pursed her lips together suddenly, staring at Genevieve
in disapproval. "You aren't going to wear that to
Glasgow, are you? You look like you're dressed for your
own burial."

Genevieve's hands flew self-consciously to her plain
black skirts. "I do?"

"I can't wear black," Annabelle informed her with
grave earnestness. "It makes my skin look horribly
sallow."

"Genevieve has other gowns to wear," Charlotte assured them.

"But they're all dark and ugly," protested Annabelle with childlike candor. "And worn."

"I'm sure she has one that doesn't look too bad." Charlotte regarded Genevieve hopefully. "You do have something nice, don't you, Genevieve?"

"Does this mean that we have the money to pay the bank?" wondered Jamie, who could not see anything wrong with Genevieve's dress.

"Not yet," Haydon replied, "but I strongly suspect that once Genevieve's paintings are handsomely framed and hung, the public will instantly be drawn to them and the works will sell. It may take a while, but—"

"And then we'll have lots of money to pay the bank and we can all live here forever!" squeaked Simon, ecstatic.

"At the very least we should make enough to satisfy the bank for a while," Haydon agreed, careful to temper their expectations. "But if this exhibition goes well, there is no reason why we couldn't arrange others, in Edinburgh, and maybe London. We shall just have to see how this one goes."

"It seems to me ye're going to be in need of some flouncier finery if ye're going to be paradin' about Glasgow as the newly wedded Mrs. Blake." Eunice studied Genevieve up and down with a critical eye. "Seein' as how yer husband is supposed to be an important friend of the artist and all."

"Well, I don't have anything better, and there's no money to be wasted on such nonsense." Genevieve's tone was brisk and pragmatic. Secretly, however, she was wishing she had something elegant to wear to the opening. It had been years since she had enjoyed the profound luxury of a new dress, and she had not had a new evening gown since before her father's death.

"Here, Eunice." Haydon pressed several bank notes into Eunice's hand. "You and Doreen take Genevieve shopping, and make sure she buys something nice for herself."

Genevieve's eyes grew round. "Where did you get that money?"

"Mr. Lytton gave me an advance against the sales. He said it was to help cover any expenses Monsieur Boulonnais might have, should he decide to travel to Glasgow. And right now," he added, grinning broadly, "it seems that Monsieur Boulonnais is in need of a new gown."

APPLE-GOLD LIGHT RIMMED THE DRAWN DRAPERIES of the main floor, sending a warm glimmer into the freezing darkness of the street. The heavy curtains effectively blocked the silhouettes of those who moved behind them, leaving Vincent staring in frustration at the home of Mr. and Mrs. Maxwell Blake.

It was only by a monumental force of will that he had managed to remain in the shadows when he had seen Haydon emerge from the front door earlier that day. His recognition of him had been immediate. Haydon had been a regular guest in his home for many years before Vincent learned that the perpetually drunken fool had helped himself to more than just the fine food and drink that Vincent so generously offered. Until then, Vincent had thought of him as little more than a trivial amusement, an insignificant but inevitable addition to any dinner or weeklong party in the country. Haydon played the role of the charming, insouciant younger brother of the Marquess of Redmond, the idle second son who had inherited all of the physical beauty of face and structure, but none of the discipline or wit required of men who actually want to make something of themselves in the world. His total lack of sobriety coupled with his undeniably handsome features and his inheritance made him utterly irresistible to women, who were drawn to him like wasps to a dollop of jam.

Vincent had been amused by the way the weaker sex contrived to throw themselves into Haydon's path at every opportunity, seeking him out for a clandestine rendezvous on the terrace, or in the rose garden, or in some dark corner where they thought their urgent gropings and halfhearted protests would go unnoticed. Haydon's conquests had been as much a form of entertainment as drinking or cards. To make it more of an event, Vincent had taken bets from the other gentlemen guests in the morning as to whose bed their drunken friend had heated the night before.

Vincent had been far from amused, however, the night Cassandra coldly informed him during a moment of pure hatred that his beloved five-year-old daughter had been sired by Haydon.

He had never thought of himself as a passionate man, capable of the capricious emotions of love and hate. He had always been cool, dignified, self-possessed, to the point where Cassandra had accused him of being frozen inside. But she was wrong. He had been cool to her, yes, because his spectacularly indulged wife had never been able to arouse any feelings within him beyond lust, for a time, and then disdain. But his love for Emmaline had surpassed any feelings he had ever held for anything else in his life. And when he learned that his precious daughter was in fact not his, but the result of some sweating, rutting tryst between his wife and a man whom Vincent had tolerated but despised, it was as if the heart that had so recently learned the exquisite pleasure of loving someone had been torn from his chest and crushed to a pulp.

What he had not understood was that love could not be eradicated merely by deciding it was over.

And that there was a far worse pain still to come.

The wash of gold rimming the windows began to be extinguished, room by room, until finally the entire house stood silent and black. Vincent thought of Haydon lying upon a warm bed inside, perhaps with his body pressing against the delicately lush form of the charitable Miss MacPhail, who had so selflessly taken it upon herself to rescue and protect him. He was alive and warm and safe, while Emmaline lay cold and rotting in the ground. The injustice of it was unbearable. Vincent wanted to storm in there and plunge a knife into Haydon's chest where he lay, to see his eyes widen with horror and surprise and watch as the blood poured hot and red across the sheets and onto the floor.

Patience, he told himself silently. *You must be patient.*

Now that he had found Haydon comfortably ensconced in his false identity as Maxwell Blake, husband and father, the mode of his demise had taken a new shape. Vincent had been somewhat alarmed when he had watched him climb into a carriage earlier that day. He had thought that perhaps Haydon was abandoning his masquerade in Inveraray and seeking refuge elsewhere. But after following him to an art gallery where he stayed for well over an hour, he observed Haydon's return to this house. What had intrigued Vincent most was the warm welcome he had received upon his return. The door had swung open and an old man clapped him on the shoulder as if he were a lad, while a jumble of children of assorted heights and ages had crowded around, grabbing him by the hands as if they couldn't wait to drag him off somewhere.

The memory of Emmaline grabbing at his own hands with her chubby little fingers suddenly filled his mind. She was not quite three years old, and she was pulling upon him as she toddled down the corridor. *Where's the puppy, Daddy?* she crooned, leading him to the room in which she had hidden one of her stuffed toys for him to find. It was a favorite game of theirs, and no matter how obvious the toy's placement, Vincent would always make a great show of investigating beneath every chair and sofa, picking up cushions and examining beneath small ornaments, huffing and frowning and looking perplexed, much to Emmaline's delight.

He could not remember precisely when he had first pulled his hand away from her. The memory was blurred because she continued to reach for him, day after day, week after week, pleading with him to follow her. Until the excruciating moment when she finally realized that her daddy didn't want to hold her hand anymore—or hug her, or kiss her, or press his cheek to hers and call her his little princess and hold her tight. Or search for her little puppy.

After that she never reached for him again.

He blinked hard, forcing himself back to the present. *Death is too easy for you, you bastard.*

Chapter Eleven

THE CITY OF GLASGOW WAS A BOISTEROUS, crowded place of exceptional beauty and horrendous despair. The cool waters of the River Clyde ran like a pulsing blue vein through its heart, linking it to the Firth of Clyde and ultimately the Atlantic Ocean. This made Glasgow perfectly situated to accommodate the needs of its rapidly expanding industry. Nearly one hundred textile mills dotted its grass-and-stone landscape, and the ironworks and coal mines of the surrounding area fed the boilermakers, shipyards, and marine-engineering shops lining the River Clyde. The flourishing manufacturing led to a nearly insatiable demand for cheap labor. Highland Scots swarmed to the city in the hopes of finding work, only to find that they had to compete with equally desperate Irish, Italian, and Jewish immigrants. Extravagant fortunes were made by a privileged few, who celebrated by erecting magnificent homes and public buildings which were then filled with the finest antiques, furnishings, and art. As for the men, women, and children who sweated and suffered gruelingly long hours in the factories, they dragged themselves home at night to the stinking foulness of the slums, where they waged an ongoing battle against hunger, disease, alcoholism, and violence. Yet even with this squalid underbelly, Glasgow was, without doubt, one of the most glorious cities in Europe.

It was the perfect place for the renowned French painter Georges Boulonnais to be introduced to Scotland.

Genevieve stared in fascination at the woman in the mirror, wondering if she had really changed as much as her reflection suggested. The gown she had chosen with the assistance of Eunice and Doreen was a simple affair of icy gray silk, trimmed with almost transparent layers of cream lace that rippled around the low neckline and fell in softly gathered pleats about the hem. It was not quite the latest fashion, nor was it as lavishly adorned as the other gowns that the woman in the shop had initially presented to her. Eunice and Doreen had swooned and sighed over the elaborate confections of dusty pink, smoky mauve, and leafy green silk, all fancifully beaded and embellished with garish ribbons and bows, ballooning over monumental hooped cages that looked as if they would have knocked over everyone and everything within a five-foot radius.

Years earlier, Genevieve would have delighted in wearing such an outlandish fashion, and would have eagerly anticipated the admiration and attention she would have drawn as she sailed confidently into a room. But that frivolous, spoiled girl did not exist anymore. The woman who stood before the looking glass was an unmarried mother of six who had struggled for years just to keep her young charges fed and dressed and off the streets. The idea of paying an outlandish sum for a ridiculous dress that could be worn only rarely, and never in the same company twice, now struck her as virtually immoral.

Despite its relative simplicity, Genevieve did think her new gown was pretty, and far nicer than anything she had owned for years. The bodice was narrowly molded to her body, creating a slim triangle from her breasts to her waist, at which point her skirts blossomed into a pearly silk bell that was supported by a modest crinoline.

The hotel had sent up a maid at her request to help her dress, as managing the complexities of her corset and crinoline and the endless row of tiny buttons and hooks at the back of the gown would have been impossible on her own. The girl was a pleasant, chatty lass by the name of Alice, who kindly offered to do Genevieve's hair. At first Genevieve protested, thinking she would merely pin it back the way she normally did and hope that it would last reasonably well through the course of the evening. But Alice had pleaded with her, telling her that she didn't often have the opportunity to work with hair as lovely and thick as Genevieve's was, and that she would be enormously grateful if Genevieve would permit her to practice a new style she had seen in a Parisian fashion publication that a friend had sent to her all the way from France. With her request presented so, it would have been almost unkind to refuse her, and so Genevieve relented and permitted the maid to try to tame the massive weight of her hair.

By the time Alice was finished, Genevieve's coral-and-gold hair had been spun into a soft bouquet of curls, which were loosely gathered and pinned low against the back of her neck. Alice had threaded a delicate cluster of tiny pink and ivory blossoms above one ear, which had the dramatic effect of adding a soft splash of color to the gray and cream of her gown. At first Genevieve feared the flowers might be a little too showy, but Alice insisted that they were most appropriate for a woman of her beauty and stature, and that as other women were certain to attend the opening wearing flouncy ostrich feathers and ribbons and even jewels in their hair, no one would think her out of place.

Darkness was creeping across the city on silent feet. Genevieve lit the oil lamps in her room and continued to study herself, unaccustomed to contemplating her appearance for any length of time. Her hair did look quite pretty, she had to admit, and while her gown was plain by the standards of the day, she thought it was entirely acceptable. It was her face, however, that interested her most. There were unfamiliar lines sketched lightly across her forehead, and a fan of smaller wrinkles edged the area around her eyes. When had she developed those? she wondered. She reminded herself that she was no longer a dewy-skinned girl of eighteen, but a twenty-six-year-old woman with countless worried, sleepless nights behind her. There were also, she hastened to add, many moments of joy, as she knew no greater pleasure than the laughter her children could bring bubbling to the surface with the smallest smile or funny gesture. She supposed it was inevitable that her face would start to reflect the evidence of her life. It was disconcerting, however, to notice how much she had changed since the last time she had really studied herself. It had been years since she had sat for any length of time before a mirror, when she was newly betrothed to Charles, and had considered herself exceptionally blessed to have won the attention of such a dashing and sophisticated gentleman as the earl of Linton.

Time had passed with dizzying speed.

There was a knock upon her door. She rose, made a final nervous adjustment to a wayward strand of hair, and went to open it.

Haydon stood in the corridor, elegantly attired in a black evening coat, immaculate white shirt, neatly tied cravat, and fitted oyster-colored trousers. He did not speak, but stared at her in silence, his gaze taking in every inch of her, from the shimmering coils of her hair to the soft flounce of lace trailing against the dark pattern of carpet beneath her. She felt his eyes rest ever so fleetingly upon the milky swell of bosom rising from her gown, then trail down the tight constriction of her bodice, over the flare of her crinolined hips and up again. Her flesh was heated merely by having his eyes graze over it, making her achingly aware that he had taken her breasts in his mouth and suckled the tips, had crushed her body against his until she could scarcely breathe, had dipped his tongue into the most intimate parts of her body and filled her with himself, thrusting into the depths of her and holding her fast until she had no inkling of time or responsibility or regret.

She turned suddenly, feeling uncomfortably hot and breathless, although the room was cool and her gown was not overly tight.

"Good evening," Haydon said, regaining the composure he had momentarily lost on first seeing Genevieve. He had always known she was beautiful, regardless of whether she was dressed in one of her faded gowns or lying naked against a rumpled swirl of cool sheets. Even so, nothing had prepared him for the loveliness radiating from her in that moment. Her gown was exquisite in its simplicity, for it made no attempt to compete with her beauty, but merely enhanced it. He entered the room and casually tossed his top hat and cloak onto a chair, resisting the urge to take her in his arms and kiss her.

She is not yours, he reminded himself stiffly. *Regardless of the liberties you have so shamelessly taken with her.*

"You look absolutely lovely tonight, Mrs. Blake," he said, adopting a lighthearted demeanor. "I have no doubt that every man in the gallery will be staring at you in awe. I can see I shall have my hands full trying to keep them at a respectable distance."

His manner was joking, but his eyes told Genevieve

that he really did find her appearance pleasing. Perhaps the lines she had seen on her face were not quite as deep and distracting as she had imagined.

"I must confess, it has been so long since I have attended an affair of any social merit, I had quite forgotten all the attention that must go into dressing for it." She made a self-conscious adjustment to her gown, which suddenly seemed entirely too low cut. "Fortunately the hotel was able to provide me with a maid who was able to assist me with my gown and my hair."

Haydon imagined plunging his hands into the soft swirl of daintily arranged curls, plucking the pins loose and dragging his fingers through the fiery-gold silk until it spilled across the snowy mounds of her breasts. As for that gown, he felt reasonably certain he could have it unhooked and slipping down the curves of her delectable body within mere moments.

Disconcerted by his thoughts, he looked away. "There is just one more thing needed to make your ensemble complete." He reached into his coat pocket and withdrew a small crimson box. "Here."

Genevieve stared at him in surprise. His expression was masked. Hesitantly, she took the box and ran her fingers over its velvety surface, enjoying the rare delight of mystery and anticipation. After a moment, she slowly opened it.

Resting upon a satin cushion lay a gleaming gold band with a small ruby stone embedded in its center.

"It is not nearly as grand as what you deserve," Haydon said, his voice slightly taut, "but I'm afraid it was the best I could do on such short notice, with rather limited funds. I did think it was about time that Mrs. Maxwell Blake had a wedding ring."

Genevieve stared in silence at the glowing circle.

At the time of her betrothal, Charles had given her a heavy, ornate ring with a trio of enormous diamonds in its center. It had been a family heirloom, he explained to her gravely at the time, and had graced the hands of three Linton countesses before her. He had then rambled on about who they were and what their accomplishments were, which mostly included stoically bearing children and being glorified hostesses. At the end of this pompous dissertation, he had informed Genevieve that she could take pride in the fact that he had chosen her above countless other potential candidates to wear this ring, and that he was certain she would do the piece justice by making him proud and never giving him cause for embarrassment. Of course, he had angrily demanded it back when their betrothal was broken, as had been his right.

She had never worn any jewelry since.

"It's lovely," she said softly.

"Here." Haydon removed the ring from the box and took her hand in his. Her skin felt silky and cool against his palm, and as he leaned closer he was suddenly aware of the delicate scent of orange blossoms. He slipped the ring over the third finger of her left hand. "I'm afraid it's a little big," he apologized. "We shall have to have it sized when we get home."

The word "home" fell easily from his mouth. He knew the moment he said it that it was wrong, but he did not correct himself, for fear of drawing them into a discussion in which they had to face the impossibility of their situation. He was well aware that he could not go on pretending to be Maxwell Blake forever. He had a life to reclaim, however empty and indulgent and meaningless it was. Moreover, he was an escaped murderer and his very presence posed a constant danger to Genevieve and her family. He closed his eyes and inhaled the scent of her again, pushing those thoughts aside. Tonight they had an art exhibition to attend, in which the cream of Glasgow's art world would cast its eyes upon the work of the artist Georges Boulonnais and determine whether or not they thought it had merit.

"Come, Genevieve," he said, gathering her evening cloak in his hands and draping it over her slim, bare shoulders. "There is a carriage outside waiting to take you to your premier exhibition." He retrieved his own hat and coat and opened the door before gallantly offering her his arm.

There would be time enough to face the stark reality of their lives in the morning.

Mr. BLAKE! OVER HERE!" ALFRED LYTTON FLUTTERED a skeletal hand in the air as he fought to negotiate his way through the crush of people surrounding him.

"Mr. Lytton," said Haydon when the bespectacled art dealer finally managed to emerge through two bodies, "it seems your gallery has attracted something of an audience. My dear, you know Mr. Lytton, do you not?" he continued, turning to Genevieve. "I believe you mentioned that your father had bought some paintings from him years ago."

"Yes, of course," said Genevieve, overwhelmed by the crowd of people staring at her paintings. The canvases had all been set in heavily carved gold frames, which gave them a far greater look of import than they had borne while strewn about her cellar. She had no idea if the people currently gaping at them loved them, hated them or were merely indifferent. "How are you, Mr. Lytton?"

"It's a madhouse!" Mr. Lytton burst out excitedly, gazing about. "An absolute madhouse! My associates had invitations delivered to our regular clientele, but because it was such short notice, we also decided to print a small advertisement in *The Herald,* thinking that we might lure a few more interested parties. Well, Mr. Stanley Chisholm, the esteemed art critic, happened to see the advertisement, and he decided to come by the gallery yesterday while we were still making preparations. It is no exaggeration to say that he was quite taken with the work. Quite taken indeed. So much so that he wrote an article for today's *Herald,* hailing Monsieur Boulonnais's work as exquisite and saying that anyone with an interest in seeing paintings of rare sensitivity must not miss this exhibition. He also happened to mention that the reclusive artist just might be making an appearance here this evening, which seems to have had the effect of rousing people's curiosity." He bobbed his head about nervously. "Do you know if Boulonnais is here?"

Haydon pretended to search the room, which was filled with elegantly attired women and men who were laughing and sipping champagne. "My wife and I have only just arrived, so I cannot be certain. If I see him, I shall let you know immediately."

"I do hope he decided to make the trip. At last count we had already sold thirteen of the twenty paintings— and the evening has scarcely begun! The Duke of Argyll purchased five of them before we had even shipped them here from Inveraray, but I told him they had to be included in the exhibition. He did not mind, of course. The exposure will only have the effect of increasing their value."

Genevieve's eyes widened incredulously. "You have sold thirteen paintings?"

"And I don't mind telling you, after we saw how glowing Mr. Chisholm's article in *The Herald* was, we adjusted the prices accordingly," Mr. Lytton admitted surreptitiously. "Your husband's commission on the sales will be even greater than we expected, Mrs. Blake, and of course his friend, Boulonnais, will profit very handsomely as well. I trust he will be so pleased that he will continue to permit our gallery to represent him in Scotland."

Haydon smiled. "I have no doubt that when he finds out how well the work was received, he will be interested in maintaining your representation."

"Excellent. Do forgive me, but Lord Hyslop is signaling to me that he wishes to purchase that painting of the girl with the rose. A magnificent piece, really. So beautiful, and yet there is something terribly melancholy about it. I should have asked more for it." He sighed with regret. "Excuse me." He straightened his spectacles and made his way across the room.

"Thirteen paintings," Genevieve repeated, stunned.

Haydon retrieved two glasses from a silver tray that was sailing by on the arm of a harried waiter. "Would you care for some champagne?"

Genevieve gripped the stem of the glass so tightly Haydon feared it might snap.

"Let's have a toast," he suggested. "To the mysteriously reclusive Georges Boulonnais. May he continue to paint and enchant the art world for many, many years." He raised his glass, took a sip, then frowned. "What's wrong, Genevieve? Don't you like champagne?"

She shook her head, distracted by all the people laughing and milling around her. "I don't remember. I haven't had any since the night my betrothal to Charles was announced. That was years ago."

"I believe you will find it tastes much better when one has something truly wonderful to celebrate. Not that your betrothal to Charles wasn't cause for a drink," he added dryly.

She gave him a mildly exasperated look before cautiously sipping her champagne. A flurry of cold bubbles danced upon her tongue and tickled her nose. She

took another sip, and then another. The crowded room
was warm and she was suddenly extremely thirsty. Another swallow and her glass was empty.

"More?" asked Haydon.

She nodded. "Please."

He dutifully retrieved another glass for her. "Perhaps
you should drink this one a little slower," he advised.
"Champagne does have a tendency to go down easily,
and then all at once make one feel rather lightheaded."

"I'll be fine," Genevieve assured him, taking another sip. "You needn't worry about me." She turned
away so she could watch a group of people who were
having an animated discussion in front of her painting
of Simon and Jamie.

The champagne and the heat of the gallery had
brought a rosy flush to her cheeks, which gave a lovely
contrast to the creamy softness of her throat and breasts.
She was easily the most beautiful woman in the room,
Haydon realized. What made her even more attractive
was the fact that she had no inkling of the effect she was
having on nearly every man who laid eyes upon her. He
saw their initial pleasure, which transformed into curiosity as they tried to deduce who she was and what her
relationship to him might be. He was glad he had had
the foresight to give her a wedding band before they set
out, or he would have been forced to chase off every
fatuous fool who came near. Genevieve was well past
the girlish bloom that must have made her completely
enchanting when she was first presented to society some
eight years earlier. But in that girl's place was a woman
of incredible strength and fortitude, who had not only
survived hardship and despair, but had constantly given
of herself in every way she could so that others could
survive as well. It was this combination of beauty, determination, and selflessness that set her apart from every
other woman around her.

"Can you imagine that all these people have come here to see my work?" Genevieve was completely awed by the thought of it. "And that they are actually buying it?"

"They would have to be blind not to see the beauty of your paintings, Genevieve. There is a poignant intimacy to your work that touches people. I recognized it the moment I saw your paintings, and I knew others would see it too."

She considered this a moment as she watched a gray-haired gentleman stare with pleasure at her painting of a weathered fishing boat gliding across the leaden surface of a loch.

"If my work does have merit, then it shouldn't matter that the artist is a woman. The work should stand on its own."

"You're right," Haydon agreed. "I hope one day that prejudice changes, but until it does, you must maintain your identity as Georges Boulonnais. As long as you can keep painting under his guise, you might be able to support yourself and your family. I realize it is unjust, Genevieve, but I hope that your financial success will be enough to counter the frustration of not having your talent recognized under your own name."

Of course it was enough, Genevieve realized, overwhelmed as she contemplated the magnitude of what Haydon had done. Haydon had orchestrated nothing less than her family's survival. He had not done it by giving her money and demanding something in return, the way Charles might have done, or for that matter any other man she had ever known. Instead of giving her charity, Haydon had found a way for her to stand on her own. She would be able to earn a living for herself and her family by doing something that she loved, which was expressing herself through her paintings.

It was by far the greatest gift that anyone could ever have given to her—the gift of self-sufficiency.

She raised her eyes to his, wanting to tell him how grateful she was. He regarded her steadily. He was unbearably handsome in his evening clothes, with his black hair curling against the fine fabric of his evening coat and his jaw cut firm and strong in the soft blaze of light afforded by countless oil lamps and candles. He seemed so refined and at ease amidst all the fashionable beauty and wealth floating about them, it was obvious to Genevieve that this was his world. And yet there was something about him that set him apart from every other man in the gallery. There was a menacing quality to him, a faint hint of danger that suggested he was not as civilized as his attire and manner suggested. It was this that was attracting the attention of many of the women in the room, who were stealing glances in his direction, trying to determine just what his relationship was to Genevieve. She felt a stab of jealousy.

Haydon frowned, wondering at the change that had suddenly come over her.

"Good God, Redmond," called an astonished voice from somewhere within the crowded room, "is that really you?"

Genevieve's breath froze in her chest.

Haydon stiffened slightly, then forced himself to affect an air of utter calm. Inhaling deeply, he slowly turned to greet the fiery-haired young man hurrying toward them.

"Hello, Rodney," he said, smiling. "Fancy meeting you here. Permit me to present you to Mrs. Maxwell Blake. Mrs. Blake, this is an old friend of mine, Mr. Rodney Caldwell."

Genevieve fought to restrain her panic. Her champagne glass gripped tightly in one hand, she graciously raised the other to the handsome man, whom she judged to be about thirty. "How do you do, Mr. Caldwell?"

"A tremendous pleasure, Mrs. Blake." He pressed a brief kiss to the back of her hand. "I can see the marquess still has an affinity for keeping company with the most beautiful woman in the room." His manner was friendly and teasing. "Haydon, you sly wretch, just where the devil have you been? We heard about some nasty business concerning a murder trial. They said you had been hanged, but clearly those stories were shamelessly exaggerated." He laughed.

Haydon sipped his champagne, looking faintly amused. "So it would seem."

"Well, I'm glad that mess is all straightened out. Just an unpleasant misunderstanding, was it?"

"I'm afraid so."

"Thank God for that. Everyone up in Inverness had given you up for dead—except for me, of course. I knew whatever scrape you'd gotten yourself into, you would somehow manage to squeak out of it. I can tell you, they'll be positively tickled when I tell them that I saw you gadding about Glasgow, drinking champagne in the company of a beautiful woman at an art exhibit."

"Really, Mr. Caldwell, you flatter me too much," protested Genevieve, forcing herself to smile. "Lord Redmond, would you mind escorting me back to my husband? If he sees me standing here talking to two such handsome men, I've no doubt that he will become insufferably jealous. You will excuse us, won't you, Mr. Caldwell?" she asked sweetly.

"Of course, Mrs. Blake." He tilted forward in a small bow. "It was a pleasure to meet you. How long are you planning to stay in Glasgow, Haydon?" he asked, turning to Haydon. "I'm here for the week. Perhaps we could dine together one evening, and you can tell me all about how you managed to escape the hangman's noose." His tone was jovial.

"Unfortunately, I'm leaving tomorrow."

"That's a pity. Are you heading for home?"

"Not directly. I expect to return within a few weeks," Haydon said evasively.

"Business matters, I suppose?"

"Yes."

Rodney sighed. "I regret to say it's the bane of us ne'er-do-wells, Mrs. Blake. We are forced to actually work occasionally so that we can go on playing in the style to which we have grown accustomed. Well then, Haydon, I suppose I shall have to wait until we are both back at home before you can regale me with your sordid tales about how you escaped your execution. I can tell you, I'm most anxious to hear all about it."

"I shall look forward to that." Haydon offered his arm to Genevieve. She obediently laid her fingers lightly upon the fabric of his sleeve. "And now, if you will excuse us, I must deliver Mrs. Blake safely back to her husband. Good night, Rodney." He smiled and turned away.

"We have to leave," he said tautly as he steered Genevieve through the crowd. "Now."

Genevieve maintained a frozen visage as Haydon retrieved their cloaks. She saw Mr. Lytton hurrying toward another prospective buyer, who was involved in an animated discussion with his wife over the merits of one of her paintings. She was vaguely aware that she had probably sold another one. People were still drinking and laughing and talking loudly. Nothing had changed in the room.

She shivered as Haydon laid her cloak over her shoulders.

Neither spoke during the carriage ride back to the hotel. Once they were safely ensconced in the privacy of Genevieve's chamber, Haydon bolted the door and leaned heavily against it, trying to think.

"Is this Mr. Caldwell a good friend of yours?"

He shook his head. He had no good friends.

"That would explain why he didn't have a clear grasp on what had happened to you," Genevieve mused.

"I suppose he was recalling whatever gossip was being churned about at social events up near Inverness," Haydon reflected. "Apparently they do not yet know of my escape. Either that, or Rodney has been away from the crowd for a bit, and is not quite on top of things."

"But now that he has seen you, he is sure to tell others."

Haydon didn't answer.

Despair began to wrap around Genevieve. For a brief moment, as they walked into the gallery together as Mr. and Mrs. Maxwell Blake, she had felt strangely happy—as if she were actually living the charade that they had so carefully constructed. No one in Inveraray had recognized Haydon as the marquess of Redmond. Her handsome, charming, apparently devoted husband bore little resemblance to the filthy, brutal drunk who had lain burning with fever upon the foulness of the jail floor. Constable Drummond had mentioned to her that the marquess had an estate in the Highlands north of Inverness. That had seemed so far away, she had not imagined that anyone Haydon knew might accidentally see him in Inveraray or Glasgow. Now that someone had, this deliciously unexpected tidbit of news would quickly fly from mouth to mouth. Eventually someone who knew that the marquess of Redmond had escaped would hear of it and they would feel compelled to share this morsel with the authorities. Haydon would instantly be linked to Mrs. Maxwell Blake, for Rodney Caldwell was not likely to spare any detail of their meeting.

Constable Drummond would be smashing down her door with an army of police officers, ready to drag Haydon away and crush his neck at the end of a rope.

She turned and looked out the frozen black pane of the window. Her hands gripped the cold wooden ledge as she studied the snow-dusted street below. A man alighted from a carriage in front of the hotel and turned to assist his young wife. It was clear the two had not been married overly long, for she giggled as he presented his hand to her, which caused him to bow gallantly before her, making her laugh even harder. Now they would go into the dining room and share a lovely meal together, Genevieve thought, accompanied by a bottle of wine. They would linger over some beautifully presented dessert, piled high with imported berries and freshly whipped cream. Then the husband might indulge in a cigar while his wife drank coffee from a tiny china cup rimmed with gold. And after all this mannered civility, they would retire to their room and he would take her into his arms and kiss her and touch her and plunge himself deep inside her, until there was nothing beyond the fire and passion burning between them. At last they would sleep, each secure in the knowledge that the other would be there when they awoke, ready to help them with their buttons as they dressed, and sit across from them over breakfast.

It was an exquisite state of familiarity and comfort, which she would never know.

"Tomorrow I will escort you back to Inveraray," Haydon was saying, restlessly pacing the room. "I have to be sure that you return safely. Caldwell is here for the week and then he is returning to Inverness, so there is no reason to think that anyone in Inveraray will learn of my identity. Once you are home, I will leave immediately. You will tell people that I have gone to France to see Boulonnais, to let him know how his exhibition went and bring him his share of his earnings. Since I was just responsible for his glorious introduction to the Scottish art world, no one should find my desire to tell him about it in person implausible. From there, you can say I am going to England to take care of a few business matters. Give the impression that I will be gone at least several weeks. After a month or two has passed, you can tell people that I have been killed—either by illness or accident, it doesn't matter."

"No."

He raised a dark brow in surprise. "What do you mean, no?"

She turned from the dark windowpane to face him. "You cannot accompany me to Inveraray, Haydon. It is too dangerous. Wherever it is you intend on going, you must leave now. You cannot be delayed because you feel I must be escorted home."

In truth, he could not bear the thought of abandoning her so suddenly. He had not prepared himself for this. The thought of Genevieve being torn from him without preamble was too painful. The return to Inveraray would take two days. That was two more days of being with her. It wasn't nearly enough, he realized hopelessly. Even so, it was better than being forced to leave her now.

That was, quite simply, unthinkable.

"I will be fine taking the coach on my own," she assured him, trying to get him to see reason. "I can tell people that you were detained here because of business matters, and that you then intend to go on to France to see your artist friend. You can slip out of this hotel right now and disappear into the night. That is far better than taking the risk of returning home with me."

"And the moment you arrive without me, you will be under a mantle of suspicion, especially if anyone hears that you were seen at the gallery conversing with the marquess of Redmond, who just happens to look exactly like the man claiming to be your husband." Haydon threw his hat and cloak onto a chair. "I won't permit you to be put at further risk, Genevieve. Appearances must be maintained—especially given that people have already found our sudden marriage somewhat odd. It will look far better for you if you return from Glasgow with your husband, and then I leave on business from there. Anything else will be suspect."

"If anyone there does hear Mr. Caldwell's tale that I was seen in the company of Lord Redmond, I will just say that I spoke with many people at the opening of Monsieur Boulonnais's exhibition, and I don't remember. There is nothing to Mr. Caldwell's tale to suggest that the marquess was in fact posing as my husband. We made a great show of your having to deliver me back to Mr. Maxwell Blake, so as far as Caldwell is concerned, I am a respectable married woman with a jealous husband lurking somewhere in the shadows."

She may be right, Haydon thought, raking his hand through his hair. He wasn't sure. All he knew was that he wasn't about to abandon her in a hotel in Glasgow, never to see her again, not knowing if she had been arrested or abducted or attacked by thieving scum on the long journey home. And he damn well wasn't going to leave without saying good-bye to the children. Each of them had suffered enough disruption and desertion in their short lives. At the very least he wanted to speak to them and make them understand that he was not abandoning them by choice, as so many others in their lives had, but of necessity.

Making them aware of that distinction was vitally important.

"I'm not leaving you now, Genevieve."

Anger flared within her. "Don't you realize that going now gives you your best chance for escape?" she snapped.

"At the cost of destroying the situation we have so carefully constructed around you as Mrs. Maxwell Blake. Were I to suddenly disappear this evening, the authorities would immediately wonder just what the devil 'business matters' were so bloody urgent that your husband had to vanish in the middle of the night like a guilty thief. I might get away, Genevieve, but you would be left to explain my abrupt disappearance, and the situation would be dangerously incriminating for you. It wouldn't take much of a leap of logic to piece together that the missing Maxwell Blake and the elusive marquess of Redmond are the same man. You would be arrested and forced to confess how you have sheltered and protected me these last few weeks."

"Whatever they do to me will not be as terrible as what they are going to do to you, Haydon. They are going to hang you for a crime you didn't commit!"

Fury glittered in her velvet-brown eyes, tinged with a wrenching fear. She stood rigid before him, her chin set with purpose, her hands gripping at the cool silken bell of her evening gown. She looked as if she were ready to do battle with him, with him and anyone else who might come crashing through the door behind him to try to take him away. She was like a lioness in that moment, all fire and courage and determination. She was still trying to protect him, he realized, feeling humbled and distinctly unworthy. She had been trying to protect him from the moment she laid eyes upon him, as if he were one of her wayward urchins that could be saved with kindness and care.

He raised his hand and caressed her cheek with the back of his fingers, telling himself that it would be enough, that he would touch her just so, and no more.

"I cannot let you do it, Genevieve." His voice was rough and steeped in regret. "I cannot permit you to risk destroying your life and the lives of all your children because of a worthless piece of refuse like me."

"You're not worthless—"

"You don't know anything about me," Haydon insisted, silencing her by laying his finger against her mouth. "And if you did, you would regret everything that you have done to help me. There is a stain upon my soul, Genevieve, and nothing I can ever say or do will ever wash it clean." He hesitated a long moment before confessing harshly, "I never deserved to be freed that night from the jail."

She stood trembling before him, imprisoned beneath his touch, though he held her with nothing but the gentleness of his hand upon her cheek and the torment burning in the shadowed blue of his eyes.

"You told me you killed that man in self-defense," she ventured, trying to understand.

He shook his head. "I'm not talking about the scum who attacked me. I did kill one of them out of necessity, and would do so again in an instant. The life I'm talking about was far more precious and innocent than that of a common murderer."

His face was carved in anguish. It pained her just to look upon him, for she could feel his suffering as surely as if she had started to bleed from within. Whatever misdeed he had committed, it was torturing him to the depths of his soul. His jaw was clenched with emotion, as if he feared that if he spoke or otherwise permitted it to relax, he might begin to weep. The knowledge that he could feel such anguish over an act of which he imagined himself responsible told her that whatever it was he had done, it must have been a horrible accident.

And the guilt of it was destroying him.

"It's all right, Haydon," she whispered, reaching out

and wrapping her arms around his enormous shoulders. "It's all right."

He didn't know which surprised him more, the incredible wonder of her granting him forgiveness without even knowing the nature of his sin, or how swiftly his body reacted to hers. She was pressing herself against him, her silky cheek buried against his neck, filling his senses with the sweet floral fragrance of her hair. She held him hard and fast, as if she would absorb his pain and suffer it herself if she could, sharing her compassion and her strength, giving of herself and her seemingly endless ability to nurture and comfort and care. He didn't deserve her. He understood that. He could not name a single act in his useless, self-absorbed existence that merited even a droplet of her tenderness. And yet suddenly he wanted nothing less than all of her. He wanted to cleave her to him so that they could never be separated, wanted her blood to course through his veins and his through hers, wanted their flesh and their souls to be melded as one.

He groaned and crushed his mouth to hers, knowing as he did so that he would not be able to stop, and not giving a damn. He would see her safely home to Inveraray and then he would leave her, not knowing if he would ever return. Until then there was only the softness of her gathered in his arms, with the keen, black cold shimmering on the streets outside and the apricot light of the oil lamps glowing warm upon her skin.

In that moment, she belonged only to him.

He lifted her into his arms and strode toward the bed, aware of the swish of silk and lace as he lowered her onto the feather mattress. He swept his tongue hungrily through the dark heat of her mouth, tasting the sweet tang of champagne. He tore off his jacket and yanked at the stiff fabric of his cravat, anxious to be rid of the bloody thing. It unraveled quickly from his neck and then his shirt followed it onto the floor, baring him to the waist. Genevieve's fingers fumbled at the buttons of his trousers, inadvertently brushing against the hardness of his arousal. She abandoned the buttons to caress him through the finely woven wool, but the sensation of her stroking him through a barrier of fabric was too much to be borne. With a groan Haydon pulled himself away so that he could peel off his trousers and stockings. Finally he stood naked before her, all hard planes and sinewy curves, his body etched in the shadows and light afforded by the bronze ripple of the small fire burning in the hearth and the soft wash of the lamps.

Genevieve stared at him, her eyes flickering with carnal desire, aroused and unashamed. She had opened herself to him before, had lain panting and writhing beneath him as he kissed her and licked her and thrust himself into the deepest recesses of her body. Any virgin sensibilities she might once have cherished were long gone, lost to the tempest of the burning splendor they had already known. She wanted Haydon with a desperate passion, wanted him touching her and covering her and filling her with himself. Soon he would leave her and she would be alone again. She had not understood the depths of her loneliness before, for she was always surrounded by her children and Oliver, Doreen and Eunice, caught in an endless blur of meals and lessons and housework and bills. But Haydon had delved beneath the carefully constructed facade of her hard-won independence. He had opened her heart and filled it with something that was brilliant and glorious and utterly agonizing.

He stretched out beside her and covered her mouth with his while his hands hungrily roamed the silk and steel barriers wrapped around her. It had taken Alice well over an hour to carefully pull and tie and hook Genevieve into the intricate enigma of her gown, corset, crinoline, and petticoats, yet Haydon was expertly versed in the art of freeing her from them. One by one the layers gave way and were tossed upon the floor, until finally she wore only her corset and drawers. Her breasts swelled above the tightly molded constriction of her corset, giving her a lush, wanton appearance, and the fine French lace trimming her drawers had ruffled up to her thighs, at which point the soft opening to the delicate undergarment lay teasingly unguarded. There was a dark sensuality to the fact that she remained clothed in her intimate apparel while he was utterly naked. She could see his desire for her in his magnificent erection and in every hard curve of muscle covering his body. As he stared at her with hunger, she sensed her power over him as the object of his lust.

She rose to her knees and pulled at the pins in her hair, releasing her elegantly arranged coiffure into a glossy cascade of coppery waves. Then she leaned over and placed her hands firmly upon his shoulders, pinning him to the bed as she lowered her mouth to his and swept her tongue inside. Haydon growled with pleasure at her unexpected dominance of him. Emboldened by this, she pulled her mouth away to trail kisses upon the rough skin of his cheek and jaw, then down the thick column of his neck to the massive granite of his chest. She nibbled and swirled her tongue in tiny circles as she explored him, taking the dark medallion of his nipple into her mouth and suckling hard, then grazing across the valley of his chest and teasingly flicking her tongue over the other one. His skin was warm and faintly salty, and he smelled clean and distinctly male, a woodsy, spicy scent that enlivened her senses as she pressed her cheek against the ebony hair on his belly and inhaled deeply. He reached for her and tried to pull her up to him, but she pushed his hands away and boldly continued her forbidden exploration.

She stroked the narrow swath of hair that grew beneath his navel, then brushed her fingers against the black curls surrounding his straining manhood, causing him to flinch and shift restlessly upon the bed. The memory of his previous torture of her came flooding back, and the thought that he might endure the same kind of scorching pleasure that he had inflicted upon her enhanced her desire. Her lips pressed gentle, teasing kisses along the iron muscles of his thighs, which tensed like massive tree trunks as she touched them. Her fingers roved the flesh of his inner thighs, then slid lightly over the rounded ballocks between, causing him to draw a sharp intake of breath. And then her mouth was skimming ever so lightly across the taut length of his arousal, her lips flitting over the warm velvet skin like the wings of a butterfly.

Haydon swore.

Genevieve hesitated, wondering if perhaps she had caused him pain. And then she remembered how desperate she had felt the first time his tongue had flicked into her coral wetness, paradoxically afraid that he would continue and terrified that he would stop.

Aroused by her newly discovered mastery over him, she took his erection in her hand and flicked her tongue across the tip, licking at him as if he were some delectable sweet that had to be slowly savored. Haydon froze, unable to so much as release the breath that was trapped within his chest. She flitted her tongue over him again and again, thoroughly excited by her ability to pleasure him with such intensity. And then she opened her mouth and surrounded him with its hot wetness, causing him to groan in torment and grasp at the rumpled blankets beneath them. Up and down she moved along the throbbing shaft, sucking gently, using her lips and her tongue to pleasure him as her hand caressed his ballocks.

He reached for her thighs, found the opening between the delicately woven linen of her drawers, and his fingers slipped inside her aching cleft. Slick dew seeped over them as he caressed the swollen petals, which were full and slippery from the incredible eroticism of being in control of his pleasure. Genevieve moaned and parted her legs wider, opening herself to his swirling exploration as she sucked and stroked him harder. He pressed a finger deep inside and began to move it in tandem with the rhythm she was inflicting upon him.

Finally she could bear it no longer, for the need to be filled by him was overwhelming. She straddled his hips and positioned herself over him, barely grazing his arousal with her hot, slick wetness. Then she laid her hands flat against his chest and planted herself upon him, sheathing him in silken heat. Haydon groaned and drove his tongue deep into her mouth, tasting her as fully as he could. Genevieve broke the kiss so she could loom over him as he thrust into her, stimulated by the sight of him lying naked beneath her, knowing nothing of the world beyond that moment and the exquisite ecstasy she was giving to him, and he to her.

Haydon gazed up at Genevieve, marveling at her beauty and sensuality. Her hair was spilling over the creamy skin of her shoulders and breasts, which had all but escaped the tight confines of her corset. She had the gorgeously rumpled look of a woman in the throes of passion, and as she stared down at him with smoky eyes, he could see that she was desperately aroused. Unwilling to leave her unfulfilled, he began to stroke the sleek nub of pleasure hidden within the satiny folds between her legs. Her breath disintegrated into frantic little gasps as he filled and caressed her, making him thrust faster as he surrendered himself to her.

He wanted to remain joined to her forever, wanted to spill himself into her and then hold her in his arms and fall asleep and know that she would be there when he wakened. He would make a life with her, he vowed feverishly, filled with long, languid days and passion-filled nights. He would drape her in beautiful gowns and cover her in jewels, not because she needed such fripperies to enhance her natural magnificence, but because she had lived far too much of her life putting herself last, dressing in faded gowns with frayed hemlines, whatever jewels she may once have worn sold to pay for the urgent necessities of food and shelter.

She pressed her hands against the slender contour of her corseted waist and he saw the plain gold wedding band he had placed upon her finger earlier that evening. It was not enough, he thought, for she deserved the most lavish jewels he could afford. But at that moment he could afford nothing. He had been robbed of his life as the marquess of Redmond and was now a common fugitive. His failure to her was absolute. There was nothing more for them but this stolen moment, and he could feel it skidding away from him as ardor gripped him in a fierce embrace.

He wanted to stop, wanted to slow the frenzied thrusts into her beautiful body, wanted to pull away and just hold her against his pounding chest while he regained some semblance of control, but the pleasure surging through him was unbearable. Genevieve cried out suddenly and rocked against him, and he drove himself deep inside her, again and again, releasing his essence into her as he called her name, a cry of reverence and despair.

She collapsed against him, her breath gusting in sweet puffs upon his shoulder. Her hair fell in a tangled web of strawberry-gold silk across his chest, and her body still gripped him tight. He wrapped his arms around her and eased her onto the mattress beside him, then tenderly brushed a strand of hair off her face.

"I cannot leave you, Genevieve," he whispered hoarsely. "Not tonight."

Tears glazed her eyes. And then they began to fall, little silvery drops of pain that leaked down her cheeks and into her hair.

"You will be caught, Haydon," she managed, her voice small and ragged. "You will be caught and you will be hanged. And I won't be able to bear it."

He pulled her into his arms and stroked her hair, trying to soothe her. "If I am to be caught, then I would rather spend my last few hours holding you than fleeing blindly into the darkness. And if I am not to be caught, then I must make sure that you are delivered home safely, and that I have a chance to say good-bye to the children. I don't want them to believe I cared so little for them that I could simply disappear without having at least a few words with them." His voice was rough with anger as he finished, "There have been enough people in their lives who have simply walked away when the time suited them."

"I would make them understand, Haydon," she assured him. "I would make certain that they did not feel betrayed."

He shook his head. "No."

"Why is it so important to you to see them again?"

Shadows veiled his eyes, shadows of pain and regret. He tried to conceal it from her by shrugging his shoulders, acting as if his desire to speak with the children was nothing more than kindness. But Genevieve was not fooled by his pretense.

"Tell me, Haydon," she urged softly. "Please."

He eased his hold on her, turned away and studied the delicate trellis of cracks upon the ceiling, saying nothing. Their bodies cooled and the fire died, eradicating the brilliant heat that had filled the chamber but moments earlier. And just when Genevieve thought that she had clumsily destroyed whatever fragile bond had formed between them, he spoke.

"I had a daughter," he said in a low, halting voice. "I abandoned her. And she killed herself."

He expected her to regard him in horror. He thought she would roll away from him, cocoon herself in a blanket, and spring from the bed. Then she would assault him with questions, demanding to know if he was married, and when was this child born, and how could he possibly have been so cruel? It was no more than he deserved, and utterly understandable for a woman who had devoted her life to rescuing and loving children, all but one of whom were not even tied to her by blood or marriage.

Instead she lay still, silently absorbing what he had told her. And then she reached out and laid her hand upon his chest, pulling herself closer as she pillowed her head upon his shoulder.

"Tell me what happened."

Her voice was gentle and void of condemnation. Her composure bewildered him. Had she not understood what he had said? Or was it that after so many years of looking after troubled children and thieving adults she had learned that life was a painful, messy affair, and that sometimes the choices one faced were invariably cruel and ugly?

She was waiting for him to explain it to her, almost childlike in her trust as she rested her cheek against him. It was this patient calm, so confusing and unexpected, that began to erode the wall he had long built around the subject of Emmaline. She would hate him after she learned the truth, he realized bleakly. She would be horrified by what a cowardly, selfish bastard he was, and she would regret the fact that she had ever tried to help him. *You deserve her contempt,* he told himself savagely. Maybe having her despise him would make it easier for him to leave. It would not affect the powerful feelings he held toward her, but it was certain to vanquish any fondness or respect she might harbor for him. The idea of enduring her hatred cut him to the core. But after everything she had done for him, he felt he at least owed her the courtesy of the truth.

"I wasn't supposed to be the marquess of Redmond," he began, staring at the ceiling. "That dubious honor belonged to my older brother, Edward. He was cosseted and coddled and told that he was going to amount to great things, while I was generally ignored and allowed to get on however I liked. I never gave a damn, because the truth of the matter was, Edward was always cautious and pragmatic, and that was exactly what the future marquess needed to be. So Edward inherited the privilege of managing the family estate and slaving long hours to try to increase his wealth, while I received a relatively handsome monthly allowance with no responsibilities whatsoever.

"I indulged in all the usual things." His mouth tightened with contempt. "Drink, gambling, women. And one of the women whose bed I shared for a brief time was the countess of Bothwell, who had married at eighteen and was insufferably bored with her husband by the tender age of twenty. Our affair lasted a few weeks, when Cassandra was twenty-four, and I was neither the first nor the last of her lovers. But soon afterward, she was most distressed to discover that she was expecting a child, whom she claimed could only have been mine."

Genevieve lay very still, her hand still pressed against the hard wall of his chest.

"There was never any question of her leaving her husband for me. Cassandra may have despised Vincent, but she positively adored her social standing as his wife, and the life he afforded her far surpassed anything I could have given her on my monthly allocation. I was twenty-nine at the time, and was unprepared to accept something as intrusive into my life as a wife for whom I cared nothing, and a child whose very creation had been nothing more than a drunken mishap. So we agreed that Cassandra would bed Vincent immediately and then tell him that the child was his, and they would raise it. It seemed the best solution at the time for all concerned.

"Cassandra gave birth to a little girl, whom she named Emmaline. I heard through the gossipmongers that while Vincent had initially hoped for a boy, he was positively enchanted with his daughter. No one was more surprised by how much he adored her than Cassandra, who found motherhood dull and tedious, despite the fact that she never actually took care of the child herself. Vincent hired the most expensive nurses he could find to care for Emmaline."

"Did you go to see her?"

Haydon shook his head. "My affair with Cassandra was over, and after enduring the misery of her pregnancy and childbirth, Cassandra had no desire to see me. Her prior inability to conceive had given her the notion that she was barren. She was most disappointed to learn that she wasn't."

"But didn't you want to see your daughter?" Genevieve was bewildered by the notion. How could a man like Haydon, who had demonstrated such immense sensitivity and compassion by risking his life for both Jack and Charlotte, not want to see his own child?

He sighed. "The simple fact is that I felt no real tie to my daughter. She was the result of a reckless moment of passion which was over and forgotten in little more than an instant. Cassandra and I broke off our affair, and quite frankly, I was relieved to be free of her. I never saw Cassandra when she was expecting, because she withdrew from all social activities so that no one would see her in her indelicate state. Once Emmaline was born, I was glad to hear that the bairn appeared to be healthy and whole. Beyond that, I believed she would be well cared for by Cassandra and Vincent, and that she would have a happy, privileged life. I felt no claim on her, and had no desire to do anything that might give her cause to question who she was or to upset the life of grandeur and stability to which she had been born. I had drunkenly participated in her conception, but there was no question in my mind that Vincent was her father. By all accounts, he was absolutely devoted to her, and she to him." He paused a moment before adding grimly, "Unfortunately, that became the problem."

Genevieve drew her brows together. "Why?"

"Cassandra continued to indulge in affairs after Emmaline was born, but her choice of suitors narrowed somewhat. She was heavier than she had been prior to her pregnancy, and she had grown even more tempestuous and self-absorbed. Vincent had never been a terribly involved husband, so he let her carry on as she wished. His world was now centered on his business holdings and Emmaline. Cassandra began to drink and mourn the loss of her youth, and gradually she became jealous of her daughter's exceptionally close relationship with Vincent. There were some dreadful fights between her and Vincent. And finally, during one drunken outburst, Cassandra shrieked at her husband that he was not Emmaline's father, and that I was."

Genevieve regarded him in horror. "That must have been terrible for him to hear."

"I imagine it was," Haydon agreed curtly. "But it didn't warrant him rejecting Emmaline like some broken piece of furniture that no longer pleased him. From that point on, he refused to have anything to do with her. Oh, he kept her under his roof and paid for her

clothes and made sure she had ample nurses and gov-
ernesses to see to her upbringing. After all, there were
appearances to be maintained. He couldn't very well
just toss her out onto the street. But he made it clear
that he no longer loved her." He paused for a moment
before bitterly adding, "She was only five years old, for
Christ's sake. How the hell was she supposed to understand?"

Genevieve could sense the anger surging through
him, mingled with despair. It was as if he wanted to
leap from the bed and do battle with someone, anyone,
in the faint hope that he might somehow be able to rec-
tify what had gone so horribly wrong. She laid her hand
soothingly against his chest.

After a long silence, he began to speak again, his
voice rough against the dark stillness. "For a long while,
their secret was confined within the walls of their estate.
I had stopped frequenting their parties and social affairs
years earlier, so I had no idea that Vincent knew that I
was Emmaline's father. But I started to hear stories that
Vincent had grown increasingly engrossed in managing
his investments, and that he and Cassandra were leading
separate lives. There was never any mention of Emmaline
whatsoever. This struck me as peculiar, because before
then everyone had talked about how utterly devoted
Vincent was to his daughter. I didn't ponder it overmuch,
however. I was far too busy finding ways to run through
my allowance before the end of each month, much to
my brother's irritation.

"Then Cassandra suddenly died. There was talk of
her having been pregnant and trying to abort the child,
but the official explanation was simply an undetermined
illness. I attended the funeral. I suppose I felt obligated
to pay my respects because Cassandra and I had once
been lovers, and while Vincent and I had never been
what one might describe as friends, I had certainly been

a guest in his home many times. Beyond that, I was curious to see how Emmaline was faring. I imagined that she must have mourned the loss of her mother, and I wanted to assure myself that she was going to be all right.

"The moment I laid eyes upon her, I knew that something was terribly wrong. She was a beautiful, slight little thing of eight, with pale-blonde hair and dark-blue eyes, just like her mother's. But while Cassandra had once been confident and sparkling with laughter, Emmaline was painfully nervous and quiet and awkward. Of course, her mother had just died, so I scarcely expected her to be brimming with mirth. But when Vincent snarled orders at her, telling her to sit in a corner and stay out of everyone's way, his monumental resentment of her was obvious to everyone. Worse, it was apparent that she was absolutely terrified of him. And that was when I realized that he knew. He knew, and he was punishing her for it. As if she had had any bloody choice in the matter."

The thought of how Emmaline must have suffered pained Genevieve. "What did you do?"

He snorted in disgust. "I left the funeral and got blinding drunk for several weeks. I felt completely helpless, and drinking helped me to forget just how inadequate I was. I could hardly charge into Vincent's home and demand that he turn my daughter, whom I'd never sought out in eight years, over to me. Even if he had agreed, just what the hell did I have to offer her? Everyone would have known that she was my bastard, which would have sentenced her to a life of being an outcast. My income at the time seemed barely enough to sustain my prodigal lifestyle. I knew nothing whatsoever about caring for a child. And so Emmaline was trapped. She was Vincent's prisoner, for him to neglect or torment as he pleased, and I convinced myself that there wasn't a damn thing I could do about it."

Genevieve said nothing.

Haydon interpreted her silence as condemnation. He knew that had she been in his position, she would have done something to rescue Emmaline.

"During my drunken sojourn, my brother died. Poor Edward, who had never been ill a day in his life that I can remember, spent his usual long day at his desk, then rose and dropped like a stone to the floor. He hadn't yet found the time to woo a woman and marry, therefore he had no heirs. And so I was suddenly thrust into the role of marquess of Redmond, with all of the trappings and responsibilities that I had so contentedly left in the capable hands of my brother over the years. I can tell you, it was an unpleasant shock to my relatives, who were convinced that I was going to squander everything that my father and Edward had worked so hard to build. I have several cousins who informed me at the time that they believed themselves to be far better candidates for marquess than I.

"Now that I had money and a title, and was considerably more sober, I decided I could not leave Emmaline at the mercy of Vincent any longer. I went to him and offered to take her and raise her myself. But Vincent flatly refused. He said he had no intention of giving up the daughter everyone believed to be his. To do so would be to make a public declaration that he had been cuckolded and was now giving his wife's bastard to her lover. He told me that he had despised me and Emmaline for years, and that I would now have to live with the knowledge that she belonged to him, to do with as he pleased.

"I argued with him long and hard. I even offered him money in exchange for her. Vincent just laughed.

He didn't care about money. All he cared about was exacting his revenge. He wanted to punish me for bedding his wife and making a child that for five years he had believed to be his own. He wanted to make me suffer with the idea that my daughter had been sentenced to a life of misery beneath his roof and that there wasn't a damn thing I could do about it. Finally I realized that I was, indeed, helpless. I had wealth and the status of my new title. But I had no legal claim upon my own daughter. There was no way for me to prove that she was actually mine by blood. Deciding that I was only making things worse for her by provoking Vincent, I left."

"Did Emmaline know that you had been there?"

"As I stormed out of Vincent's study, I caught a glimpse of her staring at me through the banister, crouched upon the stairs." His expression became tormented. "I'll never forget how small and lost she looked. She seemed so fragile, like a frightened little bird. And I realized that she had heard. She knew that I was her father, but that Vincent owned her. And that I was abandoning her. I wanted to tell her that everything was going to be all right, even though I had little confidence that it would be. But before I could say anything, Vincent came after me, waving his arms like a madman and ordering me out of his home. Emmaline raced up the stairs and disappeared, terrified that Vincent might have seen her. And I felt hopelessly, utterly helpless. I convinced myself that anything I might have said or done at that moment would only cause Emmaline more suffering. So I left."

He fell silent.

Genevieve continued to lie against him, saying nothing.

"The next day she killed herself," he finally whispered hoarsely. "She rose at dawn, rowed herself in a little boat to the center of the magnificent pond Vincent had put in years earlier, and leaped in. One of the gardeners who was just arriving for work saw her as she jumped from the boat. He raced across the lawn, dove into the pond and tried to bring her out, but the water was dark and he couldn't find her." He swallowed thickly. "It was hours before they finally were able to bring her body up. She was dressed in her nightrail, over which she had put on one of Vincent's coats. She needed a coat with deep pockets, you see, because she had gone to the trouble of filling them with heavy stones." His voice was hollow as he finished, "To help drag her down, in case she tried to fight the water as it closed over her."

His suffering was so tearing, Genevieve could no longer bear it. She sat up and grasped his jaw, forcing him to look at her. "It wasn't your fault, Haydon," she told him firmly. "There was nothing you could have done."

"You don't believe that, and neither do I." His tone was harsh. "I shouldn't have left her there. I should have grabbed her and taken her to my carriage and escaped with her. I should have told Vincent to go to bloody hell, and said he would have to kill me to get her back. I should have wrapped her in my arms and held her close and told her that no one was ever going to hurt her again. I should have done something, *anything*, except leave her there. But instead I climbed into my carriage and left her all alone, not understanding how fragile and desperate she was. And because of my stupidity and selfishness and goddamn ineptitude, my little girl jumped into a freezing black pond and drowned." His eyes were filled with raw torment as he finished, "I could have saved her, Genevieve. I could have taken her home and kept her safe. But I made the choice to leave her there, and because of that, she died."

"You didn't know," Genevieve insisted. "And even if you had taken her, Haydon, do you really think Vincent would have merely stood by and let you keep her? He would have either gone after her himself and dragged Emmaline back to his home, or he would have contacted the authorities and had the police forcibly retrieve her, either of which would have been extremely traumatic for a young girl of eight. It was an impossible situation. You had no legal right to her. By leaving her with Vincent, you believed you were doing the only thing you could."

"You had no legal right to Jamie, or Annabelle or Simon or any of the children," Haydon retorted. "Yet you managed to save each of them from a life of misery and destitution—because you were willing to fight for them."

"I did have a legal right to Jamie," Genevieve argued, "because he was my half brother—"

"You couldn't prove that."

"Perhaps not, but everyone accepted it as the truth."

"You had no right to any of the other children."

"It was different, Haydon."

"Tell me how it was goddamn different!" he raged.

"It was different because no one else wanted them." Her voice was low and gentle, a whisper of reason against his helpless fury. "Don't you see, Haydon? You couldn't have Emmaline because Vincent was unwilling to give her up. Maybe if you had had more time, you might have found a way to convince him, or to find some way to blackmail him into giving her to you, or to make him see reason and be more compassionate in his care for her. But there was no time."

He turned away and stared bleakly at the wall.

"How could you possibly have known how desperate she was?" she continued quietly. "You had never even spoken with her. But if you had known, Haydon, if you had had any inkling of the depths of her distress, I know you would have done everything within your power to take her away from Vincent and keep her safe."

He closed his eyes, trying to shut out her words of assurance. He didn't deserve them.

"The first time I saw you, you had been beaten nearly senseless after trying to save Jack from that vicious warder. You were in no condition to fight, yet you tore him off Jack and made him attack you instead. Jack wasn't your responsibility. He wasn't even your friend. He was just a filthy little thief whom nobody cared about. But you refused to stand by and watch him be brutalized, even though you knew you would be beaten and possibly even killed in the process.

"Then when Charlotte was sentenced to prison, you went to Governor Thomson and demanded that he release her. You understood that anyone at the prison might have recognized you, if not your face, then perhaps your voice or some small mannerism. Had you been discovered, you would have been imprisoned and hanged. But the threat of being executed wasn't enough to deter you. You would have died, Haydon, for a girl you had known only a couple of weeks."

"I care for Charlotte," he told her in a rough voice.

"I know you do." She reached out and laid her hand against the hard round of his shoulder. "Enough that you were willing to sacrifice yourself for her, because you felt she wasn't strong enough to survive the harshness of prison. And I know you cared for Emmaline as well. Had you been given more time, you would have found a way to help her. You feel guilty for abandoning her all those years, but until you saw her at Cassandra's funeral, you had believed that she was well and happy. And once you realized that she wasn't, you tried to help her. You didn't succeed in rescuing her from Vincent that day, Haydon, but had you been able, you would have. You just needed more time."

He stared at the wall in silence, contemplating her words. Was it possible, he wondered desperately, that there might be a grain of truth to what she was saying? He wasn't sure. All he knew was that he had laid out the blackest recesses of his soul to her, fully expecting her to recoil from him.

Instead, she was lying against him, caressing his shoulder with her slender fingers as she argued passionately on his behalf.

He turned suddenly and pulled her on top of him. He didn't want to think about any of it anymore. Not Emmaline, or Cassandra, or any of the other spectacular failures of his wasted life. He was a convicted murderer and a fugitive. It was only a matter of days or hours before the authorities realized that he had been in Glasgow that night and began to close in on him. His time with Genevieve was running out, and the realization was so excruciating he didn't think he could bear it. Cradling her face in his hands, he gazed into her eyes.

"Whatever happens to me, Genevieve, there is something you must know."

Her eyes widened slightly as she studied him.

He hesitated. Over the years he had used countless sentimental phrases on the women he had bedded. But none of them could begin to convey the feelings he was experiencing toward her. The day after tomorrow he would leave her. After that he might be caught, or spend the rest of his life trying to stay ahead of the law. He did not know if he would ever see her again. Feeling as if his heart were being torn apart, he gently swept a lock of hair back from her temple.

"There is nothing I would not have done for you,

had there been more time for us. Do you understand? Nothing."

She looked at him, feeling as if she were looking into his very heart and soul.

And then she crushed her mouth to his and kissed him deeply, holding him fast as her tears began to fall against the dark roughness of his cheeks.

Chapter Twelve

'VE PACKED A WEE LUNCH FOR YE." EUNICE
handed Haydon a colossal bundle wrapped in a blazing
red cloth. "I know ye canna go for long without a wee
bite."

Haydon stared in disbelief at the bulky package,
which looked as if it could have fed the entire household for a week. "Thank you, Eunice." He had no idea
how he was going to pack it.

"Surely ye're nae thinkin' of leavin' behind this fine
evening coat and trousers," objected Oliver, running his
gnarled hand over the woolen fabric of the garments
still hanging in the wardrobe. "They're scarcely worn."

"You may have them, Oliver." Haydon pulled a
shirt and waistcoat out of his bag in a vain attempt to
make room for Eunice's food. "I doubt I shall be at-
tending any evening affairs for a while."

Oliver chuckled. "An' just where would I be
wearin' such a fancy set?"

"Wear it around the house," Haydon suggested.
"You'll be the best-dressed butler in Inveraray."

"It's a wee bit big," Oliver observed doubtfully.

"I can fix that, Ollie," Doreen assured him. "A nip

here and a tuck there, and ye'll be as bonnie as a prince."

"Ye think so?" The idea intrigued him. He slipped the jacket off its wooden hanger and pulled it over his wizened frame, then looked in amazement at how far the sleeves flapped below his fingers. "I'm thinkin' it'll have to be more than a wee nip and tuck."

"Are ye sure ye have to go now, laddie?" fretted Eunice. "I dinna think Miss Genevieve understood that ye intended to take yer leave while she was out. She's certain to be upset that she missed saying good-bye to ye."

Haydon kept his expression neutral. "It's better this way."

He and Genevieve had returned from Glasgow late the previous evening and had spent the night passionately entwined in her bed. Haydon had risen well before dawn and retired to his own chamber. That morning they had greeted the children and elders in the dining room and regaled them over breakfast with tales of Glasgow and the dazzling success of Genevieve's premier exhibition. It had been a moment filled with happiness and warmth, tempered only by the knowledge that Haydon would soon leave.

After breakfast Genevieve had gone to meet with Mr. Humphries at the bank, to work out the details of the first payment she was going to make from the sale of her paintings. She had asked Haydon to accompany her but he had declined, explaining vaguely that he had some other matters to attend to. She had regarded him uncertainly, no doubt fearing that he was going to depart in her absence.

He had smiled and told her not to be gone too long, as if he meant to see her upon her return.

It had pained him to mislead her like that. But he had already watched her suffer deeply over the past three nights, and he had no desire to put her through any more torment than what she had already endured. It was better this way, he told himself. It would be hard enough to say good-bye to the children and Oliver, Eunice and Doreen, without having Genevieve there as well. Once he had bid them farewell, he would go down and board the coach for Edinburgh. He had instructed Genevieve to tell people that her husband was on his way to France by way of Edinburgh and London. He would book his fare and travel to Edinburgh first, so that there would be evidence that Maxwell Blake had indeed gone there.

Once in Edinburgh he would shed the identity that had become so comfortable for him and head back north to Inverness.

His only hope of reclaiming his previous life and not spending the rest of his days as a fugitive was to find out who had hired those men to kill him on that fateful night. Once he had done so, he would have to prove to the authorities that he had been the victim of a failed murder plot. He had already been working out a list of who might have reason to want him dead.

The possibilities were frustratingly numerous.

He had bedded scores of women during his life, many of whom were married at the time, so there was a bevy of disgruntled husbands out there who might well prefer to see him nailed into a coffin. Victor, of course, was one of them, but he had already had his revenge on Haydon by destroying Emmaline, so Haydon did not consider him a likely candidate. Add to the husbands the ladies themselves, some of whom had been less than pleased when their affair with Haydon came to an end, and the possibilities became overwhelming. Then there was a parade of his cousins, aunts, uncles, and other vaguely attached relatives, all of whom had shuddered with fear when he had inherited the title of marquess of

Redmond. They had quite rightly worried that he would quickly lose the Redmond holdings to drink, gambling, and his complete lack of interest in business matters. In fact, he had spent much of the last two years after Emmaline's death in a drunken haze, burning his way through as much of his fortune as possible. Surely that had to infuriate his cousin Godfrey, a pompous little arse who was all polished and ready to inherit the title should anything happen to Haydon. He doubted Godfrey was capable of murder himself, but buying the services of someone else to carry out the task seemed eminently plausible.

When he returned to Inverness, he would begin by focusing his investigation on him.

"Here now, ye're squashin' my buns," complained Eunice, watching as Haydon tried without success to cram the victuals into his bag. "Why don't ye just put yer food in another case?"

"I may have to move quickly, and I can't be burdened with two pieces of luggage." Haydon withdrew yet another shirt and a pair of trousers from his valise, then squeezed Eunice's precious lunch in and buckled the straining case closed. "There."

Doreen regarded him glumly. "All set, then?"

He nodded.

"Come on, then, laddie." Oliver shrugged out of Haydon's evening coat and carefully hung it back inside the wardrobe. "I'll leave this coat here for ye, in case ye ever find yerself back this way an' needin' it again. Can't say I fancy black much anyway—makes me look like a corpse." He closed the wardrobe door and leaned against it a moment, as if he were trying to coax the errant door to stay shut. "Ye will try to come back to her, won't ye, lad?" he demanded quietly.

"Once I succeed in clearing my name, Oliver, nothing will keep me away," Haydon vowed.

Oliver absorbed this a moment, then nodded. "I'll try to fix this door for ye while yer gone." He gave the door a final push, then turned away as it stubbornly crept back open. "Now, let's go down and have ye say yer good-byes to the children afore I drive ye to yer coach."

THE CHILDREN WERE SEATED ROUND A LITTLE FIRE IN the drawing room, watching in fascination as Jack showed them pictures of ships from the book that Genevieve had given him.

". . . and this one is a Spanish galleon," he said, pointing to a painting of a splendid ship with its sun-bleached sails puffed and taut as they harnessed a powerful wind. "They were used by the Spanish for war and exploring. They needed lots of room in the belly of the ship, so they could cram it with gold and silver and jewels to take back to Spain."

Jamie frowned. "Wouldn't all that gold and silver make the ship sink?"

"Not a ship like this," Jack assured him. "The only thing that could sink her would be if she ran aground during a storm, or if pirates blasted a hole in her hull while trying to rob her of her riches."

"How could they steal her riches if they sank her to the bottom of the ocean?" wondered Grace.

Jack shrugged. "I guess they would try to move them onto their own ship before she sank."

"That doesn't seem like a very sound plan," objected Simon. "It would take a long time to move chests of gold from one ship to another. They might find themselves sinking into the ocean with her."

Jack furrowed his brow in frustration. Why were they all so obsessed with the cargo? Weren't they impressed by how beautiful the ship itself was? "I suppose most of the time the pirates got the riches off before they sank the ship," he theorized, trying to be patient. "Now, if you look over here—"

"And then they would bury it on some remote, deserted island where no one could ever find it," Annabelle exclaimed. "Then the evil pirate captain would take his sword and skewer everyone who knew where it was buried, so that the secret would die with him." She grabbed the poker from the hearth and lunged at Simon, pretending to run him through. "Die, you black-hearted knave!"

"That's completely daft," objected Grace. "What good were all those riches if they were stuck in the ground?"

"They could always go back for it later, if they really needed it," Jamie decided. "You know, if they were having trouble with the bank."

"But suppose the pirate captain forgot where he had put it?" wondered Charlotte. "Or what if he died before he could go back and dig it up?"

"They always made a treasure map," Annabelle informed her. "And it would be found years later by a brave, handsome captain who would take the treasure home to his beautiful, sick wife, thinking now that they were rich he could buy her the medicine she needed to save her life." She tossed the poker to Simon, then raised the back of her hand to her forehead and swooned theatrically against the cushions. "Except it's too late," she continued, her voice breathy and fragile. "He returns home to find her dying, and all he can do is give her a final kiss before she closes her eyes and fades away, leaving him alone to mourn her forever with a chest of riches and a broken heart." She sighed and closed her eyes, her hands prettily clasped over her chest. "I think that would be a wonderful part for me to play—don't you?" she demanded, bolting upright again.

" 'Tis a fairy yarn if ever I heard one," sniffed Doreen, shaking her head as she entered the room. "More like the rogue would be off the next day wastin' his fortune on gambling, fancy drink, and low women."

"Hush now, Doreen, ye mustn't fill the duckies' wee heads with such twaddle," chided Eunice. "Here, sweetlings, have a biscuit."

Jack eyed Haydon suspiciously as the children flocked around Eunice. He had seen him drop his leather valise near the front door. "Are you goin' somewhere?"

"Yes."

"Where?" chirped Jamie, excited by the prospect.

Haydon hesitated. He did not want to lie to them. But there was risk to revealing the truth. If Constable Drummond grew suspicious of his absence before Genevieve declared her husband dead, he might decide to pay a visit and question the children about the whereabouts of their supposed stepfather. One of them might accidentally divulge that Haydon had planned to return to Inverness.

"I am taking the coach to Edinburgh." That part was true, at least. "I have some matters to attend to there."

Jack arched a skeptical brow. "When will you return?"

"I'm not certain."

"You mean you're not returning." His tone was flat.

Simon regarded Haydon in shock. "You're leaving us?" He sounded wounded.

"Don't you like it here?" demanded Jamie, his mouth rimmed with sugary crumbs.

A helpless feeling began to seep over Haydon. He didn't want to leave. But he had no choice. How could he possibly make them understand?

"There was a problem in Glasgow. Someone there recognized me. It is too dangerous for me to stay here any longer."

"But Glasgow is so far away," protested Charlotte, her small face pale. Haydon sensed that of all the children, she was the one who would suffer his absence the most. "No one from Glasgow ever comes here."

"Charlotte is right," said Annabelle. "I don't think you need to worry about that."

"I'm afraid it isn't that simple," Haydon replied.

He seated himself beside Charlotte and wrapped his arm around her, holding her close as he tried to make the children understand. "The person who recognized me is certain to tell other people about it, and he will mention the fact that I was with Genevieve at the time. The authorities will come here to question her. If they find me here, living under the guise of being Genevieve's husband and your stepfather, they may arrest her as well."

A glint of fear crept across their faces. He cursed himself. He did not want to frighten them. But he wanted them to understand that he wasn't leaving because he wanted to, but because he had no choice.

"From the moment I arrived here, that has always been a risk. For a while it was a risk we were willing to take, because I had to regain my strength and be well enough to travel. Now that I have healed, it is a risk I can no longer justify. It is time for me to go."

The children regarded him in dejected silence. It was obvious that they were well versed in abandonment. They had each suffered many betrayals during the course of their short lives. First by the parents who created them, then by the families who were unable or unwilling to care for them, and finally by a social system that viewed them as little more than refuse that should be locked away in prison and reformatory schools so that the rest of society could be spared the sight of their misery.

The only person who had been relentlessly steadfast and true and faithful to them from the moment she came into their lives was Genevieve.

"Are you going to come back to us?" ventured Jamie.

Haydon hesitated. He wanted to say yes. But the children had suffered enough false hope and feeble promises in their lives. He would make no assurances that he could not keep.

A sudden pounding at the door prevented him from answering.

Oliver cocked a white brow at Haydon. "Shall I answer it?"

Haydon's mind began to race. He didn't think anyone could have heard Rodney's story, made the connection that Maxwell Blake was in fact the marquess of Redmond, and traveled all the way from Glasgow to Inveraray to inform the authorities here. It was within the realm of possibility, but given the time constraints and travel involved, it seemed extremely unlikely.

He nodded. "Go ahead."

"Give an old man a minute," Oliver snapped as the banging on the door continued. He shuffled over and opened it a little, grumbling irritably, "What in the name of all the saints can be so important that ye feel ye should be breakin' down my—"

"We're here for the marquess," snarled an enormous, heavyset police officer with a greasy hank of gray hair leaking out from under his hat. The tarnished buttons of his uniform looked as if they were about to blast from his coat with his next breath of air.

"We know he's in here," added the stocky police constable next to him. He was an ugly brute, with a battered, flat nose and flared nostrils that made him resemble a pig.

"Let us in and there'll be no trouble." This dubious assurance came from a skinny young constable with a rat's nest of red hair and a profusion of pimples dotting his pale complexion.

"I dinna ken what ye're blatherin' about." Oliver idly scratched his head as he blocked their entrance with his scrawny frame. "There's no marquess here. Ye lads must have the wrong—"

"Move aside, ye bloody old fool!" The bear-framed officer heaved his shoulder into the door, sending poor Oliver reeling backward as the constables stormed into the house.

"Oliver!" cried Doreen, watching in horror as he crashed into the hall table and fell to the floor. Blood began to trickle down his forehead.

"Goddamn bastard!" raged Jack. He flew at the beefy policeman and attacked him with his fists.

"Jack—no!" shouted Haydon, bolting forward. "Stop!"

Jack landed a powerful blow squarely in the constable's face before the remaining two officers grabbed him by his shoulders and tore him away. The lad responded by sinking his teeth deep into the wrist of the one with the pig face.

"Help!" the constable squealed, whacking Jack on the shoulders as he tried to disengage his mangled wrist. "Ewan—help!"

"Get off him!" The pimply constable grabbed Jack by his hair and roughly jerked his head back. Once he had pulled him off, he wrenched Jack's arms behind his back. "Are ye all right, Harry?"

"Christ, the pissing little turd bit me like a wild animal!"

"How about you, George?"

"That wee shit broke my nose!" George raged.

"I'm going to rip his goddamn ballocks off!" Harry drew back his fist to pound Jack in the face.

"Take your hands off him," commanded Haydon savagely, "or I'll smash your friend's skull like a ripe melon."

Slowly, everyone turned to see Haydon standing in the center of the hallway, brandishing directly over George's head the brass poker that Annabelle had wielded during her swordplay.

"Let the lad go," Haydon ordered curtly. "Now."

The two constables holding Jack regarded each other uncertainly.

"For Christ's sake, do as he says!" shouted George, who was cradling his profusely bleeding nose, and had no particular desire to be bleeding from his head as well.

"We'll let him go," Harry relented, "if ye drop yer weapon."

"It's useless tryin' to escape," Ewan added, sensing Haydon's hesitation. "All of Inveraray knows who ye really are, yer lordship," he drawled sarcastically. "Ye canna get away."

Haydon felt his grip on his primitive weapon tighten. *It's over,* he realized, not quite able to accept it.

"Don't do it!" Jack was squirming wildly against his captors. "Just go!"

Haydon looked at the frightened faces of the children, who were clearly traumatized by the display of brutality they had just witnessed. All but Jack, who had not yet spent enough time away from the savagery of the streets to be intimidated by it.

No more, Haydon thought, staring with heartbreaking fondness at Jamie, Annabelle, Grace, Simon, and sweet little Charlotte. *I cannot put them through any more.*

"I will have your word," he began in a low, steady

voice, "that if I go with you willingly, you will leave the others here unharmed."

"No!" Jack pleaded. "Don't do it!"

"Fine," snapped George, whose hands were now dripping with the blood still pouring from his nose. "Drop yer weapon, and we'll just leave—with you."

Haydon felt the smooth brass rod in his palm grow warm. He had no choice, he realized grimly. He would have died rather than see harm come to any of his family. He savored the bittersweet taste of near-freedom barely a moment longer.

And then he dropped the poker.

"Got ye," snarled Harry, pouncing on him like a tiger on its prey. "Come on, Ewan, put the manacles on his wrists so he can't try anything."

The pimply youth gave Jack's arms a final painful wrench before he shoved him forward. Jack cast him a look of pure loathing, then went and knelt down before Oliver.

"Are you all right?" he demanded anxiously, dabbing at Oliver's bloodied forehead with his sleeve.

"Dinna worry about me, lad." Oliver's gaze was sober. " 'Tis his lordship we need to be worryin' about."

"I'll be fine." Haydon forced himself to appear calm as his hands were manacled behind his back.

"Sure ye will," sneered George, who was holding his arm against his nose in a clumsy effort to stanch the flow of blood. "Fine and dead."

Eunice gasped and pulled Jamie, Grace, and Charlotte tighter against her, while Doreen held fast to Annabelle and Simon. Charlotte began to cry.

"Shut your mouth," Haydon intoned softly to George, "or I'll smash in that skull of yours yet."

"That would be a pretty fancy trick, yer lordship,"

said George, sniffing against his sodden sleeve, "since ye're the one wearin' the manacles."

Haydon regarded him with dark fury, saying nothing.

"For God's sake, George, let's just get him in the carriage and go," said Harry, who was still nursing his mutilated wrist. "I need a bloody drink."

"Come on, then." Ewan shoved Haydon toward the door.

Haydon took one last look at the horror-stricken faces of the family he had come to love. There was much he wanted to say to them, but suddenly there was no time. Beyond that, any words of affection in front of the police would only incriminate them. And so he just gave them a brief, reassuring smile.

Then he turned and permitted himself to be shoved down the stairs and into the carriage waiting for him on the street.

B LACK SMOKE WAFTED IN SOOTY PLUMES ABOVE THE rooftops, weaving a shadowy veil against the leaden winter sky. The day had suddenly grown cold, and people were trying to ward off the advancing chill by tossing more precious wood and coal onto their fires. Genevieve quickly mounted the steps to her home, anxious to tell Haydon about her meeting with Mr. Humphries, the bank manager.

It had gone exceptionally well. Mr. Humphries was delighted to hear of her husband's good fortune regarding his commission on the sale of Monsieur Boulonnais's work. He was even more elated by the check Genevieve had presented to him. As the money from the sale of her paintings continued to flow in, she would eventually be able to pay off all her loans and use her earnings to support her family. Perhaps she could even afford a few special treats for the children as well. They all could do with new clothes and shoes, and there were a number of books that she wanted to purchase for their studies. She lifted the latch and hurried inside, trying not to think about the unbearable fact that Haydon would be leaving shortly. She did not want that to destroy what little time they had left together.

One look at the raw noses and scarlet-rimmed eyes of Eunice and Doreen told her that something terrible had happened.

"What is it?" she demanded abruptly, fighting to bridle her fear.

"He's gone, lass." Oliver looked old and defeated as he took her slim hand into his. "We did everythin' we could, but 'twas no use."

Genevieve stared at him blankly. "Haydon left— without saying good-bye?"

"Poor lad didn't have the chance." Eunice blew her nose noisily into her handkerchief. "Those nasty constables just shoved their way in here and dragged him out the door."

No, she thought, feeling as if her heart had been torn from her chest. *Please, God, no.*

"I tried to keep them out, lass." Oliver's aged face was twisted with remorse. "But I couldna fight the three of them. Like giants, they were, and twice as fierce!"

It was her fault, she realized bleakly. She should have made Haydon leave the minute he had been recognized in Glasgow. She should have threatened to report him to the police herself if he didn't go. Instead she had permitted him to stay with her, had permitted him to lie naked with her at night and accompany her back to Inveraray, because deep in her heart she had not been ready to give him up.

She had been a fool. A selfish, stupid fool.

"Miserable bleedin' buggers," swore Doreen in a scathing tone. "Pushed poor Oliver to the floor and cracked open his head."

"Our Jack attacked the lout who done it." Eunice dabbed at her eyes with her crumpled handkerchief. "Then the three of them started to give the poor lad a thrashing."

"So Haydon took the poker and vowed to smash the skull of the biggest bugger if they didn't unhand the lad." Oliver regarded her miserably. "He went with them quietly then, after makin' them promise that they would leave the rest of us be. He didn't want to see any of us hurt."

No, of course not. Genevieve remembered how Haydon had fought so valiantly to help Jack the night she had found him lying broken and bleeding in prison. Haydon would never stand by and watch someone else suffer. It didn't matter if it meant he would be beaten nearly to death himself.

Or led away to be hanged.

She grabbed on to the nearest chair, feeling as if she was going to be sick.

"Here, lass, sit down, ye're white as chalk," said Eunice, pulling Genevieve over to the sofa. "Doreen, be a love and fetch Miss Genevieve a glass of water. I fear the shock is too much for her."

"I'm fine," Genevieve murmured. The floor beneath her was roiling and the room had suddenly gone blazingly hot and white. She closed her eyes and sank down onto the sofa, resting her cheek against the chilled wool of her cloak. Gone. Haydon was gone. And now he would be hanged. She had heard horrible tales about how a person suffered when they were hanged. How their bodies wrenched and jerked about as they struggled helplessly for air. About how their faces turned hideous colors. She thought of Haydon, so handsome and strong and powerful, dangling helplessly at the end of a rope, fighting to fill his lungs with air.

An agonized sob escaped her lips.

"Hush, now, take a wee sip of this," soothed Eunice, easing Genevieve up so that she could drink from the glass of water.

Genevieve obediently sipped at the cool liquid.

"There now, that's better." Eunice wrapped her plump arm around Genevieve and pulled her head onto the soft pillow of her plentiful bosom. " 'Tis just the shock, lass, that's makin' ye feel so ill. Give it a moment and it will pass."

Genevieve leaned against Eunice, drawing comfort from the warm roundness of her as she held her tight.

"If only he'd had a wee bit more time," Doreen reflected sadly, "perhaps he might have been able to learn who set those ruffians upon him that night. Then this whole bleedin' mess could have been cleared up."

Had Constable Drummond and his forces been interested in doing their job, they would have made some effort to find the other men who attacked Haydon, Genevieve reflected bitterly. But because Haydon had not reported the crime himself, he had been condemned as a drunken murderer from the moment of his arrest. The authorities had no interest in trying to unearth the truth. A man was dead, and all they wanted to do was assure the frightened public that they had captured and executed the villain responsible. The scum who assaulted Haydon had failed in their attempt to kill him that night. Now the justice system would finish their work for them.

It wasn't right, she reflected, feeling anger suddenly surge through her. And she was not going to just stand by and let it happen.

"Oliver, please bring the carriage around," she said, extricating herself from the shelter of Eunice's embrace. "We're going to the prison."

Oliver regarded her with concern. "Seein' him again is only going to make ye suffer even more than ye already are, lass. I dinna think—"

"Lord Redmond isn't guilty of murder, Oliver," Genevieve interrupted. "I'm not going to let them hang him for a crime he didn't commit."

"But how will ye be able to stop them?" asked Eunice. "His sentence has already been passed by the court."

"I don't believe the court understood all the facts surrounding Haydon's case, because it went to trial so quickly. I shall speak to the judge and ask him to delay the execution on the grounds that we can provide new evidence in Lord Redmond's defense."

Oliver frowned. "And what new evidence might that be?"

"I don't know yet," Genevieve acknowledged. "But at least if we gain some time, we can do some investigating—starting right here in Inveraray. Someone must know something about the men who attacked him that night. I intend to find out who those men were and why they wanted to kill Haydon."

GOVERNOR THOMSON WAS SITTING AT HIS DESK WITH a pair of silver scissors in hand, poised to trim an obstinate strand off his otherwise impeccably manicured beard.

"Where is he?" Genevieve demanded, throwing open the door to his office.

Startled, his hand jerked, causing a gray shower of hair to fall onto the polished surface of his desk.

"Look what you did!" he cried, staring at the

amputated hairs in dismay. He held his elegant hand mirror close to the damaged area and gasped. "You made me cut a wedge in my beard!"

"Where is he?" Genevieve repeated coldly.

Governor Thomson stared forlornly at his reflection, raking his fingers through his remaining hair to see if it could be coaxed to cover up the crudely chopped gap. "Who?"

"You know very well who. Kindly take me to see Lord Redmond immediately."

He regarded her in complete bewilderment. "Lord Redmond?"

She could not understand why he was being so obtuse. "He was arrested this morning. I want to see him to assure myself that he has not been mistreated in any way, and I promise you that if I find he has been—"

"I'm afraid there must be some mistake, Mrs. Blake," Governor Thomson interrupted, laying down his mirror. "There have been no new prisoners brought here today."

"Of course there have," she insisted. "The marquess of Redmond was captured over two hours ago."

"Really?" He looked genuinely intrigued. "By whom?"

"By three police officers—I don't know their names. They must have brought him here."

Governor Thomson shook his head. "No prisoner is put into a cell without my direct authority. I have been here since seven o'clock this morning, and he has not been brought to me."

Genevieve frowned. "If he is not here, then where would the officers have taken him?"

"I can assure you that if a dangerous fugitive such as Lord Redmond had been captured, he would have been brought here and locked up forthwith."

"But he was captured—"

"How do you know?"

She stopped, suddenly uneasy. If the police had arrested Haydon, then why hadn't he been delivered here directly?

"Where is Constable Drummond?" she asked, deciding that Governor Thomson was obviously ill-informed. Constable Drummond had been leading the search for Haydon. Surely he would know about the officers who had descended upon her house that morning.

"I'm afraid you just missed him," he replied, picking up his mirror once again. "He was testifying at a trial in the courthouse, and stopped by afterward to discuss how the search for Lord Redmond is faring. Constable Drummond has been in contact with the police forces in both Glasgow and Edinburgh, as he believes the marquess may not be in Inveraray at all, but has likely escaped to—"

No, thought Genevieve, shutting out Governor Thomson's ramblings.

Like giants, they were, and twice as fierce.

Oliver hadn't said he recognized the police constables. But it didn't make sense that he wouldn't have recognized at least one of them. After all, Oliver had been a criminal in and about Inveraray for his entire life. He had been arrested and imprisoned numerous times over the years, and had made acquaintance with most, if not all, of the men who comprised its police force. Moreover, if Constable Drummond was leading the investigation to find Haydon, how could he possibly not have known about the raid on Genevieve's home? Even if he hadn't been aware of it beforehand, why hadn't he been informed by now?

Terror surged through her as the answer became horribly clear.

"—therefore he is preparing to travel to Glasgow

himself tomorrow, to investigate whether any of these reported sightings might be reliable. . . ."

Governor Thomson blinked in confusion as Genevieve tore from his office, leaving him alone to contemplate the debacle of his ridiculously clipped beard.

Chapter Thirteen

ENEVIEVE'S MIND WAS REELING AS SHE AND Oliver raced into the house. Haydon had been abducted. And he was going to be killed.

Unless he was already dead.

No, she thought, fighting the despair slashing at the frayed thread of her composure. *He is alive. He has to be.*

"Thank the Lord, ye're back," cried Eunice, wringing her handkerchief as she hurried toward them. Annabelle, Grace, Charlotte, and Simon were seated in the drawing room, their faces pale and grave. "Are the lads with ye?" Eunice demanded anxiously.

Genevieve's chest tightened until she could scarcely breathe. "What do you mean?"

"Jack and Jamie have disappeared," explained Doreen. "The children say Jack dashed out the kitchen door as those blackguards were takin' his lordship away, and Jamie took off after him. The last they saw of them, they were both running down the street in the direction the carriage had gone."

"We thought ye'd surely have found them hangin' about the prison," added Eunice.

Genevieve stared at the children, torn between fury

and fear. "Why didn't you children tell Oliver the minute Jack and Jamie were gone?"

"Jack made us swear not to." Simon looked close to
tears.

"He said that Oliver would only try to stop him,"
explained Annabelle in a small, contrite voice, "and that
if Oliver tried, then he would have to knock him to the
ground."

"He didn't want to hurt Oliver," Charlotte quickly
interjected, lest anyone misconstrue Jack's intentions.
"Jack would never hurt any of us—it's just that he was
most determined not to lose sight of the carriage that
was taking Haydon away."

"He didn't know Jamie was following him when he
set out," Grace added miserably. "But Jamie just bolted
after him and disappeared."

"We know it was wrong, Genevieve." A tear leaked
down Simon's cheek. "But we didn't see how we could
tell anyone that Jamie was gone and not have you find
out that Jack had run off as well."

" 'Twas only after Eunice and I had called the children down for their tea that we realized the boys were
missin'," finished Doreen. "By then they were long
gone. We thought ye'd just find them outside the prison
and bring them home."

"The carriage didn't go to the prison," Oliver told
her.

Eunice's plump face puckered in confusion. "Then
where did those police constables take him?"

"We don't know." His expression was grim. "No
one at the prison knew anything about the lad's arrest."

"But those police—"

"They weren't police constables," said Genevieve.

"Then who were they?"

"I don't know. All I know is they mean to kill
Haydon."

"Sweet Saint Columba!" swore Doreen. "And the boys have gone after them!"

Genevieve sank into a chair. They could be any-where, she realized, feeling as if she were drowning. A street or two away—or gone from Inveraray completely. If Jack and Jamie were discovered by Haydon's captors, they would be killed. She squeezed the heels of her hands against her eyes until they throbbed, fighting the tears that were threatening to spill from them. *I must not cry. I must not scream. I have to remain focused and think. How am I going to find them?*

"Dinna fear, now, lass," Oliver was saying as he laid a stiff hand upon her shoulder. "We'll find them. They couldn't have kept up with the carriage, so 'tis more likely that they ran until they were winded and are now walkin' back. I'll just take the carriage and go lookin'—"

The front door crashed open and Jack and Jamie staggered inside, gasping greedily for air.

"Haydon's in trouble," Jack rasped breathlessly. He hunched over and inhaled several hoarse breaths, fight-ing to replenish his lungs.

"We have to help him!" Jamie's little face was red and streaked with grime, and his trousers were filthy and torn at one knee.

With a cry Genevieve threw her arms around him, burying her face in his hair as she fought to harness her wildly fluctuating emotions. He smelled cold and sharp, and his hair was damp from exertion. He was safe. And so was Jack.

Thank you, God.

She kissed the top of Jamie's head, then wrapped her arms tightly around Jack.

Jack stood awkwardly as Genevieve held him, be-wildered by her unexpected demonstration of affection. He could not recall anyone ever embracing him so.

"We have to go after him, Genevieve," he said urgently, wondering why she was clasping him so tightly. "Those men who took him weren't the police." Had she thought that he had run away? he wondered. Even if he had, why would that make her hug him? He dismissed the question, determined to concentrate on Haydon. "We have to get him out of there!"

She broke her embrace and regarded him seriously. "Do you know where they have taken him?"

He nodded. "We followed the carriage to Devil's Den."

"That's where all the thieves and whores live," explained Jamie excitedly. "Jack told me so."

"Not only thieves and whores, though there's enough of them livin' there, to be sure," Oliver agreed. "There's mostly a rough type there, who love nothin' more than a drink and a brawl to help 'em forget the misery of their lives. I've lived there from time to time myself," he confessed, "when I was a wee bit down on my luck."

"So have I." Jack's gray eyes glittered with barely suppressed fury. "It's a place where you can beat your wife or child half to death and no one gives a bloody damn. They just bang on the walls and shout at you to stop makin' so much noise while you do it."

"That's why they've taken him there, most like," mused Doreen worriedly. "That way they can do their dirty business and no one will give them any mind—even in that crowded hellhole."

"Haydon was staggering when they pulled him out of the carriage," Jack continued. "They had taken off their uniforms so no one would notice them, and they pretended Haydon was drunk and that they were helpin' him to walk. I could see that his hands were still manacled—it looked like they had beaten him bad."

"He must have gotten in a few blows as well,"

added Jamie fiercely, "because the others didn't look so good either."

"Why bother to take him to Devil's Den?" Oliver scratched his head, thinking. "If ye're set on murderin' someone, why not just take him to the countryside and sink a knife in his belly or put a pistol to his head? That way ye can leave the body in the woods and ride away, clean and easy."

"I don't think they're plannin' to kill him right away," Jack speculated. "As they were draggin' him into a building, the big one swore at the others because Haydon was bleedin' and could hardly walk. He said something about havin' to keep him alive long enough for his lordship to see him."

Oliver frowned. "Who do they mean?"

"Whoever it is, it must be the man who wants Haydon dead," Genevieve decided. "That's why Haydon was attacked the first night he came to Inveraray. He told me he was too drunk to see the faces of his assailants clearly. The three men who came to the house today pretending to be the police may well be the same three who attacked him and then ran off that night after he killed their accomplice. It seems they have been hired by someone to kill Haydon. Perhaps they are under orders to show him to their employer before they can finish the job."

"We must tell the police straightaway," Eunice decided. "They can go to Devil's Den and get his lordship out."

Genevieve shook her head. "Constable Drummond has no interest in proving Haydon's innocence. All he wants to do is find him and make sure that this time nothing interferes with his hanging." She briskly pulled on her gloves. "Jack, I want you to show Oliver and me where they have taken Haydon. I'll find a way to get him out of there."

Oliver, Eunice, and Doreen stared at her, aghast.

"Have ye completely taken leave o' yer senses, lass?" demanded Oliver, scowling.

"A fine lady like yerself, traipsin' about Devil's Den looking for a pack of cutthroats?" Eunice looked horrified by the notion.

"Why, ye'll be lucky not to be robbed and killed yerself afore ye come anywhere near to where those black dogs are hiding his lordship!" finished Doreen.

"I'll take that chance," Genevieve replied evenly.

"Now, lass, ye're nae thinkin' clearly," Oliver chastised, gentling his voice. "I know ye'd be willing to do anythin' for the lad, but if ye go marchin' into Devil's Den and get yerself robbed and killed, ye'll nae have done anyone any good, now will ye? Best to let me and Jack go after the lad. I'm sure between the two of us we can get him out of there."

"A bent old man and a scrawny lad against three savage murderers?" Doreen snorted in disbelief. "Unless they laugh themselves to death, ye'll do naught except get yerselves killed. I'll go with ye—at least then they'll have three of us to contend with. After a lifetime of dealin' with drunken louts in a tavern, I know a thing or two about crackin' heads together!"

"I'll go as well," offered Eunice. "After all, another pair of eyes canna hurt."

"I want to go too." Grace leaped up suddenly from the sofa. "When I was picking pockets I spent some nights in Devil's Den. I know my way about, and I'll be able to look around the building without making anyone suspicious."

"Absolutely not," Genevieve said flatly.

Grace raised her chin in defiance. "Why can Jack go and not me?"

"Jack is older."

"Jack is only fourteen, and I'm nearly thirteen," Grace argued.

"I'm almost fifteen," retorted Jack. "That's a lot older than twelve."

"Well, having someone younger with you will help you look less suspicious," Grace amended, shifting her tactics. "We could pretend to be a family looking for a place to live. No one would find that strange—I could put together some outfits that would make us all look poor and wretched."

"Ye know, that's not a bad idea." Oliver stroked his grizzled chin, considering Grace's plan. "If we go as a group, we need to look as if we belong there, so folk are less likely to bother us with questions."

"If Grace is going then so am I," declared Annabelle. "Grace and I do everything together."

"And I want to go as well," said Charlotte.

"No." Jack's voice was hard.

Charlotte looked injured. "Just because I tripped the last time doesn't mean I'll do it again, Jack. Haydon helped me when I needed him, and now I want to help him."

"If Haydon were here, he would never let you go," Jack informed her.

"I know," said Charlotte softly. "And that's why I must help him."

"If everyone else is going then I'm going too," chirped Jamie. "After all, I helped Jack to follow the carriage in the first place."

"More like you kept falling and I had to keep stopping to pick you up again," Jack grumbled.

"None of you is going except for me, Oliver, and Jack," Genevieve insisted, trying to assert her authority over the situation. "It's too dangerous."

"And that's exactly why 'tis better if we all go," insisted Doreen. "The bigger we are as a group, the better our chances of dealin' with those scoundrels. Doesn't hurt to have ears and eyes on every corner, watchin' for trouble. Moreover, everyone here will be able to blend in easily with the common folk in Devil's Den."

"Except for Genevieve," pointed out Grace. "She doesn't look like she belongs there."

"I'm afraid she's right, lass," Oliver agreed, studying Genevieve with a frankly critical eye. "If there's anyone who might cause trouble for us, it's you."

Genevieve looked at him in bewilderment. "What do you mean?"

"Ye've a look of quality to ye," Doreen explained. "A bit uppity like, if ye take my meanin'."

"That's not to say that ye're snooty, ye understand," Eunice assured her, fearing that her feelings might be injured. "I've worked in many a grand household, and ye're nothin' like the folk who would just as soon have their lessers disappear down a great, black hole when they didn't need them to scrub dung off their boots or empty their chamber pots anymore. 'Tis only that with yer fancy ways and fine airs, ye dinna look like someone who belongs amongst the like of Devil's Den."

"I don't have fancy ways," Genevieve protested.

"Now, lass, dinna go feelin' all touchy," said Oliver, sensing Genevieve's hurt. "Ye could hardly be raised the daughter of a viscount in a fine house and nae have it show every time ye open yer mouth. Trouble is, there's no reason for a lady like you to be roamin' about Devil's Den with the likes of us. 'Tis best if ye stay right here and let the rest of us find the lad."

"There is absolutely no way that I am going to stay here while Haydon's life is in danger," Genevieve informed them with steely determination. "None."

Doreen sighed. "If we let ye come, ye'll nae be able to open yer mouth," she warned. "Not even a cheep out of ye."

"Fine."

Oliver looked unconvinced. "Can we do somethin'

about those uncommonly white teeth of hers—and maybe find an old hat to hide that bonny hair?"

"A little wax stuck onto her front teeth will make them look yellow and uneven," Annabelle assured him. "That's what they do in the theater."

"An' I can brush some ashes from the stove into her hair," Eunice said, eyeing the red-gold mass piled on Genevieve's head. "Take the color and shine right out, and age her nicely into the bargain."

"What about her shape?" persisted Oliver. "I dinna want any lads sniffin' after her as we walk by."

"I've an old gown that'll hang like a sack on her," Doreen offered. "Make her appear half-starved."

"And I can smudge her face with burned cork," suggested Grace. "I tried it once on Annabelle, and it gave her a wonderfully dirty look—like she'd been sleeping under the stove for a week."

Oliver sighed. "Very well, then," he relented. "See if ye can fix Miss Genevieve so that no one will have reason to look at her twice, and then fix yerselves up the same. But mind ye dinna take too long," he warned impatiently. "We've got to get to Devil's Den and find our lad quick, afore those rogues decide 'tis time to finish their work."

Chapter Fourteen

T HE DAY HAD WITHERED INTO MURKY COLD SHA-
dows by the time Genevieve and her band were making
their way through the putrid maze of Devil's Den. A tat-
tered quilt of clouds was sifting icy snow upon them,
fine as salt, which beat against their faces like a thousand
sharp pins. It was not thick enough to suffuse the filth
and muck that lay in a great, oozing mantle over the
haphazard streets, a stinking swill of human waste and
sour ale. Shattered glass lay everywhere, a testament to
the scores of men and women who crawled home each
night with a bottle of whiskey mashed against their
mouths, and after licking up the last fiery drop hurled
the vessel against the nearest wall, briefly filling the dark
with the sound of their impotent rage. The streets were
a combination of cesspool, refuse heap, and thorough-
fare, and Genevieve had to resist the impulse to instruct
the children to make their way carefully as they trudged
after Jack. She had sworn upon her beloved father's soul
that she would not speak, and therefore she remained
silent and concentrated on being as inconspicuous as
possible.

In truth, she thought that the transformation in her

appearance had been nothing short of extraordinary. Draped in Doreen's stained, shapeless dress, with her hair dulled beneath a generous application of ashes and her face and hands smudged with grime, she looked every inch the miserable young mother she was emulating, right down to the ragged bundle she carried in her arms. Oliver had insisted on her upper front teeth being masked in yellow wax, even though Genevieve had argued that as she wasn't going to speak, it wasn't necessary. The result was a lumpy, uncomfortable mold that pressed between her teeth and her inner lip, giving her mouth a misshapen appearance, almost as if she had been recently struck in the face. Doreen assured her that most of the women in Devil's Den were cuffed with brutal regularity, and that her swollen lip would help her blend better into the surrounding wretchedness.

Smoke spewed in greasy streams from the chimneys, adding the redolence of sputtering fires, wilted cabbage, and charred meat to the fetid air below. Genevieve's throat convulsed as the stench assailed her nostrils, and for a dizzying moment she thought she might vomit. She adjusted her scarf against her nose and forced herself to take tiny sips of air, fighting the quick lurch of her stomach. She had thought herself accustomed to the reek of misery, for she had spent enough time within the walls of the jail to know it intimately. But somehow, the closed stink of the prison was not nearly so overpowering as the noisome odors that assaulted her now. In prison, chamber pots were occasionally emptied and rinsed, and prisoners were required to tidy their cells each day and take a bath once a fortnight. The wretched stew that lined the streets and filled the overcrowded buildings of Devil's Den had been steeping for decades, until the very ground was rotten. As for bathing, Genevieve doubted whether any of the inhabitants here had ever enjoyed that luxury, save for the bairns that were still small enough to be hastily dunked in a battered dishpan of gray water.

"It's that one." Jack inclined his head toward a crumbling building at the end of the street.

"Ye're sure?" asked Oliver.

He nodded. "They took him through that door. I waited a bit, then slipped in after them. I think they went to the second or third floor, but before I could be certain they had disappeared into one of the apartments. It was too noisy for me to try to make out which one. Lots of screamin' and bawling goes on in these places." He gave Genevieve a hard look, trying to prepare her.

"Look!" gasped Jamie, pointing at a shifting pile of rotting scraps.

"Stay back," Doreen warned, protectively grabbing him by his shoulders. "It's a rat. The streets here are full of them."

"Really?" Jamie stared in fascination at the moving refuse. Suddenly a little orange-and-vanilla-striped head emerged from the slimy mound.

"It's a cat!" He watched with delight as the mangy creature shook off an errant bit of onionskin. Its fur was matted with grease and filth, and one ear had been torn into two pink flaps.

"Poor thing—she looks half-starved." Charlotte leaned upon her crutch and held her hand out to it. "Here, kitty."

The cat lifted her nose into the air and studied Charlotte, trying to ascertain if there was something of interest in her palm.

"Here now, dinna go touchin' that vermin-infested creature," scolded Eunice. "Lord knows what kind of nasty things are crawlin' in its fur."

Charlotte smiled as the cat came close enough for her to kneel down and stroke its sticky head. "Poor thing—she must be hungry."

"Well if she is, 'tis no concern of ours," Eunice informed her, shepherding Charlotte forward. "We've enough to worry about today without having some skinny, louse-ridden beast traipsin' after us."

Charlotte regarded her unhappily. "But if we leave her here she's going to die."

"Nonsense," scoffed Doreen. "Between the mice and the rubbish there's enough here to feed her for a year."

"Does everyone remember what our plan is?" demanded Oliver in a low voice.

The little group nodded solemnly.

"All right, then. Stay tight, and none of ye speak unless ye have to. Doreen and I will do any talkin' that's to be done. Let's go."

They trudged across the street, which was now covered with a fine, sandy snow, and bitterly cold against their roughly shod feet. Each of them had been garbed in the dullest of rags, with crushed hats and frayed coats, and they all carried a satchel of some sort. The exception to this was Genevieve, who was feigning carrying a bairn in her arms, and Charlotte, who was hobbling along with the crutch she typically tried not to use. They gave the appearance of a destitute family limping through the cold, desperately searching for a place to stay. It was far from an uncommon plight in Devil's Den. No one troubled them or asked them any questions. If anything, the people they encountered on the street made a point of quickening their pace and looking away as they tramped by. It occurred to Genevieve that they probably feared being asked for a crust of bread or a place where the bedraggled family might be able to rest and get warm.

A sickening brew of odors assailed them as they opened the door to the building. The stink of guttering fires and overly full chamber pots melded with the immediate stench of burned meats and vegetables, but there was a thicker underlying smell that permeated the very walls and floors around them. It was the reek of decades of bodies existing without benefit of bathing, a near-choking aroma of sweat and skin and scalp, and all the accompanying bodily fluids that had seeped into the clothes and mattresses and furniture around them. It was the smell of poverty and misery, but it was also the smell of defeat. Jamie wrinkled his nose in disgust. None of the others seemed to react to it. Perhaps, Genevieve reflected, they had each known that stench too well at some point in their lives to be easily offended by it.

"Yer pardon, sir," Oliver began, addressing a pinchfaced young man who was swiftly descending the stairs. "I'm lookin' for my son—"

"Go to hell." He shoved past the group and heaved open the door. "Bloody Christ!" he swore as the scrawny striped cat darted in between his legs. He drew his foot back to kick it, causing Charlotte to cry out in dismay.

"Leave it be!" snarled Jack, leaping forward to scoop the scabby creature up.

The man's eyes narrowed into dark slits. "Are ye thinkin' t' order me about?"

"Here now, we dinna want trouble," Oliver said, deftly inserting his spindly frame between Jack and the glowering tenant. "That's the lad's cat, is all. Nasty wee thing, to be sure, but good for the mice, all the same. Ye'd nae want to be rid of a good mouser, now, would ye?"

The man scowled. "Just keep the skinny bastard the hell away from me."

"I will for sure," Oliver said, not certain whether the man was referring to Jack or the cat.

The tenant stomped out the door and banged it shut behind him.

"Here," said Jack, depositing the writhing cat in Annabelle's arms. "Hold that for Charlotte."

Annabelle's eyes widened in horror as she struggled to restrain the twisting little beast. "But it's so dirty!"

"Please, Annabelle," implored Charlotte. "I'd hold her myself, but I don't think I could manage with my crutch."

"I've an idea." Simon removed his scarf and wrapped it tightly around the cat until the filthy creature resembled a small mummy. "That should keep it from moving about."

"If we're quite finished playin' with cats, could we get on with it?" demanded Doreen, growing agitated.

Oliver quickly scanned the hallway and selected an apartment that was situated close to the stairs. The sounds of children wailing and fighting could be heard behind the door, and, somewhere deeper within, a woman was screeching at them to clapper their bloody traps.

"Over here," Oliver said, directing his ragged family around him. He raised his fist and rapped upon the door.

"Dinna open it!" the woman inside shouted, but it was already too late. The door swung open and six dirty little faces stared up at them.

"I told ye nae to open it, ye bleedin' wee buggers!"

A heavily pregnant woman waddled forward, lugging over one hip a delicately boned child of about a year of age. She swatted the children away, then glared at Oliver and the others with naked hostility. Her eyes were small and set close together, and the skin around one of them bore the faded blue-and-purple mottling of an ugly bruise.

"What do ye want?" she demanded sharply.

"Forgive me for troublin' ye, missus," said Oliver,

politely removing his cap. "My wife and me are lookin'
for my son, ye see—"

The door slammed shut.

Unperturbed, Oliver herded the group to the next
door. This time a gaunt woman of about twenty answered. Her narrow body had been squeezed into a
tight corset so that her small breasts were plumped up
like two lumps of boiled dough, and her ashen face was
heavily smeared with rouge. She had arranged her oily
hair into a drab coiffure, and the sickly sweet odor of
cheap perfume wafted from her, intermingled with the
smell of old perspiration. Surprise registered upon her
face as she opened the door. It was clear to Genevieve
that she had been expecting someone else.

"Yer pardon for troublin' ye, miss," Oliver began
again, "but my wife and myself are tryin' to find our
lad, and last we heard he was livin' in this building.
Perhaps ye've seen him," he rushed on, sensing that she
was about to close the door. "Built like an ale barrel,
Harry is, with a nose laid flat from his taste for brawlin'.
Or mayhap ye've seen his mates—George is a big brute
with a belly like a swine's, while Ewan is skinny as a
weed, with hair the color of smashed turnip."

A flash of insight lit the girl's wary gaze. Clearly she
knew something about the men Oliver was describing.

"This is Harry's wife and bairns," Oliver pressed on,
pointing to Genevieve and the children. "This poor
wee bugger has never seen his da," he added, gesturing
at the ragged bundle in her arms. "Harry dinna ken that
he's gone and made another," he added, slipping into a
broader Scots than he normally used. His bony shoulders were hunched with defeat as he finished, "I'm old,
and canna go on carin' for her and her brood. 'Tis time
Harry come home and did right by them."

The children stared at her mournfully, except for

Jack, whose sullen indifference seemed entirely appropriate for an abandoned lad of fourteen. Even the motley cat let out a pitiful meow as it tried to extract itself from Annabelle's tight hold.

The girl hesitated, debating whether or not to speak. Suddenly a door banged open on a floor above them, causing her to jump.

"I dinna know nothin'," she blurted out, her eyes flitting nervously toward the staircase. She hurled the door closed.

"She knows where they are," Jack said, infuriated. He raised his fist to pound upon the door.

"Aye, o' course she does," hissed a crackling voice.

A decrepit old woman with a sparse scraggle of white hair peered at them speculatively from a doorway across the corridor. "The scurvy hoor knows every pair o' trousers that rubs together in all o' Devil's Den!" She laughed, revealing a dark cave of slippery gray gums, like snails, intermittently spiked with the occasional yellow tooth.

"A shame." Oliver shook his head as he shuffled over to her. "That's what happens to a lass when she's got nae family to help. I dinna know what'll become of these wee cubs if I canna find their da. End up on the street, most like."

"Filled yer belly and left ye to rot, did he, dearie?" The woman's watery eyes were nearly swallowed beneath the limp folds of her eyelids as she studied Genevieve. "Poor lassie. Lads today have nae honor. A quick toss of the skirts and they're off again, never mind the mess they've left behind. 'Tis a disgrace, to my way of thinkin'. If 'twere my son, I'd nae spare the whip!" She glared at Doreen, as if she bore responsibility for the transgressions of her supposed son.

"And so I shall, if I ever find him," Doreen assured her fiercely. "I dinna know where he gets it from—his da is as fine a man as ye'll ever know. He'd sooner starve himself than see one of these wee chicks go hungry." She cast a fond look at Oliver.

"Well, pleasure comes from doin' good, and that's God's truth," the woman said approvingly. "As for yer son, a wolf may lose his teeth but ne'er his nature, so even if ye drag him home by his boots, ye canna expect him to change." She studied Oliver a moment, considering. "Ye say ye think he's livin' here?"

"With friends," Oliver elaborated. "Maybe ye've seen them? Harry's short but strong as an ox, with a nose that's been walloped one time too many. Then there's George, with gray hair and a bloated belly, and tall, skinny Ewan—"

"With orange hair and red spots." The old woman nodded. "Aye, I've seen them. Not many rooms here are kept by three lads with nae lasses tae warm their beds. But they dinna get cold—not with all their visits tae that hoor across the hall." She cast a sympathetic look at Genevieve. "Yer husband's nae better nae worse than most, lassie," she assured her. "All they do is sleep and drink and fight. Today they brought yet another one home—so guttered he could nae walk, an' 'twas still practically mornin'!"

Genevieve's face grew pale.

"Where are they?" demanded Jack tersely. His hands tightened into fists.

"Angry at yer da, are ye, lad? An' so ye should be." Her scant white brows puckered together in a frown as she studied him. "Ye must have started birthin' when ye were barely weaned," she decided, turning her gaze to Genevieve.

"If ye dinna mind, missus, I'd like to find my lad an' make him come home," said Oliver, interrupting any attempt to draw Genevieve into conversation.

" 'Course ye would," the old woman agreed. "He's

up the stairs and to yer left, the last door at the end.
Should be in there now, for I've nae heard any of them
leave. Sleepin' off their whiskey, most like."

Oliver clamped a restraining hand on Jack's shoulder
to keep him from tearing up the staircase and breaking down the door. "Thank ye kindly, missus. I'm sure
Harry will be most pleased to see his family again. Most
pleased."

The old woman looked doubtful. "I dinna know
about that—what wi' all these bairns tae feed. But I expect he'll be fair surprised!" She cackled, her collapsed
mouth opening to expose her slick gray gums once more.

"Right," began Oliver in a low voice, struggling to
stay abreast of Jack as he led the little mismatched band
up the creaking staircase. "Like any job, the most important thing is, we've got to work quick. Get in, get
his lordship an' get out. Me and Jack will do any
bashin', if necessary. The rest of ye just keep 'em scur-
ryin' about while we free his lordship. Use yer weapons
if ye must, an' be sure to work together. There's but
three of them and ten of us. If we keep a quick hand
and a sharp eye, they'll be on the floor and beggin' for
mercy afore they know what they're about."

Doreen nodded in agreement. "Remember, 'tis nae
the size of the dog in the fight, but the fight in the dog!"

"Sweet saints," gasped Eunice breathlessly, clutching the rickety banister, "how many more steps are
there?"

Genevieve's heart began to beat wildly against the
cage of her ribs as the group made their way along the
dimly lit corridor. The din of men and women shouting at each other and children squealing and crying was
much the same as it had been on the floor below. Jack
had been right, she realized. The families trapped behind each of those decrepit doors were too immersed in
their own miserable lives to take any notice if someone

was being beaten or murdered in the next apartment. She unconsciously clutched the bundle she was carrying tighter to her chest. Whatever happened, they could expect no help from the other inhabitants of the dilapidated building.

Oliver motioned for them to be quiet. He pressed his ear against the door and listened for a long minute. Apparently satisfied with whatever he did or did not hear, he raised his gnarled fist and rapped upon the battered wood.

A hush of tense anticipation fell over the group. Even the wretched cat in Annabelle's arms quit struggling. There was the sound of a chair scraping against the floor and booted feet moving toward them.

Then nothing.

Oliver knocked again. There was a moment of strained silence.

Finally a heavy bolt grated across the wood and the door creaked open. Smoky light spilled from the hearth and lamps in the room beyond, illuminating the emaciated form and pimpled face of Ewan in ghostly shadows. He regarded the bedraggled assemblage in bleary confusion, showing no sign of recognition. Muffled within their ragged hats, scarves and heavy coats, their faces streaked with grime, the tatty gang bore little resemblance to the pristinely attired family whose home he and his accomplices had raided that morning.

"Yer pardon, lad, we're here to show Harry his new bairn." Oliver stepped aside to gesture at the bundle Genevieve carried, deftly inserting himself into the doorway as he did so.

Ewan gazed stupidly at the parcel of blankets. "Harry's bairn?"

"Looks just like Harry, he does," Eunice assured him cheerily. "Right down to his wee mashed nose. See for yerself."

Genevieve raised her "baby" slightly, offering Ewan a better view. Unable to restrain his curiosity, Ewan leaned forward to peer at Harry's progeny.

Quick as a whip, Doreen withdrew a heavy flatiron from her bag and brought it crashing down upon poor Ewan's head. The gangly lad stood for an instant, apparently frozen, staring blankly at Genevieve's arms.

Then his eyes rolled up into his skull and he crashed to the floor, forcing the children to scatter to make room for his crumpled body.

"That was a bloody fine blow," said Oliver, nodding at Doreen with approval.

A charming flush rose to Doreen's wrinkled cheeks. "Why, thank ye, Ollie." She girlishly adjusted a gray strand of hair that had tumbled down from her hat.

"Ewan!" growled a drunken voice from within, "what the devil's goin' on out there?"

"Here, kitty," whispered Annabelle, unraveling the cat in her arms, "go find a nice, fat mouse!" She tossed the squirming creature just beyond the door, then raced in after it, shrieking at the top of her lungs, *"Come back, kitty!"*

The other children charged through the door after her in a clamorous mob, screeching and shouting as they chased after the thoroughly agitated cat.

"What the hell is goin' on here?" demanded Harry, startled by the unexpected invasion. He shoved his chair out from the table at which he and broken-nosed George were eating their supper, and stared at them in drunken confusion.

"My kitty," wailed Annabelle, leading the children in a frenzied dance around the squalid little apartment.

"Come back, come back!" they all screeched, causing the terrified cat to race about wildly.

"Here now, ye canna be in here!" George's battered

face contorted with fury as Grace and Jamie scampered beneath the table. "Come out o' there, I say!"

Feigning compliance they obediently rose, causing the table to overturn and sending a greasy mess of fish stew and warm ale sloshing to the floor.

"What are ye thinkin', ye wee scoundrels?" demanded Eunice, storming angrily into the room, with Oliver, Doreen, and Genevieve chasing behind. "Come away from here at once, ye rotten little—"

"It's under your skirts!" Simon cried. "I think it's gone mad!"

Eunice screamed and began to whirl about, creating a tornado of petticoats as she pretended to try to evacuate the cat. "Help! Help!" She wrapped her bulky arms around George's neck and held tight, using him for support as she clambered heavily onto a chair. "Save me!"

"I . . . canna . . . breathe," George rasped, fighting to extricate himself from her strangling grip.

"Nae, he's over there!" shouted Oliver, pointing behind Harry.

Harry's eyes widened in panic as the children surged toward him in a tumultuous wave, smashing him to the floor. "Get off me, ye bloody monkeys!" he swore, trying to protect himself from their flailing arms and legs.

With the two men utterly distracted by the roiling commotion, Jack, Genevieve, and Oliver raced toward the door of the small bedroom at the back of the miserable apartment. Jack pushed it open to find Haydon lying upon the floor, bound hand and foot to an overturned chair, a length of bloodstained rag cinched tightly over his mouth. It was obvious he was trying to get closer to some fragments of shattered glass that were scattered in a pool of kerosene, the remnants of a lamp that he had managed to knock from a table. Shocked disbelief flared in his eyes as the bedraggled trio rushed toward him.

"So this is where ye be hidin'." Oliver produced two thin lengths of metal from his pocket and bent down so he could pick the lock of the manacles securing Haydon's wrists behind his back.

"You've looked worse," Jack assured Haydon tautly. He slipped a sharp dirk from his boot and sawed at the bonds lashing Haydon's ankles.

Genevieve choked back a sob as she swiftly unraveled the bloodstained rag from Haydon's bruised mouth. *He is alive,* she told herself, fighting the tears blurring her vision. Beaten and bloody, but alive. Now all they had to do was get him out of there.

"For Christ's sake, Genevieve," Haydon swore, his voice a harsh rasp as he tossed the ragged lengths of his bonds aside, "what the hell are you doing here?"

"Well, lad, she had her heart set on comin' to fetch ye, an' there was no way we were goin' to stand by an' let her do it alone," Oliver cheerfully explained. "Now, if ye dinna mind, I think we'd best take care of Harry and George so we can all go——"

"I'll kill ye!" roared George, his enormous frame blocking the bedroom doorway. His expression contorted with savage rage, he withdrew a gleaming dagger from his belt. "I'll kill all of ye!" He raised his dagger and barreled toward them.

Charlotte appeared suddenly and thrust her crutch between his ankles, causing him to crash to the floor. Quick as a whip, Jamie darted inside and dumped a blinding blizzard of flour from his satchel onto George's head. The enormous brute howled in fury and turned on Jamie, his eyes two glowering black nuggets beneath a terrifying chalk mask.

"Ye're dead now, ye pissin' little piece of——"

Eunice sailed into the chamber wielding her rolling pin and briskly cracked it against his powdery head, putting an end to both his threats and his foul language.

A floury cloud billowed into the air as George toppled nose first into the floor. Jack was on him in an instant, pinning him down with his knee as he roughly secured his hands and feet with the very same manacles and rope that had been used to bind Haydon.

"Right—just one more to attend to and we can all go home." Oliver rubbed his gnarled hands together with anticipation, looking as if he was enjoying himself immensely.

In the other room Grace and Simon were running circles around Harry, who might have been better able to foil their dizzying attack if not for the vast quantity of ale swashing through his veins. Doreen stood at the ready with her flatiron, poised to bash Harry on the head the moment the opportunity presented itself.

"Take that, foul knave!" shouted Simon, prodding and thrusting at Harry with the brass poker he was wielding as a sword.

"And that, and that!" cried Grace, handily whacking him in the arse with a brass warming pan.

Provoked beyond endurance, Harry let out an infuriated bellow and wrenched the instruments of his torture from the pesky children's grasp.

"I'll teach ye a lesson ye'll nae soon forget, ye sodding little bastards!" he raged, charging toward them.

"Harry, quick—save your bairn!" Genevieve pitched her ragged bundle at him.

His expression teetering somewhere between astonishment and panic, Harry instantly dropped the poker and warming pan in favor of catching the flying bairn.

"I got him!" he bellowed, triumphant.

Confusion washed across his face as he looked down at the disheveled blankets cozily swaddling a plump, ten-pound sack of oatmeal. "What the hell—"

Haydon's fist smashed into his jaw, cracking his teeth together in a sickening crunch. Harry regarded him in a daze, still protectively clutching the swaddled oatmeal. Haydon struck him once more, and Harry fell back like a tossed caber, the oatmeal still warm and secure within his beefy arms.

"Right—that about does it, then," said Oliver, nodding with satisfaction. "These lads will sleep 'til morn."

"Mind ye remember to take yer things with ye, children," instructed Doreen as she put her trusty iron back in her bag. "There's no sense in losin' a perfectly good warmin' pan."

"Where's the cat?" asked Charlotte, looking about the littered room.

Jamie pointed toward the door, where the traumatized little beast was surreptitiously trying to make its escape from the mayhem. "He's over there."

"Come back, kitty," called Annabelle, scampering toward it.

The cat meowed in protest and streaked into the corridor.

"No, kitty—come back!" Annabelle flung the door wide to chase after it.

And crashed directly into Vincent.

The sight of Ewan lying in a scrawny heap in the corridor had alerted the earl of Bothwell that all was not going according to his plan. And so he grabbed Annabelle and pressed his pistol firmly against her head, pragmatically deciding he might need some sort of leverage in dealing with Haydon.

"Let me go!" she shrieked, kicking him hard in the shin with her worn boot.

"Be still," Vincent hissed, wincing with pain, "or I'll blast a hole through that pretty little head of yours!" He wrenched her arm behind her back, forcing her to comply. Once she was satisfactorily subjugated, he raked his infuriated gaze over the stunned assemblage before him.

"Good evening, Haydon," he drawled, his voice coldly formal as he forced Annabelle back inside and closed the door. "I must confess, I had not expected to find you entertaining quite so many guests. I would have preferred to settle this matter between us without an audience."

Haydon regarded Vincent with an air of carefully constructed calm. He gave no hint of his concern for Annabelle's welfare, or for any of the others within the crowded chamber. To do so would only enhance the perverse pleasure Vincent was currently enjoying and place them all in even greater danger. Haydon had seen that chillingly satisfied look before, on the day he had pleaded with Vincent to grant him custody of Emmaline.

He had erroneously believed that Vincent had exacted his revenge upon him by tormenting Emmaline until she couldn't bear to live. He had thought that must have been enough for him—the horrendously lonely death of the child whom Haydon had wanted so desperately to help, and the subsequent disintegration of Haydon's life into the ashes of alcohol, guilt, and shame. Vincent knew about his appalling financial losses, and his reputation for drunkenness and brawling had become legendary. But in that frozen, hideous moment, it was clear that for the man whose wife Haydon had so selfishly bedded and gotten with child, Haydon's suffering had been wholly insufficient.

Only his death could assuage the humiliation and betrayal that Vincent had been forced to endure.

"Hello, Vincent," Haydon said pleasantly. "I must say, I didn't expect to find you traipsing about in a sordid place like this. How have you been?"

"The ever urbane marquess of Redmond." Vincent's tone was laden with bitter contempt. "No matter how unpalatable the situation, you always had a proclivity for being unfailingly polite. Even when you were ramming yourself between my wife's thighs all night beneath my own roof, you were excessively courteous and droll with me over breakfast the following morning. I suppose that made the game all the more amusing for you, didn't it."

Haydon said nothing. He had no desire to further antagonize Vincent. Moreover, there really was no adequate excuse for his contemptible behavior.

"I believe I would prefer it if all of you would toss whatever weapons you might be holding onto the floor," Vincent instructed, raking his gaze over the others.

His brow lifted as Eunice's rolling pin, Doreen's flatiron, Simon's poker, and Grace's warming pan clattered heavily to the floor. Oliver hesitated a moment, then reluctantly dropped a knife he had tucked inside his belt.

Vincent regarded Haydon and Jack expectantly.

"I'm afraid I don't have anything." Haydon raised his empty hands.

Vincent shifted his attention to Jack, who had deftly slipped his dirk up his sleeve. "Me neither." He regarded Vincent with barely contained loathing.

Vincent's eyes narrowed. "You're lying."

Jack glared at him. "No, I'm not."

"I believe you are," Vincent asserted calmly. "And unless you produce your weapon within the next five seconds, I shall be forced to blast a hole into your pretty little friend here."

A tiny, frightened whimper escaped Annabelle's throat.

Realizing he had no choice, Jack reluctantly allowed the dirk he had been hiding to slip through his fingers and clatter to the floor.

A triumphant smile lifted the corners of Vincent's mouth. "Very good."

"Let her go, Vincent." Haydon's voice was low and remarkably mild. "This is between us."

"You really have been most tiresome, you know," Vincent informed him, not relinquishing his hold on Annabelle. "I thought when I arranged for your little investment excursion here that these idiots I had hired would kill you and that would be the end of it. Instead you managed to slay one and scare these other imbeciles away. I must say, I found that rather vexing."

"Forgive me for disappointing you," Haydon apologized dryly. "I had no idea you had gone to so much trouble."

"After you were sentenced to be hanged, it ceased to matter. I decided that having you dangle at the end of a rope on the scaffold was infinitely better than having your chest swiftly split in some dark alley. There was also the added enjoyment of the scandal your trial created, and the ugly stain you had brought upon the Redmond name. It was a most appropriate ending to what has been, by my accounting, a perfectly worthless life."

Haydon did not argue.

"Unfortunately, however, you had to go and interfere." Vincent cast an irritated look at Genevieve. "Of course, you cannot be blamed entirely for your feminine weakness, Miss MacPhail. I understand you have a bizarre penchant for helping worthless criminals, as is evidenced by the scum with which you have elected to surround yourself." His lip curled with faint disgust as he swept his gaze over the unkempt children and elders crowding the room. "Moreover, the marquess here does have, what my slut of a wife took great pains to describe to me as, exceptional abilities when it comes to rutting—as I'm sure you have discovered."

Eunice gasped in horror.

"Keep yer filthy tongue to yerself afore I rip it from yer mouth!" Oliver's voice was quivering with fury and his ancient hands had knotted into fists.

"Did yer ma nae teach ye not to speak so in front of children?" demanded Doreen, looking as if she wanted to slap him. "I've a mind to wash yer mouth with a good chunk of lye soap!"

"Forgive me." Vincent tipped his head in mannerly apology, amused by the elderly trio's scandalized reaction. "I had forgotten that there were children present. They are such mysterious, fragile creatures, aren't they, Haydon?" He adjusted his hold on Annabelle while he studied the anxious faces of Jamie, Grace, Charlotte, and Simon. Jack was glaring at him with poisonous loathing. "Although these children, I suspect, are not nearly as fragile as little Emmaline was."

Despite his resolve not to antagonize him, Haydon found he could not keep silent. "You would know best about that, Vincent. After all, you tormented her to death."

"Shut your mouth, you goddamn bastard," Vincent snarled. "You, who crawled between my wife's legs night after night in a drunken haze of lust, with no thought whatsoever to the fact that a child might result from your sordid couplings! A child who was nothing more to you than spilled seed, and whom you passed off as my own while you sniggered behind my back about how clever you were! You haven't the right to speak her name, do you hear?"

His eyes were burning with rage. But there was something more there, buried deeper, masked within the swirling depths of fury and loathing. Haydon was far too consumed with his own wrath and his fear for Annabelle and the others to see it. But Genevieve recognized it instantly. All the years of ministering to the lost and broken souls of her children, each of whom had been so cruelly wounded before coming into her gentle care, enabled her to see beneath the suffocating layers of Vincent's hatred for Haydon. However much she despised him for threatening Annabelle and wanting to kill Haydon, she could not help but be moved by the raw pain she saw twisting deep within the shadows of his gaze.

This, she realized with piercing clarity, was a man who was drowning in agony.

"Do you dare think that you are better than me, Redmond?" Vincent continued savagely. "That your actions are above reproach? Or have you deluded yourself into believing that you are somehow the hero in all of this, and that you actually loved Emmaline because you accidentally planted her in my wife's womb?"

"I loved her enough to want to save her from you, Vincent," Haydon retaliated, finding it increasingly difficult to maintain his calm facade. "I loved her enough to be willing to acknowledge her as my own, and to care for her and support her for the rest of her life. But you refused me—not because you gave a damn about Emmaline, but because you despised her very existence, and wanted to punish her for the fact that she was mine and not yours."

"She was never yours!" Vincent's voice was hoarse, like the cry of an injured animal. *"She belonged to me!"*

"And that's why you treated her so cruelly, isn't it, Vincent?" demanded Haydon. "You wanted to show the world that she was your possession, to revere or destroy as you wished. And that's exactly what you did, you goddamn heartless bastard. You tortured her by denying her even the simplest acts of kindness and care, until finally she couldn't bear your cruelties a moment longer. You murdered her, Vincent, as surely as if you had thrown her into that pond and held her head down while she thrashed about gasping for air—"

"That's enough, Haydon."

Genevieve's voice was sharp, cutting through his tirade with the efficacy of a razor. Haydon stopped and looked at her in surprise. But Genevieve's attention was riveted on Vincent, who had tightened his grip on Annabelle as if he needed her for support, his pistol still positioned precariously at her head.

"Forgive me, Lord Bothwell," Genevieve began, her tone infinitely gentle. "I don't believe Lord Redmond understands. You did love Emmaline very much, didn't you?"

A mantle of deafening silence fell over the room as Vincent stared at Genevieve in bewilderment.

"I can see it," she persisted quietly. "And I can feel it. You loved her terribly, and when she died, you didn't think you could bear it."

The room was frozen as everyone waited for Vincent's response.

"She was . . . everything," he finally managed, the words breaking from his mouth like painful, shattered fragments.

"That's a bloody lie," countered Haydon. "If you loved her, then you never would have spurned her the way you did."

"It was terrible for you to discover that she wasn't your own child, wasn't it?" Genevieve continued softly, her gaze locked upon Vincent as if he were the only other person in the room.

Vincent didn't reply.

"And in your anger and your pain, you couldn't bring yourself to be near her, could you?"

His mouth tightened.

"And so you tried to cut her from your heart."

He stared at her in silence, fighting the demons clawing at his soul. And then a helpless, pained sound, part laugh and part sob, escaped his throat. "My wife laughed when she told me. She said I was a fool, and that she and Redmond would spend the rest of their lives laughing at me, because I had not been able to see that the child I had so willingly claimed as my own for five years was not really mine at all."

"That doesn't make you a fool, Lord Bothwell," Genevieve told him adamantly. "You loved her. She was your daughter."

He shook his head. "I wasn't her father."

"Not in blood, perhaps. But blood is not what forges the strongest bonds of love, nor is it what makes a family. Just ask any of my children."

He looked about helplessly at the children's faces before him.

"Emmaline could not be held accountable for the circumstances of her creation, any more than any of us can," Genevieve continued. "It was wrong for you to punish her for something in which she was a victim, just as you were. But I don't believe you intended to drive her to such sorrow. I believe you found your love for her too painful to endure, and so you erected a wall and tried to push her to the other side. And she couldn't bear it."

"I didn't understand how delicate she was," he confessed, his eyes shadowed with regret. He loosened his hold on Annabelle slightly, as if he suddenly feared that she, too, might be more delicate than he had imagined. "I thought she would simply turn away from me and focus her attention on other things. I convinced myself that was best, because I feared that one day she would learn the truth. I thought it would be easier for her to bear if she hadn't spent her whole life clinging to my hand. But instead I destroyed her." He turned his gaze to Haydon. "And so did you, Redmond. You carelessly created her with a woman who was incapable of having any tender feelings toward her own child, which is why it was inevitable that I would someday learn that you had sired her. Cassandra cared nothing for how that piece of information would affect Emmaline. Instead of loving her and wanting to protect her, she was jealous of her own daughter's relationship with me. She wanted to punish me, and on some despicable, incomprehensible level, she wanted to punish Emmaline as well—I suppose because she was a constant reminder of you. And I was too blind with fury to see it." His voice was ragged with emotion as he finished, "You should have bloody well grabbed her and taken her with you that day. Had you done so, my beautiful little daughter would still be alive."

Haydon stared at him helplessly, feeling as if he had suddenly been set adrift. He had hated Vincent with a sickening intensity for two long years. He had nurtured that hatred freely, for it had helped to mitigate the crushing weight of his own responsibility in Emmaline's pitiful existence and tragic death. But as he looked at Vincent in that moment and saw how broken and haunted he was, he found he could no longer summon the loathing he had once felt toward him. He could not despise a man who was so filled with anguish over the death of his only child. Vincent was lashing out at Haydon because he believed Haydon was the architect of his suffering.

And he was right.

"I'm sorry, Vincent," he began, the words rough with remorse. "I failed her, and I am deeply ashamed for that. But Emmaline is gone, and there is nothing left but her memory. Let us not mar it with any more hatred and misery and death. Let us bring this matter to an end." He took a slow step forward and held out his hand. "Give me your gun, Vincent."

Vincent regarded him helplessly, looking trapped. "You will kill me."

"No," Haydon assured him solemnly. "I won't."

"But I tried to kill you—"

"And you failed."

"Then you will turn me over to the authorities so that I will suffer the same indignities you were forced to suffer—"

"No. I won't."

Vincent stared at him, bewildered.

"It is over, Vincent," Haydon told him adamantly. "Let Emmaline rest. Release Annabelle and give me your gun. She is only a child herself, Vincent. I know you do not really want to frighten her."

Vincent looked down at Annabelle in surprise, as if he had forgotten that he still held her. Her enormous blue eyes were wide with fear, and her face was pale against the soft spill of lamplight in the room. He lowered his pistol.

"Emmaline," he murmured, gently laying his hand against the silky blonde length of Annabelle's hair. "Forgive me." He leaned forward and pressed a tender kiss upon her forehead.

Then he straightened, raised his pistol to his temple and squeezed the trigger.

Chapter Fifteen

RIBBONS OF PEACH LIGHT SPILLED FROM THE enormous fire crackling in the hearth, rippling across the faded pattern of the aged wool carpet and sending warm caresses across a collection of small, slippered feet.

". . . and so between the evidence, the confessions of the three men, who also admitted to their earlier attack on Haydon in which their accomplice was killed, and the body of Lord Bothwell, the judge realized he had no choice but to drop the charges against Haydon immediately," Genevieve explained to the little flock of nightgown-clad children surrounding her.

It was the following evening, and all the children had anxiously waited up to hear what had transpired during her and Haydon's lengthy visit to the prison and courthouse that day.

Jack was leaning against the wall, his expression guarded and his body tense, as if he still expected the authorities to come crashing through the door at any moment. Genevieve suspected it would be a long time before the lad stopped fearing that either he or Haydon was on the verge of being arrested.

"Why would those three bother to confess?" he demanded, eyeing Haydon seriously.

"I suppose because Constable Drummond explained to them that it would be in their best interest to tell the truth." That seemed a fairly gentle way of putting it, Haydon decided.

He was seated on the sofa with his arms wrapped around Charlotte and Annabelle, feeling overwhelmingly protective of the family assembled before him. Any one of them could have been injured or killed as they tried to rescue him, he realized, appalled by the risks they had taken. The sight of Annabelle being held at Vincent's mercy with a pistol pressing into her head had unleashed a paralyzing fear within him, just as the sight of Emmaline peering at him through the banister had some two years earlier. Even though Annabelle was now safe and seemed to have recovered from her ordeal, he still felt a need to stay close to her and reassure himself that she truly was unharmed.

"More likely the crack of Constable Drummond's stick against their big fat crowns loosened their tongues." Doreen snorted with satisfaction. "I'd have done the same with my iron if I'd had the chance."

"Aye, all ye need is for one dog to yelp an' ye'd be surprised how quick the rest o' them start to bark," said Oliver, chuckling.

"Then 'tis every man for himself and God for us all." Eunice passed around a plate of ginger biscuits. "Each points the finger at the other and they all get thrown into the pot like bones for a soup. Those ruffians may not hang for tryin' to kill his lordship, here, but I warrant they'll spend a good long time in prison, just the same. Time enough to make them wish they had never agreed to go along with Lord Bothwell's murdering scheme, no matter how much he offered to pay them."

348 *Karyn Monk*

"Poor Lord Bothwell," Charlotte murmured sadly. "Of course, it's terrible what he did," she qualified, seeing Jack's look of incredulity, "but even so, I cannot help but feel sorry from him."

"He must have missed his daughter very much," Grace reflected, "to be so filled with hatred for Haydon."

Annabelle nestled closer to Haydon, disliking the thought of anyone hating him. "If he loved her that much, then why was he so cruel to her?"

"Sometimes people get confused about their feelings," Genevieve began, trying to help the children understand. She was aware the subject was intensely difficult for Haydon, but she felt it was important that the children have some comprehension of what had motivated Vincent to act as he had, and ultimately to take his own life. "Lord Bothwell's love for Emmaline was deeply painful to him because when he discovered she was not truly his daughter, he felt horribly betrayed—and worse, I think he felt lost. Sometimes we try to distance ourselves from those we love most, not because we no longer love them, but because loving them becomes almost too painful to endure."

"I would never do that," Simon declared with childish certainty. "If I loved somebody, I would want to stay close to them and make sure they were happy and safe."

"Me, too." Jamie yawned and snuggled sleepily against Genevieve. "Wouldn't you, Genevieve?"

"Of course I would." She tenderly ruffled his berry-tinted hair, then stroked Simon's freckled cheek. "I'm just saying that we must not judge Lord Bothwell too harshly. It takes some people a long time to learn about the complexities of love. In Lord Bothwell's case, he didn't understand until it was too late."

"Speakin' of it bein' late, I believe 'tis nigh time ye lads and lassies were tucked in yer beds," said Doreen

briskly. "Tomorrow is laundry day, and I'll be expectin'
ye to help with the sorting and washin' and ironin' before ye settle down to whatever lessons Miss Genevieve
may have planned for ye."

"But I'm not tired," protested Annabelle, who had
dark smudges of exhaustion beneath her eyes.

Jamie yawned and burrowed even closer to Genevieve. "Neither am I," he assured her adamantly.

"You don't have to go to sleep right away." Years of
putting weary children to bed had taught Genevieve
that the surest way to snap them into wakefulness was to
insist that they were tired when they were protesting
otherwise. "But it is time for you to go upstairs. Brush
your teeth and climb into bed, and, if you like, you may
tell each other stories until you're tired—as long as you
remember to whisper."

Appeased by that compromise and quite confident
that they could stay awake far longer than Genevieve
anticipated, the children rose and crowded around her
to kiss her good night. Jack stood off to one side,
slouched against the wall with his thin arms folded
across his chest, watching. Genevieve sensed that despite
his affectation of utter apathy, something about the children's nightly ritual touched him. It was clear he believed himself far too old for such childish nonsense as
good night hugs and kisses and giggles. But she wondered if somewhere buried beneath the battered shield
of his hard-won maturity, he wished that he could
lower his guard, just for a moment, and permit himself
to be a mere lad once again.

As the children were bidding Haydon good night
and scampering up the stairs with Oliver, Doreen, and
Eunice, she went over to where Jack stood.

"It has occurred to me, Jack, that a young man of
your age should not have the same bedtime as the children."

His brow lifted in surprise.

"Starting tomorrow evening, you may stay up an additional hour if you like. This will be your time, and you may spend it however you wish. There are many fine books in the library that you might enjoy looking at. Or you may want to join Oliver, Eunice, and Doreen in the kitchen for a cup of tea—I'm sure they would be delighted to have your company. The time is entirely your own, to do with as you please."

Jack straightened, clearly pleased to have had his maturity recognized with the granting of such a privilege. "Fine." As an afterthought he awkwardly added, "Thank you."

Genevieve hesitated. "I was just wondering, Jack," she ventured quietly, "will you be staying?"

His gaze became shuttered. "What do you mean?"

"I know that you are quite capable of taking care of yourself, as you have for so many years before you came here," she elaborated. "And I also realize you sometimes think you would prefer to be on your own again."

Jack remained silent, neither confirming or denying her conjecture.

"It's just that I'm afraid I'm finding managing this household rather difficult," she continued, sighing. "With all the painting I shall be doing over the next while for my future exhibitions, I don't know how I will be able to accomplish everything else. Oliver, Eunice, and Doreen already have their hands full with a hundred different chores. I could never expect one of them to take on a challenge such as maintaining our financial accounts, for example, which requires quite a lot of concentration and attention to detail."

Jack regarded her in astonishment. "You want me to keep your accounts?"

"Of course, you would begin with simple equations,

and I would review your work once it was done," Genevieve assured him. "But I'm confident that eventually
you would be able to manage the task completely on
your own, as you have demonstrated a very quick mind
when it comes to addition and subtraction."

A thin ray of pride lit his face.

"There are many other responsibilities that could be
given to you, were you willing to take them on," she
continued. "You're certainly old enough, and there is
no question that you have the intelligence and maturity
to handle them. It would be an enormous help to me if
you would assume some of my duties—but I would
delegate them to you only if I knew you were going to
stay."

His shifted uncomfortably and looked away. It was
clear he had no desire to lie to her.

Bitter disappointment washed over her. Genevieve
had prayed that Jack would be so delighted by her confidence in him that he would accept her proposition
outright. Evidently that was too much to hope for.

"You don't have to answer me tonight," she told
him, somehow managing not to sound completely defeated. "I would not want you to make a commitment
that you might later feel compelled to break. All I ask,
Jack," she finished earnestly, "is that you give it some
consideration."

"Fine."

She regarded him uncertainly. "You mean you will
consider it?"

"No, I mean I'll stay."

A hesitant smile crept across her face. "You're sure?"

"Not forever," he swiftly qualified.

He didn't want Genevieve to think he was planning
to spend the rest of his life living off of her charity. But
if he was honest with himself, part of him desperately

wanted to stay. Of course he disliked being told what
to do all the time, and he hated peeling bloody potatoes and chopping up stinking fish and washing dishes,
and it chafed not being allowed to just come and go
as he pleased. Furthermore, he would never understand
Genevieve's maddening obsession with bathing and
manners and such. But despite these things, he found he
actually liked living with this odd family of thieves and
outcasts. For the first time in his life, he felt accepted for
exactly who he was—and more, he actually felt *wanted*.
Most of all, there was Charlotte. A terrible sense of
helpless rage filled him every time he watched her limp
awkwardly across the room, or prop her leg up and try
to rub away some of the pain that plagued her constantly. He could not bear the thought of leaving her—
not yet, anyway.

Charlotte needed him to watch out for her.

"I'll stay for two years, the length of my sentence.
That way you won't be gettin' into any trouble with the
governor when I leave." He had not forgotten how anxious the children had been when he had told them he
was going to Glasgow. "As long as you think I can be
some help." He wanted to make it clear that he intended to earn his keep.

So great was Genevieve's relief, she wrapped her
arms around him, embracing him in a long, fierce hug.
Jack froze, uncertain how to respond. She smelled
sweetly crisp and clean to him, like a rain-soaked field
of grass, and utterly different from his filmy remem-
brances of his mother, which now reminded him of
cheap perfume and ripe wool. He closed his eyes and
leaned into her, just a little, feeling strangely childlike as
she held him. It was as if the years suddenly melted
away and he was a little boy clinging to his mother,
tearfully begging her not to leave him. But Genevieve
was not leaving him. A tentative gust of happiness

filtered through him, so new and unfamiliar, he scarcely knew what it was. She was asking *him* not to leave *her*.

He raised his arms and draped them around her, awkwardly returning her embrace.

"Thanks, Genevieve," he whispered fiercely, "for takin' me out of prison and bringin' me here."

He dropped his arms and cleared his throat, suddenly embarrassed by his emotionalism. " 'Night," he said, casting a cursory glance in Haydon's direction as he sauntered out of the drawing room.

"Good night, Jack," Genevieve returned, smiling as she closed the doors.

Haydon rose from the sofa and went to the fire, suddenly ill at ease now that he and Genevieve were finally alone. He grasped the poker and jabbed at the logs piled in the hearth, which were burning satisfactorily and in no need of adjustment whatsoever. He then carefully selected another piece of wood and added it to the pyre, watching as the flames licked ravenously against the dry wood. Uncertain what to do next, he braced one arm against the mantel and stared at the blaze, feeling hopelessly lost.

Just as abruptly as his life had been stripped from him, so it had unexpectedly been restored. He was the marquess of Redmond once again, a free man with a clear name, other than the distinction of his sordid past and the freshly minted scandal of his recent troubles. That would provide fodder for the gossipmongers for years to come—or at least until some other deliciously shocking event came along to eclipse it. His legacy was as seamy and despicable as his father had once predicted it would be, although the old bastard had never imagined that Haydon would actually bear the Redmond title while he was dragging his family's name through the mire.

Haydon had never given a damn about his reputation

or the sanctity of his family pedigree. But neither had he ever imagined himself caring about a woman with the relentlessly moral spirit of Genevieve MacPhail. Hers was not the kind of morality that took pious delight in judging the rest of the world according to the narrow dictates of religion and the law, the way people like Governor Thomson's wife and Constable Drummond did. No, what Genevieve lived by was an inherent morality of gentle compassion and selflessness.

From the moment she so willingly sacrificed both her position in society and any hope of a life of ease as the wife of the earl of Linton, pompous ass though Charles may be, she had detached herself from the rarefied world of privilege and acceptance that she had always known. All for the sake of rescuing a dead maid's bastard, which any other gently bred woman in her position would have been satisfied to see quietly sent off to an orphanage to languish a while and then die.

But Genevieve was not like any other woman, he realized, feeling awed and humbled by her. There was a magnificent brilliance to her that defied analysis, like the silvery flare of a faraway star. At the youthful age of eighteen she had elected to leap from the path of familiarity and comfort that had been laid before her and fight to survive on her own, not because she wanted to, but because there was a helpless child who needed her. She had promptly been discarded by the man who had vowed to make her his wife, and rejected by the very society that had once celebrated her for being so young and lovely and charming.

What that society could not accept was that she was also profoundly ethical and caring and humane, and these attributes could not be stifled beneath lavish homes and expensive jewels and shallow gestures of carefully calculated generosity. Instead of being revered for her selflessness and determination, she had been ostracized and called mad, as if it were unfathomable that a young, eminently desirable woman might choose to save a bastard child's life over becoming a pampered wife and countess. And then, because her tender spirit found true joy in helping children, who were surely the most vulnerable members of society, she had gone on to rescue five more. Not because she felt driven by a sanctimonious need to please God, or to earn a better place in heaven, or to feel morally superior to the rest of the world. Genevieve helped others because within her breast beat a noble and caring heart, which rendered her incapable of walking away from the pain of someone else's suffering.

Even a brutal, condemned murderer on the eve of his execution.

He had always known that he was unworthy of her. He who had so casually destroyed the lives of not one, but now two people, each ending in a self-inflicted death. But he had never imagined coming to love her so deeply that he would have gladly given up anything and everything for the sole privilege of being the man with whom she shared her life. What he could not do, no matter how much he wished it, was escape the ugly black stains upon his soul. They would torment him forever—the memory of an innocent child's suffering and a betrayed father's unbearable anguish. How could a woman like Genevieve, who had devoted her life to easing the misery of others, accept a callow, selfish bastard like him as her husband and the father to her precious children?

Genevieve watched Haydon uneasily, dreading whatever it was that he was struggling to tell her. Caught in the vortex of events that had consumed her so absolutely during the last two days, she had not permitted herself to consider what was to become of them. But seeing Haydon standing rigid before the fire, his expression twisted with a mixture of guilt and remorse, she knew what he was about to say.

"You're leaving," she concluded dully.

He nodded, not turning to look at her. "Tomorrow morning. I'm taking Vincent's casket by coach to Oban. From there, I've arranged for a ship to sail us north to Inverness." His voice was hollow as he finished, "I want to ensure that he is buried next to Emmaline."

Of course. His title had been restored and his name was cleared. What had she thought he would do? Genevieve wondered. Had she actually thought he might stay with her and—what? Marry her? An outcast spinster living in a shabby old debt-ridden house with her eccentric brood of aged thieves and semi-rehabilitated urchins? The idea was ludicrous—she could see that now as plainly as anyone. Something within her began to crack, like a thin sheet of ice beneath the crushing wheel of a carriage. She gripped the threadbare arm of the sofa, fighting to maintain some semblance of dignity. The gold ring that Haydon had given her in Glasgow gleamed against her finger, a mocking reminder of their charade as husband and wife. For one sweet, shimmering moment she had foolishly allowed herself to forget that it was all a pretense. Somewhere between the nights of feeling his heart pound against her as they joined their bodies and their souls, and the agony of believing she had lost him forever, she had forgotten that they were not truly wedded. But they were not, and they never would be. It was as simple, and as heartbreaking, as that.

She plumbed the depths of her composure, fighting to shield her feelings from him. Realizing how terribly difficult the task of taking Vincent's body back would be for him, she found the poise to comment quietly, "I'm certain Vincent would have appreciated your concern for him, Haydon."

A harsh, dry laugh erupted from his throat. "I doubt that. Vincent despised me, and he had every right to." He turned away from the fire, his face shadowed with torment. "I killed him, Genevieve, as surely as if I had been holding that goddamn pistol myself."

"I don't believe that and neither should you." Her protectiveness of him instantly overwhelmed her own feelings of anguish. "Vincent was going to kill you, Haydon, as he had been planning to for months, or perhaps even years. But when he realized you were not the monster he had envisioned you to be, he could not bring himself to do it—"

"So he killed himself instead," Haydon finished harshly, "because I had destroyed his life." The words were raw with self-loathing.

"You injured him terribly by creating a child that Cassandra convinced him was his own," Genevieve acknowledged. "But you didn't destroy him, Haydon, and you certainly didn't make him kill himself. It was Vincent's choice to erect a wall between himself and Emmaline. Perhaps at the time he felt he had no choice, but I believe he did. We cannot control much of what happens to us in our lives—we can only control how we allow ourselves to react to it." Her voice softened as she continued, "Vincent was devastated to learn that Emmaline wasn't his daughter by blood, but no one forced him to withhold his love from her. That was his choice. And the consequences of that choice were insufferable, both for Emmaline and for him."

Haydon shook his head, unconvinced. "If I had never fathered her—"

"If you had never fathered her then Vincent might never have known the precious love he experienced for her during those first five years," she interjected, "and the love he continued to feel toward her afterward. Or Cassandra may have become pregnant by one of her other lovers and that child would have been presented as Vincent's own. It is impossible to speculate upon what might have happened, Haydon. Our lives have unfolded as they have, and we have both made choices in response to the situations we have been faced with. When Jamie was born and his mother died, I raged against God for creating him, because I was given the impossible choice of having to either take responsibility for him, or close my eyes and walk away."

"But you didn't walk away, Genevieve."

"No, I didn't. And everything that has happened in my life since then has been inextricably tied to the choice I made that day. It awakened me to the plight of unwanted children who exist so tenuously in the dark corners of our society. It brought me my children and Oliver, Eunice and Doreen, who have become my family and filled my life with unparalleled joy. And finally, incredibly," she finished, her voice beginning to break, "it brought me you."

She stopped abruptly. She could not bear the thought of him knowing how much he had come to mean to her. Not when he was going to leave her. She could suffer almost anything, but she did not think she could endure his pity.

Haydon regarded her with surprise. She looked away, avoiding his gaze, her hand clutching desperately at the arm of the sofa. In the span of a heartbeat she had gone from being strong and sure and full of fire as she defended his life and his actions to him, to being achingly fragile and uncertain.

And finally, incredibly, it brought me you.

He closed the distance between them in two strides. Kneeling down, he took her chin between his fingers and gently tipped her face up. Her eyes were shimmering with tears as she stared at him, a glaze of agony that cut through his soul. Slowly, tentatively, she grasped his hand and held it hard against her heart.

And then her teardrops began to fall, glittering upon her cheek like diamonds.

Haydon stared at her in awe, feeling the warm softness of her heart beating rapidly against his palm. And suddenly he understood. Genevieve did not condemn him for the dark transgressions of his past, any more than she condemned any one of her children for the lives they had led before coming to the sanctuary of her home. Somehow, she believed that deep within him there was actually good. That was why she had helped him to escape from prison and then risked everything to protect him from the authorities and his kidnappers. It was also why she had permitted him to become part of her closely guarded family. But it was not the reason she had given herself to him, sharing a magnificent, reckless passion that he had never known with any other woman. Nor was it why she now sat drowning in pain, his hand clutched tightly against her heart. The reason for that was far more bewildering and glorious.

She loved him.

A brilliant shaft of joy blazed through him, obliterating the leaden shadows of his tortured past and replacing them with healing light.

"I love you, Genevieve," he managed hoarsely, leaning into her until his lips were but a breath away from hers. "More than life itself. I have loved you from the moment I first laid eyes upon you in the bleakness of prison, and I have grown to love you more every day since. And if you give me the chance, I will spend the rest of my life surrounding you with that love."

Genevieve stared at him in silence, unable to accept what he was telling her.

"I will also cherish and protect each of our children

to the very depths of my soul," Haydon pledged, wanting her to understand that he would never again fail a child the way he once had. "And I will happily welcome any other children you bring into our lives, whether from the prison or the street, or as a result of our devotion to each other."

"But—you are a marquess," she protested tearfully, still clasping his hand tightly against her heart.

"I was hoping you would not hold that against me."

"You could marry anyone," Genevieve clarified.

"I'm flattered that you think so. Shall I take it, then, that your answer is 'yes'?"

She shook her head in misery. "You cannot want to marry me, Haydon," she told him with painful certainty. "You only think you do because you have been away from your home for so long. My children and I don't belong in the society in which you live—surely you can see that. They would never be accepted by your friends and family, any more than they have been accepted here by those who once welcomed me into their homes as a guest and an equal." Feeling as if she were tearing out her own heart, she slowly released his hand. "I could not bear to see you scorned because of me and my children, Haydon, just as I could not bear to see my children despised by narrow-minded people who are blinded by the trappings of their titles and wealth."

"Then I'll give up the bloody title," he swore fiercely. "I'll sell my estate and my house in Inverness, so none of our children ever have to go there and endure being the subject of idle gossip. We can live here, or we can move somewhere else and begin anew. I don't give a damn about any of it, Genevieve," he assured her with harsh finality. "Not the title, or the holdings, or what people think about me or my choice for a wife. The only thing that matters is that we are together, as a family. Marry me, Genevieve," he finished in a raw, pleading voice. "Marry me, and let me spend the rest of my life loving you." He brushed a silky strand of hair off her face, capturing a silvery drop of her anguish on his hand as he did so. "Please."

Genevieve bit her trembling lip, staring at him in awe. Firelight was playing across the chiseled planes of his face, etching his grim expression in shadows of gold. There was determination in his eyes, the granite-hard resolve of a man who was accustomed to having his way in virtually every challenge he undertook. But there was fear there as well, like a ragged, bleeding gash from which his very soul seemed to pour as he tensely waited for her answer.

And suddenly she knew that she could never let him go.

With a little cry she wrapped her arms around him and crushed her lips to his, kissing him deeply as she sank to her knees on the floor and pressed herself against him.

"Yes," she breathed, feeling joy flood through her, washing away her fear as it filled her with newfound strength. And then, because she had no wish to force him to relinquish his title and turn his back on his family and his heritage in order to win her hand, she added with just a hint of playfulness, "I suppose I will marry you, Lord Redmond."

He laughed and kissed her hungrily, cradling her against his body as he lowered her onto the carpet before the hearth. He pulled the pins from her hair and let it spill in silky waves around her, fascinated by the dance of coral light against the creamy skin pouring from the neckline of her gown.

"There is something I feel I must bring to your attention," he murmured, nuzzling the tender hollow of her throat as his hands roamed the lush hills and valleys of her breasts. The tiny round buttons of her gown were quickly released, enabling him to free her from the confines of her corset. Haydon ran his tongue over the claret tip of her breast before drawing it deep into his mouth.

Genevieve sighed and twined her arms around his shoulders, enjoying the hardness of his arousal pressing against her as he worshiped her. Honeyed heat began to course through her veins, causing her to shift restlessly beneath him. His hand trailed up the length of her thighs and into the opening of her undergarment.

"Did you hear me, Genevieve?" he asked, slipping his fingers inside her.

"Yes!" she gasped.

"Given your penchant for rescuing urchins," Haydon reflected, languidly stroking her as he rained kisses across the warm satin sheet of her skin, "and the amount of time I intend to devote to showing you just how much I love you, we are apt to have a ridiculously large family." He paused in his ministrations and gave her a teasing grin.

"Fortunately, I adore large families," returned Genevieve, unfastening his trousers. She peeled them down the sculpted muscles of his legs, then slid off her hooped petticoat and her drawers before lying back down before the fire. "Does your estate have a fair number of bedchambers?"

Haydon shrugged out of his coat and shirt and stretched naked over her, pushing the froth of her skirts up to her hips as he positioned himself between her legs.

"I believe it has enough to suffice for a time, should you decide you would like to live there. Once we have them all filled, we can always look for something larger."

"How many bedrooms does it have?"

"Eighteen." He smiled as her eyes widened in

astonishment. "Thirty-four if you count the servants' quarters. Do you think you can fill all of them?"

"I can certainly try." She raised her hips and pulled him down into her, sheathing him tightly within her hot clasp.

"Jesus." His face contorted with effort as he fought to regain his control.

"Come, my lord," said Genevieve, flexing impatiently beneath him. "I do believe I shall require your assistance in this matter."

Haydon managed a strangled laugh. "As you wish, my love. I am, and forever will be, your prisoner."

He lowered his head and kissed her deeply, feeling his heart grow whole and the scars of his past fade as they pulsed together in the amber flicker of firelight.

ABOUT THE AUTHOR

KARYN MONK has been writing since she was a girl. In university she discovered a love for history. After several years working in the highly charged world of advertising, she turned to writing historical romance. She is married to a wonderfully romantic husband, Philip, who she allows to believe is the model for her heroes.

The delightful cast of
characters from

THE PRISONER

lives on in Karyn Monk's
upcoming trilogy.

Look for Jack's story
in late 2002 . . .

Karyn Monk

Once a Warrior

A medieval Scottish tale of a Highland beauty desperate to save her clan, and a shattered hero fighting for redemption—and fighting for love.

The Witch and the Warrior

A tale of an unearthly beauty, wrongly condemned for witchcraft, and the fierce and handsome Highland warrior who saves her from death so that she may save his dying son.

The Rose and the Warrior

The eagerly anticipated follow-up to the Witch and the Warrior—where an infamous thief falls in love with the warrior who is intent on catching her.

FN 13 6/01

Bestselling Historical Women's Fiction

IRIS JOHANSEN

THE WIND DANCER	$6.99/$9.99
THE TIGER PRINCE	$6.99/$8.99
THE MAGNIFICENT ROGUE	$6.99/$8.99
BELOVED SCOUNDREL	$6.99/$8.99
MIDNIGHT WARRIOR	$6.99/$8.99
DARK RIDER	$6.99/$8.99
LION'S BRIDE	$6.99/$8.99
THE UGLY DUCKLING	$6.99/$8.99
LONG AFTER MIDNIGHT	$6.99/$8.99
AND THEN YOU DIE	$6.99/$8.99
THE FACE OF DECEPTION	$6.99/$9.99

TERESA MEDEIROS

HEATHER AND VELVET	$5.99/$7.50
ONCE AN ANGEL	$5.99/$7.99
A WHISPER OF ROSES	$5.99/$7.99
THIEF OF HEARTS	$5.99/$7.99
FAIREST OF THEM ALL	$5.99/$7.50
BREATH OF MAGIC	$5.99/$7.99
SHADOWS AND LACE	$5.99/$7.99
TOUCH OF ENCHANTMENT	$5.99/$7.99
NOBODY'S DARLING	$5.99/$7.99
CHARMING THE PRINCE	$5.99/$8.99